D.A.S.P.O.

AN UNHINGED NOVEL OF VIETNAM

JEROLD A. GREENFIELD
AND
RONALD B. FENSTER

Based on the adventurous
Vietnam tour of duty
of
Lt. Ronald B. Fenster

For Information Contact:

Creative Projects International Ltd.
4001 Santa Barbara Blvd.
Suite 404
Naples, Florida 34104

ISBN: 978-0-9818222-6-6

Library of Congress: 2014907260

Cover Design: Len Eckert
        iconDo, Inc.

D.A.S.P.O.
DEPARTMENT OF THE ARMY SPECIAL PHOTOGRAPHIC OFFICE

The photographing of military operations is as old as photography itself. However, official military photographic units had their beginning during World War I, when cameramen were sent to document battles in Europe. During World War II, the Army Pictorial Center became the main audio-visual arm of the American military, and fielded film crews throughout the world. Film directors such as Frank Capra received their early training in these units.

In the 1960s the Department of the Army Special Photographic Office (DASPO) was established to produce motion pictures for "documentation and historical purposes." DASPO officers and enlisted men held State Department diplomatic passports and high-level security clearance. They customarily wore civilian clothes, had permission to carry concealed weapons, and were authorized to travel anywhere in the world to make films that were deemed "of interest" to the Department of the Army. They were not combat photographers, but that fact didn't keep them out of the line of fire.

This book, based on the exploits and experiences of DASPO units during the Vietnam War, is a work of fiction. The historical facts and dates relating to the events of that war are accurate, but some characters are compilations of people who served in DASPO units in the time and place described. No resemblance to any actual person is intended or should be inferred.

DEDICATION

The characters in this book are a compilation of many of the men who served in DASPO in the Far East. They went into the jungles by day and returned to a wartime night life in their villa in downtown Saigon where they partied hard till the sun came up. I dedicate this book to all the men of DASPO.

And of course, to my children, Mikael, Banesha, Renaud, Eddie, and Kevin. You are the proudest shots I ever produced.

This book is also dedicated to Debi Greenfield, who loves us and puts up with us.

ALSO BY JEROLD A. GREENFIELD

Maverick: The Personal War of a Vietnam Cobra Pilot
    with Dennis Marvicsin

Secrets of the Wine Whisperer:
        Or
How I Learned to Drink Wine and Found Ecstasy, Joy,
Peace, Happiness, Life, and Salvation

FOREWORD

"...it is no secret that use of marijuana by American soldiers in Vietnam is so extensive that it has produced a pot subculture among U.S. troops."

Newsweek April 21, 1969

"[V. Adm. William P. Mack] said less than 1 per cent of troops have been found to have used marijuana..."

U.S. News & World Report April 6, 1970

"The war against drug use by Americans in Vietnam is faring badly. Possible reason: Some top men in the Saigon regime may be in on the racket."

U.S. News & World Report May 10, 1971

"A report...estimates that some 30,000 to 40,000 servicemen in Vietnam are heroin addicts – which means roughly 10 to 15 per cent of all GIs in the country."

Newsweek May 24, 1971

"The Army's ineptness in trying to educate soldiers to the dangers of heroin has been matched by its failure to control the drug traffic."

Newsweek May 24, 1971

"Dope is hope."

Vietnam soldiers' motto

CHAPTER 1
THE ROOFTOP

Wednesday, June 17, 1970

Dusk.

At that darkening time of day, Foster and some of the troops would sit out on the roof of the villa, the jumble of the city spread before them, rendered in tile, terra-cotta and colorful tin. They would listen to the sounds of the night: traffic noises slowly diminishing, the occasional gunshot or explosion, including the grenade the previous evening that demolished the little sandwich stand in the alley behind the building. From their perch, they would witness the transformation of Saigon, and feel the new energies being released into the air. The difference between the days and nights was so extreme as to be almost spiritual.

Out on the sidewalk, in front of the villa, the day teemed with people in endless motion, thousands of them, men in light-colored shirts, women creating an endless sea of conical straw hats, bobbing on the surface of the traffic. Troung Minh Ky ran parallel to Cong Ly, the main boulevard between downtown Saigon and the American Military base at Tan Son Nhut. It was half as wide as the big street, but carried just as many cars and trucks, so every day was one long gridlock that was bad enough before the Americans arrived, but compounded over the years by military trucks and Jeeps. There was also the occasional 2-1/2 ton truck, the deuce and a half, loaded with GIs playing chicken with the people on the sidewalk. They'd swivel the mounted 50-caliber machine gun around, pointing it at the unfortunate old men and women huddling on the side of the road.

The air never lost its smell of oil and cheap gasoline. Those who were desperate enough to eat something from one of the *shin-to* stands would inevitably taste a strong savor of 10-W-

40. Press all those vapors to the ground with tropical heat and humidity, and that was the aura of the day.

But at dusk, when the sun turned the faded white walls to a succulent orange, when the patches of mildew melted into the surrounding darkness, brick and tar gave up the flame of day, and newer, more unusual aromas washed over the walls. Cooking. The fumes of Mamasan concocting dinner downstairs, aided and abetted by her daughter Young Dung, combined with the odors of other exotic recipes wafting in from down the block, Former Sergeant First Class Harris' English Leather, Weinberg's Canoe, the inevitable Old Spice, and the merest hint of pot smoke that always seemed to drift around the villa's makeshift rooftop terrace.

Best of all, the traffic would thin out, the noise from the ciclos diminish, and military trucks and Jeeps virtually disappear. The crowds that pushed and hurried during the day magically lost mobility, like the tide going out. They simply stood around, thousands of people transformed by the hour, bicycle rickshaws with girls decked out in elegant *au dais*, their drivers, like Cinderella's mice, magically changed into their business agent for the night.

Foster realized: he'd been in country three months to the day.

* * * *

Ninety days earlier: Wednesday, March 18, 1970

WHUMP! Front row seat. Right over *there*, not fifty yards away, a huge gout of red earth and flame erupted from the ground, close enough so that he saw it, felt it and heard it all at the same time. Little pieces of rock and dirt singed his skin. The first, wispy, ever-so-slight smells of combat drifted up to him. Without thinking, Foster sucked in a lungful of air. He knew Tan Son Nhut would smell like this...he knew it. Then the sirens kicked in, a high, keening wail, shaking the air.

To his left, a troop he'd seen on his flight was sniffing the air with an expression of unlikely and completely inappropriate enthusiasm. It was Warrant Officer 2 Samuel Taylor ("Spider") Webb, who had walked off the United Airlines charter flight directly behind Foster, and directly into the first mortar attack of his life. He was delighted.

As Webb bent over to pick up his bag, he heard the rocket in the air just slightly before it crunched into the other side of the runway, a kind of *deja vu* sound, an oddly familiar noise even though he'd never experienced it in all his 24 years, because mortar shells fell so infrequently in Milwaukee. Music. The sounds of combat. Exactly what he'd signed up for.

Nothing like walking into a war on your birthday, said his little voice. *Happy 24th. I hope we see a few more. So that's what a mortar explosion looks like. Probably a lot more where this came from. But as long as you can see them, you're okay.*

"What the hell's going on?" yelled a voice from behind him. A real voice, not like the ones from inside his head, a high thin nervous voice, shaking with tension.

Webb spun around. *WHUMP!* Another explosion, a bit farther away, but he still felt it. It was then that he noticed the ashen-faced and trembling lieutenant who'd stumbled aboard the plane in Hawaii with about 40 cases of camera equipment. His name plate said "Foster."

"It's a mortar attack. Sir."

"Shouldn't we take cover?" yelled Foster. Webb really didn't want to, because the sound of the rockets, the explosions, were right out of those old John Wayne movies. Exactly why he'd come to Vietnam. He didn't want to miss a minute of it, but another huge *WHUMP!*, uncomfortably close this time, lifted both of them about an inch off the ground, and made him understand that strolling around in that kind of storm wasn't the smartest thing he could do. Even the Duke would run for cover in a situation like this. "We have to find a bunker," Foster yelled.

"Over there!" Webb pointed to a group of soldiers, running as fast as they could, crouched over, all in the same direction like a herd of stampeding buffalo with their asses in the air, toward a low structure made of sandbags, covered with steel planking and more sandbags. Webb took off, then looked back to see if the lieutenant was following. He wasn't.

"But...what about all my stuff?" Foster bleated. *Great*, Webb's voice commented. *The first guy you meet in country is both an officer and an asshole.*

"Forget your stuff. Follow me. The bunker's over there!"

They sprinted toward the bunker, diving into the dirt once or twice as a couple of close rounds shook them off their feet. Together they tumbled into the opening, along with what seemed like half a million other troops, and found a place to huddle.

WHUMP!

"I'm Webb."

"Leon Foster. Call me Lenny."

"Today's my birthday. Do you believe it?"

"Yes."

"Where you headed, sir?" Webb asked.

"DASPO," Foster said, looking around, dazed. "Department of the Army Special Photographic Office. I'm the Officer In Charge of F-Troop based here in Saigon. I'm here for three months of TDY."

"You a photographer?"

Foster seemed offended. "No, I'm not a photographer. I'm an 8511 MOS."

"And that is...?"

"I'm a director, a *filmmaker*. You?"

"I fly choppers. Just got out of Ft. Wolters. Supposed to go up to Tay Ninh."

WHUMP! Another explosion. The roof shook, and the men in the bunker were blessed with a fine dusting of red sand.

"This shit's not supposed to happen," said Foster. "Hope my stuff doesn't get blown up."

Foster took a breath, or tried to. It was March in Saigon. He'd heard about March in Saigon: with the monsoons approaching the heat and humidity were strangling, and when you stayed in a bunker for more than ten minutes, you crawled out soaked with nasty sweat. There were probably 40 to 50 troops huddled in the bunker and the stench was overwhelming. But Sgt. Goodhardt told him before he left Hawaii that you never hear the mortar that lands right on top of you, so as long as you could take in the stink, you were still alive.

As hard as he tried not to stare, Webb couldn't help looking at the men sitting around him in the pallid subterranean light, leaning forward with their elbows on their knees.

"Look at these guys," he whispered to Foster. The two men were sitting well apart from the rest of the group, even though the bunker was crowded.   Nobody wanted to be near a Fuckin' New Guy in any combat situation. Bad luck.

"How come they all look older than us?" Foster wondered. And indeed, they did. "Great bunch of faces, though. They'd look good on camera. 'The Countenance of War.' Maybe I'll write a script."

"You nuts?" Webb tried not to stare. The faces of the men he'd gone through helicopter training with at Ft. Wolters were young and smooth and full, eager and promising. Like his. So were the ones on the flight over. But these, these were older. No. Not older...aged. Faces chiseled in the harsh peculiar orange light of the bunker.

Y'know," Webb whispered to Foster, squeezed in next to him on the bench, "when I was a kid, I showed up to baseball practice with a brand new glove. The other kids' gloves were all beat up and used, like they were playing pro all their lives. But my glove told everybody I was new. Right now, I feel like I walked in here with a new glove." Foster just nodded, and looked up at the ceiling of the bunker, as if he could see the little rockets raining down from the sky.

He averted his eyes from those around him, glancing up just briefly, and infrequently. He'd heard of the thousand-yard-stare, but had never seen one up close. After making films for a year at the Army Pictorial Center in Astoria, New York, Foster looked at Webb, and at everyone else, as if they were centered in his viewfinder. One of his instructors in his college film program told him to always notice details, and he took the advice to heart. He started to notice Webb.

Painfully ordinary normal brown hair above a high forehead, with a little bit of baby-pink scalp showing through in the back. He'd be bald some day, probably sooner than later. Normal brown eyes, deep-set and intense, a kind of longish, narrow face with maybe a little too much in the chin, but not so much that it would set him apart. Thin lips, and cheeks that were perhaps a bit too smooth for his age. Aside from that, he looked exactly like any Midwestern kid who just arrived at the war. This guy, thought Foster, looks like exactly nobody. Almost everyone has had another person come up to them and say, "You look like Dustin Hoffman," or "You remind me of my Uncle Sol." Nobody ever said that to Webb. In an attempt to set himself off, he'd given himself a mustache for his birthday, which he had started growing the previous day. Foster didn't think he'd look too great on camera.

Both men wore formerly spotless uniforms, painfully pressed, sinfully starched, and, except for the red smears they'd picked up from diving into the dirt on the way to the bunker, they were not much the worse for the overnight flight from Honolulu.

The troops around them also wore uniforms, but those were more like green skins or pelts, well lived-in, crusted with red dirt and sweat, some adorned with telling rips and tears, each one a story. Webb wanted his to look the same.

"Looks like these guys were on their way out," said Webb.

"Waiting for the plane we came in on. 'Gentlemen, the captain has informed us that our takeoff time will be delayed due to the weather. There is a slight mortar shower in the area, but we expect it to clear up soon.'"

"You're some funny guy. Sir." Webb looked at Foster sideways. "Take a look around. Think you're going to some kind of party?"

"Actually, yes."

"What do you mean?"

"Never mind." Foster considered this brief spell in the bunker a temporary setback. Before he left New York, and for weeks at DASPO headquarters in Hawaii, he'd been told that his time in-country would be a combination picnic, beer blast, and sex orgy. DASPO troops lived in some kind of palatial villa in Saigon, he'd been told, with servants and private quarters and real bathrooms. And air conditioning.

Webb's thoughts ran in a contrary direction. *Great*, his voice mused. *You spent months as a warrant officer candidate at Fort Wolters, letting those TAC officers shit all over you, doing all those goddam pushups, and now you're a newby all over again. The TAC officers didn't care whether you lived or died, and neither do these guys.*

The worst thing about mortars is how *random* they are. Outside, a thunderstorm of them was rolling across the sky, some distant, some not so distant, cottony *whumps*, heard through the sandbags and pierced steel that made up the roof. Webb looked up, too, wondering when one would come crashing through. Nobody else looked up. Only the newbys.

"Fuck this shit," the sergeant next to him whispered, half to himself.

"Did you hear about Carlson?" said a kid across from Webb. Jesus, thought Webb, that guy can't be more than seventeen.

"Carlson who?" someone asked.

"Assistant cook. Sat down in the latrine last night and got a bouncing Betty up the ass."

"Fuck this shit," the sergeant whispered again. Outside, the abrupt sounds of the mortars continued to pound against the roof, far and near. The place was beyond hot. Webb and Foster were sticky with sweat.

Webb knew he was in for it the second his toes touched the tarmac that day. His voice whispered to him, generating a tingle of anticipation, kind of like stage fright, scared and excited at the same time. It wasn't because of the airfield, even though the planes crowded in rows along the apron did lean heavily toward olive drab, and except for the gleaming white DC-8s chartered from United, any aircraft that looked even vaguely commercial were conspicuous by the simple but elegant absence of identifying marks. No friendly skies in Vietnam, it seemed, and the price of a ticket home was likely to be very high, indeed.

Once out of the bunker, the terminal didn't give him a clue either, because it looked, surprisingly enough, like any passenger's lounge at any fairly decent airport in any number of third world countries or, come to think of it, almost any airport in the small towns around Milwaukee.

"Some airport, huh?" said Foster, trying to get the conversation going again. He was the only one, and he felt uncomfortable, like talking in a crowded elevator. Outside, the little he'd been able to notice before things started blowing up was too familiar, too ordinary. It looked like any old day of the week at the busiest airport on the planet. A little noisier than most airports, maybe, but that was only because in March of 1970 the sky above Saigon was a magic portal out of which streamed a literally unending supply of metal and meat. Great place to start a cargo cult, because flying trucks settled to the hot earth around the clock, disgorging their explosives, supplies, materiel, provisions, boxes, crates and barrels, pallets, entire boxcars of hard goods, soft goods,

goods that explode, and the soldiers, all the soldiers, the softest goods of all.

Too familiar, even so. Too normal. Except for the slight matter of the mortar attack, it didn't look much like combat, but it certainly looked like the military, especially to a brand new hot shot chopper jock just out of Ft. Rucker, Alabama by way of Ft. Wolters, Texas, and a frustrated filmmaker just out of New York City by way of Honolulu and Miami Beach.

After the mortar storm roiled off into the distance, Webb and Foster crawled out of the underground, no longer clean and pressed, unbending themselves, squinting in the fading orange light of early evening. Webb took a deep breath.

"Smell that?" It was gunpowder, saltpeter and burnt earth. "I love it."

Foster walked aimlessly in circles, his arms flapping loosely at his sides.

"Now, where's my stuff? Where's my goddam *stuff?* There's supposed to be 40 cases of equipment, and I signed for it. Maybe it's over there. Somebody's supposed to pick me up...." He wandered off, muttering to himself.

"Have a nice war," Webb said to his retreating back. But he was gone. Asshole.

CHAPTER 2
THE FIVE O'CLOCK FOLLIES

Thursday, March 19, 1970

The movie screen at the Joint US Public Affairs Office headquarters in Saigon glimmered with the image of five soldiers urinating. Though the audience for this unorthodox spectacle could not properly appreciate the fact, the soldiers were performing this act in military fashion, by the numbers, according to a new set of Army regulations which detailed for G.I.s returning to the states the correct procedure for producing a urine specimen. Their backs were, mercifully, to the camera, the ritual taking place in a barracks bathroom, closely supervised by an obviously uncomfortable young lieutenant perched on a chair at the end of the line of urinals, and observed in stunned disbelief by fifty or sixty assorted news correspondents assembled in the featureless briefing room. Many of them had been covering the war in Vietnam for quite some time, and until this instant, thought they had seen it all.

Dan Rather from CBS was in the room that day, taking time out from a quick tour of the country because of what a correspondent from NBC had told him.

"Everybody calls it the Five O'clock Follies, even though they hold it at four thirty. You don't want to miss it."

A writer from *Playboy* sat along the back wall fidgeting with his cassette recorder, his unlikely presence explained by the upcoming Bunny tour of remote firebases.

The reporters sat patiently. They were world-weary, war-weary, and knew that the Follies was intended to be, just like every other military briefing from the dawn of time, more a profession of faith than pronouncement of fact. On the tiny JUSPAO stage, in front of the screen, Colonel Herman Berner wielded a wicked collapsible metal pointer with a red plastic tip, and began his daily ritual of oversimplification.

"We've been running these drug tests," said Colonel Berner, "on troops rotating back to the States, and they've been extremely successful in curbing heroin use." Some of the reporters barely stifled a smirk.

Colonel Berner was a small round pale, moist man, and what he lacked in neck he made up in forehead. Nobody could look at him without remarking the uncanny resemblance he bore to the actor Broderick Crawford. He was the head of the Joint US Public Affairs Office, JUSPAO in Saigon, chiefly responsible for disseminating information to the international press corps. It was his job -- indeed, it was his pleasure -- to paste a positive face on every event, be it triumph or tragedy, the US military experienced in Southeast Asia. A believer in the cause, a committed career officer, and an accomplished briefer, Colonel Berner fiercely loved and fiercely defended a job that nobody else on the planet would have taken on a bet. It was on his desk, at the very bottom of the chain of command, that the problem of the notorious Sergeant Ledbetter and the orders from CINCPAC and USARV finally came to rest. He'd spent the earlier part of the war trying, through assiduous recitation of hard facts, body counts which almost nobody believed, and other statistics, to prove that the war was being won. But even he had given that up, and was now professing victories in another war. The heroin epidemic, and general drug abuse in the military, were his favorite topics -- especially since USARV had specifically ordered him to come up with positive stories on the military's fight against drugs, even if he had to pull them from his fevered imagination. He'd never been tasked with that type of assignment before, and even though the drug abuse project had flowed downhill past half a dozen buck-passing commands before it pooled in his lap, Berner had convinced himself that his orders had come from his Commander in Chief, Richard Milhous Nixon, directly and personally to him. There was a saying in Vietnam that there were only two ways to make General: by fighting or by briefing. Colonel Berner had stars in his eyes.

The men on the screen, micturition mission accomplished, zipped up and put their little half-yellow plastic cups on a metal table. There was an uncomfortable silence in the briefing room, punctuated only by the distant *WHUMP!* of mortar explosions. The correspondents shifted from cheek to cheek in their chairs and tried not to look at each other.

"I feel it incumbent upon myself," said Colonel Berner, "to give you my personal analysis on the drug problem in Southeast Asia."

"Shit," whispered half the men in the room, but that didn't stop him.

Between 1968 and that afternoon in March of 1970, the use of marijuana among US troops had rocketed from 25 to 50 per cent, and heroin use was climbing at an even more alarming rate. No longer able to maintain its blindness to the epidemic, the Military Assistance Command finally mobilized huge campaigns against it, the on-camera pissing contest being the most recent. Drug sniffing dogs. A special crime lab. Prosecutors and DEA agents flown in from the states to detect and prosecute drug users. In 1969, they arrested over 8,000 soldiers, and never made the slightest dent in the problem.

"Looks like they're really trying to do something," said the young man from a German syndicate to the overweight AP stringer next to him.

"You're not from around here, are ya? A lot of these kids don't want to be here, so they stay as stoned as they can. And besides, you can buy ready made joints real cheap on any streetcorner. They got stuff inside that'll blow the top of your head off. And they dip 'em in opium oil."

"They do?"

"Yeah. Here, you can have one of mine. Save it for later, and don't take more than two or three hits or you won't be able to walk for hours."

Colonel Berner cleared his throat. "No sooner did the military mount a campaign against pot than heroin made an emphatic and perhaps somewhat overdue appearance." It was, in fact, absolutely everywhere, coming from laboratories along the borders of Thailand, Laos and Cambodia, carried in by Americans returning from R&R, corrupt South Vietnamese government functionaries, Thai and Laotian Air Force pilots, American military cargo flights. Sometimes they knew it was on board, sometimes they didn't. The traffic was so pervasive, Colonel Berner reminded the correspondents as he was halfway through the second of his carefully structured three points (all military briefers had to make three points, no more, no less), and the supply so bountiful, that a typical soldier could support a full-scale heroin addiction for about two dollars a day. What the colonel did not say, and did not need to say, was that the drug traffic ran insidious tendrils into so many areas of the war effort that everybody was scared shitless. The reporters knew, for example, that US Ambassador Ellsworth Bunker's command pilot had been arrested with $8 million worth of heroin on the ambassadorial aircraft. Then there was that Military Assistance Command colonel who wound up in front of a court martial for shipping heroin back to the States inside decorative (and hand painted) plaster Oriental elephants. And nobody needed to remind them that teenage girls sold it at roadside shin-to stands, most of it almost a hundred per cent pure.

Berner, despite the dearness of the subject to his heart, was a master at maintaining eye contact, another critical briefing skill. The eyes of his audience were beginning to glaze over at exactly the right time, so he carefully tied his three points together.

"Now, I'm proud to announce that the Army has developed even more effective methods to combat this menace to our morale and our war effort.

"We have formed," he continued, "an elite drug interdiction unit that will put a stop to the flow of opium and refined heroin into this country from Burma, Laos and Cambodia. Of course, the details are confidential for security reasons, but I do have the honor of introducing the unit's new commanding officer."

Colonel Berner went on to rhapsodize at length about this brave officer and gentleman, a paragon of military virtue, dedicated, eager to meet the challenge.

"I'd like you to meet...Colonel Xoan."

A tall, thin, elegant Vietnamese officer stood up to a smattering of halfhearted applause. His cheekbones were elegantly high, his teeth painfully white, his eyes deep and flashing. He could have been an Asiatic Erroll Flynn, and his *éclat* was enhanced, in some peculiar way, by the flowing white aviator's scarf he wore around his neck.

"What's the story on the scarf?" the *Playboy* reporter said to the AP stringer.

"The latest fad among Vietnamese Air Force officers. Most of 'em look like shmucks with scarves around their necks, but this guy kind of makes it work."

Berner had a good deal more to say about the prodigious task awaiting Colonel Xoan, and how he was going to receive the full cooperation and vigorous support of every single man, woman and child in the American Military Establishment, regardless of race, creed, color, religion, or national origin, but he could sense the restlessness among the reporters. Many of them had actually regained consciousness, and were shifting in their wooden folding chairs, making scraping sounds on the floor. The rest were edging toward the door, anxious to bolt back across the street to the verandah of the Continental Hotel, or the Caravelle. It was getting dangerously close to happy hour, so Berner made a few lame concluding remarks, thanked Colonel Xoan, and let them go.

CHAPTER 3
THE RECRUITER

Thursday, March 19, 1970

At an Army recruiting office a few steps off Times Square, the following conversation took place between Master Sergeant Warren Ledbetter and a potential soldier.

"Ever been arrested?"

"Couple times."

"What for?"

"Fighting." Good. A warrior, Sergeant Ledbetter thought.

"Anything else?"

"Inciting to riot at a Knicks game."

"Inciting to riot?"

"The ref made a really bad call." Okay. He's a leader.

"Oh. And there was a burglary charge, but they couldn't make it stick." Hmmm. Possible procurement specialist.

"Ever convicted?"

"Naw. They gimme probation every time."

"Why do you want to enlist in the Army?"

"That probation guy told me I could do a couple years with Uncle Sam, or a couple years in the can. This looks like a better deal." Ledbetter eyed him carefully once again, and decided to take the plunge.

"You're a smart guy, so I know you'll understand all the important opportunities the Army can provide for a young man in your position. Here's what I recommend. You can join up now and go to basic. I'll make sure they send you right to Nam where you can stay fucked up from the day you arrive till the day you leave."

"What? Really? You allowed to tell me shit like this?"

"What do you think? Of course not. This is between you and me, and if you tell anybody I said it, I'll deny it, and they always believe me. Besides, I ain't telling you something you don't know. Like I said, I can see you're a smart guy. You know the dope in Southeast Asia is the best in the world."

"Yeah...I saw something about that on TV."

"Well, it's true. And it's really cheap, too. They roll their joints in opium oil."

"No shit? But what if I get killed?" They always asked that.

"You're not gonna get killed. Look. Over a hundred thousand guys have gone over there, and how many of them got killed? Under ten per cent. Besides, the war is winding down. There's no action. No shooting. Your odds are pretty good. Especially if you're smart and stay out of trouble. Besides, the shit is so good, you won't even know you're gone until you get wherever it is you go. And if you're real smart, I'll put you in touch with some people who can set you up in your own little business. If you know what I mean." They always knew what he meant. "We got a deal?"

The young man gulped once and nodded his head. "Great. Why don't you wait outside while I finish up the paperwork, and we'll get you all signed up."

Master Sergeant Warren Ledbetter was feeling more than moderately pleased with himself. He leaned back in his slightly-creaking swivel chair behind his gray metal desk, clasped his hands behind his head, watched the young man leave his office, and permitted himself a small, satisfied stretch. Once again, for the seventeenth month in a row, he had exceeded his recruitment quota. He strolled to the marker board on the wall and wrote "B. Jackson," the name of the latest underprivileged young man who had made the mistake of believing him.

"God damn," said Sgt. Ashley from across the room. "How the hell do you do it?"

SFC Ledbetter wasn't just any recruiting sergeant. He was, in fact, the Army's top recruiting sergeant. Stationed in New York City, he had consistently exceeded his quota for enlistees by at least 100% every month. The brass couldn't figure it out, but they certainly didn't try to stop him. Even though the war was in the ostensible process of being "Vietnamized," there was still plenty of need for manpower in the military.

March 19, 1970. He had exactly one month left at the New

York office, and the Army was going to give him a medal. His chest was already a fruit salad of various awards, commendations, and citations from his two tours of Vietnam, none of them earned in combat. But he was a whiz at logistics, and had made his not-inconsiderable reputation by being the best supervisor and purchasing agent in Southeast Asia, and perhaps in the entire Far East. His specialty: retail merchandise and liquor for the Army's base exchanges, officers' clubs, and NCO clubs. He had, in fact, gone into a kind of business with three other top sergeants, all of whom managed to get themselves transferred from posting to posting as a group, and to put their shell company cleverly between the people who sold merchandise to the base exchanges and the people who bought it. Throughout Southeast Asia, millions of dollars flowed through their corporation, plenty of it stuck to their hands, and they never had to touch the goods. Sure, a few of his partners had taken a fall in 1969 for all the kickbacks and bribes they received, and a general or two kind of got put through the wringer, but Ledbetter, with his characteristic good fortune, managed to skate.

After his third tour, he'd been rewarded with a posting to New York, not far from where he'd grown up. He belonged to the city, and felt most at home on its streetcorners, in its bars, and on the sidewalks in front of its less savory nightclubs. He was expecting yet another promotion, and more than anything, he wanted to be a Sergeant Major, with a nice comfy posting to Europe, and a job heading up the biggest NCO clubs. Torrejon in Spain, maybe. Or someplace in Italy. He didn't need the money. He just wanted it.

His glow of smug satisfaction lasted a pitifully short time. Moments after B. Jackson had made his misguided commitment to serve his country, a Captain from the CID strode in. On his heels was the largest MP Ledbetter had ever seen in his life.

"Sergeant Ledbetter?"

"Yes, sir." He jumped to his feet.

"Master Sergeant Warren Ledbetter?"

Gulp. They used his first name. A bad sign.

"Yes, sir."

"I'm Captain Harold Weitzman from the Criminal Investigation

Division. Do you have a couple of minutes? I'd like to ask you a few questions."

A few questions? Ledbetter got that sinking sensation in his stomach, like the time his chopper loaded with black market scotch and color Polaroid film got shot down near Hue, dropping out from under him, whirling toward the impenetrable green below. That day, he'd been truly afraid he would die, or be captured and tortured by the VC. He'd lost thousands of dollars in that crash. This was worse, and in a perverse way, he'd almost been waiting for it.

Ledbetter became a recruitment superstar because he thought to offer the kind of peculiar incentive he had proposed to B. Jackson. The young men he dealt with were of two types: the patriotic adventurer, looking for the chance to see a war up close, lusting for the medals and glory and masculine fulfillment they foolishly believed could be achieved only through intensive participation in armed conflict. They were easy to sign up, because they had sold themselves on the military before they ever walked into the office. Ledbetter had only to demonstrate that of all the branches of service, the Army offered the best opportunity for the particular type of satisfaction they sought. He neglected to tell them that in March, 1970 most of the troops out in the Vietnam boonies were bored stiff, with nothing to do but smoke pot as soon as the sun went down.

The second type, like B. Jackson, was running away from something, rather than toward, and they were even easier. These boys were the misfits, the miscreants, the incipient felons, desperate to get away from home, flee the ghettos of the south Bronx or put themselves beyond the reach of the law. It was among them that Ledbetter had his greatest success because he had an almost supernatural ability to judge character, or the lack of it.

In many cases, of course, the prospective inductee had already been caught up with. Faced with the choice, most of them concluded that the Army would be a better hitch than jail. Most of them were right, and this made Ledbetter's job much easier.

Ledbetter's walk-in traffic increased enormously in the weeks after Walter Cronkite had run a story on CBS News, showing troops in Vietnam smoking their brains out in the field using a double-barreled shotgun as a huge bong.

Experts at evil have a perverse gift. Abnormal charisma, the talent of easy persuasion, something. Ledbetter's gift was the ability to unerringly recognize people like himself. He never said the wrong thing to the wrong person. No potential recruit ever dreamed of reporting him.

But by 1970, so many troops were returning home hooked on heroin that the military, try as it might, could no longer ignore the problem. The boys were smoking pot and hash oil, or taking pills, which, some authorities believed led to the upsurge of fragging and the mysterious demise of young lieutenants and many of the veteran by-the-book-die-for-your-country sergeants. The drug problem had become a depressingly frequent mention on the network news, like the body count, and it was causing a series of intense high level meetings at the Pentagon. The military told the public they had programs in place, which they did, but nothing worked. The White House Office of Drug Abuse handed the problem to the Joint Chiefs of Staff, who bumped it to CINCPAC, the Commander in Chief Pacific, who immediately tasked MACV, the Military Assistance Command/Vietnam, which immediately tasked USARV, the US Army/Vietnam command, to get results right this minute. USARV rose to the challenge by letting the problem flow down the chain of command in time honored fecal fashion until it eventually landed on the Saigon desk of one very excited public affairs Colonel who immediately recognized the problem as his greatest career assignment.

The military, however, hadn't been completely lax in meeting the challenge. There were drug testing programs, lectures, posters ("Marijuana Means Trouble"), rehab centers, spasms of arrests in Saigon and other places, but the news media and the Americans who watched faithfully over their dinners every night wanted something a bit more dramatic. Then, on March 19, 1970, Captain Weitzman walked into the office of Master Sergeant Warren Ledbetter.

"The Army," said Weitzman, "has known about your activities for some time. It may make you feel better if I tell you that some of the brass wanted us to leave you alone because you were signing up so many recruits, and they didn't care how you did it. But we can't ignore the problem any longer. We need dramatic arrests. Front page news. You're it."

Ledbetter leaned back in his chair. He didn't get where he was by being stupid, just dishonest and immoral. He knew at once that he had to keep his time in Leavenworth to a minimum, or avoid the place completely so he could enjoy the riches he had stashed in his three Cayman Island bank accounts. Honor among thieves being a persistent myth, the Sergeant talked...and talked...and talked. First, he ascertained that anything he said would help him out in the long run, and anybody he turned in would be traded for reduced punishment. Then, for the better part of three hours, he spoke volumes into a cheap, tiny microphone attached to a cheap, tiny cassette recorder. He was, he claimed, the smallest of the fish, but he would show the JAG office where the big fish were, and provide them with buckets full of bait.

It took Weitzman four days to transcribe the tapes and write his report, stopping every so often for a muttered "God damn," or "son of a bitch," or other expression of incredulity. When he proudly turned it in and began preparing for Ledbetter's court martial, his boss told him the whole thing was ridiculous, impossible, farfetched, and fictitious. But procedure is procedure, and the report was duly passed along to the Inspector General, who confided his opinion only to his aide.

"If this confession gets out," the Inspector General whispered, "Congress is going to jump right down our throats, even if it's not true. So will the hippies and the rest of the peaceniks."

"Begging your pardon, sir. But what if it *is* true?"

"Then we're really fucked."

In characteristic fashion, he passed the whole mess up the line to his four-star-general superior with a big red stamp and a note:

"It is not possible that corruption can exist within our military establishment on such an organized scale. If we believe these tapes, we must accept that there is a chain of criminal activity that reaches from the villages of Vietnam through the Vietnamese government to the top levels of the

Pentagon. These accusations have been made by a dishonored soldier who is seeking to avoid a harsh sentence. However, I respectfully recommend that we take a strong proactive posture on this matter, and attack it with every public relations tool at our disposal."

And so they did.

CHAPTER 4
THE MAGIC FINGERS

Thursday, March 19, 1970

"This can't be right," Kyle Longacre muttered. He coughed once, twice, from the exhaust of the passing ciclos. The raucous little motorbikes burned diesel fuel with such marginal efficiency that riding behind one was like putting your face in the cone of a CO_2 fire extinguisher and taking a deep, enthusiastic breath. A huge hit of noxious fumes, right down the lungs...part of the accepted ambiance of a ride through the streets of Saigon. It was late in the day, so the boulevards were full of ciclos, a constant ear-shattering racket that filled the steaming afternoon air with black carbonized mist.

He looked at the address, then down at his orders one more time. Troung Minh Ky? Right. Number 842? Okay. Magic Fingers Massage Salon, one flight up. A GI relaxation paradise.

"This *can't* be right," he said again. He was anything but happy to be there, exhausted from the heat, little dribbles of sweat making his uniform stick to his back, trickling through his intense eyebrows. Across the street was a line of villas, almost small mansions, once occupied by the Americans' well-to-do French predecessors. Longacre tried not to think of what happened to them. On his side of the crowded street was a line of shin-to stands, skinny people selling things on what passed for a sidewalk, all kinds of things. One woman sat proudly behind a huge pile of buttons. An old man presided over a tattered blanket spread out with the guts of ancient radios. Vacuum tubes, transformers, knobs and dials. There was the stolen liquor from the PX and just about anything else that could be heisted from the Americans. In front of each blanket, a grunt or two was haggling with mama and papasan for something to take back to the base... something that might make the next few days bearable.

The blankets all had eyelets sewn into the corners, with a rope running through them. When the police came, the vendors could gather up their wares with one pull of the rope, and run away.

The crowd in front of one particular stall was especially thick. "Ten dollars," one grunt shouted. "Twelve," yelled another. One glance through the crunch of people to the booty on the rough wooden table was enough to make him understand. In country, everyone inevitably suffered prolonged paroxysms of diarrhea from the orange malaria pills Uncle Sam handed out, and until their bodies adjusted, they'd kill for a bottle of Pepto Bismol. Mamasan had hit it big. She'd scored a fabulous array of black market bubble-gum-colored bottles that were precious beyond measure. She was holding out for $20 apiece, and getting it.

Longacre trudged up the block one more time, dragging his duffel, which was gradually becoming more of a burden, made a decision, and hauled himself up a flight of narrow musty stairs to the Magic Fingers Massage Salon. A hot pink door, with flowers painted on it, and a crude sign, "Please Knock." He did. The hallway smelled like fish sauce. Everything smelled like fish sauce.

The door opened a crack and an eye appeared. An Oriental eye, possibly belonging to a young man in his twenties.

"We're closed," he said in perfect American English. It was the last thing Longacre expected to hear.

"Wait. Is this 842 Troung Minh Ky?"

"Yeah. Come back around five. Best massage in town."

"I'm Longacre. Here to see..."

"Oh," said the eye. "Hang on a sec."

The eye and the crack disappeared like a startled prairie dog. Longacre put aside his curiosity about the man behind the door and looked around the small landing. The walls were covered with photographs, old 8x10 glossies behind glass, curling and faded, young Vietnamese women in various undignified yet undeniably provocative postures. Some photos were in frames covered with tinfoil, peeling and shabby. The women in the pictures fell into two groups:

beautiful and more than beautiful. The very thin girls had strong bony faces. These were the beautiful ones --the pure Vietnamese. The second more than beautiful group had fuller and far more sensual features. These were the Eurasians, another gift from the long-departed interbreeding French.

In the glass, Longacre saw his reflection. He realized he hadn't really looked at himself for quite some time. His name suited him exactly. Everything about him was long, his fingers, his chin, his nose, all parts of him presenting an unmistakable aspect of attenuation. His hair, thick, straight and abundant, was so black it was almost blue, combed straight back from his forehead. His eyes were the same deep tunnel color set off underneath by poochy hangdog bags the shade of old liver. He was twenty-eight, and felt a lot older. He looked it, too.

The door opened. He turned, and saw the owner of the eye, who was indeed a young Vietnamese man in his twenties, about five-eight, taller than most.

"Okay, pal. Right this way." The door opened and the young man started off down a long hallway. Longacre had to brush past a painfully thin woman, certainly well over a hundred and sixty years old, who pointed at him with a gnarled finger. If Longacre had paid attention in high school English class, he would have remembered the Three Weird Sisters, asking Macbeth to step right up to the boiling cauldron and read his future therein. He was treated to another whiff of *nuoc mam*, the fermented fish concoction most GIs called "armpit sauce," stronger this time.

He stopped, startled. Aside from the fish sauce, the air inside the Magic Fingers was blessedly cool. Jesus, he thought, this place is actually air conditioned. The establishment obviously catered to an elevated clientele, because air conditioning in Saigon was practically priceless.

He followed the man uncertainly through the inevitable beaded curtain, down a hallway lined with doors on both sides. The place was like no other massage parlor he had ever seen in Vietnam. The wallpaper was lush, stylish, and tasteful (as well as he could determine), the carpeting deep and quiet, and if he'd known what French Provincial was, he would have seen excellent examples of it in the sitting rooms and bedrooms off the hallway. Compared to the normal

Saigon steam and cream parlor, the Magic Fingers was the Taj Mahal.

If he hadn't been so absorbed in the atmosphere of the place, and wondering where his guide had learned to speak English like he was from Oklahoma, he'd never have been knocked sideways by the ravishing Vietnamese girl who came pounding down a set of stairs to his right, long straight black hair streaming furiously behind. She was yelling as loud as she could, so enraged he could see her trembling.

"You huckin' numba ten GI bastard! You son bitch!" "*Dit me!*"

Longacre recognized the phrase. Vietnamese for "fuck your mother," with that delightful scurrilous maternal implication thrown in.

The girl was yelling back up the stairs at a short GI with fuzzy black hair who stumbled across the upper landing, pulling his white boxer shorts up over chunky legs. "Thi Lanh! Wait a minute, goddamit!" He struggled with a pair of round black-framed glasses.

"*Ma y chet di!*" she screamed. Longacre was on his second tour, and he'd heard *ma y chet di* plenty out in the boonies. Go fucking die.

"You huck you motha!" Louder, this time. The Vietnamese language, like most Oriental tongues, has no words that began with the letter "F," so even people with the best English accents only managed to pucker up and blow a little, getting across a kind of "f" sound. They never really got their front teeth down on the lower lip for a true labio-dental fricative. Most of them, if they spoke English at all, spoke it like Thi Lanh.

The American got about halfway down the stairs, missed a step and somersaulted to the bottom, one foot in his shorts, the other out, rolling down the last eight or nine steps like an oblong bowling ball, making the same kind of noises, planting his face squarely on the scarred wood floor, about six inches from Longacre's boot. He lifted himself painfully to all fours in front of the girl, who towered over him, all five feet of her, fabulous legs coated by the most magical black micromesh stockings Longacre had ever seen, teasing seams up the back, elevated by the preposterously high black platform shoes she teetered on and one of which she let the GI have right under the chin.   His head snapped back, his round glasses went spinning across the hallway, and he rolled over onto his side. Longacre's eyes expanded like somebody had used a bicycle pump on them.

"I no put dirty thing there.   Put soup there, you huckin' numba ten sumbitch.   You want blowjob, you get goddam American girl put dirty thing in mouth.   I good girl.   I put soup in mouth.   You go make pictures of fish!   Huck you!" She cocked an exquisite black-nyloned leg back to kick him again, but found herself grabbed from behind by the man who had opened the door.   She whirled, glared at him, and fired off some more accelerated Vietnamese, which he answered, even sharper and faster.

The woman glanced at Longacre, stared hard at the man who still had a solid grip on her elbow, then looked around the empty hallway, her head jerking from place to place like a very small bird, long straight black shiny hair flinging itself around her head.   Her blazing eyes found Longacre's.   "Ah, goddam numba ten American GI asshole bastard. *Cai thaing cha de!*" He thought it meant son of a bitch.   She jerked her arm away from the man's grip and flung herself out the front door, skirt flashing around her thighs, giving him a too-brief glimpse of her lacy stocking bands, disappearing down the dark passage.

"Goddam it, Weinberg," the Vietnamese man said in perfect idiomatic English.   "Don't you know better than to ask a hooker around here for a blow job?   Gimme a hand here, will ya, buddy?"

Longacre helped the man pull Weinberg to his feet.   The unfortunate GI fumbled his glasses onto his face, wiped his mouth, looked at his hand, stared at Longacre for a long stunned second, shook his head, and limped back up the stairs.   At the end of the hallway, a door opened.

"Sorry about that.   Your guy's in there," the Vietnamese said, and abruptly vanished.   Longacre took a deep breath. They'd told him to report to a whorehouse.   It was a very good sign.   And a very nice whorehouse.

He let himself into a room that was bare, save for an elegant carved-wood desk, two engulfing leather armchairs, and delicately-tinted wallpaper that depicted sprays of roses.   This room, too, smelled like fish sauce.   The door opened again.

"Thanks, Walter," the man inside called to the retreating Vietnamese. "Sit down, Longacre." The man made it to the other side of the desk in three long, determined strides.

First impressions are lasting ones, and Longacre would never forget his first look at Major Alvin P. Sanderson. Of course, Longacre didn't know his name, didn't know he was a major, didn't know anything at all right then except that he was an American, dressed in a blue oxford shirt with button down collar, so heavily starched it could have stood up by itself and perhaps even walked a little, tan chinos, argyle socks and brown penny loafers. The kind of outfit an Ivy League college senior would be wearing in the States right about then, if he wasn't busy smoking dope and demonstrating against the war, the kind of outfit Longacre would have worn, if he'd gone to college instead of learning to fly a helicopter in Fort Wolters, Texas.

But Sanderson was no college student, and his face had not been gazing recently on any halls of ivy. It was a face like broken glass, atop a lean and craggy body, topped with brown hair straight back, a little longer than the US Army might have preferred. A low forehead, a heavy ridge of bone running just above his eye sockets, protecting the entrance to the tunnels that contained his eyes, wet places deep inside, shining like the goo in carnivorous plants that entices insects to tumble to the bottom.

Longacre stared at him. This is the kind of guy who'd have a bluebird tattooed on the head of his dick, and know how to make it flap its wings.

"Let me see your orders." Longacre handed them over. The man towered behind the table, riffled through the three stapled sheets, and handed them back.

"You *volunteered* for this? You don't even know what it is."

"I don't much care. I been flying ash & trash in the boonies for two tours, and if there's a chance I can get in on some action, I'll take it."

The major looked at Longacre like a huge penis had suddenly sprouted from his forehead. "They must be trying to get rid of you."

"I been thinking that."

"You're crazier than most. Okay, here goes. I'm Major Alvin P. Sanderson. What I'm about to tell you is classified under the Official Secrets Act. If you divulge any of this information to anyone, you will be court-martialed and executed."

"What if they find me innocent?" Longacre couldn't help asking.

"They won't. And don't ask smartass questions. Do you understand?"

"Yes. Sir."

"Good. At this very moment, Colonel Herman Berner..."

Longacre sat up in his chair, the legs scraping noisily on the tile floor.

"You know who Berner is?"

"Sorry, sir. Just a twitch. But yeah, I've heard the name. Who hasn't?"

"He's briefing the war correspondents about a special unit being set up to stop the flow of opium and heroin into Vietnam. And if I know Colonel Berner, he's making the whole thing sound like his idea.

"It's my unit. And it has to be kept secret to guard against sabotage by corrupt Vietnamese officials and military people involved in the drug trade, of which there are plenty. We operate out of our own compound at Tan Son Nhut, and we can be vulnerable to attack even by our own people. So we live off base, and we wear civilian clothes. There are some other sweet surprises, but I'll have Larue fill you in later. First, get rid of that uniform. Change in here, then I'll take you over to the villa. It's across the street."

As Longacre had noticed on his way in, the villas on the far side of the racketing street were in various stages of benign degeneration, but the one Sanderson led him toward was in somewhat better shape than the rest. The two men, dressed like aging college seniors, took their lives in their hands and darted through the maniacal traffic, narrowly missed by a Jeep that turned into the villa next door. Longacre got a glimpse of a ridiculously thin enlisted man behind the wheel, and an obviously terrified newby lieutenant hanging on to the passenger seat.

Hearts pounding, they made it to the opposite curb. Up close, Longacre could see high walls with jagged pieces of broken glass cemented into the top, a freshly-painted black wrought iron gate, and a faded, moderately gracious two-story building beyond.

We gotta get out of this place
If it's the last thing we ever dooooo.....

From the building next door, where the Jeep had turned in, reverberation shook the air. Heavy bass line, lots of percussion. It reminded Longacre of the stereo they'd had in their hooch back up in Cu Chi during his first tour. You could measure the volume on the Richter scale.

"Assholes," grumbled Sanderson. "I'd shoot 'em all, but we're supposed to be civilians."

"Who are they?"

"Some kind of goddam Army photographic unit. There's two or three film crews based in Hawaii and they come over here on temporary duty. I can't decide which bunch of the degenerate motherfuckers I hate the worst."

High-pitched screams and laughter floated over the walls from the house next door. Crashing sounds, rock and roll, the plaintive wail of lunatic dogs. As they walked past the gate, Longacre peered into the courtyard, where the GI from the massage parlor was surrounded by a horde of soldiers, laughing and patting him on the back.

Then, a scream. Longacre looked up. A huge, blonde suntanned woman, gloriously naked except for a tiny pink nurse's hat and surgical mask, exploded out of a window on the third floor balcony that fronted the villa, running for her life.

"Jesus," muttered Longacre, "look at those tits." The appendages in question bounced joyously as she ran, while behind her, a short dark troop with a ducktail haircut and a black movie camera on his shoulder stumbled along in determined pursuit. She disappeared into a window around the corner. So did he. Longacre heard another shriek, and a whoop.

He followed Sanderson to the villa next door, up a set of wide, cracked front steps, trying to make sense of what he'd just seen. Visions of naked ladies danced in his head like Christmas treats. He hadn't seen an unclothed Caucasian woman for a *very* long time, and he couldn't bring himself to go to bed with a Vietnamese woman, no matter how much he hated them.

The villa was unlike anyplace else he'd been in Vietnam.

A *real house*, not a hooch, with real rooms and ceiling fans and floors and hallways, two bathrooms on the first floor and one more on the second. He almost started to forgive Colonel Berner for screwing him so viciously. After more than twenty months of standing in the way of death, he'd finally walked into paradise.

"This is Larue," said Sanderson. "Get Longacre a bed and fill him in. I've gotta meet Colonel Xoan at the Continental. See you guys at the stadium." He disappeared again.

"Your room's upstairs," Larue said. He had thick brown hair that he wore combed straight back, and teeth so white they didn't look real. "I'll show you."

Longacre couldn't help asking. "The major said you'd fill me in. How 'bout starting with what you're doing here?"

Larue stopped on the stairs and turned around, his head level with Longacre's who was two steps below.

"Your first lesson. Most of us are here because we fucked up in ways they don't want people to know about. Get it?"

Longacre was stopped short. "Uhhh...sure."

"Don't suppose you'd like to tell me how *you* got here?" Larue inquired.

"I didn't do it. Besides, I've been flying Hueys in this shithole for twenty months, and so far I managed to keep myself under control. But right now I'm hot, I'm tired, I've had a very long day, some guy I never met before threatened me with a court martial in a whorehouse, this gorgeous hooker kicked a GI in the face because he wanted a blowjob, and I just saw a blonde bimbo with monster jugs run out a window. So I'm not really sure how twisted this situation is gonna get. And one more goddam thing. That asshole Colonel named Berner who I flew around fucked me over to cover his own ass. You lemme know when you got a couple of hours, because it's a real. Good. Story."

"Some other time," said Larue, backing off just a bit. "Come on."

"Hey," Longacre called up after him. "Nobody told me what you call this unit."

"The Shadows," Larue said, turning back toward him. "You're in the Shadows."

CHAPTER 5
FORMER SERGEANT FIRST CLASS HARRIS

Thursday, March 19, 1970

To begin with, there was Former Sergeant First Class Harris. Actually, he was a sergeant to the third power, since he'd served in practically every armed force known to man. He was inevitably the first person that DASPO troops encountered when they arrived at the villa on Troung Minh Ky.

Former Sergeant First Class Harris was the rarest of all jewels: a black man whose 30 years in the Army had really taught him how things worked. His talents for unorthodox procurement were as critical as they were legendary, because the military was not in the business of making motion pictures, and when the Department of the Army Special Photographic Office made films, they always required the acquisition of goods and services outrageously beyond the scope of the Army's Table of Organization & Equipment. The war was only incidentally a movie set, so the DASPO crews often had to get creative. Harris "knew people." He seemed to possess a special connection with sources of supply and methods of distribution that were laughably illegitimate. Nobody asked, and nobody wanted to know, which made Harris worth his weight in diamonds. He knew it, but he also knew that those diamonds would be glass once he was out of the service, a black man with virtually no education back on the streets in civvies.

He loved the Army, and would have stayed a soldier forever, but the previous year he'd been forced to confront the repugnant reality of retirement. Panicked, he immediately built the foundation for his new career. When Foster arrived at the villa, Harris had retired only the month before, after thirty years. He had long since decided that when the clock struck midnight, he would take his Army separation in Saigon and continue his career as a soldier of fortune instead of a soldier. His talents being virtually indispensable, the commanding officer had agreed to let him keep his room at the villa until he found another place to stay. He had no intention of finding another place to stay, because DASPO, and its continuously rotating film crews, were an unending source of revenue.

The first step in his retirement planning was to get a travel agent's license, and start booking charter flights from the States to Bangkok so the servicemen in country could fly their wives and sweethearts over when they pulled R&R. His second step was to establish a "talent agency" that booked bands into clubs on military bases all across the Pacific.

He loved everything about Vietnam, but three things enchanted him in particular. First, he loved the modest fortune he was making booking the flights. Second, he loved the somewhat larger fortune that flowed to him from booking sickly Filipino rock bands into all the downtown Saigon clubs, because he paid the bands about a fifth of what the clubs paid him. Harris routinely promised any group who signed with him that he'd get them a guest shot on the Ed Sullivan Show. Ed Sullivan hadn't done a TV show in years, but that didn't seem to bother Harris.

The third thing he loved -- even though it had no discernible effect on his net worth -- was watching a newby's expression when he saw the DASPO villa for the first time. He treasured those moments, and they were plentiful, because DASPO film crews rotated in and out about every three months. As he stood in the packed dirt courtyard, waiting for Ironman to bestow Lt. Foster on him, a luxurious expression crossed his face the way fine Swiss chocolate melts and flows upon the tongue.

Former Sergeant First Class Harris liked the fact that everyone was always so...*appalled* by it all. Especially the new lieutenants, which is exactly what Foster was supposed to be. And especially when they came out, like Foster, for the first time from Honolulu. From the air, Vietnam looked just like Hawaii, except for the bomb craters and the Agent Orange-d jungles. When you flew high over the cliffs and beaches on the approach to Tan Son Nhut, all you saw was paradise. On the ground, Former Sergeant First Class Harris would say, "That's a horse of a different wheelbase."

Ah, the newbys. When they pulled into the courtyard they would get out of the Jeep, heads swimming from the wild ride through the confused city with its swirling dirt, teeming traffic, through the huddled masses of people yearning, so the US Army told them, to breathe free. But nobody breathed free in Saigon, because the ciclos burned pure oil and farted enormous clouds of greasy black carcinogenic vapor.

"The first thing they always say," Former Sergeant First Class Harris would tell the troops, "is, 'This isn't what I expected.'" He was right. It was the first thing they always said.

Since Hawaii was DASPO's permanent station in the Pacific Theatre, the temporary duty in Vietnam entitled each of them to a princely (in the context of the mutilated Vietnamese economy) per diem of $26.25 per day. DASPO Lieutenants and Captains who stayed in-country long enough made in per diem about as much as a Brigadier General. They had few expenses, other than what they spent on beer and "massage therapy," which rarely if ever involved muscular manipulation, or even any contact at all above the waist. Even the enlisted men made almost as much as Colonels and everybody hated them. Since DASPO generally operated without rather than within traditional structure, those who were committed to running things in a strictly military fashion hated them the most. In any case, instead of paying to stay in hotels, their communal wealth allowed them to rent what was, from a military standpoint, practically a palace. Former Sergeant First Class Harris had found it, bought it from some Vietnamese businessman, and rented it back to the military through some kind of front company.

Finally, after a night in the officer's quarters recovering from the mortar attack, Foster was on his way to the villa. He'd heard about the place endlessly ever since he'd arrived at DASPO's Honolulu headquarters. The villa was legendary, and the unit's lore was rife with fantastic stories about the parties, orgies, alcoholic excesses, and drug-induced lunacies that had taken place there since around 1965. When the Army closed down the Astoria studios across the river from

Manhattan, Foster had fought for a transfer to DASPO, even making an audacious trip to the Pentagon to lobby for it personally, and celebrated the day his TDY orders had invited him onto a MACV flight to Saigon.

Vietnam was, after all, a war zone, offering not many benefits that would give military life any semblance of sanity. However, among the entitlements DASPO could muster up for the villa were two and a half servants, air conditioning for each of the seven bedrooms and five baths, along with the unit's own generator, two guard dogs, three hot squares a day, nightly feature films courtesy of their direct line to the Army Air Force Movie exchange, and an expansive rooftop terrace with a wet bar. There was no view, except for the spectacle of the sky at night, when flares and tracers lit the city. Foster was more than ready for the massage parlors, the hookers, and yes, even a smoke or two. He was even willing to write off the mortar attack at the airport as a mere aberration, along with the vehicular near-homicide they'd committed on the two men in civvies who were crossing the street as they drove up. But this was 1970, the Year of the Dog, and Foster, along with many others, would suffer severe disappointment.

In the Saigon of the time, regular troops lived in the barracks on the sprawling MAC-V base adjoining Tan Son Nhut. But the troops who wound up in DASPO were anything but regular. The unit was made up of film students who hadn't managed to beat the draft, still photographers aching to get that Pulitzer shot of people caught in napalm attacks so they could peddle them to *LIFE* magazine, and officers like Foster, who'd gone through ROTC so the Army would pay for his graduate school. They were creative artists, men of tender sensibility and poetic impulse who had analyzed the brooding cinematic images of Bergman *ad nauseam*, who had seen "Battleship Potemkin" thirty times, who had hung on their dormitory walls the crisp black-and-white compositions of Ansel Adams, who could quote every line in "Casablanca." They weren't soldiers, they were *filmmakers*, with Hollywood ambitions if not necessarily Hollywood talent. When Foster boarded the flight to Saigon he thought he was going to heaven. There was a war on, and the Army wanted pictures of *everything*.

The Jeep honked at the gate, barely heard above the constant racketing from the street and the laboring grunts of Hilda the generator. This was a sour, ill-tempered machine that sat against the wall on the far side of the villa trembling like a hippopotamus in estrus. Harris had hustled the generator from...somewhere...in his own special way. Otherwise, they'd have sat in the dark one night out of three.

Corporal D'Amato opened the big black rusted wrought iron gates and Ironman, clinging to the wheel of the Jeep with white knuckles, bounced a not-yet-disillusioned Lt. Foster cruelly into the courtyard.

Foster's stomach gripped him from deep within. He'd been on that airplane all night from Hawaii to Saigon, he was jet-lagged, welcomed by explosives that fell from the sky, still smelly from that spell in the underground bunker, sore from the way Ironman had vibrated him in the Jeep, short of breath from the ciclo fumes, and terrified that Ironman's driving had come *this* close to murdering two American civilians in the middle of the street. Wisps of his sandy hair stood out from his head at random angles. He was oily, he had gritty little specks in his blue eyes and in the creases of his forehead. People called them laugh lines, and he tried to believe it, though they made him look older than twenty-five. He didn't feel much like laughing at the moment.

He'd had a hint, though, of the way things were going to be on the way in from the airport. The streets were full of blue buses transporting American soldiers, and they all had wire mesh over the windows.

"What's the screens for?" Foster had asked Ironman.

"Well, Lieutenant, it seems that once in a while, the citizens of this fair city, whose lives and liberty and sacred honor we're helping to defend, will buzz up alongside a bus on a ciclo and chuck a grenade inside."

"Really?" Ironman just looked at him, a man who was wild-eyed, breathing hard, his knuckles white as old bone.

"Welcome to the villa, Lieutenant," Former Sergeant First Class Harris said, saluting, and then sticking out a scarred hand the size of a house pet. Foster tried not to notice the generous coils of concertina wire that ringed the building. He blinked at Harris once, twice, then automatically returned the salute, fumbling with his shoulder bag and clutching at the scabby, callused appendage like it had suddenly appeared from above, reaching down into the depths to save him from drowning.

"Thank you...uh?" Foster blinked at him.

"Harris, sir, William S. Former Sergeant First Class."

"The famous Sergeant Harris. I've heard of you. This, uh...isn't exactly what I expected."

Former Sergeant First Class Harris allowed himself a brief, toothy grin at Corporal D'Amato, who grinned back.

"Well, it's home sweet home for the boys from DASPO, sir." Foster had no idea how unmercifully he was being put on.

"This here is Weinberg, one of the still photographers with your unit."

Spec-4 Weinberg, black-framed glasses, curly black hair, scurried out from the depths of the villa, saluted sloppily and extended to Foster a moist, discouragingly slack hand. At that very moment, the villa's two psychotic dogs made a sudden and enthusiastic appearance.

"I like this part the best," mumbled Weinberg. Foster had no idea what he meant, until he got a good look at Jack and Little Shit.

They were slavering creatures that could only have been birthed in Saigon -- scrofulous, dishonest, violent and devious, curs in the literal and curs in the figurative, black fur cratered, matted, and crusted. For the past few weeks, Ironman had been smearing them with oil from the crankcase of the Jeep. "Supposed to cure the mange," he said.

Their yellow dripping eyes rolled in a frenzy, from heaven to earth, from earth to heaven, their tongues dead black, moving like maddened snakes, not part of the dogs themselves but just sort of lurking inside their mouths, flopping blindly from one side to the other, oozing indescribable fluids. They were dogs gone mindstruck from seeing the life of Saigon from the knees down.

The two of them exploded into the courtyard as if expelled under intense pressure from Dog Hell after an eternity of starvation and torture. They slid sideways around the corner like those dumb animals in the cartoons and covered the distance to the steps with two or three leaps and a series of furious wounded yelps. Howling, Jack instantly bit into Foster's sleeve while Little Shit grappled himself to Foster's right leg and began pumping for all he was worth.

"God DAMN!" yelled Weinberg, doing his best to look outraged, but his lips clamped over the giggle that bubbled up and broke behind his nose, forcing itself outward in wet little snorts. He didn't exactly blow his nose all over the front of his face, but he came close.

"Get him off me! Jesus! Let GO!" Foster shook his leg furiously. Jack finally gave up, but Little Shit hung on to the erotic leg like a sailor back from a desperately long voyage, until Ironman gave him a vicious crack on the head with one of Foster's camera bags. The dog rolled over backwards in the dirt, scrambled to his feet and stood there, four legs splayed outward, drooling, panting, ready to go again.

"Ironman will get your bags, sir," said Harris. Come on in."

Both statements were cruel jokes. Ironman's name was the first. He could only dream of the day he would bulk up to 100 pounds. You could suck him through a straw. The second was the mountain of gear Foster had brought over from Hawaii: replacement photographic equipment for the unit, bags and boxes and cases piled into the back of the Jeep as though legions of Hebrew slaves had placed them there piece by meticulous piece since the days of the Pharoahs. There were cases of 16mm film, tripods, filters, and a new Arriflex camera and telephoto lens to replace the one Dennis had dropped when the footbridge blew up.

The invitation to come in was another minor joy for Former Sergeant First Class Harris, because the only thing better than a newby's face when he first saw the outside of the villa was that same face when he first saw the inside.

"Your office is here on the main floor, just off the kitchen," explained Weinberg. "I sleep upstairs with the EMs."

"Where's the head?" Weinberg knew Foster would ask that sooner or later, so, with something of a flourish, he pushed open the door. Much as he hated to admit it, he, too, got a Harrislike kick out of the villa's effect on newcomers.

Foster's eyes opened so wide his eyelids almost bled. His breathing stopped (part of it was the fight or flight reaction triggered by the sight of the bathroom, and part was that nobody could walk in there the first time and continue to breathe), mouth agape. He put out his hand to support himself against the wall, thought better of it, and just stood with his arms at his sides.

"What are all those brown stains around the faucets?"

"They drip. The water stains the bowl."

"They're not dripping now."

"There's no water now. Actually there hardly ever is, so they don't drip very often."

"Can't we complain to the landlord?"

"Only one who's ever seen him is Harris. He never even comes to collect the rent."

"How does he get paid?" Foster inquired.

"He has us put the rent money in a film can and give it to some weirdass civilians who live in the villa next door. I think they do construction work or engineering or something. Come on, Harris will show you around upstairs."

"Hello, Lieutelan, you welcome Vietnam!" This enthusiastic greeting issued from a small, wiry Vietnamese man who had emerged from a tiny room underneath the stairs. He was Yak Dung, the butler, steward, houseboy, janitor. The British would call him the dogsbody.

You could spend all day guessing his age without ever getting close. His huge mouth was crammed with teeth the size of piano keys. They looked like he'd covered them with bleu cheese, and he showed them to you every chance he got. He never stopped smiling.

His name wasn't really Yak Dung, but Weinberg introduced him that way, and nobody ever did find out what his real name was. Behind him clustered his wife ("At least we think she's his wife," said Weinberg. "For all we know, he could own her."), a buttery woman in a long plain nightdress with a round glistening face creased into a permanent frown. They called her Mama-san. And huddling behind with wide eyes was his daughter of twelve or fourteen. She'd told everyone her name a dozen times but nobody could catch it, even if they wanted to, which few of them did, so they called her Young Dung.

Foster followed Weinberg to the dark staircase at the rear of the building, and climbed. The walls of the stairway, in fact most of the inside walls in every room, were covered with black and white glossy photos of DASPO exploits on various missions. Stuck up with duct tape, there were shots of film crews at fire bases, film crews in the middle of Saigon traffic, in operating rooms, barracks, everywhere they worked they took stills, and used them for wallpaper. For Foster, it was a crash course in the history of the unit, and gave him a quick and somewhat frightening idea of what he was in for.

At the top was a hallway and four good-sized rooms. He peered into one.

"Who lives here?"

"I do," said Weinberg. Unlike the rest of the villa, the walls of this room were not completely covered with photos of DASPO personnel and exploits. Instead, they were completely covered with brilliantly tinted drawings of fish. Not exotic fish, not majestic marlins or other game fish, just...fish.

"Is that a...snook?" Foster asked.

"*Centropomus unidecimalis*," quoted Weinberg. "And this is a mahi-mahi. *Coryphaena hippurus*."

"My God."

The drawing was brilliantly done in colored pencil, capturing the deep iridescent blue of the body, the profound silver and yellow around the eyes, all in exquisite detail, almost every spine, every scale, rendered with agonizing precision. They were more like portraits than drawings, huge, measuring two or three feet across. Each one must have taken weeks – months – to complete.

"And there's a *melanogrammus aeglefinus*, a *scomber scombrus...*" Flounder and snapper, tuna and mackerel, each done with the same depth of color and detail, the same sensitivity and interpretation, the wavy bars on the back of the mackerel seeming to jump off the paper. Fabulous.

"But...why?" asked Foster.

"Fish are pretty."

Foster shook his head and continued down the hall, joined by Former Sergeant First Class Harris. One room contained the unit's film editing equipment, another had square silver camera cases scattered about, and one was filled with shoddy chairs. There was an irregular sodden green lump which Foster surmised had been a sofa in a previous incarnation, sitting in front of a white sheet that hung from two bent nails pounded into the wall. In the far corner, a Bell & Howell 16mm film projector perched on a high table, next to three earthenware pots of various sizes. They looked unimaginably old.

"What's with the pots?"

"Antiques, Lieutenant," said Harris. "Some of the guys buy them here and send them home. See those markings?" He pointed to two ideograms incised into the clay near the bottom. "Shows they're from one of Vietnam's most ancient dynasties. Worth seven, eight hundred bucks, but you can pick them up for about fifty if you know what to look for, and know where to go."

"And you do?"

"Well, I know a few of the markings, and I can write down which ones to look for. And I do happen to know one shop across town where you can get these pretty cheap. Guy doesn't know what he's sittin' on. Take 'em home and sell 'em, you'll make a couple grand."

Foster turned and looked at the window, then stopped. He pointed with a shaking hand at a cracked plastic gridwork that protruded from the base of one of the windows. In a day filled with new and unusual sights, this was by far the most astonishing.

"Is this an...*air conditioner*?" Perhaps the tales of the villa as Shangri-La were true after all.

"Yes, sir," said Harris. "All the rooms have them."

"It must be a hundred degrees in here. Why aren't they on?"

"None of them work. They break down all the time."

"Can't you get them fixed?" Foster started feeling like he was Alice, talking to the white rabbit.

"We're not authorized to have air conditioners, sir, so we're not authorized to get them repaired. But I'm working on it. Now, this is where the enlisted men sleep." Harris pushed open the door to a room full of metal framed beds.

"What's that sticking out from under the bed?" Foster asked.

"Where?"

"There." Foster waved his hand at a piece of pointed metal, sharp and triangular.

"Oh," Harris said, bending down to throw back the sheet that hung down the side. "Them are LAW anti-tank rockets."

Under the bed sat exactly fifteen little rockets, pudgy and gray, in a precise pile. Foster felt like he'd been axed. His military education, except for basic training, had been short on the weaponry aspect of war, and his assignment as a photographic specialist didn't involve the use of explosive projectiles.

Foster glanced under the next bed and his eyes widened. Hand grenades, bunches of them, like ripe fruit in the marketplace. He stood up, went to the third bed and threw back the sheet. Stacks of olive green rectangular tins, like big sardine cans, but curved. Maybe sixty pieces. On the top, concave surface was stamped, in emphatic letters, "THIS SIDE TOWARD ENEMY."

"Aren't these Claymore mines?"

"Good for you, sir." Harris smiled. "Ever used one?"

"I did a film on them once, but...Jesus, there's enough stuff here to blow this villa into a parallel universe. You got any other goodies I should know about? Bazookas? Nukes?"

"I can help you on the first one, Lieutenant," he grinned, "but there's a waiting list on the nukes."

Foster started to sit down on the nearest cot, but thought better of it. They'd sent him over to take command of Foxtrot Troop, and then he'd found out that he'd have responsibility for Delta Troop, too. This was his first trip, and not even an experienced officer directed two film crews at the same time. He'd been willing to overlook the mortar attack, his first terrifying ride through the streets of Saigon was hardly a memory, the deposit Little Shit had left on his pants leg was starting to dry, and the stench from the bathroom downstairs was fading, albeit slowly. But this? This was making his knees rubbery, so he sat down, running a hand through his greasy hair and looking up at Harris' face. Yellow light worked its way into the room, outlining forbidding features.

"Harris, you got enough firepower here to take out half the city."

"Naw. Probably just a few square blocks, sir. I figured it out once."

"But...we're not supposed to have stuff like this! We're not combat troops."

"This is Vietnam, Lieutenant. Everybody's a combat troop."

In spite of the fact that his illusions and expectations had taken several powerful blows since he'd arrived, Foster wasn't quite ready to abandon his "life is a cabaret" approach to the DASPO mission in Saigon, especially since he'd spent so much time building his expectations. However, the Vietnam War wasted little time in showing him its ugly, grinning face, and he got his first glimpse that very same night, at his first production meeting. Just before the soon-to-depart Captain Wagner took him out for a tour of the immediate neighborhood, including the massage parlors, steam and cream salons, and all the street corners where old women and teenagers sold drugs, and just after Mama-San and Young Dung served them dinner, the DASPO crews settled in around the scarred wooden table in the dining room.

It all struck Foster as uncommonly strange, surreal, even. Maybe it was the jet lag, or the bowl of mysterious goop over rice Young Dung had thrown down in front of him, maybe it was the dim light from the single undersized flickering fluorescent tube high in the ceiling, bouncing off the beads of sweat on all the faces, and the sickening greenish hue of the walls, but all the men around the table seemed cadaverous, hollow-eyed, embalmed in a watery green glow. He couldn't remember any of their names.

"The mortuary cosmetology films are coming up and now we're in the middle of a film on the care of napalm and white phosphorus victims," said Ironman in his thin voice. He was the production coordinator, responsible for scheduling, keeping track of what they'd shot, where it all was. The light gave the papers in his hands, and his skin, too, a discouraging greenish cast. "Lieutenant Garcia was directing, but now that he's...uh...gone, I guess you'll just have to step in."

"Did he really fall over his tripod and break his neck?" That was what they'd told Foster in the States. He'd been in Hawaii only a few days, just long enough to get loaded up with equipment, then they'd shoved him onto the flight.

The question made Svoboda sit up straight. He liked Garcia. Or he *had* liked him.

"Goddam pigfucking bastards!" Svoboda yelled. "Never tell what really is. He died he vas a hero!" It would take Foster a while to get used to his accent. Georj Svoboda was a Czech or a Hungarian or a Yugoslavian or some other kind of Eastern European in his late thirties, broad-shouldered, barrel-chested, pale and squat, with a huge head, no neck, and baleful brown eyes set closely on either side of a nose that wandered across his face like Moses in the desert. His hair was a sixteenth of an inch long, and no particular color. His voice, resonating in his prodigious cranial cavities, came all the way up from the basement of his balls. Svoboda was an American citizen and proud of it. He wasted no time telling Foster that he could speak six languages, but Foster didn't think English was one of them.

"A crocodile ate him." Ironman's face was surprisingly serious.

"Goddam crocodile bastards!" yelled Svoboda. "We vas shooting aerials from a Huey, and him leaning out the door. Not too high, you know, maybe hundred, hundred-fifty feet over Song Ba river. Harness come apart, he fall into river. Not so bad, he was alive. But...."

"Before the chopper could get down to pick him up," continued D'Amato, "a crocodile ate his ass."

Foster just sat there, his mind racing. "Okay, guys. I'm new here, first day in country, but do you really expect me to believe that shit? Just how big was this crocodile?" He strained to keep the smile off his face.

"This part of the world they get pretty big. 'Bout 15-20 feet," said D'Amato. "See?" He pointed to a picture among a clutch of others stuck up on the wall, an enlargement of himself and some of the other DASPO troops clustered around the dead, bloody form of the biggest, most prehistorically vicious reptile any of them had ever seen...well-fed, but the victim nonetheless of a screaming door gunner and his trusty M-60.

Foster knew it was possible to get killed in a war, but thought that the privilege was reserved for people who carry guns, like combat troops, the guys out in the shit. Former Sergeant First Class Harris had, only a few hours earlier, told him one of the Big Truths upstairs, but he didn't really understand it yet. He'd discover for himself what everybody else already knew. Everybody is a combat troop. There were no front lines, there was no Forward Edge of Battle Area, no demilitarized zone. You didn't have to go into battle to get killed. It could happen in the bar, or in your bed. The enemy was all around, there were pit vipers and vermin, the people hated you, even the *animals* hated you, and nobody ever was safe. But crocodiles?

Foster managed to choke out a question. "What's that in his mouth?"

"Garcia's arm," said Svoboda.

"His left one," D'Amato chimed in, "and some chunks of a 16mm Arriflex."

"Welcome to the Republic of Vietnam, sir," said Former Sergeant First Class Harris. It seemed to be a favorite phrase.

I, thought Foster, have a morale problem on my hands. He looked at all the new faces, struggling to put names with them, and failing. There were Weinberg and White, Svoboda's punished nose, D'Amato and Moose and Ironman, all ninety-seven pounds of him, who hunched over the table, trying to be invisible and succeeding. There wasn't much of him to see, anyway.

"Okay." Foster took a deep breath, let it out slowly. "Tell me about the film."

"We're scheduled to shoot at Cong Hoa Hospital tomorrow at 0800," said D'Amato, sliding a shot sheet across the table. "Army training film Number One-Zero-Seven Slash Three: 'Care and Maintenance of Napalm and White Phosphorus Victims.' This American female Bird Colonel type surgeon is gonna slice and dice some guy who has a butt full of Willie Peter. Should be fun." D'Amato ran his hands back through his thick black hair. He wore it the way they did in the Fifties, almost a duck-tail. Foster thought he'd caught a whiff of Brylcreem, and wondered, does anybody really still use that stuff?

"Cut the sarcasm," said Foster, trying manfully to assert his authority.

"He's right, sir. Sorry," said White. Ironman just maintained his woeful gaze. "This shoot's been a pain for weeks. The older Vietnamese doctors got their training at the University in Hanoi or in Paris or someplace. They're okay. But the young guys go to med school for two years, tops. And the nurses get the kind of on the job training that'd make you cry real blood. There's the possibility of some dramatic conflict."

"Every good drama has conflict," observed Weinberg. In addition to his painstaking labor on the fish drawings, he was taking a correspondence course in screenwriting. D'Amato punched him.

"After the surgery, we get some wild shots of napalm victims, stuff like that."

"I like that, too," grinned D'Amato. It was Foster's turn to stare at him.

"Never mind," said Foster. "I brought a project with me." Everybody sat up a little straighter. They all liked starting new film shoots. "We've been tasked with the production of a one-hour documentary in the Army Big Picture series, about the Vietnamization of the war, and the success of the military's campaigns to eliminate the use of drugs among the troops."

The totally spontaneous wall of hysterical laughter hit him so hard his chair slid back. There were yuks and guffaws, chortles and giggles, every possible expression of human risibility, from every single man at the table, all at the same time. Ironman laughed so hard that half a can of Coke came out his nose, and D'Amato put his head down and pounded on the table with his fist. Even Svoboda permitted himself a broad grin and a chuckle.

"What's so funny? What?"

CHAPTER 6
NOT THAT FAR FROM HOME

Saturday, March 21, 1970

It took Webb three days of waiting and standing in line and waiting and chasing around and waiting and being bored to find out his orders had been changed en route, and instead of going to his original assignment, an aviation battalion in the Delta, he found himself, much like Jonah, and in the same condition of imminent annihilation, in the belly of a cavernous Caribou, nose pressed to the clear plastic of the window, landing at Tay Ninh.

After innumerable wrong turns, he was directed to a hooch with a huge, egotistical sign in front that said "Vampires." It was painted -- a professional job -- in blood colors on black, with dripping letters, streams of brilliant vermilion that flowed down the background and pooled at the bottom. They reminded him of the opening titles of a late-night horror movie.

It was a typical hooch. He'd seen pictures in the Hall of Fame at Fort Wolters, the place where they displayed all the memorabilia of the war to date, the place where you could look at the pictures -- so many pictures -- of all the flight school graduates who hadn't made it back.

The place was an exactly square slab of concrete with a little patio out front, a few steps up to the front screen door. High tin roof, big overhang so the rain wouldn't come in, canvas shutters that opened up from the bottom. The walls came only halfway up, and screening ran all around the structure from about waist high to the top. Around the walls were sandbags. Lots of sandbags. On the ground, were little mounds of sand in the shape of anthills. The sand had leaked from small holes in the bags.

The dirt street and walkway outside the hooch were crawling

with troops, American civilians, and Vietnamese. Tay Ninh, presided over by the brooding four-thousand-foot ebony presence of Nui ba Denh, one of Vietnam's few mountains, was busy, almost frantic. Nobody stopped to talk to him.

Webb hauled his bag up the rough wooden steps to the rough wooden porch, tripped over a board that stuck up a little in the center, and peered in through the screen door, one hand cupping the side of his face. Nobody. He stepped inside, right foot first. His mother always said it was good luck. He didn't believe in luck, but he figured what the hell.

He just stared, smelling the peculiar odors of young men living in common, feeling that curious disorientation that occurs when when you find yourself alone in the house of a stranger. Then it caught up with him, all at once. For weeks he'd been embroiled in the whirl of graduating flight school at Fort Rucker, one last leave to spend some time with his parents in Milwaukee (it had turned out just like he'd been afraid it would), the trip to Travis Air Force Base in San Francisco, a day of what he thought had been imaginative debauchery but was perfectly ordinary debauchery, since a young man of 24 who had never been all that far from Milwaukee can think of only so many things to do with one woman in one night. He knew the score pretty well, he thought, but she had taught him some new lyrics.

There were the 22 hours on a 707 crowded in with all the other troops, which did absolutely nothing for his hangover, but the forced immobility helped the mending of his abused reproductive equipment. Stops in Hawaii, and that dumb lieutenant got on the plane with his tons of equipment, then Wake Island, then the Philippines. It took forever.

At Tan Son Nhut, they had settled out of a crystal sky to a velvet green coastline with beaches as pure as the Blessed Virgin, the last place you'd expect to find a war. He was on full sensory overload...the rattling scream of airplanes pouring endlessly out of the sky for twenty-seven and a half hours every day, the flight to Tay Ninh. He couldn't believe he'd gone so far from Milwaukee that if he kept going he'd be coming back.

Suddenly he knew what the feeling was.

Viet Fucking Nam. He was *there*. They'd taught him all about it in flight school, the TAC officers were combat veterans, the flight instructors, too, and they'd all said, "In *Vietnam*, Candidate, it's like this," or "If you were in *combat* right now, Candidate, your ass would be just another sorry fucking statistic." All of them had been in the shit, they'd made their own war stories. But war in general, and this war in particular, wasn't something you could pick up from others. You have to touch the hot stove for yourself, at least once, to feel the burn. If it's so terrible, said his little voice, how come everybody loves it so goddam much? And what are we doing here?

He'd fought his way through 12 weeks of flight school at Fort Wolters, Texas, slamming himself into a brace against the wall for the contemptuous TAC officers, doing their pushups, taking their abuse. He'd been yelled at and screamed at and belittled, humiliated and embarrassed, all in the name of building the kind of character that the book says a Military Aviator is supposed to possess in abundance.

Coincidentally, he'd even learned how to fly a helicopter, a feat which amazed him, because if there was ever a machine invented for a purpose that it shouldn't fulfill, it was the rotary-winged aircraft. They didn't want to be flown, are not even designed to leave the ground, not really, but he, and most of his classmates (except poor Eddie) had lived through the training, survived their mistakes, even mastered the machine. Webb, at best, had come to terms with it. At least he'd graduated. He didn't know at the time that the Army needed helicopter pilots so badly by 1970 they'd have graduated any life form that was warm blooded, breathed air, and walked on fewer than four legs.

Then there was advanced training at Fort Rucker, the Hueys, with the bigger turbine engine and improved rotor system. He'd gotten through that, too, along with Murphy and Gonzalez and the rest, except Eddie, just so he could be exactly where he was. He had wings on his shirt. He was a pilot.

The hooch had a central hallway, with a door on each end, smelling of oil and leather, tobacco, ashes, and stale beer. Two large rooms, the one on the right a featureless cube, containing two standard Army issue cots, neatly made, blankets tight across. Except for the continual clatter of choppers overhead, it was quiet, almost peaceful.

The other room was a different experience. Webb had never been to college but he imagined that if he joined the most insane, most delinquent, most morally bankrupt and ethically depraved fraternity on campus, the brothers would have created living quarters just like this.

About two feet inside the door, the floor had been raised with a platform to make a kind of sitting area, and in the corner two cots sat on another riser, up in the air like an altar where Mayan priests cut the hearts out of live virgins.

Camouflage parachutes drooped from the ceiling, a makeshift bar stood in the corner opposite the bunks, with fish netting all over it, a few sand dollars -- Webb guessed that's what they were -- some starfish. There were American flags, Vietnamese flags, captured Viet Cong colors and banners along the walls, some kind of diseased gray nubby third-hand carpeting on the floor with huge ugly sickening stains all over it, dried puddles of unspeakable substances, and, in the corner, a stereo system with speakers the size of toll booths.

"We usually make the fuckin' new guys sleep outside, Mister," a voice said from the porch. Webb had never heard the footsteps, but he knew the sound at once. War creates the most intense coincidence, both good and bad.

"I don't fucking believe it." Webb's mouth gaped as he turned around. On the other side of the door, half hidden in shadow, his perfectly-shaped nose pressed against the screen, stood O'Connell, Murphy W., Warrant Officer Two in the Army of the United States of America, recently anointed helicopter pilot.

"There's a lot around here you're not gonna fucking believe," Murphy said, opening the door and holding out his hand. "Welcome to the Republic of Vietnam, Your Southeast Asian Vacation Paradise." Webb grabbed onto the front of Murphy's shirt and pulled him into an embrace so fierce they both almost fell over.

"Easy! I'm glad you're here, but people will talk."

"God damn, Murph. God *damn*. I was just standing here feeling...well, never mind...and then you...here...shit, it's good to see you." Webb really meant it.

"You, too, but I ain't gonna kiss you 'cause you always use your tongue."

Webb just stared at him for a long moment, feeling an embarrassing warm flush. Murphy O'Connell. How come people didn't kill him just for looking so good? Almost everyone who saw him asked if he was a movie star, or at least somebody famous. People were always convinced that they'd seen him on some TV show or soap opera because they stared at him, they asked for his autograph, they whispered and nudged each other behind his back when he passed. He was like that Richard Corey in the poem Webb once had to memorize in school, clean favored and imperially slim. He glittered when he walked.

Knowing that his face could be his fortune, Murphy had, in fact, gone west and tried to break into show business. But three months of working at a California Pizza Kitchen in West Hollywood convinced him that looks were one thing, determination another and talent yet a third. So he joined up. He didn't have anything else to do, he'd never seen a war up close, and they happened to be holding one at exactly the right time.

Webb just goggled at him, understanding how Robinson Crusoe must have felt when he discovered that single footprint on the empty beach. I'm not alone. Murphy's here. I don't have to be the only asshole newby.

"Here I am in the middle of the foreignest country I've ever seen, and I suddenly hear the voice of my favorite asshole flight school roommate, Murphy 'Crash and Burn' O'Connell. Excuse me for being a little overwhelmed, okay?"

"Pretty far from Milwaukee, huh?"

"Pretty far from Tinseltown, too, for you."

"Eleven thousand, eight hundred sixty-three miles," said Murphy, "from this spot to Sunset and La Cienega. I looked it up."

"You probably paced it off. What are you...I mean, how did....?"

"I got sent direct from Fort Rucker," he said, picking up Webb's bag and carrying it into the den of iniquity to the left of the hallway. "Maybe a day or two before you. Your name was on the new personnel roster yesterday. I'm your welcome wagon."

"Jesus, that's great. Wait. I'm not staying in this room?" O'Connell was quiet for a second.

"They had...an unexpected vacancy. You're rooming with a guy named Berryman. I think they call him Huck. Handy, ain't he?"

"More enthusiasm than taste, you ask me."

Murphy stepped up to the platform and dropped Webb's bag onto the empty bunk, which immediately collapsed. He turned and started toward the front of the hooch.

"Come with me, I got something to show you." He opened the door.

"But I gotta report...."

"The platoon's on a mission. You can't report till they get back. Just come on."

Murphy walked him through the streets of the base, past painfully precise rows of hooches, each with its own individual sign and platoon insignia, each one named something more aggressive and hostile than the last. Vicious predators were a favorite, followed by anything that had to do with irreverence, or the sudden, unanticipated infliction of mayhem, chaos, death and destruction. Vietnam was full of Assassins and Cobras and Outlaws, Razorbacks, and Mad Dogs. And they were the friendlies.

On one block, there was a hole in the middle of a row, like a missing tooth. A hooch should have been there, but what remained was only charred earth, and burn marks on the walls of the structures alongside.

"Direct hit," O'Connell told him.

Tay Ninh was a regular little tent city, like that Boy Scout jamboree at Valley Forge every year. Webb's head was on a swivel, trying to look everywhere at once. The place was full of Americans, but it sure didn't feel like home.

"See that?" Murphy pointed to a Huey on the flight line. It had a big red X hanging in the cockpit -- down for maintenance. "That is your basic UH-1C Huey, the Charlie Model."

"I know what the fuck it is, Murphy, I fly one too, just like you."

"Not like this one, you don't. In case you haven't noticed, this particular specimen is a gunship. It has armament up the ass, miniguns, rocket pods, a couple of 60mm machine guns out the sides, everything but a low-yield tactical thermonuclear device."

"Does it have a crossbow?"

"Shut up." Murphy grabbed Webb by the bicep and pulled him closer to the machine. "I show you this because tomorrow at 0800 hours I start taking my in-country check rides in this very aircraft. If they get the goddam thing fixed."

"We're flying *guns*?" A warm, wet enraptured feeling flooded over him. "Thank you, God," he said, even though a clattering machine full of lethal weapons is an odd request to make of the Heavenly Father. His breathing actually heavied up as he walked around the Huey, like a sixteen year old kid whose father has just driven up after work in a brand new red Ferrari.

"You didn't know?"

"How come no Cobras?" It wasn't enough that Webb had landed, by sheer luck, in a gunship platoon. He wanted more, he wanted those long sleek menacing AH1-G Cobra gunships, not the old Hueys, fat and slow.

"You don't ask too much, do you? Some other units got broken down and they spread around all the bastard aircraft. Seems the Vampires had some Cobras one time, but they lost a bunch of 'em."

Webb didn't ask how.

* * * *

The noise level in the sky picked up considerably as Webb and O'Connell strolled back to the Vampire hooch. It was the *whupwhupwhup* of rotor blades, announcing the arrival of several sections of choppers: four or five Hueys, called slicks because they were unarmed except for the M-60 machine guns sticking out the cargo bay doors, carrying infantry troops (they didn't bring back as many as they'd left with), two or three small scout helicopters, called Loaches, and gunships galore, a mix of Hueys and the sinister Cobras.

Dunno why they call them Snakes, Webb's voice opined. *Look more like some kind of poisonous lizard to me.* He watched as they circled in the sky, the comparison to angry grasshoppers or locusts also occurring to him, an infestation of heavily armed machinery flying the traffic pattern down to the runway, fluttering to earth one by one. On one hand, he wanted to be among them at that very second. On the other, he had a delicious tingle of anticipation, the kind you get when you really want to open that one special Christmas present, but you make yourself save it for last. This is what he had trained for.

"That's the Vampires," said O'Connell. "Come on. We'll meet them when they get out of Ops."

It was a long walk, practically all the way across the base, to the Operations shack, and Webb could hardly keep himself from breaking into a run. But the second he saw his new platoon, all his bubbling enthusiasm deserted him, dribbling out like someone had pulled his plug.

White sweaty faces, dark sweaty flight suits, a group of angry, discouraged men with unruly hair grouped outside the low tan building, helmets tucked under their arms. Some leaned against the wall, others sat on the ground. It was like they'd come out the door and all the air went out of them; they were stuck there, deflated, unable to move. Except for the constant roaring in the sky, it was quiet. Dead quiet.

O'Connell, in his usual effervescent style, practically bounded up to one of the silent men, loud and smiling.

"Lieutenant, the new guy's here. Name's Webb. Come on over here, Spider."

The lieutenant didn't smile, didn't hold out his hand. Faces swam in front of Webb like dead things floating in a grey sea.

"Spider Webb, huh? Welcome to the Vampires."

"Bloodsuckers," said one of the men sitting on the ground.

"Motherfuckers," chimed in two or three more, automatically, with little feeling.

"Boy, am I happy to see you." The lieutenant didn't sound happy, he didn't look happy, he was miles short of happy in every direction. His voice sounded like it came out of a deep hole, issuing up from the bowels of the earth. "Especially today. I'm Anders, first section leader. Let's see...that's Berryman, Doctor Watson, Roth, Iglesias, Godwin...." He stopped, as though he was used to reeling off more names in that particular situation. But there were no more names. Some people were inexplicably absent.

All the grim mouths, the disappointed eyes, ran together for Webb, one melting into the other. *Don't worry*, said his voice, *you can straighten it all out later. Right now, just grab the hands one at a time, that's right, nod, say hello. Good. Try not to notice that they're looking at you like you're the second*

Fuckin' New Guy that's been dumped into their laps this week. And try to ignore the suspicion and fear in their faces. You don't need to be social right now. Got the feeling these boys are in no mood for it. Besides, the way the Army was rotating people in and out of the units, some of them might not be there long enough to worry about.

Webb was to discover one of the worst things about how the war in Vietnam was being fought. Units didn't travel together, they didn't stay together, and they didn't develop any of the *esprit de corps* that held soldiers together under stress in previous wars. Fuckin' New Guys were always showing up to join combat veterans in infantry and aviation units, endangering them with their inexperience and ignorance. After a month or so of combat, you automatically forgot that you'd been an FNG not that long ago, and you hated the new ones who were always appearing, and whose stupid mistakes could cost you your life.

"Come on back to the hooch. I'll fill you in. We gotta get both of you up to speed in a hurry. We lost two more today."

A bit later, in the beery air of the hooch, Anders leaned forward, crushed a can in his fist, and looked at Webb with deep dark eyes. "Gibson didn't come back. Neither did his co-pilot. Son of a bitch just got his in-country checkout, too. Damn." The crew chief didn't make it either, or the gunner.

Watson told the story, his voice almost reverent. They had been covering some slicks hauling ammunition and food into a firebase that had been hot for two days, tracers all over the place, red and green whizzes in the sky, crossing back and forth, Cobras and Huey gunships circling, climbing for altitude then diving in, making gun runs one after the other, plunging through the grey smoke, the red smoke, dodging the fire in the sky. No help. Enemy artillery and anti-aircraft fire kept pouring in like generous donations to one of those television evangelists.

They flew in fireteams of two gunships each, Gibson the team leader, below Watson and to the left, hanging improbably in the sky, ready to begin the next run at the treeline about half a kilometer from the wire. Together, they lifted themselves to the right, Watson following in perfect formation, lined up on the skid supports of Gibson's machine. They'd been flying as a fireteam for two months, and Watson knew exactly what to do. Again, they turned, lining up for the run, the trees a deep green wall dead in front of them.

"Three-two, you with me, ol' buddy?" Gibson talked like that. He was from Amarillo, Texas, and even though he was a city boy, when he put on a flight helmet it felt like a ten-gallon hat to him, when he seized the controls of his chopper he saw in his mind callused brown hands running a strap around a horse's belly, tightening the girth, he saw a pointed boot sliding into a stirrup. The cyclic stuck up between his knees, the stick that controlled the motion of the machine forward, reverse, and side to side. With his left hand, he grasped the collective, like an emergency brake handle with a motorcycle-type twist throttle on the end. This controlled the angle for the rotor blades and the speed of the engine, providing lift. Both hands on the controls, the drawl took over.

"Bet your ass," Watson said. He was scared, but he couldn't wait. They tilted forward, gathering speed, ready to drop in.

Gibson and Monroe went first, directly into the muzzle flashes from the treeline, twinkling lights, deceptively festive. The fat Huey dropped toward the wall of trees, miniguns buzzing, throwing thousands of rounds a minute, rockets raced away, dancing on delicate strings of exhaust smoke, making bright orange puffs below. Gibson hit the bottom of his dive just when he was supposed to, and Watson went down right behind him.

Gibson was supposed to break up and to the right at the bottom of the dive, but he didn't. The practiced lift on the collective never happened, nor did the emphatic twist to the throttle. He just kept on going, down and down, straight toward the adamant earth at dive speed, almost like he was doing it on purpose. He hit the trees so fast that Watson never had time to yell. The words "Pull up! Pull up!" caught in his throat like fishhooks.

POOF! Gibson's Huey incandesced right before their eyes in a glorious eruption of yellow fire and greasy black smoke. Watson was so shocked and amazed and shaken that he aborted his run and flew right through the cloud of fire, up and out the other side, smoke swirling all around him.

There was the usual screaming on the radio as Watson and Godwin shouted "Mayday" both at once. Anders got on the frequency, but there was no way anyone could help. First, it was obvious the ship had blown completely apart. If they could get in close enough to see what had survived, they would find precious little except a sad black smear in the earth. Second, even if there had been some remote chance of survival, Gibson had crashed into the very center of a concentration of enemy troops, and nobody could have gotten in, no matter how badly they wanted to. They could only hope he'd taken some of the enemy with him.

In the dim yellow light that streamed through the heavy air from the screened walls of the hooch, Webb sat appalled, and listened without a word, trying to keep his jaw from dropping. He'd heard stories from the TAC officers in flight school, but this, this was the Real Thing, this had happened today, a few hours ago, not ten miles from this spot. It was his first small exposure to the violence of war. A remote contact, to be sure, but contact nonetheless. The rest of it, he was confident, would come soon enough. He knew he'd be ready.

Nobody felt like going to the mess tent, so they sat around outside the hooch devouring as many beers as they could, silent, dulled. Webb knew enough to keep his mouth shut. Apparently Gibson had been a favorite. Short-timer, too, and the Vampires were taking it harder than usual. Webb spent his time listening, trying to put the names with the faces.

Anders had his Swedish or Finnish ancestry drawn on him with broad strokes. He was about as blonde as people can get without being absolutely albino. Yellow hair, cut very short, long, straight nose, pointed a little. Square chin.

Berryman, his new roommate, was short and ruddy and round, probably skirting the edge of the weight requirement for helicopter pilots. Dark brown hair, waving straight back from his high forehead, mild brown eyes. He looked like he was made out of balloons.

Then black-haired Iglesias, with black eyes and those high Hispanic cheekbones, Godwin, tall and painfully thin, Roth, who looked like a Beagle puppy. He'd never get them all straight. Probably not worth learning the names anyway. You never knew who'd be there the next day, or week. Another factor that drove the men apart, instead of bringing them together as a unit.

They all sat silent for a minute or two, until a dark figure shuffled up the path toward the subdued group. Stooped, round-shouldered, a kind of Ichabod Crane shadow against the dimming sky.

"Webb and O'Connell," he pronounced.

"Yo," said O'Connell, scrambling to his feet. Webb did the same.

"I'm Captain Parker, the platoon commander. You guys wanna come with me." It wasn't a question. "Lieutenant?" Anders heaved himself to his feet and followed the trio down the path.

They walked in silence toward the mess tent, boots crunching in the dirt. Webb could barely see Parker, towering above him in the dim light from the row of hooches behind. It was getting darker.

"I'm gonna make this short and sweet." *Well*, said Webb's voice, *he sure launches into it, doesn't he? Intense fucker, too.* "We lost two good pilots today, plus the crew chief and gunner. That makes six in the last two weeks, two from here and four from the other section. What with troop pullouts and Vietnamization and all, we're so under strength it isn't even funny. I suppose you know that Sihanouk got thrown out. He never wanted us in Cambodia, but this new guy, Lon Nol, does. In fact, he's invited the ARVN to mount some operations across the border, so in a few days, they're taking a couple hundred troops over toward the Parrot's Beak." Webb had heard of it. A section of the Cambodian border that curled into Vietnam describing that peculiar shape on the maps. "Two gunship platoons will provide air support. We're one of them. That means we have to get you two up to speed right now. I want you checked out instantly. Tomorrow should be quiet, so get with Ferguson at first light. He'll take you, O'Connell, and I'll take Webb. You're both quick studies, right?"

* * * *

Webb lay in his new bunk that night, head swimming in beer, listening to Berryman's rasping breath in the cot next to him, the sights and sounds of the day racing in his head. In the course of the increasingly slurred conversation, he'd been brought up to date on their situation.

In the middle of March the heaviest fighting of the last six months was starting to occur along the DMZ.   There were serious clashes in Cambodia, even though President Thieu had rolled his eyes heavenward, placed his right hand upon his heart and innocently denied his troops had ever crossed the border. The previous week, the Vietnamese death toll was the second highest in the entire war. In the midst of all the carnage, almost 13,000 Marines had packed up, getting ready to pull out in the third phase of President Nixon's troop withdrawals and much-hoped-for "Vietnamization"program. *All that shit going on,* said Webb's voice late that night, *you play your cards right, you could be the last man killed in this war.*

CHAPTER 7
A LETTER TO BENNY #1

Sunday, March 22, 1970

Dear Benny...

Yes, it's your brother, Second Lieutenant Leon Foster, saying greetings from DASPO and the Republic of South Vietnam!

This cassette recorder you gave me is the greatest thing. Now I can just sit and talk to my favorite little brother instead of going to the trouble of writing it all out. We've got a couple of those nice IBM Selectric typewriters, but talking to you is a lot better. Besides, I don't think I could sit down and write anything because I only just got here two days ago. Three? Maybe four. Feels like I've been here a month. I'm kind of overwhelmed, but I wanted to talk to you for a few minutes before I try and get some sleep. I won't fill up both sides of the cassette right now, because it's over an hour long, but I'll talk to you every time I get a chance. That way you'll get maybe a week's worth of stories from me at one time.

You have to promise me one thing, though. Never, never let Mom and Dad hear these tapes. There's a whole bunch of shit going on around here, like fighting and bombing and killing, and there's enough of it on the news, what with the body counts and all, so they really don't need to hear about it in my voice. Besides, there's a massage parlor right across the street, and from the stories I hear, they massage very specialized parts of the body, so I'll probably be telling you things that are just between us guys. Understand?

They sent me over to take charge of a film crew squad called F Troop, which I think is pretty funny. But when I got here I found out that there's some shortage of personnel and I'm actually commanding two squads. I've never even commanded one, but I'm an 8511, thanks to an act of Congress, so I must be able to.

Captain Wagner, the guy I'm replacing, took me out the night I arrived for a familiarization tour of the neighborhood, which seems to consist of a bunch of these old semi-ruined villas, tiny shops, people selling things on the street, and bars. Lots of bars. The local favorite is the Number One Club, where I found myself around two in the morning, listening to some incredible stories. There was this shitfaced captain sitting next to me, I guess around thirty, with big wet eyes and lenses in his glasses that must have been three inches thick. Tells me his name is Norman and he's with the Judge Advocate General's office, in country investigating the drug trade, with a little military supply graft and corruption thrown in. Now, I'm sure black markets spring up anyplace there's a war on, but from what this guy told me, Vietnam graduates first in the class, with honors. He was half blasted – maybe more than half – and went on and on about all the money and merchandise and materiel that's disappearing from the bases, and from the whole BX system, in fact. The brass figures they're losing millions of dollars a year because of it. Makes you wonder. I read somewhere that it costs a million dollars to kill one VC, but they're worried about a few missing cases of Johnny Walker Black.

The first thing he tells me about is this guy named Wooldridge. He was a veteran of three wars, even a veteran of the D-Day Landing in 1944, and his service record was so distinguished that Lyndon Johnson made him First Sergeant Major of the Army back in '66. He got accused last year of running a huge supply scam. Along with three or four other top sergeants, he formed a company called Maredem, buying merchandise from manufacturers and reselling it to base exchanges all over the world...at a huge markup. Plus, they think these guys were in control of the entertainers that got booked into the enlisted men's clubs, and got enormous kickbacks from that, too. Oh, and they skimmed money from the slot machines in the clubs, too. There were some colonels in on it, and a general, but they haven't proved it all yet. It goes on and on.

Then there's the money scam. US currency is illegal over here, so we exchange our dollars for Military Payment

Certificates that we use in the base exchange and places like
that. One buck, one MPC. But on the black market, one
dollar will get you two MPCs, which you then exchange for
Vietnamese piasters at 400 to one, instead of the legal rate of
100 to one. Problem is, what do you do with all those
piasters, because they aren't worth shit anywhere in the
world.

Norman tells me that guys loaded with piasters buy this
"rare" ancient dynasty pottery that's supposed to be worth a
fortune from these shops all around the city. The stuff has
certain markings on it that prove how ancient it is, and the
guys go from store to store, looking for it so they can send it
home and make money selling it when they get back. Of
course, these rare ancient pots are made out in the alley, and
they're worth about a buck each, if you stretch it a little.

You can also use your MPCs to buy something expensive at
the BX, like a refrigerator for a hundred bucks. Then you can
sell it on the black market for five hundred. Plenty of ways to
get rich around here.

Then this Norman guy asks me what my MOS is, and I tell
him I'm with DASPO.

"DASPO, huh? You're the guys we love to hate."

"What's that supposed to mean?"

"You got the cushiest job in Saigon, short of being a general.
Private villa, servants, wild parties, hookers, air conditioners..."
I was going to tell him they don't work, but thought I should
keep my mouth shut.

So he's investigating money laundering, and the way huge
amounts of stuff keep disappearing from the docks and
supply depots, finding its way to the black market. You go in
to the BX and the shelves are mostly bare, because all the
goods are being "diverted" before they ever get there. The
black market is about the only place you can get Pepto-
Bismol, Polaroid film and other stuff like that, because it
vanishes the second it comes off the boat.

"Who's responsible for all this?" I asked him. Sounded like
a good idea for a film.

"Walter Crawley," he tells me. The guy is apparently a
Vietnamese, but he's really an American. Or maybe he's an
American who's really a Vietnamese. It was late, I was drunk
and tired, and I didn't understand a word of it. Crawley has

been here since 1964 or so, and has contracts for juke boxes in the clubs, wholesale deals for liquor, and bulk rates on rubbers, nylon stockings, and toilet paper, for all I know. We could use a guy like that in DASPO.

Norman says people are making millions on stuff they steal from the military. Especially Walter. There's weapons and ammo, vehicles, uniforms, cameras, stereos, God knows what. They think Crawley is in the middle of it all, and probably involved in the drug trade, but everybody's involved in the drug trade. They can't prove anything, and I don't care. We've got a villa in the middle of town, a houseboy with black and green teeth who could be a hundred and fifty years old, with a greasy wife and chubby daughter, a bathroom that works sometimes, another one that never works at all, and at least I'm not out in some hellhole firebase getting shot at and shitting my pants. What's not to like?

It's late. I'm exhausted. I'll tell you more about Vietnam after I find my way around. They sent me over here to make movies, and that's what I'm going to do.

I almost forgot the best part. Just before I leave, this Norman guy looks at me real close and says, "you sure you never heard of Walter Crawley?" I say no, because I just arrived in country and why should I know Walter Crawley?

"He used to own your villa. Sergeant Harris bought it from him."

How the hell does he know that?

CHAPTER 8
WALTER CRAWLEY

Tuesday, February 3, 1953

If there's one thing Walter Crawley didn't look like, it was a young man named Walter Crawley. He was, in fact, a full-blooded Vietnamese, and owed his name to the compassionate but somewhat misguided missionary couple that managed to rescue him after the fall of Dienbienphu.

Marion and Marilyn Crawley had labored as members of a church outreach mission in French Indochina for five years, until their village and the school they'd built with their own hands were overrun, burned, and sacked. Any of the inhabitants who managed to survive scattered and disappeared into the jungle, including the parents and cousins of one ten-year-old boy who had been too sick to run.

In the confusion of the time, it wasn't too difficult for the couple to take the boy with them back to the States, and the church helped finagle some refugee papers for him. They adopted him officially, because it was certain that nobody else would want him, and named him Walter, after Marilyn's grandfather. Then they made a series of well-meaning errors in judgment that would affect thousands of lives two decades later.

The first thing they did wrong was to leave the church. Marilyn made it plain that she wasn't cut out for any more missionary work, especially the kind that involves having people burn down your house and shoot at you. So Marion got a job teaching at a small semi-religious private college smack in the middle of a square state in the Midwest, in a small town floating in a sea of cornfields that extended hundreds of miles in every direction.

Their second mistake, also an understandable one, was having too much faith in their fellow men. They were idealists, believers in God and the ultimate perfectibility of humankind, and it never occurred to them that a white couple raising an Asiatic child in the American heartland in 1954 might suffer in a chill wind of xenophobia that would batter them incessantly from every direction.

The third mistake they made was leaving Walter to deal with it on his own, which he did in the most non-constructive possible ways.

Walter was a good looking kid, wiry and strong, but the differences between him and the huge, round-faced, beefy, strapping, corn-fed farm boys he went to school with would have been insurmountable under the best of conditions. Throw in the natural suspicion of strangers in a small town, add the inevitable racial overtones, and then recall that America had just finished fighting a brutal war against people who looked just like him (the corn farmers not caring about the physiognomic differences between Japanese, Koreans, and Vietnamese), and young Walter didn't have many friends. Continually tired of being called Creepy Crawley, he had lots of fights, most of which he won because he fought dirty.

He ran away from home on Easter Sunday in 1963, excusing himself in the middle of the church service and vanishing into the endless rows of corn. The Crawleys never saw or heard from him again and were, frankly, not all that devastated at his disappearance. The good people of the town had made them suffer quite enough for the good deed they'd performed ten years earlier.

The Crawleys had made yet another mistake in raising little Walter, though it too sprang from the absolute best of intentions. On one hand they wanted him to be absorbed into the great American melting pot, even though they picked a bad place to do it. On the other hand, they were decades ahead of their time in the matter of ethnic pride and diversity, wanting Walter to know about the culture, heritage and history he'd come from, giving him the books they'd brought back about Southeast Asia, somehow keeping up on events in the country that became Vietnam. They'd also kept in touch, through letters that took months to arrive, with some of their missionary friends who had stayed behind, and were as up to date as possible on the events taking place in a part of the world that most American had yet to hear of.

They told Walter about Southeast Asia in glowing, affectionate terms, because they had loved their life there, at least while the French had everything under control. They had loved the people, and the magnificence of the scenery, the rivers and endless rows of rubber trees on the plantations. They were moderately fluent in the language, albeit a little out of practice, and helped him not to lose what he had learned. Gradually, and not surprisingly, Walter got it into his head that Vietnam was some kind of lost paradise. Through the stories his adoptive parents told, the country began to call to him, and when he walked out of the church that Sunday morning, he headed west, to San Francisco and beyond. Less than two years later, at somewhere around twenty years old, he stepped off the small boat that had brought him down the Mekong from Penang to Saigon, and was instantly illuminated by his destiny.

It was just then that the very first American "advisors" were arriving on a well-meaning mission to train the South Vietnamese in ways to repel the depredations of their neighbors to the north. They lived on military bases, went out every morning, conducted a few missions, and came home every night in time for dinner. Walter, with a prescience that few people possessed at the time, understood America with a clarity that only outsiders can command, believed that more Americans would follow, and immediately set about making himself useful.

The Americans around Saigon were delighted to find an enthusiastic, smiling Vietnamese in his late teens who spoke perfect idiomatic English, was awash in American culture and slang, and was, best of all, on their side. It didn't take him long to become an interpreter, gofer, intermediary, liaison, maker of deals, puller of strings, cultural authority, soother of ruffled native feathers, an indispensable part of the supply chain in armaments, PX liquor, whatever deal was working at the time, and deals were always working. In about a year it was well known in American military circles, and among the gradually expanding foreign press corps, that if there was something you needed, especially if it was something esoteric, unconventional, or illegal, Walter Crawley could get it for you. For a price. Best of all nobody ever had the remotest idea of how much he hated them.

As his connections and fortunes grew (which, given the burgeoning, artificial military economy, didn't take long), and as he began to extend his "help" to securing the supply of liquor, jukeboxes, attractive young women, and all the other things military officers and their troops require to wage war on foreign soil, he dedicated himself to another goal: finding the cousins who had left him behind when his village was overrun a decade earlier. He wasn't sure whether he wanted to execute them or embrace them, but blood calls to blood. He'd been able to find out that the oldest, who had been about twenty at the time of the attack, was a colonel in the Vietnamese Air Force. The other, a little younger, had disappeared into Laos, or perhaps Burma. Nobody claimed to know a thing about him. There were just rumors. Walter kept asking.

CHAPTER 9
LONGACRE LEARNS TO SHOOT

Friday, March 29, 1970

It takes a while to learn to fly gunships, but Longacre knew he could do it. He'd been flying slicks for more than two years, sorry missions out in the boonies, Ash and Trash missions, hauling soldiers into the field, carrying cargo to the firebases, all because of Colonel Berner. He longed to fly guns, be part of the action, part of the real war, but he was certain that Berner's unscrupulous influence, somehow, some way, was keeping him out of it. Rat bastard.

Even the best pilots, the most instinctive aviators, need time to attain any reasonable marksmanship with the miniguns and rockets. First, you have to do all the normal things, like fly the ship, and a helicopter demands to be flown every second. You can't just set the controls, sit back and enjoy the ride. Meanwhile, you have to navigate and maneuver in formation, trying to make sense of bedsheet-sized maps with the names of the villages printed in type of an insectile size. Add to that the precision of making a gun run with another gunship or two in front or close behind, squinting through the reticle to aim the miniguns, pointing the ship so you can fire the rockets, all the buttons and switches and triggers, and you're trying to do all this in combat, so there's the small matter of the tracers and the noise and the bullets popping through the thin skin of the chopper, the minor distraction that all those people down there want you dead, and right now. It's easy to lose focus.

So Sanderson and Larue taught Longacre to fly guns in a huge hurry, working out of the anonymous hooch in the corner of the base. They took him out day after day to a free fire zone near the base, taught him to sight the miniguns first through the reticle, then with a BOT, a burst on target, zeroing in by eye on numberless logs floating in the canals, or on huge conical termite mounds that stood as much as six feet above the flat earth. He learned how to spray the tree-lines with ripping fire, how to walk the tracers toward the target, how to swivel the guns directly downward and squeeze off the rounds to cover himself as the ship wheeled, and surged up and away.

He flew from the right seat, too, pointing the ship toward a target on the ground, a ruined hooch, a tree, matching up the objective with little yellow grease pencil marks on the plexiglas, sending the buzzing rockets to earth, watching the bursts of orange fire. His experience was eerily parallel to Webb's, who was learning to fly guns many miles away, with just as much urgency.

They filled him in on the mission. Everybody in the unit had "volunteered," just like he did, each of them there because they'd fucked up in some way that was so imaginative and inspired the Army didn't know what else to do with them. Predictably, none of them wanted to talk about what they'd done, and Longacre couldn't, because he wasn't sure he'd done anything.

Their mission, under the direction of the seldom-seen Colonel Xoan, was to somehow stop the onrush of heroin, opium, and marijuana that flooded from the Cambodian border into Vietnam, keeping them out of the bloodstreams of otherwise healthy young American soldiers, though nobody was exactly sure how to do it. Larue didn't know. Sanderson didn't know. Longacre certainly didn't know. When he was flying grunts into battle in the north, they'd walk through fields of marijuana plants that grew eight and ten feet high, pulling off sticky buds and stuffing them into their packs.

But Colonel Xoan, when he did show up, seemed to know, as he had the Shadows point their gunships at this village or that, claiming they were havens for drug caravans, or storage depots for opium, or were populated with smugglers, and ordering them obliterated.

Not long after Longacre arrived, he and LaRue flew Xoan out to a secret fire support base for a meeting with some of his contacts. Longacre was navigating from the right seat when he noticed that the coordinates of the base are just *this* much to the west of the border...inside Laos.

"Hey, Larue. We're getting into number ten country here. This place is about six clicks over the line. We should tell the Colonel that this place is in Laos."

"No, it's not."

"What do you mean, no it's not? I flew over the border one time before and didn't like it. I don't want to do it again."

"I personally guarantee that the Colonel's map will show that FOB 26-Charlie is at least three clicks on our side of the line."

"But..."

"He has these black ops meetings a couple times a month. We fly him in, he talks to the same guy every time, they kiss, they hug, they have tea, they pass all these envelopes back and forth, and we're home by dinner."

"And if we get shot down in Laos, who's going to get our asses out?"

"We can't get shot down," Larue answered.

"And why the fuck not?" Longacre shot back.

"Because we don't exist."

CHAPTER 10
BLOODSUCKERS. MOTHERFUCKERS.

Thursday, April 6, 1970

One day in early April, the VC had killed 14 Americans and wounded over 40 by booby-trapping one of their artillery shells. The following morning, Samuel Taylor Webb, now known by his call sign, "Spider," opened the left hand door of the Huey and hoisted himself up into the thick slab of steel that covered the seat. He pulled his chicken plate over his head, settling it on his chest. It was a kind of metal vest, meant to protect him from enemy fire. He was doubtful. And he was doubtful about the steel plate that had been welded under his seat, to keep bullets from flying up his ass. His hands were coated with a thin film of oily sweat.

It was a weird feeling, like he'd never been in one of these hulking green machines before. Of course, he'd been flying every day since he'd arrived, learning, more or less, to fly and shoot at the same time. In fact, Parker had told him he had a real talent for it, a kind of instinct. Truth was, it had felt good, the swinging of the ship in the air, the percussion of the rockets as they launched, the high buzz of the miniguns. Six whirling barrels spitting two thousand rounds a minute, you could cut the jungle in half with one of them, and you did.

Parker was right. Webb *was* good at it, and they'd assigned him to fly with Anders, the Vampires section leader.

"Get us out of here," said Anders from the right seat. "I'll take it when we get to the AO."

"Clear right," said Link, the crew chief, from behind him.

"Clear left," said Gomez, the gunner, from the other side.

The area of operations that day lay to the northwest of Tay Ninh, near a village called Nang Ra, in the middle of dense jungle, laced with streams and wetlands.

"Tough place to work," Captain Parker had told them the night before, towering in the cold greenwhite light of the ops shack. "We're flying support for a troop extraction, a platoon of grunts and ARVNS. They've been prowling around in the jungle, being careful, of course, to stay on our side of the border."

"Wink, wink," Berryman had whispered, nudging Webb with his elbow, just a little too hard.

Webb lifted the chopper into a low hover and backed it out of the walls of steel and sandbags that surrounded him, too close, swallowed hard, shifted in his seat, but he kept it smooth.

"Last I heard, the grunts weren't in position yet," said Anders, yawning. "But they should be there time we arrive. We'll rendezvous with the slicks on station." Webb swiveled the ship around, floated down the taxiway and led the platoon as they all lifted smoothly into the orange morning air.

"Going hot," he said. Fingers tickled the switches that armed the guns and rockets.

There wasn't a single helicopter pilot in Vietnam who didn't love flying more than just about anything. That included the pilots who flew the unarmed Hueys, called slicks because of their lack of armament, hauling troops and supplies, the ones like Webb and O'Connell who flew guns, the Loach pilots, who may have been the craziest of all, flying those little two-seaters down among the trees, ten feet from a Vietcong surprise party, the Medevac pilots, brave maniacs who flew any time, anywhere, under any conditions. They must have loved it, because they were even willing to do it in skies full of hot metal and boiling smoke.

Webb was no exception. As they floated above the emerald green countryside, the forbidding bulk of Nui ba Den receding behind them, he was not exactly relaxed, since this was his first real mission, and not exactly comfortable, either, but he was suffused with the same deep satisfaction experienced by anyone who controls a machine that flies, who looks down upon the earth from superior height.

The collective was in his left hand, emerging from the floor like an emergency brake handle, controlling the pitch of the rotor blades and engine RPM. The cyclic that came up between his legs rested benignly in his fingers. He nudged it easily from side to side, pointing the chopper where he wanted it to go.

The Huey vibrated contentedly around him. Like cruising the main drag in your Chevy on a Saturday night.

Since he was flying with the section leader, the rest of the choppers were low and behind. He could feel them back there, all eyes on his machine, lined up in a nice straight right echelon, the pilots sighting on his skid supports to stay in position, trailing him through the uncertain beginnings of a perfect morning. Before him the jungle endlessly unrolled, behind him the sky began to paint itself, a Shakespearian dawn, rosy-fingered.

"There they are." Anders pointed to the left, about ten o'clock low. Webb looked down through the chin bubble to see four slicks approaching from the south, just below them, dark shapes hanging in the morning air, M-60s poking out the cargo bay doors like skinny sticks.

Some crosstalk on the radio, Anders setting up the formation. The landing zone was about five kilometers ahead, and word was that the platoon was in position and ready, even eager, for extraction.

"Jesus," said Gomez from the back. "Sure hope this doesn't turn into a RF."

Webb had been there at least long enough to find out what a Rat Fuck was. Back in the dim recesses of the beginning of the war, the letters had stood for a Reaction in Force, an armed response to enemy activity. Gradually, though, the meaning changed, deteriorated, as meanings are wont to do, especially under the pressure of extreme circumstances, especially under the crushing weight of sad experience. He reflected briefly on how the RF was just one phrase in a long history of military abbreviations describing how things could go wrong. Long before his career, there had been the SNAFU (Situation Normal, All Fucked Up), followed by the FUBAR (Fucked Up Beyond All Recognition). Vietnam had spawned its very own lexicon, including the popular BOHICA (Bend Over, Here It Comes Again.) Before Webb got there an RF had become a rat fuck, a mission that started in the ordinary normal fashion, dropping in, picking up troops, taking them home, and ended up as a kind of horror show nobody could begin to imagine. They never really knew what they'd be flying into, the same way that they never really knew who was the enemy and who wasn't.

You lived your life always, always fearing the worst. But it was such a beautiful day.

They orbited for a few minutes and finally got everything straightened out, after much crosstalk, all the ships in position, the Vampires ready to show their bloodsucking, motherfucking stuff, and fervently hoping they wouldn't have to.

"Vampire Three, Eagle Four. We're in position, come and get us."

"Pop smoke," replied Anders.

In seconds, a stream of hazy green billowed up ahead of them, at the far edge of a clearing, flowing to the south.

"Roger," Anders told them. "We're seeing the color of money."

"You got it, Vampire."

"Confirmation," Anders said to Webb. "If the enemy knows what color the smoke's gonna be, sometimes they pop one and we land right in the middle of them."

Webb gulped and looked around as Anders flew the ship at support altitude, watching for activity on the ground but mostly watching the slicks circle onto their final approach from the south, into the wind indicated by the smoke, rotors flailing the air, one, two, three, four, settling in to the clearing, rocking on their skids inches above the ground, along the far tree line, where he could just make out the dark forms of the waiting troops, twenty-five or thirty of them. The clearing was a brown smear in the center of dense emerald foliage, probably created in a microsecond by a daisy cutter bomb. They had a fuse that made them detonate a few feet above the ground, which caused less cratering. The explosion was a perfect circle that wasted and flattened the earth. Instant landing zone. The jungle wasn't the heavy triple-canopy kind, but it was thick enough to hold a surprise or two. So he'd been told.

"Keep your eyes on the troops," said Anders. "The door gunners'll watch the jungle on both sides."

Three Vampires circled above the clearing spaced 120 degrees apart, while Anders and Webb racketed in orbit above. O'Connell was down there in Two-Five, flying with Berryman. Watson, too, with Godwin in the left seat, and Roth, who'd been made an Aircraft Commander for the same reason Webb and O'Connell had passed their check rides so quickly, flying with a newby named Kirkland.

The Hueys settled down, and the grunts started clambering aboard, throwing their rifles and rucksacks up into the cargo bays, six or seven to each chopper. The pilots kept the machines light on the skids, just barely hovering in case they had to get out quickly. Good thing, too, because they needed whatever edge they could manage when the clearing blew up in a rush of bullets, mortars and smoke.

Webb's eyes went wide as the dark forms of the grunts started falling to earth. *Amazing, ain't it,* said Webb's voice, chiming in as it often did at the least opportune times, *how easy you can tell which ones drop because they want to, and which ones drop because they got to?*

"Well, bite me on the ass," said Anders when all the firing started, all at once. "These fuckers must be crazy." There was thin, high-pitched screaming on the radio, the Hueys lifting off as fast as they could, with whoever happened to be aboard at the time, leaving the rest of the grunts on the ground. The three Vampires were equally surprised, rising quickly to altitude to shape up for a run at the jungle around the clearing.

Mortars sailed in, and tracers whistled across the open area from the near side, explosions and smoke everywhere, red smoke, too, from a grenade somebody had popped to indicate that things had suddenly gotten hot, as if nobody could tell. Anders started barking orders.

"Huck, you and the Doctor fly the perimeter and take out whatever you find. Roth, come with me and wax those mortars. You go south and west."

Webb knew that the chance of them getting hit in midair by an incoming round was not even worth mentioning, but he couldn't help looking up as Anders wrenched the trembling Huey around to the north. Jungle uncoiled beneath them.

"Watch for puffs of smoke," said Anders, pushing the cyclic forward for airspeed, his eyes undoubtedly scanning the horizon behind his helmet visor.

"Got one, sir," yelled Iglesias, "nine o'clock your position."

Anders whipped the machine around.

"Crazy-ass fuckers," mumbled Anders in the intercom. "They know there's gonna be gunships supporting the slicks, they know we can spot the mortar positions from the air. They must want us real bad."

Another puff of white smoke from the jungle, another mortar round headed for the clearing, to rain down on the heads of the ambushed troops. Anders headed straight for it, dropping in for the run.

Webb gripped the gunsight with both hands, staring at the red dot in the middle of the reticle. He couldn't see where the smoke had been, not through the gunsight, so he just started squeezing off rounds straight ahead of the plummeting ship, burst on target, following the path of the rockets that streamed into the jungle trailing grey smoke and orange fire. Fountains of fiery vegetation spurted up below them as the rockets plunged in. Webb could feel the percussion of the door guns, Gomez and Link sending suppressing fire into the jungle around them.

Up, around, suddenly feeling heavy under the G-force as Anders showed the machine no mercy. In position again, dropping, dropping, rockets flying away from them in pairs, Webb shaking, sweating, aiming his miniguns by eye, on a crazy carnival ride, trying desperately to concentrate, trying not to fall apart under fire for the first time, determined to prove what he'd come to prove. He was doing a sensational job, whether he knew it or not, his pulse pounding in his ears, feeling very good about the whole situation, until his attention was distracted by the abrupt and explosive disintegration of the chin bubble.

SMACK! SMACK! Two heavy rounds burst into his world, literally right before his eyes, brilliant shards of plexiglass whirred and flew around him, gales blew, things started falling apart.

"Fuck me for life," yelled Anders, equally surprised. "They got a 51-cal down there somewhere."

It was a trap within a trap. The VC or NVA were not such crazy ass fuckers after all. They'd staked out the LZ for an ambush, and lured two of the gunships away by firing those fat, juicy little mortar rounds, knowing that the gunnies would have to come out and find the positions.

They did, too, just as planned, but the mortar emplacements were traps themselves, defended by their totally unexpected and thoroughly lethal 51-caliber machine guns. These were Chinese or Russian-made weapons that threw huge rounds, big fat bullets that could take a helicopter out of the air in a heartbeat. But Webb and Anders were lucky. All they had to deal with was 70 knots of wind rushing toward them from the front, and who knows how many knots coming down from the rotor wash.

"Everybody all right?" yelled Anders, his hands full, trying to control the ship in the middle of the windstorm. Everybody was.

Holy damn, piped up Webb's voice yet again, *Look how sucky this thing flies when it's all shot to shit.*

At least it flies, Webb answered, something he rarely did.

"We're getting out of here," said Anders. "Better off helping them clear that LZ."

Back to the landing zone, in the teeth of the rushing wind, flattened against their seats, barely in control. Red and green and yellow smoke billowed around the clearing, so they could hardly see below them, but they did see one of the slicks on the ground, one in the air, and two others being devoured by grunts trying to crawl aboard, eager for extraction. Meanwhile, Berryman and Watson circled in their ships, pouring fire straight down into the jungle. It seemed to help, but only a little.

"Like pissing on a three-alarm fire," Anders muttered.

Webb went to his gunsight again, like he'd been doing it all his life, peering at the ground, trying to find a target. Anders wrestled with the ship, maneuvering for position, wanting to save the few rockets he had left. Roth's Huey swam into view from the south.

"Vampire Two One," crackled Roth. "We got the fucker. Two mortars."

"Great," yelled Anders. "Now how about a nice run along the north side?"

"Roger that," Roth said. "You hire, we fire."

"Cocky fucker," mumbled Anders. "He's gonna be one of the great ones."

It went on for...ten minutes? Twenty? A month and a half? Webb couldn't tell, and he had absolutely no time to be scared. It was all he could do to keep his cold damp hands on the handles of his gunsight, twisting, squeezing off the buzzing rounds, sending them down into the jungle as though he were forcing them up out of his own guts, into the smoke and fire and boiling madness.

And when he finally did lift his head into the fierce wind, he saw the dark forms, bodies on the ground, lying like broken twigs. A realization shook him. They were the first dead people he'd ever seen that weren't relatives laid out in a funeral home in mahogany caskets, brass fittings gleaming, consoling music in the air, women weeping into lace handkerchiefs.

Finally, enough grunts had been killed and fallen off so the remaining Hueys could struggle into the sky. Even so, there were two crazed men hanging from the skids, tiny dark shadows, dangling, silhouetted against the ascending smoke.

The slicks clawed their way out of the area any way they could, beating the air, fat and heavy, with the Vampires above, but the enemy had gotten enough of them for one day. Behind, in the wretched smear of clearing, the smoke settled around the bodies, a soft, warm blanket.

CHAPTER 11
THE WATERMELON MAN

Monday, April 12, 1970

Dear Benny,

This is my second tape to you, and a lot has happened since the last one.

I've been here a few weeks, now, and all I see is dirty guys in filthy greens. It's like they give you one set of jungle fatigues with a tag like you find on pillows...do not remove under penalty of law. And the funny thing is no one seems to mind smelling like they've been dead for a month. I mean, I know it's a war zone and all, but when they told me about the villa and the servants, I expected everything to be a lot more...civilized.

It feels like I've been here forever, and what I've seen of Saigon is like a movie that Salvador Dali would direct if he took about six hits of bad acid. Only thing missing is the melting watches. The heat is enormous, rising off the streets and sidewalks in huge shimmering waves. The people glide through it, they appear and disappear, like hallucinations. Even though Saigon has apartment houses, and four-or-five-story buildings, and old French villas like ours, it's all so very not familiar. It should look like someplace, and it doesn't. I'll tell you more about it later. They tell me that in the fifties and early sixties, before the Americans came, Saigon was one of the most gracious, elegant cities in the world. You'd never know it now. It's pretty fucked up.

I guess I shouldn't tell you this, but part of what's weird about this place is that everybody packs heat. I mean, I had firearms training in basic, and I've qualified on the range like any other troop, but it's not the same as loading up a real .45 and strapping it to your hip before you go out to the bars at night. I look around, thinking, "What the fuck." Do I look like a newby, or what?

In spite of the abundance of firearms, it may sound a little weird when I say I'm perfectly safe. If you have to be in the military and you have to be in a war zone, you'd want to be in DASPO. I think I told you the joke...only two officers from DASPO have ever died in combat. One of them died when he fell over a camera tripod and hit his head, and the second one died laughing watching the first. We're not combat photographers, all we do is stay back here and make movies. I know there's a lot of guys out there in the shit, getting wounded and killed, and we think about them a lot, but this villa seems like a pretty safe place to be.

I sure could use some rest. I still have jet lag, and the shits. They tell me the diarrhea will be permanent. The unit is really busy, and I've been getting up to speed on all the shoots that are going on. The other day, I helped this guy Weinberg – he draws pictures of fish – I helped him edit together some footage they'd shot in a hospital that treats American drug addicts. Apparently, there's thousands of them, because heroin is practically free around here.

So I'm watching a scene where this poor son of a bitch is going cold turkey, and he's strapped down to a bed, sweating, twitching, screaming, pissing on himself, throwing up, and he's yelling something about the watermelon man. He's screaming, "Where's the watermelon man?" and "Tell Mama-San I want the watermelon man!"

Weinberg tells me this guy was a private named Billy Jackson from the Bronx, in-country hardly any time at all, living on the base, and for a dollar and a half a day he was supporting a heroin habit that would've cost $200 in the states. He started shooting up about two minutes after he got off the plane, and it turns out he joined up because some recruiting sergeant in New York had told him how cheap it was to buy drugs over here. He's getting the stuff from this Vietnamese guy who delivers watermelons and other kinds of fruit and produce to the barracks, and inside they're all hollowed out and stuffed with smack, pot, pills, even morphine and opium, all dirt cheap. God knows how the stuff gets here. Every barracks has a Mamasan who cleans the place up, and every Mamasan knows the watermelon man, or somebody like him. The troops order it from them, right in the barracks. Jesus.

That's about it. I've got to help the crew get the equipment ready for our shoot tomorrow. It's my first time as a motion picture director in the US Army, and I'm not looking forward to it. We're going to some hospital to take pictures of people who've been burned up by napalm and white phosphorus. Terrific.

CHAPTER 12
THE MAN IN THE TANK

Tuesday, April 13, 1970

The morning of the hospital shoot, Foster woke up about six and spent some long moments staring up at the coffee-colored water stains on the ceiling of his room, listening to his stomach making frightening, pre-natal noises. His head hurt. He firmly believed that he hadn't slept in days.

Back in Hawaii, they'd told him his stomach would desert him completely in Vietnam, and return only on his arrival back in The World. He was beginning to believe it.

He'd had weird dreams, about lust-crazed dogs dripping with crankcase oil driving buses with metal mesh on the windows, buses full of 30-foot crocodiles. All night long, the motorbikes passing on the street outside poured chainsaw noises over the dingy gray walls.

"Jesus, said Foster to Weinberg later that morning. "Didn't these people *ever* sleep? Didn't any one hear about the ten o'clock curfew? Does anyone care?"

"It's like living next to the railroad tracks," Weinberg told him. "Pretty soon you won't even notice it." Foster had his doubts.

Former Sergeant First Class Harris had two Jeeps ready for them right at seven, in spite of the fact he'd been out in the clubs all night looking after his "talent." Foster could barely drag himself out of bed. He felt very, very far from home.

When he dragged himself out to the Jeep, he took another look back at the villa, still having trouble getting his mind around the situation. His arrival had been such a tornado of new sights, sounds and smells that most of what he'd seen hadn't registered, except, of course, the first sight of those two dogs.

Due to the cultural heritage of the area, the place had a

charming, if slightly rancid, flavor of the French. Whoever built the villa had waved a lunatic Gallic sensibility over it the way a skilled bartender waves vermouth over a martini, but not with anywhere near the same bracing effect. It was comparatively luxurious, by the standards of the time and place, but not as classy as the villa next door populated by an indefinite number of spooky American civilians. Nobody knew them. Nobody wanted to.

There was a high dull white concrete block wall all around, blotched with discouraging black patches of mildew, the plaster peeling off in more than a few places, as though it were suffering from an unspeakable disease of the skin. The packed dirt and gravel courtyard lay behind a wrought iron gate that looked more imposing than it really was. Along the top of the wall ran razor wire and the inevitable cruel shards of broken glass. They were foolish enough to think that no VC, regardless of the depth of his dedication to The Cause, would brave that mess just to kill some Americans who made movies for Uncle Sam. But the VC never believed for an instant that the DASPO troops were there to make movies, because they'd never met an enemy who sent the war back home on the six o'clock news. To find out for sure, Foster was told, two sappers came over the wall during the 1968 Tet Offensive. They were shot twice. First by an M-16 rifle belonging to Former Sergeant First Class Harris, then by a 16mm Arriflex movie camera belonging to Corporal D'Amato.

The walls were probably white at one time, and they were full of little pits and pockmarks. For a brief instant, Foster wondered what caused them. Then he realized they were bullet holes. The sun was like a knife.

Cong Hoa hospital looked more like a motorcycle factory than a medical facility, but so few things in Vietnam looked like what they actually were. The place squatted along the road like a constipated St. Bernard, a low, dusty gray structure, plain concrete block, square and without feature.

"What are all these people doing here?" Foster asked. "They seem healthy enough."

"There's no such thing as visiting hours," said Weinberg as he helped Foster push through the crowds. "When somebody's sick or hurt, the whole family just moves right in."

The unit had filmed in the hospital several times, and maybe most of the guys were used to it, but in Vietnam it was traditional not to give the newbys any break at all. You let them find out things on their own, and mostly they did, or they died in the process. So Foster wasn't prepared for what he saw, because nobody tipped him off. While Weinberg, White and Svoboda dragged the camera and tripod and film magazines and cases into position, Foster got his first look at one small result of the war, and his stomach raced for the basement. He saw the man in the tank.

In the middle of the operating room there was a man lying in a tank of water. He couldn't have been more than about five-two, but he was heavier than any of the Vietnamese Foster had seen since his arrival (was it really only yesterday?). The man was a lump of sweaty brown butter. He didn't look good.

Through the clear side of the tank, Foster stared, aghast. The man's left leg was horribly reddened, perforated with angry gashes and holes, the flesh looking like it had melted. There was no blood.

"Thing about Willie Peter," said D'Amato, his eyes alive with interest above his mask, "-- that's white phosphorus -- is that it burns on contact with air. Now, this gook's got some pieces of it buried in his leg and his blood and tissues're keeping it wet. If you just took it out of him, it'd burn up so fast it's almost an explosion. So they take it out under water. The water has this copper shit in it. Turn the particles purple so the docs can see it. Great stuff."

"Today," mumbled Svoboda, "we are to going in for tze close-ups."

"I can't wait," said Foster.

"Is not so bad," grunted Svoboda. "Yesterday ve only puke twice."

To Foster, it seemed like the operation took forever. Three Vietnamese doctors, accompanied by an American doctor -- and a female colonel at that -- cut on the guy until all traces of the horrible, purple, melted flesh were gone. Foster puked only once.

The filming was bad enough, but then, back in the editing room at the villa, they had to screen the footage over and over again, as they selected the shots to edit into the final version of the project. Foster was to see the man in the tank dozens of times. They told him he'd get used to it, but he didn't. Fortunately, the DASPO crews had a choice of retreats from the horrors they were forced to watch in living color, magnified on the ground glass of their camera viewfinders, and on the small screens of the editing tables.

CHAPTER 13
AP DO

Friday, April 17, 1970

Nothing was moving on the ground. All Longacre could see below him as he hung there in the ironically calm morning light were blackened hooches, the ones that were standing at all, a few pitiful pigs rooting around in the smoldering earth, gray plumes of smoke, emptiness. The bodies were gone.

The village of Ap Do hadn't been much to begin with, but now it was even more sadly diminished. The invisible Col. Xoan had decided a few days before that, innocent-looking as it was, the place was a hotbed of drug activity, a fetid pit overflowing with seething masses of heroin dealers, oozing, slimy creatures who slept in heaps and squirmed all over each other just for the chance to peddle dope to brave American soldiers.

The word had come from the colonel through Major Sanderson. Ap Do, situated as it was due west of Saigon, was a perfect rallying point for NVA and VC troops mounting operations back and forth across the Cambodian border. Just look here on the map, Sanderson said. They could barely pick it out. It must be destroyed, he said. The sooner the better.

So in the early morning they rose into the sky and pointed their trembling machines toward the unfortunate and unsuspecting village of Ap Do. The Marines would call it snoopin' and poopin'...just going out to look around and see what they could see.

Ap Do had been a classic mission, perfectly executed. Three fire teams, two choppers each. They'd gone in low, very low, pulling a steep climb up and over the treetops, and spraying everything in sight with machine gun fire, grenades, and high explosive rockets.

It was over almost before it started. No return fire, no resistance, just a ragged gaggle of people, old men and women, mostly, running around on the ground below them, diving into their hooches as though a thatched roof could protect them from the storm of lead and all the other things that exploded from the sky. They didn't look like drug smugglers to Longacre, but he had his orders.

Now it was the next day. Longacre and Harrell were sent back to assess the damage.

"Nothing left here," said Longacre into his mike.

"Not a goddam thing," said Harrell from the other Cobra, high and to the right, flying cover. He'd been in broadcasting school before he volunteered for the Warrant Officer program, and sounded just like a disk jockey. "Want to head back?"

"Roger that," said Longacre. "Shortstop, take us back to base." Up front, the copilot took his eyes from the ground and laid his hand gently on the tiny cyclic that stuck up from his right armrest. He moved his wrist just a bit and the slim, sinister machine pointed its nose into the rising sun. Harrell and Larson did the same.

In contrast to the fiery thunder of the war, Vietnam had the ability, at times, to repose in early morning tranquility. Nothing stirred except the bronze sunlight on the brown water of the rice paddies.

There were days when Longacre had been aloft, skimming over the hills, and actually forgot about the war, even if only for a minute. This was that kind of day, until Harrell saw the troops on the horizon.

"Hey, Longacre," said Harrell from above. "You see what I see?"

"Looks like eight troops. No, maybe nine. Let's drop it down and get a visual on this shit."

The two Cobras settled gently toward the wavering water of the paddies. Amid enormous roar and clatter, they approached the straggling line of figures at the speed of a fast walk, hanging above the surface, swinging in the early light.

"I make it eight," said Longacre.

"Roger that," replied Harrell. "But what's that first guy got on his goddam head?"

Shortstop took out his binoculars, flipped up his visor and leaned forward in his seat.

"Some kind of weirdass hat," he said. "Looks like a -- whaddayacallit -- a porkpie."

"Of course," said Longacre. "There's some asshole running around the middle of Vietnam wearing a porkpie hat. That makes sense. Better check this out."

Silhouetted against the morning sky, light streaming from behind him, the leader of the little parade, unmistakably a Caucasian, sported an equally-unmistakable smartass hat, like the kind you'd wear to hang around the candy store on a streetcorner in Brooklyn, or if you were singing with a Fifties doo-wop group.

The rest of the troops wore miscellaneous articles of clothing, military and non. Web belts, armaments and gear dangled from each of them. They carried carbines and ancient Thompson submachine guns that gave Longacre a quick flash of Chicago gangsters out for a little Valentine's Day celebration.

"Catch this action," said Larson. As Longacre and Harrell guided their roaring machines around the column and dangled in the air to the east, the tall leader pushed his hat back on his head, put one hand in front of his face to shield his eyes, and waved to them. The seven tiny figures strung out behind him did the same.

He was only about five ten, but still towered significantly above his companions. Jeans, a t-shirt that had once been white but was now far from it, and a safari vest with dozens of pockets.

The two Cobras moved even closer, malignant shapes above the water, stirring up enormous spray, so narrow that they almost disappeared when seen head on, except for the wing stores bristling out from the sides, rocket pods and miniguns and grenade launchers. It takes uncommon courage to stand in front of such an apparition. But the motley bunch waved again. Every one of them.

"Looks like nice folks," said Harrell. "Neighborly enough."

The gunships swung in the air alongside the paddy dike.

"Shadow Base, this is Shadow Two Five Niner," Longacre keyed the radio on the secure headquarters channel. "We got some troops in the area, about a klick north of Ap Do, eight men on a paddy dike."

His headset crackled. "Shadow Two Five Niner, we have

no operations in that area. Stand by and we'll get back to you."

"Well, fuck," Longacre muttered to Shortstop. "What does he think this is? Harrell...let's get back to what we were doing. Those guys don't know jack shit."

So the Cobras wheeled off in a circle around the band of men, who lifted their hands in friendly salute once again, and went back to look for survivors in the village, or anything at all that moved so they could complete the annihilation, but there was nothing.

"Shadow Two Five Niner, reconfirm troop sighting."

Reconfirm? What the hell for, Longacre thought. I told them what I saw. Well, shit.

Back they went, rupturing the air just above the paddy dikes, across the flat land toward the little line of men. The straggle of men had made it across one dike and were headed off at an angle to their original direction.

The machines came much closer, 30-40 meters, Longacre along the treeline low, Harrell up high for cover, because you just never know. They approached from the rear.

"Like I said before, Shadow Base. One Caucasian in some kind of dinky little hat, seven Asians dressed lots of ways, weapons, Thompsons, stuff like that. What's this all about?"

"Stand by one," the radio crackled.

"Harrell, what do you think?" Longacre's joy of flying was leaving him. The sun was higher now, the Cobra cockpit under its glass canopy going into its greenhouse mode. The sweat would be pouring soon and nobody cared who those people on the paddy dike were.

"Shadow Two Five Niner, describe the Caucasian."

Shortstop piped up on the intercom. "I would, but they all look alike to me."

"About five eight or ten," Longacre responded. "Tanned, lean, wiry. Jeans, t-shirt, khaki vest and a little round hat."

"Is he wearing cowboy boots?"

"Is he wearing *boots*? Baby Jesus," Longacre said to Harrell, "What the fuck's going on?"

"Dunno. Maybe somebody back at the base needs a pair of Tony Lamas."

"Roger that, Shadow Base. The Caucasian is in fact wearing boots. Could be snakeskin, maybe elephant, but it's tough to tell from here." The sarcasm didn't carry through on the radio.

"Roger, Two Five Niner. Stand by. Remain in the area, and don't lose sight of those troops."

Once again Longacre and Harrell pulled up on their collectives, causing the rotors to take a big bite out of the air and lift them wheeling off into the sky, once again everybody waved, like they were making home movies.

For about ten minutes they circled in the air, hovering here, hovering there, about a kilometer or two from the rice paddy, pretending to be doing something else, just floating in their expensive machines.

"Shadow Two Five Niner, this is Shadow Six. Do you read?"

"Holy shit," said Harrell. "That's Colonel Xoan."

"You sure?"

"Nobody else on earth talks like that. Shadow Two Five Niner. Read you five square."

"Do you have those troops in sight?"

"Uh...roger that, Shadow Six. Troops are in sight."

"Good. Go back there and take care of them."

Longacre felt a lurch in his stomach. He hated it when things got strange.

"Harrell, what's this guy want?"

"Beats the fuckall out of me. Better answer him."

"Shadow Six, this is Shadow Two Five Niner. We are in Cobras. We have no facilities to pick those troops up."

The voice came back. "I do not want you to pick them up, I want you to take them out. Do you read?"

"Uh, you're breaking up, Shadow Six. Stand by one."

Longacre got Harrell on the RF. "Hey, are you catching this shit?"

"I hear what you hear, buddy. He wants us to wax those guys."

Longacre tried again.

"Shadow Six, Shadow Six. Sir, I do not copy. I'm not reading you correctly. There is a Caucasian leading this bunch...are you telling me you want these people wasted?"

"That is affirmative."

Three little words. But not the ones Longacre wanted to hear. Then three more. "Report mission accomplished." Longacre felt his breakfast turn to concrete in his stomach.   Familiar sensation.

"Shortstop," he said on the intercom, "Tell me what you heard."

"To put it as humorously as possible, Col. Xoan has ordered us to kill the shit out of eight seemingly innocent people."

"That's what I heard, too." The heat in the bubble cockpit had kicked up a couple of notches. Longacre was sweating. He had nothing against killing VC. In fact, he believed, like many others, that it was the whole point of the war. And during the previous twenty months of his tours, he'd longed for the opportunity fervently enough.   But his combat fantasies were just that. Combat. He never expected to be ordered to assassinate people before, not in a non-combat situation.   His only comfort was his sure and certain knowledge that in Vietnam it was nearly impossible to tell who you were supposed to kill, and who you were supposed to save. Caucasians were about the only people you didn't kill.

"Harrell, I'm asking you this formally. What did you hear on the headquarters channel?"   Harrell's voice came back, never more serious.

"Mr. Longacre, I heard Shadow Six order you to kill those men. Do you want me to reconfirm that order?"

"Goddam right I do," Harrell said. "If the man wants those guys waxed so bad, he won't mind saying it again."

Longacre came back up on the HQ frequency.

"Shadow Two Five Niner to Shadow Six. Sir. I want to confirm that your first orders were to waste the eight personnel that we just reported."

"How many times do you have to hear it, son?" A new voice, Sanderson's voice, and short of patience. "Get on with it. We don't want to say that again. Now, do you copy?"

Longacre took a deep breath. "Affirmative. Harrell, let's get this over with. Standard approach."

They circled around for almost a kilometer so they could come up innocently from behind, both at about a thousand feet, and then shoved their cyclics forward, dropping down for a classic gun run. Longacre first, Harrell right behind and higher.

The tiny figures below loomed larger and larger as the Cobras stooped like falcons launched from the arm of some medieval king. The men on the ground started waving with all their might, radiating warmth, brotherhood, and pure good will into the golden morning air, but it didn't help. First, Shortstop coughed up a few grenades, then Longacre squeezed off the buzzing rounds from the miniguns. Spurts of water flew into the air all around the men on the dike, the silly little porkpie hat jumped into the air as the gangling Caucasian dropped for cover. But there was no cover from Harrell's merciless rockets, the long gray strings of smoke unraveling toward the ground. Longacre saw them as he pulled up and to the right, orange flame of motors, gray smoke, red bursts of explosions on the dike, in the water.

It was over quickly, just like Longacre wanted it. From his sky seat he examined the bodies on the ground, like tiny broken dolls, most in the paddy, some draped across the dike. The Caucasian lay half in and half out, the absurd hat bobbing in the water alongside.

"Harrell, call this in." Longacre mumbled as they turned back toward the base. He was sick.

Harrell and Longacre wearily set the Cobras on the pads in the Shadows compound, shut them down. Sweet silence.

"Sanderson wants to see you guys in his office," the crew chief said to Longacre as he flipped open the canopy. It was a long walk to the compound, but Longacre didn't mind, because he knew as soon as he got inside he'd be face to face at long last with the mythical Col. Xoan.

Major Sanderson arranged the four pilots in front of his desk. Col. Xoan was nowhere to be seen. Nobody asked where he was, so Longacre didn't, either.

"Good work," said Sanderson to the four empty men. Harrell had been in the shit plenty of times, but never heard himself praised for an act of premeditated murder. Is this what the Shadow platoon is all about?

"The guy you just waxed is actually a Spaniard. Nobody knows his real name so they call him Juan Wayne. Worked for a Frenchman named Henri LeCrane who owned a rubber plantation back in the late forties. Been in Vietnam most of his life. Quite a guy. Jumped into the culture with both feet. Learned the language, married a Vietnamese woman, quite respected. When the French got into trouble, he was one of the first people the Americans tried to win over."

"Excuse me, sir," Longacre ventured. "How do you know all this?"

"Got it all from Colonel Xoan. I never heard of this guy in any of the briefings, but Xoan's known about him for years. He's been a major league drug smuggler ever since the French bit the big one at Dienbienphu. The troops with him were part of his militia. He works – or worked – out of an area east of the Golden Triangle. Sanderson paused for a second and looked out the window.

"Don't understand how he let himself get caught in the open like that. He sure wasn't supposed to be there."

"Neither were we," Harrell said.

"Can't tell you how many American boys are strung out or dead because of him. You guys did good, taking him out. If anybody knew we existed, you'd get a medal. But they don't, so you won't."

Longacre's feet dragged as he walked out of the office. Before him, he saw those broken bodies lying on the ground, twitching, that sorry, silly hat floating in the muddy brown water, the looks of fatal surprise as he'd opened fire. They were the enemy, so why should he feel so empty about it all? Was it because he'd never been that close before? Was it because he'd never attacked without being provoked or fired upon? If this is being a hero, it sure as shit doesn't feel like it.

CHAPTER 14
COLONEL BERNER ACTS OUT

Saturday, April 25, 1970

Even though everybody said it was the best show in town, Foster hadn't had a chance to attend the Five O'Clock Follies, and had therefore never met Colonel Berner. But he was amazed at the fine job the man had done in building his reputation around Saigon. Everybody knew who Berner was, down to the pedicab drivers and pot washers at the Caravelle Hotel. Foster had heard the name dozens of times since he'd been in country, and it was always, always, recited as "thatassholecolonelberner." One word, verbatim, every time.

Berner had singlehandedly created a personal distinction that assumed a life of its own, a renown that ran before him like a messenger dashing from one village to another, announcing the arrival of the king. Everybody knew who he was, and everybody referred to him in exactly the same way. Foster had, however, spoken to Berner once on the phone, but that was because the Colonel had accused Svoboda of being a communist.

Svoboda and Berner had had a minor *contretemps* in some downtown Saigon tea room. Berner, in spite of the joy he took in his job, was, at heart, a sour, embittered, spiritually rancid human being. He loved the military, but he hated the Army.

"He's been on the list for Brigadier General for two years," Weinberg told Foster, "but keeps getting passed over." For some reason, the Congress of the United States continually refused to elevate him to his proper and (he believed) well-deserved level of incompetence. Tired of waiting, he spent most of his time dreaming of creative ways to call attention to himself, and his pragmatic side led him to the conclusion that his way up through the ranks lay in the production of self-aggrandizing motion pictures. Sight, sound and motion were the most persuasive forces on the planet, and of all the units in Vietnam, only DASPO knew how to use them, and Berner thought he knew how to use DASPO. In a fashion that was unique to his personality, he believed in vinegar instead of honey.

But about the communist accusation: in the club, Svoboda picked up a bar girl whose acquaintance Berner had been cultivating with every fiber of his being. The Colonel didn't take kindly to the way he was moved in on and deprived of relatively inexpensive feminine companionship. Svoboda hadn't exercised the best judgment in trying to take the girl away from a superior officer, but she thought Berner was an asshole anyway, even if she didn't know who he was, and was much more interested in Svoboda. She'd seen "The Blue Angel" once and liked Svoboda because he talked like Erich Von Stroheim. Berner, who was more than half in the bag at the time, heard Svoboda's accent and, in his alcoholic haze, jumped to a conclusion about his antidemocratic political position. Since everybody was in civilian clothes, Berner didn't know Svoboda was a US troop, and of course, couldn't possibly know he was in DASPO.

People were always accusing Svoboda of being a pinko or commie or fellow traveler, or some kind of Bolshevik, even if they didn't really know what a Bolshevik was, and the insults stung him worse than anyone could imagine. He'd risked his life escaping from behind the Iron Curtain, spending endless frigid nights in the hills of Czechoslovakia, sleeping in trees, eating bugs and roots, working his way westward. He'd struggled to become an American citizen, and his family and friends had suffered more pain and disaster at the hands of the communists than he could possibly ever speak of. So when Berner loudly and belligerently accused him of Trotskyite tendencies, Svoboda drew himself up to his full five feet five inches, and steeled himself for a savage attack. But luckily, just at that moment, the QC, the South Vietnamese police, who were better known among Americans as the White Mice because of their white helmets and gloves, pulled one of their periodic raids, because they had nothing better to do that night, and it always amused them to haul away the hookers. Berner had the QC arrest Svoboda so Foster got the

2AM phone call to come to the MP station and get him out of jail, because the QC handed him over to the MPs when they found out he was military.

The next day Berner got Foster on the phone. Foster was always surprised at how well the phone system worked in Vietnam. He could call the DASPO headquarters in Honolulu, and they sounded like they were around the block. He could hear Berner just fine. Unfortunately.

Do you have a communist agitator named Svoboda in your unit? No, sir, it must be some other communist agitator named Svoboda in some other unit. Berner hung up.

Foster finally met the infamous colonel face to face because he had been summoned to JUSPAO headquarters. An exec officer had called the villa the night before and "requested" the officer in charge of the DASPO troop to visit Colonel Berner the following morning, promptly at nine. Promptly.

This particular Saturday morning had started out cheerfully enough. Foster's diarrhea had gone on vacation for a day or two, giving him a welcome respite, the sky was clearer than usual, even at street level, and for some mysterious reason, the air was almost dry. It was, for Saigon, relatively quiet.

Foster sat in the cramped lobby of what had once been a prestigious office building, and now was occupied by the Joint United States Public Affairs Office. Even though he was there at Berner's command, he had some business with the Colonel, too. They were almost finished with a film on the QC, shooting with different units all over the country, documenting the training by American advisors whose job it was to instruct the Vietnamese in the latest techniques in law enforcement. Just like the military, the civilian peacekeeping forces were being Vietnamized. Someday soon, he hoped, they would be going it alone. The one-hour film was called "Progress to Peace," a part of the Army Big Picture series. It was the most complex production he'd ever done, and the most important. He didn't feel qualified to produce or direct such a big film, but the Army had dubbed him an 8511, and that meant he was.

He riffled through the papers in the ragged file folder he carried, reviewing all the orders and clearances he'd obtained, all the paperwork that had been sent to him authorizing the production. He examined one smaller piece of paper for the dozenth time, because it was different from the rest. It was on White House letterhead. No fancy stationery, no flowery prose, just a simple direct order requesting that a film entitled Progress to Peace be produced, edited, and delivered by a certain date. At the bottom of the letter, there wasn't even a name. Just a title: The President.

One segment of the project required access to the Vietnamese Psychological Warfare Department, and though Foster had been able to clear most of the production through local public affairs offices, he felt he had to go to the top for this one. It was Colonel Berner's job, theoretically, to coordinate between the Americans and Vietnamese in matters on this level.

Berner kept him waiting for over forty-five minutes, a period of silent reflection interrupted only by occasional bouts of screaming from the inner offices. He couldn't hear the words, but it was apparent that some unfortunate underling was being provided with an additional excretory orifice.

After a particularly vicious round of yelling, a thin, ashen-faced Major appeared at the end of the hall. His hands shook.

"Lieutenant Foster. I'm Major Perry. Colonel Berner will see you now."

The hallway reminded Foster of the walk Jimmy Cagney had taken to the gas chamber in "Angels with Dirty Faces." It was long, dark and narrow, and it smelled of dusty despair.

"At ease, *Lieutenant*," Berner said, making sure Foster was aware of the vast difference in their ranks. His high forehead gleamed with sweat and oil, even though it wasn't especially humid that day. His hair started halfway back on his skull, making his face look long and puffy. Worst of all, he combed what hair he had sideways across his head, the few sparse wisps clinging pathetically and desperately to his gleaming skull.

"I want you to make room in your schedule to shoot a film for me. Thursday of next week at 1100 hours at a location I will specify later. Sound and color, about twenty to thirty minutes. Two cameras. Got me?"

"Sir? Thursday of next week?" Foster looked at the schedule sheet he'd brought along. "I'm sorry, sir, but both

my crews are up-country that day. If you could possibly give
us a bit more notice...."

"I don't give a SHIT what you have booked that day!"
Foster's eyes went wide, and he actually leaned back a bit
from the force of Berner's unexpected outburst. For some
reason, he thought the man would be at least marginally
reasonable, in spite of his notoriety. "Next Thursday. Cancel
something else."

"Sir, if you could tell me what we'll be shooting...."

"You don't need to know that."

"Or how many people...."

"You don't need to know that, either. I'll tell you where in a
day or two. Just be there. Two cameras. Tape recorder.
Plenty of film. Got me?"

"Uh....but sir....if...."

"Got me?" Foster felt like he'd been sucker punched.

"Sir. Yes, sir." Deep breath.

Berner sat back in his chair and knit his fingers over the
rise of his stomach. There are wasps that sting their prey
enough to paralyze them, then suck out their intestines while
their victim is still alive. Foster was reminded. He was,
incidentally, still standing. There were two perfectly
serviceable chairs right next to him, but Berner hadn't offered
him one.

"Thursday morning. Eleven hundred hours. You're
dismissed." Berner looked down at his desk and started to
scribble on a yellow legal pad. Foster took another breath,
and tried to decide whether it would be the biggest mistake of
his life to ask Berner about the Progress for Peace project. It
was.

"Excuse me, sir...but may I ask the Colonel a question?"

"Hmmfp?" Berner kept writing, didn't look up. Foster
plunged on. He'd rather have waited till Berner deflated a bit,
but the project was pressing and he needed some action right
away.

"We've been assigned to shoot the last film on
Vietnamization for the Army Big Picture series. The order for
this film comes right from the President's office. I'd like to
request ...."

Berner vaulted to his feet so fast that Foster stumbled
backward. The redness rose in his face, veins pounding on

both sides of his neck, especially a little squiggly one that ran right down the center of his forehead to the bridge of his nose. Foster could actually *feel* the man's temperature rise, if not his blood pressure, and half expected to see steam come bursting out of his ears, along with that train-whistle sound effect, like in the cartoons. The colonel didn't exactly lose his temper, he set it free with both hands, abandoned it, hurling what little self control he owned explosively into space.

"*Who* in the hell do you think you *are*, throwing the President's name around like that in front of *me*? You're a second lieutenant! I'm a colonel! *You* don't get orders from the President!"

Foster stood his ground, but just barely, bravely confronting the raw fury that poured at him across the desk. With trembling hands, he held out his precious folder, but Berner didn't even glance down.

"I know about you DASPO assholes, coming over here, dropping names, you think you can do whatever the hell you want, go anywhere. Maybe you can get away with it someplace else, but this is *Vietnam*, Lieutenant, and you won't get away with it *here*. Now, what do you want, before I bring you up on charges. I think we'll start with insubordination."

Foster felt little twitches, spasms, and convulsions in his lower bowel. He'd seen cartoons where characters were so scared their knees started knocking together. He never thought such a physical response was possible, until that moment. Part of his anxiety came from the fact that a superior officer could conceivably make up a reason to put him in front of a firing squad, and part was because he'd never seen that much rage come out of a single human being before.

"Beg your pardon, sir, but I didn't mean to drop the President's name. All I said was that these orders...."

"I *hate* you guys. Know why?" Berner didn't wait for an answer. "Because you come waltzing over here on TDY with your precious per diem, and you wind up making more than I do. How long you been in the Army, Lieutenant?"

"Eleven months, sir." And two weeks, three days and sixteen hours.

"I've been in the Army for twenty nine years, and I sure

could use the extra seven hundred a month you're getting.

"Know what else I hate? Your goddam villa and the hookers who fall out the windows all hours of the night. I hate your servants and your goddam air conditioners -- think nobody knows about your air conditioners? -- and you know what I hate most of all? *Most* of all?" He bit off each word. "You get first crack at all the good movies!"

That last, unfortunately, was true. Whenever new feature films came over from the States, the DASPO troops, thanks to their connections with the other photographic units, almost always saw them first. Foster tried to get the next part out all in one sentence, before Berner cleared himself for a second orbit. Now or never.

"Sir, we've been shooting an Army Big Picture on the American efforts at Vietnamization. We're about sixty per cent complete and I need some assistance to get the support of the Vietnamese Psychological Operations people." Suddenly, Foster was inspired to grovel. "It's well known in the community that you've developed excellent relationships with our Vietnamese allies, and that they think very highly of you. You may be the only one with enough status, respect, and influence to clear the way for us."

Foster stopped, watching Berner, awaiting the benign results of his soothing words. He got exactly the reaction he didn't expect. The Colonel started bouncing up and down, like he was gathering himself for a leap across the desk.

"What? You mean to tell me you've shot more than half this film without clearing it with *me*? You took it upon yourself to go out and shoot whatever the hell you wanted and didn't tell *me* about it? You mean...."

"Sir. I did have official clearance for everything we shot."

"From who?" His voice went up a notch. He'd have a sore throat by nightfall.

"From the commanding officers of every unit we dealt with."

"Not good enough! Not good! Not! This type of coordination is MY responsibility, and everything goes through this office. Got me? *Nothing* is filmed without my approval. *Our* approval. If you think you got a problem with me, wait till the Vietnamese News Bureau gets hold of you. You can watch them burn every single foot of that film. Major!"

The major had been standing there all the time, slowly backing into a corner to make himself invisible and give Berner's fury a bit more room to take flight.

"Perry, take this man to Colonel La right now. I'll call ahead and tell him what we're dealing with. Out. Both of you."

On the way over to the Vietnamese office Major Perry didn't say a word to Foster, acting much like the prison guard who walks condemned men down the last mile. Foster's mind raced, trying to figure the whole thing out. DASPO had been operating in Vietnam for the entire war, and nobody had ever cleared any of their film projects with Berner. Could Berner crucify him, even though DASPO wasn't under his command and the unit's orders came directly from the Department of the Army? What if Colonel La didn't care whose orders he was under? What if he declared DASPO a security risk and kicked the whole unit out of Vietnam?

"That's him," said Perry, pointing out one of three officers standing on the steps of the low building, chatting to a tall, thin, good-natured Vietnamese civilian. Their obvious good spirits gave Foster hope. When he climbed the stairs toward them, one of the officers, the only one who hadn't been laughing, turned and, to Foster's surprise, saluted him.

"I am Colonel La. Wait one moment."

Desperately, Foster tried to read his face, his eyes, his body language, looking for a sign, a flicker of expression. But no. La was the first prize winner in the Mount Rushmore lookalike contest. Narrow eyes, mouth frozen in a straight line, midnight black hair, combed straight back. Two crooked teeth in the top row.

The Colonel surprised Foster again. He turned back to the civilian and said, "Delighted to see you again, Walter. I will take care of everything." They gave each other a warm embrace, with much kissing of the air and patting of the back.

La and the other officers on the steps escorted Foster and the major into a small windowless room that smelled damp, like the ceiling had leaked. As one, the three of them took seats behind a long table, and signaled to Foster to sit in the single chair that faced them. Foster's mind raced. The colonel had called the civilian Walter. Could he be...?

Back to the situation before him. Foster had seen plenty of

war movies, and if this didn't look like a setup for a court martial, he'd eat his whole folder, including the letter from the President. He sat so far on the edge of the chair that only his paranoia kept him from sliding to the floor.

Colonel La took a sip of Coca-Cola from a tall soda glass and using a long spoon started slurping it off large chunks of ice. It was one of the first things Foster had noticed about the Vietnamese. They all drank Coca Cola the same way, pouring it over large chunks of ice and slurping. The other two officers obediently did the same, slurping and eyeing Foster and Perry.

"This is Major Doh on my right, and Colonel Thi." They nodded with fixed faces. "What can we do for you gentlemen? Colonel Berner made this sound like a serious matter." His English was painfully perfect. He pronounced every word with a sharp edge, and enunciated every letter. He said "gen-tel-men," instead of "gennulmun."

Foster poured out the story, looking at La, Thi, and Do, from one set of staring eyes to another, searching for understanding, sympathy, a flash of recognition, anything.

"...And so, Colonel Berner believes we may have violated procedure by not clearing all this other filming with you."

La was puzzled. "But you say you cleared your filming with the local commanders?"

"Yes, sir. Every one of them." Foster pushed his folder across the table. La glanced through the stack of official documents.

"Well, Lieutenant, these all seem to be in excellent order. Very thorough, in fact. Your Colonel Berner told me you were sneaking around the country taking photographs of secret installations without clearance, possibly committing espionage or treason or some other offense that is punishable by death. No doubt he misunderstood. It seems to me you have all the authorizations you require. If I had arranged this matter myself, I doubt I could have done as fine a job."

Foster opened his mouth, then closed it again. "Will there be anything else?" Foster could have sworn that La almost smiled at him. He decided to push his luck.

"Well, sir, I was hoping that you could arrange for us to get some footage of the Psy Ops instruction your people are taking."

"This is a fortunate coincidence. Major Doh here is the commanding officer of that program."

"This is correct," said Major Doh in English even more agonizingly correct than La's. "Of course, some of what we do is classified, but I will be delighted to extend every courtesy to you and your men. Please contact me at your convenience."

Foster could hardly heave himself to his feet. He stammered his thanks, threw smiles at all concerned, saluted, and lurched out of the room. As he left, La fired off a string of Vietnamese to his companions. Foster didn't know any of the language except "fuck off" and a few other niceties, but he did manage to catch the words "Berner" and "asshole." It's the same in any language, he supposed.

On the way back to the center of town, Foster wondered how they would tell Berner about the meeting. Foster was none too eager to face him again, especially after they walked out of the Vietnamese HQ with everything they came for, including total support, eager cooperation, and an almost-promise of lifelong friendship.

"Don't worry, Lieutenant," said Major Perry. "I'll tell him."

"Really?"

"Oh, yes. I want to. I really do."

CHAPTER 15

DEPARTMENT OF THE ARMY
HQ U.S ARMY STRATEGIC COMMUNICATIONS COMMAND
SIGNAL GROUP, HAWAII
APO San Francisco 96557

SCCPH-A   April 28, 1970
COMMUNICATIONS NUMBER 04-21
SUBJECT: DOD FILM PROPOSAL

TO: FOSTER, LEONARD B. 266-90-4235
     2LT MOS 8511 MOS
     US SPECIAL PHOTO DET.
     Pac. (W1X9) APO SF 96558

Lieutenant Foster:

Your script proposal for the US Army Big Picture film subject "The Vietnamization of the War in Southeast Asia" has been forwarded to me by the commanding officer of the DASPO unit in Honolulu. This proposal is hereby rejected.

Your desire to focus on drug use among American troops in Vietnam is unnecessary, inaccurate, and inappropriate. Many reports on the scope of the situation have been presented to the US Congress and the Pentagon, and the facts vary widely. It is not your place to deal with this minor issue when entrusted with a documentary project of such scope and importance.

In fact, several high-ranking officers in the Department of Defense have quite recently testified before Congress and stated that less than 1 per cent of troops in Vietnam have used marijuana.

In your proposal, you mention that your "sources" in Saigon tell you of widespread narcotics smuggling conspiracies and involvement in these conspiracies by high military and civilian officials. I assure you that your sources are severely misrepresenting both the extent and the seriousness of the situation. I strongly advise that you not be taken in by misinformation and propaganda spread by those who are working only for our country's defeat and humiliation.

You are directed to submit a new proposal deleting all references to the use of drugs by the brave men and women who are fighting for the cause of freedom and democracy in Southeast Asia. I expect to have this revised document in my hands no later than 5 May.
FOR THE COMMANDER

Col. H.T. Frye
Adjutant
DISTRIBUTION: D-Plus Z-FAO, ATTN: IA Br.
* * * *

Thursday, May 7, 1970

"Set your stuff up over there," Colonel Berner growled at Ironman, sounding more like Broderick Crawford than usual. He would have growled at Foster or just about anybody else, but Ironman was the first one through the door. He was loaded down with silver metal cases, tripods, light stands, everything D'Amato could pile onto his frail frame.

Berner had phoned with the location. It was an out-of-the-way hooch not far from the morgue on Tan Son Nhut Air Force Base. There were dozens of similar buildings on the base, most with no signs on them, and no indication of their real purpose. This was one of them. They were in a kind of ready room, big and bare and dark. In the middle of the room sat two plain wooden chairs and a table. When Ironman set the lights up and turned them on, he thought it looked like the kind of place you'd take somebody when you wanted painfully honest answers to hard questions, and were ready to obtain them through physically demanding interrogation.

"I am not to go in there," Svoboda whispered to Foster as they unloaded the Jeep. "Berner vill try to kill me, and I vill haf to kill him first."

"There was nobody else to bring," Foster said. "Besides, you said Berner was shitfaced that night, so he may not recognize you. But he might be able to place the accent, so keep your mouth shut."

Berner's hatred of DASPO was as famous as his crippled personality, but nobody, especially not Foster, understood how much Berner cherished the hatred, nurtured it, fanned the flame of it, and watched it grow. He hated them because he needed them so badly, and lived with the certain fear that someday they'd commit to film something he didn't want committed. That they'd have their cameras pointed at the wrong spot at exactly the right time, and he would have to summon all his public relations skills and minor connections among the press to cover it all up. Subversive bastards. It was bile and wormwood to him that he had no official authority over them. The DASPO brass made sure everyone knew that the film crews answered directly to the Chief of Staff for Communications and Electronics. When Berner became particularly difficult, one needed only suggest that he take his case to the four star general who held the Chief of Staff position.

Berner couldn't command, but he could bully, and that was usually enough. Worst of all, he could barely look at Foster after the humiliation Colonel La had dished out, but he had to eat it, knowing that the young lieutenant and his crew could quite possibly represent his ladder up to Brigadier.

He hovered uncomfortably, shifting from one foot to the other as Ironman plugged some lights into an enormous converter box. Foster had never seen anything like it in his life, but Svoboda explained that there were three kinds of electricity in Vietnam, and the deity only knew how many different kinds of plugs and sockets. The monster box could convert anything to anything. To Foster, it looked like it ran on steam.

"You'll be shooting me interviewing a Vietnamese Air Force colonel," Berner said. "I want this dramatic, like the CBS Evening News. People tell me I come across like Walter Cronkite. Same kind of dignity and credibility. You'll shoot me from my right side -- I'll be sitting here -- with just a little kick around the shoulders. Kind of like Hollywood lighting. Got me?" Svoboda and Ironman exchanged skeptical glances.

"Everything around us falls off to black limbo. I don't want anybody watching this to know where we are."

"When will the VNAF colonel arrive, sir?" Foster asked.

"You don't need to know that. When he gets here, we'll do about a twenty-minute interview. This film needs to go directly to Washington. The Chairman of the Joint Chiefs called me personally."

"Bullshit," whispered D'Amato to Ironman.

Just as Foster got both cameras set up and ran off a few feet of film, Colonel Xoan, timing his entrance perfectly, swept into the room, white scarf flowing, trailed by a couple of young VNAF captains who toddled along at his heels like demented baby ducks.

After effusive greetings, hugs, and handshakes between the two colonels, they sat down in their individual dramatic pools of light, the cameras rolled, and they got to work.

"Colonel Xoan," intoned Berner, sneaking a look at the camera to make sure he was properly framed, "the United States Army and the Army of the Republic of Vietnam have done brilliant work here in Southeast Asia choking off the flow of drugs across the border. Now, you're taking charge of confidential drug interdiction efforts, and your headquarters are right here in this secret location. Can you tell us where these drugs are coming from?"

"As if anybody around here doesn't know," whispered Ironman again.

Xoan answered him in perfect English, accented with the Cockney of his au pair when he was a child, the French he'd picked up in whorehouses of Paris during his college days, the Gaelic of his personal tutor, mixed in with some kind of Dixie white trash twang that nobody could figure out.

"Holy shit," muttered Foster, as Xoan gave Berner (and his presumed friends at the Joint Chiefs) a concise yet complete remedial course on the history of drug trafficking in Southeast Asia. Even in its short form, the story took quite a while, with Berner interrupting every so often to ask a question, then quietly congratulating himself on his incisiveness and pithy phrasing.

Xoan warmed to his subject quickly, and talked like an expert. He told about places like Klong Toey and other slums in Bangkok, where nobody in their right mind would ever go unless they lived there or sold opium.

But Klong Toey is only one of the places in Thailand and

Cambodia where opium is distributed to factories along the borders, said Xoan. Chemists trained in China and Hong Kong turn it into Grade 4 heroin for sale around the world. The poppies are grown by peasants in the infamous Golden Triangle, in the easternmost part of Burma's Shan State, where Laos, Thailand and Burma all come together. They've been doing it for centuries, and would never dream of growing anything else. If they planted soybeans or corn or whatever else might grow up around 4000 feet, they'd have to drag their crops miles to the nearest large town, and be subject to the vagaries of uncertain market conditions and unstable prices. But when they grow poppies, the buyers are all too happy to come to them, and the demand is absolutely guaranteed.

"Tell me, Colonel, from your vast experience combating drugs in Southeast Asia, who is our worst enemy?"

"His name is...Wo Minh," said Xoan, with a certain dramatic flair. Svoboda squinted through his eyepiece and zoomed in for a tighter shot. The Colonel's Boston Blackie mustache gleamed against his upper lip. Ironman had done a good job with the lighting.

"There are many, but he is the worst, the most evil of all. A murdering guerrilla fighter with his own private army, over 5,000 troops, and he controls a significant portion of the drug trade around the world." According to Xoan, Wo Minh lorded over an area the size of several US counties in the Shan state of Burma. In his main village, there was a school, a hospital, barracks for the soldiers, even a movie once in a while. Thousands of men, women and children lived there, and all of them either grew opium, guarded it, transported it, or shot people who tried to steal it.

"And how does this evil drug lord exercise such power over the region?"

Xoan was only too happy to explain. Depending on where you have the misfortune to dwell in that part of the world, your life might be under control of any one of a number of private armies, some of them numbering up to 10,000 troops. There's the remnant of the Kuomintang, Chinese forces who took refuge in the area after the victory of Mao Tse Dung. There are the tribes of the Wa, who are fabled to use human heads as legal tender. There are the Yunnanese, plus private individual warlords, and dozens of other minor fiefdoms.

"Where do they get their troops?" Berner asked.

"These despicable scum raid the villages. If a family has three boys, they take one."

"But they don't do the same thing with...the girls?" Berner tried to sound appropriately shocked. He knew exactly what they did with the girls.

"No. The drug lords kidnap the girls and sell them."

"Oh, my God. But I understand our Thai and Cambodian neighbors are doing quite a bit to help us."

"Most certainly. Our very good friends in Thailand are making every effort to stamp out the drug trade," said Xoan, beaming. "The border officials are risking their lives to stop these caravans from coming into our beloved country."

"Tell us how the opium travels," said Berner, leaning forward in what he hoped was an intelligent, interested posture.

An even more shocking story flowed from the Colonel's lips, this one about the route of the opium down from the mountains to Vientiane, to the factories along the border, then into Vietnam on the backs of mules and enslaved children. Foster was fascinated. "What we must now fight against," gritted Xoan, "is the transport of drugs from Cambodia to Saigon. Here, in this very building, we headquarter a special drug interdiction unit, but where the troops will come from is classified. They will help us wipe out the villages that are used as storage and transport points. They will destroy the criminals who are responsible for these abominations. This unit is now being assembled."

Berner lobbed softballs to Xoan for about ten more minutes, stopping only when Svoboda, who was careful to keep himself back in the dark, needed to change film. Foster took notes for the editing they'd do when they got the footage back from the lab. The crew was getting a real education, even though Berner's shameless hamming for the camera caused breakfast to lurch somewhat in the stomach. With a stern face, Xoan told them that even though only a very few brave fighting men were hooked on heroin, one was too many. This was a lie. Between 1968 and 1970, heroin addiction among US troops had doubled. Many of them stayed in country for additional tours because they couldn't afford to support their habits at home.

"In addition to your courageous and dedicated efforts, what other actions are the Americans taking to put a stop to this terrible plague?"

Xoan gushed about the wonderful things Americans were doing to solve the problem, glowed with the chances of their success, and gave his audience glittering assurances that the people of the countryside were every bit as concerned as he was, and every bit as dedicated to the cause of eradication.

"Kill the lights," Foster said when both men got to their feet and embraced each other fervently once again, dripping with cross-cultural cordiality. As they started packing up, D'Amato leaned toward Svoboda's ear.

"Remember that film we did with the guys pissing?"

"Ya."

"How long ago was that?"

"Tree months, maybe."

"Right. So what's this guy been up to all this time?"

The hugging and kissing gradually came to an end, and Xoan departed as grandly as he had arrived, his entourage scrambling for the honor of opening his door.

"Process that film, soldier," commanded Berner, as though Foster might have some other ideas about what to do with it. "I want a work print in my office in 72 hours. The Joint Chiefs are waiting. Got me?"

CHAPTER 16
THE CITY IN THE JUNGLE

Saturday, May 9, 1970

"In case you don't remember this," the intelligence officer told the assembled Vampires that Saturday evening, "about six weeks ago, 18 March, to be exact, Prince Sihanouk of Cambodia was overthrown in a bloodless coup."

"About the only bloodless thing going on in this asshole part of the world," whispered Huck.

"What happened to him?" asked Watson. He really didn't care, but would rather have stood on his head in untreated sewage than listen to an intelligence briefing.

"It doesn't matter," said the major, standing at the front of the room with his pointer in the air. "What we...."

"Where is he now? Is he okay?" Huck sounded genuinely concerned. Webb smothered a giggle.

"He's in exile somewhere," the major said. "Russia. North Vietnam. I don't know."

"Didn't he used to play the saxophone?" asked Iglesias.

"Yes, but it doesn't *matter*," repeated the major.

"Does if he was any good," said Iglesias.

Little beads of sweat started to pop from the tight skin of the major's high forehead. At what point, he wondered, did I lose control of this briefing? He took one more stab at it.

"Gentlemen." He paused for a breath and looked around the dim, low-ceilinged room. "What *does* matter is that his successor, a man named Lon Nol, who used to be his prime minister, closest advisor, and dearest friend, has completely abandoned the Parrot's Beak and Fishhook areas to the Communists."

"Jesus H. Motherfucking Christ," whispered O'Connell.

"What's Lon Nol spelled backwards?" Berryman asked.

Previously, Sihanouk had tried to ignore the Communists,

making only token attempts to have his troops drive them out.
They'd been keeping house over there, *de facto* if not *de jure*,
for quite some time. Lon Nol was merely making it official.

"And I'm sure you also know that our troops have been
crossing the border into Cambodia for almost a month."

"Nooooo!" gasped O'Connell, with all the wide-eyed
breathless incredulity he could muster. Webb smacked him.

"Which is why our Commander in Chief announced on
national television that we are beginning, notice I said
beginning to send US and South Vietnamese troops into
Cambodia to take out the supply depots, hidey-holes,
everything we can find."

"Sounds like an invasion," Webb observed.

"No!" said the major with surprising vehemence. "It's NOT
an invasion. It's...expeditionary support." Webb wondered
how he could say things like that with a straight face.

He flipped over a page of his chart. The paper rattled. "All
platoons will be involved...aerorifle, scout and guns. You'll
get specific assignments from your troop commanders. But
let me give you the big picture."

Just like the major said, the picture was big, and it was
ugly. It took him a full hour to explain it, but that included
the interruptions by questions, comments, snide remarks,
and farts. The Vampires listened in spite of themselves,
because they knew their lives depended on whatever
information they could get, even if some of it was
"intelligence."

Two days later, they heard that the village of Hiep Duc,
only 40 miles south of Danang, had fallen to the NVA, after
three days of fighting. The Vampires, along with every other
platoon at Tay Ninh that could put a chopper in the air,
walked through orange apricot sunrise and swirling red
dust to the flight line to take off in support of the 2nd of the
63rd, and all the other US troops and ARVNS who were to
charge screaming over the border on a massive raid into the
Fishhook, along the Cambodian border not far from Tay
Ninh.

"The commies have been there forever," Watson
complained, dragging his feet in the dirt. "They're dug in."

"Probably have subways, adult book stores, bars..." mused
Huck, taking apart the little that was left of his Chesterfield.

It was cool and damp that morning, a low mist idling just above the ground. Over the low walls of the revetments, the rotor blades of the Hueys and Cobras hung limp and wilted, like discouraged flags at half mast.

This, said Webb's voice, *is not going to be one of our better days.*

Shut up, said Webb. He was starting to answer more often than he used to.

* * * *

The mission, as the beleaguered major had bravely struggled to explain, required the Vampires to station themselves behind the known and supposed enemy positions, a good twenty or thirty kilometers into Cambodia. The battle plan was for the ground forces attacking from the south under artillery and air cover to drive the panicked, retreating VC northward so the gunships, the Vampires among them, could wipe out whoever came running by.

By the time of the raids, Webb was a full aircraft commander, with his own Huey. So was O'Connell. It had happened quickly, too quickly, only because so many of the other ACs had been killed, or returned home, so many units disbanded, so many others "Vietnamized." Still no Cobras, because the President was afraid that mobilization of newer equipment would be seen as counter to his efforts to "wind down" the war.

Huck Berryman was section leader, off to Webb's right in the slowly brightening morning air. Beyond him, back to the left in echelon formation, the fat green forms hung in the sky, shifting slightly up and down like a school of whales as they made their way northeast. O'Connell with an FNG in the third machine, Roth in the last. Godwin was gone, too, leaving them, as Anders had said right at the beginning, to do more and more with less and less. Above, Captain Parker would orbit in the command and control ship, expecting to coordinate the utter destruction of the retreating VC multitudes.

"This looks like the spot," said Kirkland, from the left seat. To Webb, it looked just like any other spot. Huck set up a circle pattern, and the rest of the choppers fell in. The push had started almost an hour before. In the far distance, beyond the endless disheartening green expanse of jungle, they could see abrupt puffs of black smoke from the artillery barrage.

Webb tried not to listen to the insidious whisper of his little voice. The war had been slowing down, and aside from the reception he got on his first mission with Anders, not much had happened in the previous thirty days. Just some escort missions and resupply, no spreads of the dead on the ground, no smoke, no fire. Just making sure nothing inappropriate happened to all the VIPs who were showing up to watch the war being gradually turned over to the South Vietnamese, and to take credit for it.

But his voice wouldn't shut up. *Today's the day, it told him. You've been cruelly deceived. This does not, it whispered, smell like a simple fish-in-a-barrel operation. You will not, it hissed, simply hang here in the sky and pick off these poor suckers as they run past your sights. Have I ever been wrong? it insisted. Have I?*

Captain Parker came up on the radio. "If all this works out, we should see some action pretty soon. Let's get the scouts going a little back toward the south."

The Loaches dropped down to the trees, fluttering in and out among the deep green branches, tiny dragonfly machines, rotor wash causing great stir among the leaves. Their blades had white stripes painted on the upper surface to make them more visible from above. Webb watched the white circles buzzing below.

The surprise was not long in coming.

"Holy shit!" Brandon yelled from one of the scouts. "I don't believe this!" Webb looked out and down at Brandon's Loach as it broke away from the canopy of jungle. His words were followed instantly by a trail of thick white haze from his smoke grenade, marking his position. A thick knot began to coil in Webb's stomach.

"Kirkland, you see anything?"

"No, sir, but somebody sure did."

The other Loach scurried toward them from the west, where he'd been puttering around in the high trees.

"Are you taking fire?" Webb's voice tightened a notch, right along with his stomach.

"Negative, but we sure as shit got something here,"

Brandon continued, his voice shaking from excitement, fear, surprise. "Can't tell what it is yet...."

That's as far as he got before his chopper exploded. Against the dense green of the jungle, the fireball was a gorgeous orange, tinged with red around the edges, pulsing veins of black smoke in the middle. Everybody started screaming at once.

"Jesus Bartholomew Christ," O'Connell said on the RF. "What the hell...?"

"Brandon! Oh, my God!"

The other Loach zipped into position over the spot where the shards of Brandon's chopper drifted down. A hand pulled a smoke grenade from the doorpost, threw it to the ground. A column of red pulsed up to the sky, fluttered and spread.

"Receiving fire! Receiving fire!" the other scout yelled as he broke his machine hard, hard to the right. A spray of bullets burst from the tiny helicopter hurrying madly away to the south. Automatically, the gunships broke into two teams, Berryman and Webb in one, O'Connell and Roth in the other.

"They got a little city down there," yelled the scout pilot. "Couldn't see much, it's all buried under the canopy. But...my God, there's more of it over here!"

They would have attacked, but they didn't know where to start. There was enemy where Brandon's chopper got blown up, and the remaining Loach reported enemy to the south, too. The gunships pulled up to attack altitude, above the kill zone where small arms fire from the ground couldn't reach.

"Shit, there's more stuff down here," said the Loach.

"Great," said O'Connell. "'Cept nobody but you can see it."

"Bunkers, I think. Shelters. God *damn*!"

As soon as Webb heard the last "God damn," the world blew sky-high into a fog of hot flying metal, smoke and confusion.

"Break to the north!" yelled Berryman. "Form up and orbit!"

The fat green forms hurled themselves over onto their sides and executed what is politely termed a "retrograde operation." They retreated, as far and as fast as they could, to form up and work out a plan that would deal with the disagreeable little surprise. There were enemy troops down there, lots of them, that absolutely nobody had known about. They were a

good thirty klicks from the border, so they couldn't call in
artillery, and any air support that could help them at that
moment was otherwise occupied. At least that's what Captain
Parker was told when he called in. He screamed for artillery,
air strikes, a little napalm, white phosphorus, a few
screaming A-7s, slingshots, catapults, crossbows, anything,
but the resources were "committed elsewhere."

The Loach stayed where it was, throwing red smoke to the
four winds, thick columns billowing up from the intense green
below.

Told you, said Webb's voice. Shut up, said Webb. He
hated it when he had to answer back.

The four Hueys circled in the sky, their pilots and crews
looking back to the north, trying to see through the puffy
clouds of red smoke. Discussion ensued, mostly between
Parker and Berryman, trying to decide how to handle this
startling turn of events.

"One thing's obvious," said Berryman, to anybody who
would listen. "They were hoping we wouldn't get this far.
They never expected us to find anything back here."

"Well, the fuckers know we're here now," put in Roth.

"Surprise isn't exactly on our side," agreed Webb.

"Must be a refuge for troops along the border," offered
O'Connell. "If they retreat from the south, I bet they head
straight for here."

"Murph, you dog," said Webb, "We can always count on
you for keen analysis."

"Send it up the Hershey highway, ol' buddy," said
O'Connell.

Webb smiled. Nobody had as many terms for the lower
bowel as Murphy did.

"Knock it off," warned Parker. "We just gotta make sure
there's nothing here for them when they arrive. Racetrack
runs. Huck and Spider on the right pattern, the other two on
the left."

Webb pushed his cyclic forward. The rotors tilted in the
same direction, pulling the chopper, gathering speed. He let
the collective drop, changing the angle of the blades, losing
lift, and the ground rushed up toward him. Over the
intercom, he could hear Kirkland's breathing heavy up. In
back, Link and Gomez wiggled themselves on the pillows that

covered their armor-plated seats, checked their machine guns, yanked on their harnesses yet one more time, took deep breaths, blew them out between pursed lips. Gomez crossed himself.

"Give 'em hell, Murph," said Webb.

"Right in the old fudge factory," he replied.

"Let's rock and roll," said Berryman.

The four Hueys ran straight for the clouds of smoke. Webb, his hands sweaty, tried to keep a relaxed grip on the cyclic, sure that Kirkland would be able to see his white knuckles right through his flying gloves. *This is what you came for*, his voice reminded him. *Now you can show your father what you're really made of.* Leave my father out of this, Webb mumbled.

"Say again?" asked Kirkland.

"Nothing," muttered Webb. "You just put those miniguns where they'll do the most good." They flew into the fire.

A racetrack run is just what it sounds like. The choppers follow each other around in a roughly oval pattern, like a racetrack, but it is easier said than done. There was red smoke below them, around them, even above them as they paired off and began the steep drop. Whoever was down there controlled a decent slice of real estate because the wiggling red tracers reached for them almost at once, from almost every direction. Webb needed no reminder that every single red streak he could see represented five chubby slugs that he couldn't.

Racetrack runs. The gunships would head straight toward the base of the red smoke, Huck first, Webb far behind. When Huck broke to the right, Webb would be on the straightaway, coming in low with his rockets, Kirkland on the miniguns, the boys in back playing counterpoint on their M-60s, making deadly music. Two long straightaways, one inbound and one outbound, a tight 180 at either end. A bit to the west, O'Connell and Roth would do the same, except to the left.

Nose down, the Huey near redline power, rattling and shaking around them, Kirkland with his face to the reticle, ready to let go with the miniguns, the ground rolling by not very far below, hearts pounding, stomachs tight.

Huck barreled into the confusion, his Huey disappearing

for an instant inside all the billowing red smoke, miniguns spinning madly, six barrels spraying right and left, exactly at the moment when every major anti-aircraft gun in southeast Asia spoke up, each making its presence known in gruff, deep, authoritative voices. Red streaking tracers came from everywhere, brilliant white flashes, puffs of dirty orange from shrapnel, 12.75s, maybe some radar-guided anti-aircraft weaponry contributed by the Chinese. Even in the bright of day, the sky radiated a streaking psychopyrotechnic spectacle of glowing deadly colors.

Huck was through the mess, miraculously untouched and breaking to the right. It was Webb's turn.

"Kirkland, I hope you got a firm overlapping grip on your balls," Webb said, his eyes riveted on a cloud of smoke ahead. He had his little grease pencil marks on the windscreen lined up, ready to send his rockets toward whatever was down there, airmail, special delivery.

"Shit, yes," Kirkland said. There was no mistaking the excitement in his voice.

Closer. And lower. Wisps of red smoke rushed by alongside, mixed with the gray from the explosion of Huck's earlier rockets. Chatter in his helmet, something from Link about the two huge ragged holes that had miraculously appeared in the fuselage next to his head, obscene Spanish from Gomez -- *Me cago en la leche de tu puta madre,*" or something like that -- who squeezed the rounds out of his M-60 as fast as they would go, sitting in a spray of golden hot ejecting shell casings.

Burst on target from Kirkland. He'd gotten better with the miniguns. Webb pushed the button and two rockets escaped from the ship, trailing gray smoke and orange fire. Explosions on the ground, explosions in the air.

"Taking hits! Taking hits!" Hey, thought Webb, who isn't? But it was O'Connell's voice, far to the left as Webb broke around for another pass.

"It's the tail rotor! We took one in the tail rotor!" Murph's co-pilot, whatever his name was.

"Take this thing," Webb yelled to Kirkland, and immediately put his visor up, scanning out his window for any sign of O'Connell. If they got his tail rotor, he was in the most excremental of conditions, and no doubt about it.

The tail rotor counteracts the torque produced by the main rotor shaft, and keeps a helicopter from turning in the same direction as the rotating blades. When it goes out, the chopper spins helplessly to the right, all control gone.

In theory, there's an emergency procedure for that kind of situation, and every good warrant officer candidate practices it all through Fort Rucker. Works every time. In theory.

Webb could scarcely see O'Connell's ship in the distance, but he knew right away that no emergency procedure was going to help. The wounded helicopter, trailing dark hydraulic fluid out the back, made a lame erratic spinning path directly toward the heart of the hostility below.

"Maydaymaydaymayday! We're going in!"

"Can you make it?" Captain Parker, his gangling figure no doubt leaning out of his Command and Control Huey above them, trying to stay in touch.

"Affirmative," said O'Connell, his voice sounded like steel cables that hold up high-voltage lines. "Little busy right now. I'll report on the ground."

But he didn't. Long seconds went by. Webb got crazy.

"Captain! We need to go get him. I'm on my way!"

"Hold your station, Mister! Continue the run."

"Sir...."

"That's an order!"

Webb felt like he'd been bludgeoned. He could see the exact spot where O'Connell's chopper had gone in. There was smoke over it, white and gray, some small explosions, and the tracers, of course, which just kept coming, lighting the sky. The cry of "mayday" echoed inside his helmet, infinite and far away.

He put it all aside, just for a second, as hard as that was for him to do. His friend was down. Down! And in the worst possible place, at the worst possible time. *You have to do something*, his voice said. *Now.*

His training took over for one more run. Numbly, he watched Huck hurtle through the mess and break right for the second time, and he followed.

"I got it," he told Kirkland. He tightened his jaw without knowing it, clamping down on his teeth so hard that little iron bolts of pain shot up through his ears. Cyclic forward, fast, fast, the guns whirring, the ship shaking, red smoke thinner now, still rushing by in baby-fine wisps, rockets thumping out of the pods, streaking, glowing.

"Okay, let's fall back," Captain Parker said. If disgust could drip, Webb would have heard a puddle of it in his voice.

"Sir, what about O'Connell? We gotta...."

"There's nothing we can do," Parker told him. The three Hueys wandered back toward the south about a klick, out of range of the little enemy city they'd run into. Webb listened to the voice in his helmet, acutely aware that everybody else was listening, too.

"But...."

"How much fuel you got left, huh?" Parker asked him. "How much ammo? We're way out of our league. There's boocoo heavy shit down there. We'll head back over the border to the FRB and report this. Form up on Huck and let's get the fuck out of this place."

Webb collapsed back into his seat, his hands in his lap, his neck slack, head to one side, again with that deflated, drained sensation. Startled, Kirkland grabbed the cyclic, took over, brought the ship around, formed up on Berryman's Huey, and headed south toward the forward refueling base.

At the FRB, the situation was tense. Parker and Webb were facing off.

"I said, they'll take care of it," Parker insisted.

"And I said, he's my friend and I have to go get his ass out of there. Right now. All due respect. Sir."

There was, however, no respect whatsoever in his voice. Parker, having dealt with dozens of equally deranged young pilots, stood patiently next to the chopper, his boots digging in to the dead, dry beaten-down grass. He knew he'd just have to take it while this stressed-out, angry, heartbroken troop in front of him worked it all out. He'd seen it so many times before.

"I saw where he went in, I know right where it is, all we have to do is go in there with a few guys, and...."

"Forget it. And get some sense, okay? I'm sorry about O'Connell, really. He's a good troop. And from what I saw, there's a better than even shot he's alive. They'll get him out." What Parker didn't say was that if O'Connell *was* alive, he was also, beyond the shadow of any doubt, in the unsympathetic clutches of dozens, probably hundreds, of grinning unfriendlies.

"We stumbled into an installation they call the City. It's huge. They knew it was there someplace, but nobody knew where. It's their biggest base. We could all get medals."

"I'm thrilled." Parker let it pass.

"No wonder there was so much firepower. They're bringing in more troops. Including, I'm told, 2,000 Cambodian mercenaries."

Was that supposed to make Webb happy? It didn't. He had a *friend* in there, probably in terrible shape, and he didn't care how many Cambodian mercenaries got brought in. None of them would be looking to rescue O'Connell.

"Just take it easy, okay?" Parker slouched away. Webb sat at the edge of the cargo bay trying not to think.

CHAPTER 17
DEAR BENNY

Sunday, May 10, 1970

Dear Benny,

Here's another installment of the continuing DASPO saga. Sorry it's taken me so long, but things have been really busy. Today is Sunday, so I have a little time to catch you up on everything that's happened so far.

Now that you know I'm at the war but not actually <u>in</u> the war, here's my first war story. As soon as I got to Saigon, I had to step into the middle of shooting a film on the medical care of people who'd been burned by napalm or white phosphorus. They call 'em crispy critters. The Army must have a dozen films on how to burn people up, and we have to do one on how to fix 'em afterwards.

We were shooting at Cong Hoa Hospital, a good-sized Vietnamese clinic not far from our villa. Yeah, we have a villa, but that's a story for another time, too. Trust me, it's not like on the Mediterranean with Zorba the Greek and dancing girls on the beach. From what I hear, there happen to be some dancing girls right here in Saigon, but if I tell you about them, you can't say a word to Mom and Dad. Remember?

I'll skip the details, but the guy we were filming, in addition to being roasted by napalm, had half a grenade up his ass, and we got to watch them pull it out.

Right after that, we had to shoot some stuff at the American hospital in Cam Ranh Bay, but when we got there people started boiling around in the corridors, running back and forth like they were going nuts. You'd think that the Surgeon General had suddenly popped in for a surprise inspection.

Well, the Surgeon General had suddenly popped in for a surprise inspection, and the place went right to shit the second he walked in the door. What happened was, two

American doctors had gone fishing out in the bay a few hours earlier, in a small aluminum boat powered by the first outboard motor ever made on earth. The thing conked out about two miles from shore, so they called on their walkie-talkie for a chopper to pick them up. They were late for their shift and didn't have time to mess with the motor.

Out of the sky drops this medevac chopper. It's a Huey, like the kind you've seen on television, with the big wide doors on the side. It has pontoons, so it lands on the water and takes the two of them aboard. They decide to let the boat go, but the motor wasn't totally worthless so they pull it off the boat and take it with them, securing it the only way they could in a medevac chopper, by strapping it to a stretcher.

These guys are *really* late for their shift, so the chopper pilot puts them down on the dustoff pad right outside the operating room. Now, nobody ever lands there, not ever, unless there's wounded aboard. So when they radio that they're coming in, everybody says, "Great! A chopper full of bleeding, dying wounded guys, just in time for us to show the Surgeon General what crack troops we are, how efficient in coming to the aid of our boys who are fighting for the cause."

The sound of the rotors above the hospital jump-starts everybody into action, and suddenly it's showtime.

The very second the chopper touches down every single member of the hospital's emergency staff, dozens of people all dressed in white, pour onto the pad, wheeling gurneys, carrying IV tubes, bottles of plasma, bright green tanks of oxygen, bandages, running all over the place, heads low, shoulders hunched under the rotor blades. The Surgeon General, swept along by this flood of medical mercy, has a front row seat for the drama about to unfold.

Remember, this is my first assignment. When we were shooting, I had the major shits, I couldn't eat, couldn't see straight, and we're loaded with cameras and film, walking into the middle of an actual Media Event, so I grab the equipment and crew (at least now I know all their names) and we bolt outside with the rest of them, cameras and all, urged along in no uncertain terms by the Vietnamese hospital director who anticipates glory, lots of face, the respect of his departed ancestors, and tons of bucks after the war if he can just get some film of himself helping the Surgeon General of the

United States with an honest-to-God medical emergency. Everybody's trying to get into the act.

Svoboda bounces down the corridor with the camera on his shoulder, Weinberg grabs some cable -- turns out I'm not the only Jew in Vietnam -- and we all rush outside to the pad.

The orderlies deal with lots of wounded...it's kind of their job, and they go into action on autopilot. They push the Surgeon General to the front, his face lights up, he's right there, in the middle of it all, and these people are doing their drill like a...a... water ballet or something. These guys are *good*.

They fling open the huge side cargo door of the chopper, and the two American docs hop out, all smiles, wearing jeans and t-shirts, boots and flop hats with lures pinned all over them, looking for all the world like they've just had a great helicopter ride back from a brief fishing holiday, which is exactly what they had.

Of course, they're a little confused by the reception, but they're taking it in stride. The orderlies release the stretcher and slide it onto the gurney.

Svoboda pushes closer with the camera, the Surgeon General presses in to monitor the response, a nurse pulls the blanket aside and the ER doctor plunks his stethoscope down on the hard cold metal casing of the outboard motor. I bet it hurt.

I can't wait till we process the film. I jumped on Svoboda right away to get some footage of the Surgeon General's face, and he assures me he did. Hope it comes out.

Looks like I have a little more time, so here's another one.

I guess the papers at home are full of news about how the war is being "Vietnamized." That means a lot of Americans are going home – except me, of course – leaving the Vietnamese to figure it out for themselves. Here at DASPO, we're doing our part to spread the word. The unit just finished a film for the Army Big Picture series about how we're training the Vietnamese police in our enlightened methods of dealing with criminals and crazies, except we never told them about electric chairs and gas chambers. Didn't have to. Here, they just take you outside and shoot you. One part of the film was on the prison system, so they gave us the grand tour of their finest correctional facilities. Holy shit.

The first was a more or less traditional military prison or

something like that, you know, big building with bars on the windows, high walls all around. We walked in with all our equipment, and there are these two American guys in the yard, just two of them, among all the Vietnamese prisoners. They looked like shit, all skinny and dirty. God knows what they get to eat in a place like that. The guard told us they'd been arrested by the QC on drug charges. I thought if they put every American who was doing drugs in jail, the war would be over in a hurry, because there wouldn't be anybody left to fight it. But these two sorry bastards were unlucky enough to get caught, and why they weren't in the American jail at Long Binh is anybody's guess. The American military police and justice system can't arrest or prosecute the Vietnamese, but they can arrest us. Long story short, you don't want to spend too much time figuring out how things work around here.

One of the Americans told us his name was Larry, and started whispering about what a pit the place was, about how he and the other guy got beat up by the guards all the time because they hated what the Americans were doing to their country.

The other American, Bill, or Will, or something like that, was older than the first, probably around thirty-five or so, but he looked sixty. Told us he was an ex-GI who took his ETS in Vietnam – that's his discharge – and went to work as a civilian for this guy named Walter Crawley who supplies all the base exchanges and clubs with liquor. Maybe you remember that the guy in the bar who told me about him? Bill was a pilot, and used to fly this guy around the back country in a chopper with a bunch of Vietnamese Air Force colonels and some other civilians, taking them to all sorts of villages and places they weren't supposed to be. One day he decided to find out what was going on, like what was in the boxes they were hauling from place to place, and the next thing he knew the QC were dragging him off to jail at three in the morning on drug smuggling charges. He'd been there a year. Apparently the Vietnamese constitution doesn't guarantee the right to a speedy trial. You know that old saying, Benny, about believing none of what you hear and half of what you see? Well, over here, it's hard to believe anything at all.

That's about all the story we got, because when the guards saw him talking to us they hauled him off. We were all pretty upset about it, but there was nothing we could do.

For the second part, they flew us out to some penal institution on a place called Cong Song island. Jesus, Benny, you wouldn't've believed it. Let's just say that when it comes to jails, this particular culture doesn't choose to invest in infrastructure nearly the way we do. These people put prisoners in holes in the ground, they cover the top with a bamboo grid, and forget about them. Tiger cages. I think there's been some press about them lately back in the states.

We're walking around out there, and the warden is telling me that Cong Song is one of the nicer prisons. At least you had fresh air and a bath when it rained. In the monsoon season, your tiger cage turns into a swimming pool. The other prisons are supposed to be worse, which I just can't imagine. But I made the mistake of looking down into one of the holes, and that's when I saw Uncle Dung.

I think I already told you about the people who work in our villa. The family Dung. There's Yak Dung, who chews betel nuts all the time so his teeth are totally black, and when he smiles at you, you hope to God he won't do it again, and then he does. There's his wife Mamasan and their daughter Young Dung, too. A few weeks ago I found out Yak had an older brother, so we called him Uncle Dung. Until recently, Uncle Dung had his own sidewalk soup kitchen down the street. A lot of Vietnamese are living on the sidewalk, or doing business there. This guy's got a huge open pot on a few chips of burning coal, and inside the pot is...well, you don't want to know. Stuff that used to be noodles, unidentifiable vegetables and chunks of something that was maybe alive at one time. You know...mystery meat. Gave me an idea for a new cooking show called "Recipes From the Gutter." Could be a hit.

Now imagine a man who looks about 200 years old, but he's probably only around 50, about four and a half feet tall, but when he squats down on the ground he has the uncanny ability to compact himself into a little two-foot ball of a human being. Young Dung told me that her family had been making soup on the same streetcorner for generations. I think it's still the same soup.

Last week, President Thieu announced another one of his

stellar programs to curb inflation. Any citizen who raised prices in his store or restaurant would be arrested, and sentenced to seven years to life. In a jail around here, seven years is already a life sentence, because it's tough to last much longer than that. Anyway. Thieu makes this decree and he orders the White Mice – that's the civilian police -- to go out and make some examples so everybody else will fall into line.

Now, get this. Two days ago, the guys and I went to La Dolce Vita, a great restaurant right next to the Continental Hotel. Because of the price freeze, we ate a seven course meal for about $1.70 American. When we left, we ran right into one of Thieu's raids. Guess who the cops were making an example of.

Right. I recognized Uncle Dung because he was wearing a DASPO T-shirt. One of the guys had them made in Okinawa. They say "DASPO Brothers Flying Circus and Freak Show," and our company slogan, "Ars gratia per diem." There's a drawing of a fist holding a wad of money, all wrapped up in film. Mamasan steals our t-shirts when she does the laundry, but we don't mind. They need 'em more than we do.

According to the Family Dung, Uncle charged about 50 piasters for a bowl of soup...around 12 cents American, but they hit you for an extra 10P if you want a clean bowl. Uncle, who probably doesn't even know Thieu is president, was caught raising the price of his cuisine about two cents. He claimed he was only covering the expense of adding more high quality ingredients, but the cops didn't buy it.

So we had to stand there and watch as they hauled this poor shrunken 200 year old guy off to jail. Next thing I know he shows up at the bottom of a hole. Talk about winning hearts and minds.

We were still upset about Larry and the other American guy, but we couldn't do anything about them because they were in a military jail. Uncle Dung was in a civilian facility, and even though it's pretty easy to get thrown in jail in Vietnam, it's even easier to get out. All it takes is money, and not a whole hell of a lot of it. Each of the guys in the platoon kicked in five bucks and we gave it to Yak Dung, who showed us two rows of perfectly black teeth, went to the jail, paid off the right people, and Uncle was free in twenty minutes. Pretty good system.

Gotta run. I'm okay. Really.

CHAPTER 18
THE GIRL WITH ONE GREEN LEG

Saturday, May 16, 1970

It was only because Foster couldn't face the prospect of spending yet another night drunk in the bars that he met the girl with one green leg. He had come to understand that it wasn't really possible to stay drunk all the time, though many people tried to. Some nights there was nothing else to do but sit at home.

They'd been shooting every day, finishing up the National Police film for the Army Big Picture series. Colonels La, Thi, and Do had been as gracious and hospitable as promised, and the brass back at the base in Hawaii had sent their congratulations. The unit was ready to start on a new safety film, a gripping epic entitled "Hazards of Vehicle Operation in Vietnam," but most of the GIs already knew how hazardous it was, because they'd either been run over, or had run over someone else, or been through enough close calls to learn the hard way. Foster was beset by a growing stack of other projects, too, either starting, finishing, or somewhere in the middle. They'd been spending days in the field, up at firebases, training camps, flying back and forth. When they were in the city, they'd unpack their gear, go out, get drunk, come home, and fall into bed. The hundred-degree heat and gritty red dust of the firebases and hilltops out in the boonies had taken their toll, and there were nights they couldn't even drag themselves out the door. The other major deterrent to chronic alcohol abuse was that it didn't do any favors for the inexhaustible diarrhea they suffered from the malaria pills, or from the burning liquid agony of Ho Chi Minh's revenge which was not, despite the old saying, best served cold. And besides, drinking did absolutely no good if you had the clap, because it made you piss a lot, and it burned.

Foster had so far escaped that particular affliction, but almost everybody had it at one time or another. Since venereal diseases were so epidemic, the military believed in treating them aggressively and enthusiastically. Sufferers received two horse needle shots, about a quart apiece, the first time they showed up at the dispensary with the famous symptoms, then a follow-up series three days in a row after that. There were so many cases that the dispensary had a special entrance for clap sufferers, and every day hundreds of men, from privates to full bird colonels, would line up for their shots. None of them spoke to each other, ever. They just stood there outside the door, silent, shuffling along, gazing at the ground.

It was Saturday, but Foster didn't feel like drinking, and for some reason he didn't feel like surrendering himself to the lubricious delights of the Magic Fingers across the street. He'd discovered, much to his disappointment, that there really could be too much of a good thing. He was fresh out of ejaculate.

So he did something simple. He went for a walk.

"You help?" Foster didn't even turn around. There were always people on the street, asking for one thing or another.

"You help? You Foster, yes? You help me?" That made him look. Who would know his name? He turned to see a Vietnamese girl, face reddish and flushed, hollow-eyed, ragged, hobbling toward him on a set of homemade crutches. She was wearing shorts, a blouse that had once been white, holding a bandaged leg up off the ground as she made her painful way along the sidewalk toward him. Long black hair, big eyes, and she probably would have been attractive enough if she hadn't been on the verge of collapse.

Foster looked once, then twice. "Thi Lanh?" He could hardly believe it. He knew her from the massage parlor, and for a while she'd been Former Sergeant First Class Harris' girlfriend. But she refused to set foot in the villa ever since she'd kicked Weinberg down the stairs because he asked her for a blowjob at the Magic Fingers. The last time he saw her, she was decked out in her party finery, skintight skirt, low-cut blouse, wicked black stockings, shocking pink high heels. Now, woefully reduced, she looked like she'd crawled up out of Uncle Dung's pot of soup.

"Foster, you help?"

"Jesus! You look like you got hit by a truck. What happened?"

"I hit by truck. Come home from party one night with boy, and I fall off ciclo. Truck hit me. Break leg real bad."

He looked down. Former Sergeant First Class Harris loved her legs. So did everybody else. The inhabitants of the villa would turn out en masse, clogging the first floor hallway, just to watch her walk up the stairs, and her legs in those black stockings with their seams up the back and retro Fifties-style Cuban heels were the stuff of many a fevered fantasy. Harris had found the hosiery in an old French lingerie shop somewhere, and given her six or eight pair, on condition that she wear them only at the villa. But her legs didn't look all that appetizing now. The right one was bruised and scraped, with ugly red scratches all along her outer thigh. The left one was bandaged around the calf with a piece of cloth that looked like it came off the floor of a garage.

"I need money. Can not be girlfriend with broke leg."

"But didn't you go to the doctor?" He had to ask, because it looked like she hadn't.

"Yes. Doctor fix. But it still hurt, so I go back, and he fix again. It is not well. See?"

Before he could stop her, she eased herself down to the crumbling sidewalk, with people stepping over and around her, unwrapped the sticky bandage, and showed him something he could have lived the rest of his life without seeing.

"Oh, holy Christ." His stomach lurched, and he could feel Mamasan's noodle dinner struggling to escape. Her entire leg from the knee down was the color of rancid pea soup and bad eggplant. It was mostly green, but there were purple overtones, too, spattered with furious red blotches of infection. Bits of flesh hung from a ragged gray wound, which made him conclude that she'd had a compound fracture and nobody had even reset the bone or put a cast on it or done much of anything but slap on a rag. If there had ever been a dressing, it was long since gone. Veins of red ran out from the wound. He'd never seen blood poisoning before, but this was certainly it. The whole thing had obviously gone septic, she could even have gangrene, her leg oozing and suppurating. He held his breath, because he had some fearful idea about what the whole thing would smell like, even from where he stood.   He remembered the amputees in Cong Hoa hospital. It wasn't just because of the war.

"Hurts very bad. You give me money, I go to a real doctor, French man." She struggled to stand up, and Foster put out an arm to help her, but she passed out anyway, almost knocking him over as her eyes rolled up in her head, and she fainted against him.   Her crutches clattered to the broken sidewalk.

Somehow, he wrestled her halfway back up the block to the gate of the villa, just in time to see Ironman coming out.

"Trolling for hookers, Lieutenant?"

"Cute. Help me get her inside." Ironman took a good look at Thi Lanh, not recognizing her.

"Y'know, there are six million stories in the naked city. You can't help 'em all."

"We can help one. Give me a hand."

Mercifully, Jack and Little Shit didn't come howling around the building in their normal fuck frenzy as Foster and Ironman carried her across the courtyard and up the steps. Inside the door, Foster looked for someplace to set her down, but the dining room table was occupied by Huggins and some supply corporal he knew from the base, who were interviewing two Vietnamese girls about their abundant if not particularly fulfilling sex lives. He had his Nagra tape recorder on the table, the silver spools whirling.   The Nagra was a plain, cheap-looking machine, nothing like the space-age tape recorders the GIs bought in the duty free shops of Tokyo, with all the flashing lights, dials and buttons. It was just a simple aluminum-colored box with a few plain silver knobs, but it was painstakingly built and calibrated with scientific precision, made especially to synchronize with movie cameras and record sound for motion pictures. The dumpy-looking thing cost about four thousand dollars, but the government had paid eight.   Huggins also had the unit's best, most expensive Sennheiser microphone picking up every detail of the girls' innumerable and not terribly imaginative liaisons with American soldiers. Huggins could barely write, but he was sure there was a book or a screenplay in there somewhere.

Thi Lanh started to come around, her head flopping lazily from one side to the other. They dragged her up to the second floor, but couldn't find any room there, either. Svoboda was taking pictures of two naked women in the projection room, having set up quite a complete little photo studio with strobe lights and five or six different textured backgrounds. Weinberg was hunched over a pad of drawing paper, his glasses held together with camera tape, colored pencils flying, busily completing a life-size portrait of a flounder, and behind the other closed doors, the sounds of energetic, athletic sex rumbled and thundered into the hallway amid random whiffs of pot smoke. One of the EMs had bought a set of black silk sheets, and he and his dates slid out of bed onto the floor with a resounding thump two or three times a night.

Up one more flight. Finally, they laid her down on a spare bed in Foster's room, which was the last place he wanted her, but the only available spot. When they lifted her broken leg onto the bed, she suddenly came to and started to scream.

She shrieked and moaned, her exclamations carrying down the hall, down the stairs, ringing all through the villa. From below, cheers and exclamations echoed back.

"All RIGHT, Lieutenant!" "Way to go!" They'd heard sounds like that from the upper floors on many nights, sounds of ecstatic young women with their American "boyfriends." To them, it sounded like Foster was showing her a very good time, and the crutches were just there for a little extra kinky touch.

"Are we done?" Ironman asked.

"This isn't gonna work," Foster observed. "We have to get her to the hospital. She could lose that leg."

"Won't be the first one."

"You helping or not?"

"The hospital only treats Americans."

"We'll see about that. Come on."

Accompanied by more screams and moans, and more cheers from downstairs, they picked her up and dragged her down to a Jeep in the courtyard. The 3rd Field Hospital was just around the corner, and as soon as Foster carried her in the door, everybody in the place snapped into action. They didn't care if she was American, or Vietnamese or Martian, all they saw was a young woman with a leg that looked like it would rot and fall off any second. A nurse and orderly grabbed her from Foster and Ironman, put her on a gurney, clattered down the hallway and disappeared.

Foster hadn't given any thought to what would happen next, but he had to when a doctor and nurse brought her back two hours later, leg set in a bright white cast, stoned and delirious with antibiotics and high-end painkillers. She was totally inert, draped over them and sliding to the floor.

"We got it just in time," the American doctor said. He wasn't much older than Foster. "Had to cut away some of the flesh around the calf because of the gangrene, so she'll probably walk with a limp. Her leg ain't gonna look that great, but another day or two and she would have lost it completely." In spite of the situation a brief regret flitted across Foster's mind. No more black stockings.

"Hey," Foster asked, trying to hold her up. "What did you give her?"

"Just about everything we had."

"Yeah? How much?"

"Tons."

The doctor stuffed Foster's pockets with little brown bottles of pills, told him if everything went well he could bring her back in six weeks to have the cast removed. They gave him a quick explanation about changing her dressing, told him how many pills to give her and when, handed her over, and rushed off to their life of constant crisis.

Foster just stood there for a minute, looking at her semiconscious and now cleaner and moderately more attractive face, holding her up, trying to decide what to do next. Put her back where he found her? Unthinkable. Deliver her to her family? He realized that even though she'd been a fixture around the villa, he knew nothing about her. Had no idea where she lived, if she even had a family. She'd been just another "girlfriend." Now she was all his.

There's not much difference between helping people and adopting them. Once you pull some unfortunate lost soul out of the gutter, give him a meal, patch him up, he's yours. What else do you do with him? Give somebody a hand, you own them. At that point, Foster owned Thi Lanh. Now what?

Ironman had long since disappeared into the bars a few

blocks away, so Foster had to get her back into the Jeep by himself. A wheelchair would have helped, but the place was teeming with people and all the equipment seemed to be taken. So he wandered the halls till he found a laundry basket, folded her gently into it and wheeled her out the door. The villa needed a good laundry basket.

Another arm would have helped, too, on the drive back, because his left hand was frantically engaged clutching the wheel, dodging the innumerable ciclos, pedicabs, and tiny cars piloted by Vietnamese who had never actually learned to drive in any sort of structured or formal sense. That's why they were doing the traffic safety film. Foster wasn't sure, but he'd heard you didn't need a license in Vietnam; there were no driving schools, no written tests, no taking the sweaty-palmed ride with the state trooper. You could be eleven years old, but if you could acquire a vehicle and reach the pedals with either your hands or your feet, you were the king of the road. Dozens of soldiers and Vietnamese were buying it on the highways, as if there weren't enough people dying already out in the bush.

His right hand did double duty. He was using it to shift, grinding back and forth between gears, lurching through the decomposing streets. Every time he shifted he had to let go of Thi Lanh, but when he did she would simply roll off her seat and onto the road. After she fell out the second time, he tried to be more careful, but he lost her once more before he got the hang of it. He'd get her stabilized in the seat and she'd start listing to starboard, her head lolled aimlessly from side to side, speaking in tongues, and seriously off-balance to her right. Her crutches clattered in the back while Foster's flailing arm and the weight of her cast kept her from going overboard yet again and being lost forever.

Even Jack and Little Shit had the sense to keep their distance as he bundled her out of the Jeep and wrestled her up the stairs. She sweated in his bed all night, head rolling from side to side, mumbling in ancient tribal tongues, drenching the sheets as the antibiotics fought to keep her leg attached. Foster mopped up while Svoboda, once he'd sent his nude models home and found out what was going on, stayed with her, and so did a few of the newbys who didn't know any better. Everybody helped. Foster never expected it.

The Dung family didn't help, and didn't say why. But Former Sergeant First Class Harris had told him months before. They were deeply offended by what had happened to the young women of the country when the Americans moved in. It had taken the society 12 years to get over the French, and they hadn't even completed the process yet when all the American mother's sons showed up, young and healthy, with a serious imbalance in their testosterone and adrenalin levels caused by the conditions in which they found themselves. They wanted and needed plenty of entertainment opportunities, and many young Vietnamese women were quick to learn a key tenet of free enterprise: when demand exists, supply always rises to meet it. Just like any war. Yak Dung (his real family name went back 1500 years, and was of the nobility) was a father. He and Mamasan had a twelve- or fourteen-year-old daughter. The only way she'd have any kind of childhood was if the war was over and the Americans gone. The Dungs didn't much care who won.

It took about five days before Thi Lanh came completely back. Foster went out shooting with his crew almost every day, and had to leave her alone, but they took turns staying up nights, forcing pills down her throat, changing the repulsive bandages through the space in her cast. Slowly, her color returned, and when she talked, she almost made sense.

CHAPTER 19
O'CONNELL IS RESCUED, BUT NOT WELL

Saturday, May 23, 1970

The first thing, the very first thing, they teach you in survival training is never *ever* get captured. If you're captured, you're up the fecal waterway with no means of propulsion. If you're captured, you're probably better off dead, provided you can make it reasonably quick and painless. Anything is better than captured.

Webb learned the lesson again as soon as he joined the Vampires, but the pedagogical methodology was more immediate, and therefore more visceral. Sitting around the hooch at night, listening to Berryman, Harrell and the rest, he realized that the type of survival training he was getting now was a lab, not a lecture, teaching by flesh and blood example, a place where lessons are learned by seeing up close and personal that, as in most wars, the captor looks upon the captive with eyes less than kind. Back at Fort Wolters, if you screwed up, the TAC officer would say, "If this was *Vietnam*, you'd be fucked right now."

Theory had become reality. It *was* Vietnam, and if he wasn't fucked, O'Connell certainly was. He was fighting against (and often for) people whose armies and police summarily executed prisoners at high noon on a main street with cameras rolling, people who absolutely did not share his uniquely American sense of fair play, due process, or habeas corpus. Worse yet, they hated him for his beliefs, and used them against him. He started to understand that the cross-cultural relationships were not all they could be. He was fighting people with peculiar cultural predilections toward things he considered cruel and unusual. After two thousand years of fighting they'd become quite skilled at it. The inflicting of prolonged and excruciating punishment was not only a pastime, but something of a high art. He'd heard how they buried those two guys in the ground up to their necks and left them for the fire ants. As he thought about O'Connell, down behind enemy lines for two weeks, his voice chattered incessantly: You can hold all the conventions in Geneva you want to, Yankee, but out here in the jungle it's just you and me, kid.

Webb had always been a mild sort, not given to wide ranges of emotion. His family came from proper British stock some time back, and the reserved personality, the quiet desperation, had been passed along. So he was shocked at the emotions that kept him staring at the ceiling at night, and not a little puzzled. He was seething, nervous, downright pissed off in the most classic sense. First of all, those National Guard troops had shot a few kids at some university in Ohio, and every other college in the country was just about shut down. People were in the streets. Armed Forces Radio didn't want anyone to know about it, but the jungle telegraph was remarkably effective. Word got around, and it didn't make flying helicopters in combat any easier.

He was even more sincerely pissed by the fact that he couldn't do anything about O'Connell. Hanging there, Hueyed high in the morning along the Cambodian border, he'd stopped caring about how beautiful a day it was or how smooth the air, or how nice his Charlie-Model was humming along, or how they hadn't been shot at all morning, and what a nice surprise it was. He was getting real tired of it all, and he still had seven months to go.

Godwin was flying from the left seat, delighted that Webb had finally let him take over for a change, which gave Webb even more leisure to ignore his surroundings.

But he didn't give up his aircraft just to let Godwin have some fun. He gave it up because he was too furious to fly, and was trying to understand the feeling, the gnashing anger in his gut. It was real, it was writhing, and he just didn't feel like doing the delicate little dance you have to do when you fly and shoot at the same time.

O'Connell, Murphy W., Warrant Officer Two, had been missing ever since that God-cursed mission into Cambodia on May 9. Webb may have been surprised at the way all the new emotions felt, but he was even more astounded at the political sensibilities he was starting to develop. When you're in combat, the actions of your Commander in Chief deserve some attention. Webb's voice continued to chatter at him: Thank you very fucking much, President Nixon; if you'd known they were going to throw Prince Sihanouk out on his ass, none of this would've happened.

("This is nice," he'd said to Godwin the night before in the hooch, "We support Sihanouk because he's democratic, but he lets the NVA use his country as a base. Now there's this Lon Nol guy. When those goddam college kids hear we're raiding Cambodia, they're gonna go even crazier than they already are.")

All Webb knew was that O'Connell could be sitting in a tiger cage somewhere in Cambodia even as he and Godwin, with Baldwin and Iglesias in the back, made their way through the Asian air in their thunderous machine.

More galling still was that Webb knew --*knew* -- that O'Connell was not far away, perhaps just over the border, maybe even right over *there*, couple of klicks or so, a place that Webb could see from his seat in the sky. That's what the intelligence officers had said. He *could* be over there.

Webb wasn't the only one who dozed through intelligence briefings, because they'd all caught the act too many times. The intelligence officers, clean and pressed, stood up there, rhapsodizing with their maps and charts and pointers. They loved those collapsible pointers, the kind like car radio antennas, with little red plastic tips.

"Late at night," O'Connell had whispered to him during one particularly insulting briefing, "in their hooches, these guys have bull sessions about different kinds of pointers, which is better, ash or elm, or maybe oak."

Blithely, they customarily assured the assembled gunny and slick pilots of a nice, quiet routine mission. Too bad when those assurances turned out to be achingly empty, tragically mistaken. They'd stand up there, never hearing the low murmurs of "rat fuck, rat fuck," from the unwilling audience.

He could still hear it in his head, his best friend yelling "Mayday" (from the French m'aidez, meaning "help me" in the imperative mood) as his smoking machine plunged into the deep Cambodian jungle. Probably done in by a 51-cal right along the ground, he was told. O'Connell's co-pilot, a newby named Allis, was found the next day, nailed to a tree about a hundred yards from the crash site. The wreckage was remarkably intact. Allis was not. O'Connell was gone.

Webb's voice told him, *Hey, come on. So what, right? Murphy got shot down. Comes with the job. You been here three months, it happens all the time. Not to you, of course. Not yet. That's why they call those Reaction in Force missions Rat Fucks, because you never, ever know what'll be waiting.* Right. If it's a surprise, it's never a good one, never a birthday party or a new car in the driveway when you wake up Christmas morning, never anything like that. It's always the hot flying metal kind of surprise, the fire, the noise, the dying.

Since O'Connell went missing, the voice had not stopped for a second. Webb didn't even mind that he heard it, it'd been with him so long. Besides, it was usually right, which scared him more than his hearing it in the first place. It whispered sick little suggestions. *Hey...ain't it somethin' how just one or two little shots can put this rattling hulk of flying metal on the ground in a heartbeat? Amazing how those 51-cals can open up on you from the treeline when you least expect it.* Sometimes you get hit, the controls get arthritis on you, so you pull this nice little autorotation, a gentle bump to Mother Earth, the slicks come, drop from the sky and take you home. Sometimes the enemy gets to you first. It's only gotta happen once.

Anybody can get shot down, anybody can wind up in one of those cute little VC bamboo efficiencies, the voice went on. *Yup, just enough room for three quarters of an American aviator, no luxuries, no air conditioning, no whirlpool, no weight room, no recreational facilities of any kind, and zero square meals a day.*

You gotta help your friends, he told his voice.

Why?

You just do.

He tried to keep himself from hoping Murphy was dead. Not captured, please. Jesus, that's the last thing I'd want to be, he thought, watching the emerald jungle roll by below him. Dead is better. He knew of pilots that kept Derringers in their flight suits, a couple of tiny .22s to make sure that

death came before dishonor. He couldn't bring himself to get
one. There's always hope, he thought, always. But Murphy
O'Connell would, at that moment, have told him a very
different story. He'd know by now. If he was still alive he'd be
learning things he wished he didn't know.

There was a possibility – actually a hint of a rumor of a
possibility -- that Montagnard or Hmong scouts had sighted
him in Cambodia, being moved from village to village at night,
not far away. If he was alive, and if it was O'Connell at all,
the scouts said he was right around the block.

But Cambodia, as Webb continually had to remind himself,
was off limits today. Last month, it was very much part of the
war, but the college kids went as crazy as Webb had
predicted, crazier, even, and today was different. If things
were happening in Cambodia, and they were, nobody was
talking about it.

If rumors were bubbling about O'Connell, there was even
more buzz about what the VC were up to. They had tunnels
running from the heart of that mountain near Tay Ninh
straight toward the Cambodian border. The Cambodians
were being gracious hosts, especially since Prince Sihanouk
got deposed. There was so much going on over the border,
right over *there*, that it made Webb's heart hurt. His mind
wouldn't let him feel for everybody who was suffering in the
war; he knew that there were hundreds of POWs somewhere
and they escaped so seldom it wasn't worth hoping for. But
O'Connell was his friend, somebody he'd done push-ups with
on that broiling Texas tarmac. You have to help your friends
when they're in trouble. It was something Webb believed from
childhood, ever since what happened to Douglas when he was
six.

The belief narrowed his prodding pain, focused it down
from everyone who was being damaged in the war to a single
individual, which makes it more real, and more meaningful.
The process had been continuing since he'd learned what
Vietnam was all about. First Gibson and Monroe the very day
he'd arrived, then Jacoby, then all those others. Had it really
been only three months? Then there was O'Connell, Murphy
W., probably sitting in his little bamboo room, just across the
border, spending his days, if indeed he was still alive, saying
goodbye to himself.

"I'll take it," Webb said to Godwin, who glanced over at him.

"Aww, and I was having such a good time."

"The fun is just beginning. We're going for a little ride. Doctor!" Webb screamed to his wingman on the radio, the other half of his fire team, hanging up to his right in the bright morning air. "Doctor Watson! Will you accompany me northwestward?"

"With pleasure, sir," Watson shot back. All the Vampires called him Doctor, and never stopped telling him how elementary everything was. They all tried to talk to him like Sherlock Holmes, but of all the Vampires, Webb was marginally the most literate, and was best at it. His mother was a high school art teacher, and had always poured literature and painting on him. When he was about fourteen, his mother took him to the Art Institute in Chicago and showed him the glistening gardens and ponds and bridges of Monet. He gazed at them for long moments, becoming so transfixed that his mother bought him a print in the museum store and hung it in his room. Hanging there in the early Asian day, looking down on the sparkle of sun on water, he remembered that painting, how it shimmered as if by its own light, the little green bridge, plants floating on the water, far away. Far away.

"However," Watson continued, "if I'm not mistaken, that direction would take us into Number Ten Country."

"Naah," Webb's voice crackled in the radio. "All them goddam little rivers and streams down there dry up and change shape every day. These maps suck. I'm absolutely certain we're nowhere near Cambodia."

Godwin, catching the drift of the conversation at once, started wrestling with an area map the size of a bedsheet. A huge green piece of paper, much too big to be any use in a Huey cockpit, marked off in little squares of 1,000 meters, very small scale, very fine detail, tiny type, showing every wart and dimple of the terrain below. Worthless.

Watson wasn't stupid. If Webb wanted to take a look over the border, he was going to, and he was the fire team leader.

"You're the ranking guy in the sky," said Watson. "Orders is orders."

On any other day, Godwin would have made a few humble

suggestions to Webb as to how it might not be in their best personal interests to fly into Cambodia. But after the briefing, after finding out that O'Connell could still be alive, thinking he was perhaps even within a few kilometers of them, they'd stayed up half the night talking about him with that peculiar mixture of bravado and silliness that you get sometimes in a war, far from home, at 12 beer o'clock.

"Jesus, that poor bastard," said one.

"Nice if we could get him out," said the second.

"Must be the shits, sitting in that tiger cage all day," said yet a third.

"You don't know if they're gonna blow you away, or do the bag job on you...."

"Let's not talk about the bag job," said the Doctor. A classmate of his from Fort Wolters had died like that, in the hands of the enemy, a burlap bag over his head, soaking wet, allowing him to drown tied to a chair, on dry land, in the privacy of a VC hooch.

They all wanted to do something about O'Connell, but Webb pushed it more than the others.

"I mean," said Berryman, "I know he's your friend and I understand all that. But why are you so jacked up about all this?" Webb wouldn't tell him.

"I know that stream," said Webb, pointing down to the right. Buzzing in the air, the two gunships swung slightly to the north. At a place where the little river narrowed and curved was the border with Cambodia, exactly due west of Tay Ninh, about 18 klicks.

Webb pretended not to see it. As they passed the point, he expected Watson's "Ahem" in his headset, but didn't get it.

"Let's take it down," he said, and the two choppers settled smoothly toward the waving green treetops below. Slowly, about 50 knots, they skimmed gently through the morning air.

"Vampire Three-Four, report your position." The section leader, in the operations shack, was getting nervous about the prolonged silence.

Webb looked over at Godwin in the left seat. "Tell him. But take off a few klicks."

"Vampire Three-Four," stammered Godwin, "We're due west of the base, about fifteen klicks, um, eastbound."

"Good boy," said Webb.

"Return to base. We have a briefing on tomorrow's mission and you guys need to be there."

"Ahhhh, roger that," said Godwin, looking at Webb through his visor, eyes wide. Webb took matters into his own hands.

"This is the AC," he said, keying his mike. "We spotted something out here, want to get a better look. Be back soon."

"What is it? Do you want to scramble the blues?" The section leader's voice went up a notch. He lived for the action.

"Negative, negative on that," said Webb. "It's probably nothing. Just a...."

The sentence never got finished. It hung there, a semi-stream of electromagnetic vibration between his Huey and the base, ominously incomplete.

"Say again, Vampire Three-Four."

Godwin took over. He'd seen what made Webb's voice abandon him, but he could still talk. Ahead of them, on the bank of the river, were four small men in khaki shorts and pith helmets. They were splashing themselves with water. Occasionally they threw a bucketful at the huddled form inside the bamboo cage on the riverbank.

"Jesus Christ, Son of God and Savior," muttered Watson, from above and behind. "Right out in the open."

"They knew we'd never come over here," said Webb. "They think they're safe. Watson, pull up and around to the right. I gotta wax those fuckers before they have a chance to wax O'Connell."

Watson knew exactly what to do. He soared aloft and disappeared, circling around to the other side of the river. The wind was blowing toward the choppers, so the men in the river didn't hear the sound of the rotors.

"Tighten up on those nuts, Godwin," muttered Webb. "It's showtime."

Webb's hand pushed forward on the cyclic, the chopper's nose went down, building airspeed, heading straight for the soldiers on the bank, toward O'Connell, a tiny black form, curled up in his cage.

"We gotta lay down fire between the NVA and the cage," said Webb. "If we don't take those assholes out, they'll shoot O'Connell."

"How do you know?" asked Godwin.

"Wouldn't you?"

The ship rushed over the riverbank, fifty feet in the air, spitting minigun fire, Godwin trying desperately to place it right between the cage and the soldiers around it.

The NVA didn't hear them till the last minute. Suddenly, they looked up at the percussive noise in the air and dashed away from the little splats in the mud around the cage, toward the trees for their weapons, leaving the small cruel cage by itself on the riverbank, alone and exposed.

In hiding under the trees, the NVA soldiers suddenly realized that if they'd stayed right next to the cage the gunships would never have shot at them. All four of them made a maniacal dash from the treeline across the broad flat exposed riverbank toward O'Connell's cage.

Webb rolled in, pointing Godwin toward the area between the cage and the treeline. The co-pilot seized the reticle with both hands, put the little red ring on the tiny brown figures, and squeezed. The miniguns sang their little buzzing song, red fingers of tracers tickling the mud.

Webb was too busy to look at the cage on the first pass, because he knew Watson would be coming in from the other side to make the snatch. But if he had looked down he would have seen O'Connell, a tiny bearded figure in black pajamas huddled in the corner with his hands over his head, as if he could shield himself from the enormity of the explosions that issued from the sky. They were being as careful as they could, but shooting at moving targets from a moving helicopter is not an exact science, and their rounds puffed into the mud around O'Connell, one of them an inch from his ass, another not much farther away from his left hand, which clung to one of the cage's bamboo rods, till a stray round demolished it, leaving his arm singing with pain.

One small figure, a black spot against the light brown mud of the riverbank, scuttled faster than the rest. He gained the treeline, grabbed his rifle with two skinny arms, sat down and started squeezing off rounds toward the tiger cage as fast as his finger would wiggle.

Then the action kicked up a level. From the village no more than a hundred meters away came the telltale twinkling flashes of small weapons fire, followed by the chatter of something very like an M-60, and then, the unmistakable impact of a 51-cal. Webb's abused Huey jolted from the strain, vibrated from the big heavy slugs that popped through the thin metal skin.

The gunship spun around in the other direction, suddenly pointed back toward the one remaining NVA, who, given enough time, would eventually improve his panicked aim and kill O'Connell.

On impulse, Webb let go with a salvo of rockets. He didn't know what else to do. In an instant, the tree disappeared, the NVA disappeared, and three feet of earth became dust, all in a sudden spurt of orange fire.

"Nice shooting," said Godwin.

"Praise the Lard," said Webb.

"Vampire Three Four, report your position," said the radio. Like an emphatic period at the end of the demand, a fat 51-cal slug ripped through the plexi right in front of Godwin, pelting his visor with bright glistening shards.

"Well, shit," said Webb, just as he heard exactly the same phrase in his headset from Baldwin in the back.

"Doctor, we gotta take out whatever that is. I'll go high. You get the cage."

"Roger that," said Watson, already on his way from the far side of the stream.

"Vampire Three Four, I say again, report your position." We don't have time for this shit, Webb thought. We really don't.

"You're breaking up, Vampire Five. We do not read."

Webb could see the section leader sitting there in the ops shack, choking the microphone, looking at the radio speakers as if he expected to see pictures moving inside them, stuttering.

A push forward on the cyclic, a vicious twist of the throttle, the machine rattled and shook, pouring heat into the sky, climbing right into the middle of the kill zone, directly in range of the small arms fire from the ground.

Below, they saw nothing but a small gathering of hooches huddled in some brown mud, a few dozen yards up from the river. Thatch roofs, little holes in the middle to let the smoke out, vivid green all around. Then, miraculously, from the far side of the treeline, like a Satanic apparition, a slim, snaky Cobra floated into sight.

"What the fuck?" muttered Webb. He'd found himself doing a lot of muttering lately. "Who the hell is that?"

The Cobra was painted flat black, not a mark or number or insignia on it. Webb and the rest of them knew instantly that it was friendly, because the enemy didn't have helicopters, but they'd never seen an unmarked gunship before, and certainly not out here on the bad side of the border. Webb pulled back on the cyclic, stopping his ship right in the middle of the air, as the Cobra wasted no time throwing a whole fistful of rockets at the village. Explosions occurred, and the sorry clutch of huts began to disappear. Orange and red, yellow flames, against the green of the trees, rapidly turning brown and crumbling. Bursting fire lurched into the air, greasy black smoke. The Cobra wheeled around and disappeared as quickly as it had come, dropping low again, down behind the trees.

"Well, fuck me with a meathook," said Baldwin from the back. "What was *that* all about?"

Webb didn't have time to wonder, and didn't have time to explain to the guys in the back what a *deus ex machina* was. The shooting from the ground had started up again, with renewed zest, and O'Connell still needed rescuing.

Webb wrenched the Huey into a steep turn to the right, hoping the boys in back were holding on, circled, came in low and fast. He spat the rockets, Godwin twisted out the hot rounds from the miniguns.

Around again, one more pass. Fewer twinkles from the ground this time, but they were still down there, right at the edge of the village clearing.

"Vampire Three Four, are you engaging in activity against the enemy? Report your position."

"Negative," said Webb. Ain't no enemy in friendly Cambodia, and besides, could you maybe call back later?

More rockets, dancing like marionettes on their strings of gray smoke, racing downward. More fire, more bursts, more shattering.

"Just some target practice for the boys, out here in the free fire zone," he said, wrestling with the machine. "We're just fine."

"We're hit! Vampire Three Five, we're hit."

Watson's voice, sounding very elementary indeed, a simple tone, sharp and piercing. Fear.

"Can you keep it in the air?" *Fuck*, said his voice. *It wasn't supposed to turn out like this.*

"Negative. No control. I gotta put it down on the riverbank."

Webb could see him, just settling in behind the trees. But where had the shots come from?

One more pass over the village. Nothing down there. What had been green was brown. What had been dry was burning. What had been houses were holes. What had been people were...not any more.

Webb put the nose down to gain speed and raced back to the river, just in time to see Watson's chopper plop into the mud as though it had been dropped from a hundred feet.

"Guy's already made two emergency landings," said Webb to nobody in particular, "and he screws them up every time."

Webb settled in next to them, keeping the Huey slightly in the air, dangling, the skids just above the mud. Furious wind swirled around him. Iglesias and Baldwin jumped out of the back, ran, hunched over, to the tiger cage to help Watson's crew pull O'Connell out. Webb's reason began to desert him. He could feel it ebbing away.

"Take it," he yelled to Godwin, and immediately released the controls. The chopper lurched in the air. Webb threw open his door, jumped to the ground and squished into the mud up to his ankles. He pulled himself loose with an obscene sucking sound and slogged over to the cage. The sight of O'Connell put a lancing, stabbing pain into his heart.

"Jesus, look at him," Iglesias said, wiping his nose. Iglesias was always wiping his nose.

O'Connell was lying in a heap on the bottom of the cage, bright red seeping through the black of his filthy wet pajamas. Webb put his hand through the bars and felt his neck.

"At least he's alive. Let's get him out of there."

"No time," said Watson's gunner. "How about we pick up the whole thing?"

They heaved the tiger cage up out of the mud and slid it, dragged it, hauled it, across the slimy surface, then stopped.

"This'll never work," panted Webb, just before the machine guns opened up from across the river.

"Stuck," groaned Baldwin, pushing up on a corner with his shoulder. The bullets kept coming. Godwin swung the chopper around, pointed the nose across the river and let the miniguns speak for themselves. The bullets kept singing.

"Bust it open! Get him out!"

"It'll take a machete," said Watson. "It's in the chopper." They all looked at each other. Getting the machete meant that one of them would have to run directly into the line of fire, pitifully shielded by the downed Huey. Nobody's hand shot up.

"Hey! We're under some fuckin' fire here," said Watson's gunner. "No time. We gotta leave him. Let's go!" Webb looked at the man with eyes that nailed him to the spot, eyes that scared him more than the enemy fire from across the river, more, perhaps, than he'd ever been scared.

"Roll it!" yelled Iglesias, and everybody stopped, in spite of the rattling noise of the chopper, the buzz of the miniguns and the whipping sound of the machine gun bullets pouring in from across the river, the little soft pops in the mud all around their feet. They looked at him like he'd just turned purple and grown another head.

"We'll kill him if we do that, you asshole," screamed Baldwin.

"Kill us if we don't, you <u>bugarón</u>," yelled Iglesias, grabbing his corner and pulling up.

Dire extremity is the mother of quick decision. They all grabbed a side of the cage.

Thunk! The cage rolled one-quarter turn, and Murphy rolled with it, *flup flup*, thudding to the bottom and screaming. Godwin brought the Huey in as close as he dared, putting the machine between the struggling men and the river, taking hits, taking hits. Baldwin looked at the situation one time and decided he could do more good on the 60mm that hung on bungee cords from the cargo bay door than he could pulling on Murphy's cage, so he made a run for the chopper.

Thunk! The cage clumped onto its other side, rolled again, and again, Watson and the rest gritted their teeth and shut their eyes every time the wounded Murphy flopped to the bottom and hollered. He tried holding on to the bars but he was just too weak.

"We're gonna kill him like this," yelled Webb, tears in his eyes from watching the helpless O'Connell roll around inside his little prison. "We gotta get him out."

Webb started to tear at the chain and lock with his bare hands, slipping in the mud, sitting down heavily. The rest of the men, Watson and his co-pilot, Iglesias, Watson's gunner and crew chief, just stared at him, their heads hunched into their shoulders. Then they joined in.

All this took mere seconds, because Godwin was still rocking his chopper next to them, just above the ground, firing madly into the treeline across the river. He would have sent some rockets across, but he had only two left and besides, the enemy was too close. The rockets wouldn't arm until they reached a certain speed, and that required more distance than he had. He couldn't use the grenade launcher on the chin bubble, either, because he needed more altitude.

Baldwin had the M-60 off the bungee cord and was leaning out the huge cargo bay door, firing with one hand and feeding the linked rounds with the other.

It was one of those times when human desire overcomes human limitation, when the mind wants something so badly that the body just does it, whether the physical resources are there or not. Webb was crazed, frenzied, he gave the phrase "out of his mind" a whole new meaning because, in truth, rational process had deserted him completely. There was only the reality of his friend, probably dying in that cage, which he simply could not permit, the reality of all that inimical ammunition buzzing around him, the reality of long bamboo rods lashed together at the corners, the door of the cage held shut by a small but adequate rusty chain, and a brand new, gleaming improbably American Master padlock.

Somehow, the cage came open. Hands reached in and dragged the insensible O'Connell out onto the riverbank. They picked him up, started to run, dropped him with a sick sploosh into the mud, picked him up again, and staggered to the dangling chopper. With one last desperate heave, the men in the mud threw the limp form into the cargo bay, sucked their boots out of the riverbed and clambered into the rocking Huey.

"Everybody aboard?" Webb yelled.

"Just get us the fuck out of here. Sir." said Baldwin, putting a few extra bursts into the jungle across the river.

Watson and his crew huddled in the back, Iglesias and

Baldwin clung to O'Connell so he wouldn't roll out the cargo bay door, possibly bleeding to death.

Webb half staggered, half crawled into the cockpit.

"Up! Up! Let's go, Goddammit!" He pounded on Godwin's helmet. The copilot wrenched the cyclic to the left, pulled up on the collective, twisted the throttle handle, desperately trying to gain altitude.

Then Webb found out how Watson got shot down.

Another 51-cal, somewhere out there in the jungle, not far from the village, started spitting its fat slugs into the clearing all around them. Webb took over, willed the machine into the air, putting the nose down and skimming along the mud to pick up airspeed. The thing was heavy, heavy, with seven men in the back, two in the front, and still about half a load of grenades, rockets and assorted weaponry.

SNICK! The windshield directly in front of Webb's face disappeared in a breathtaking shower of glittering sharp-edged plexi.

"Why the fuck does it always do that?" Webb asked, but nobody heard him because he hadn't had time to put his helmet back on. He could feel the *whup* sounds of the slugs pounding into the fuselage.

"Takin' hits back here, sir," Iglesias' voice quivered in Godwin's headphones.

As Webb wrestled to keep the machine in the air, the black Cobra appeared again from the other side of the village, higher this time.

"Look! He's back," someone said on the radio. Webb couldn't see what was going on, but the Cobra wheeled quickly away from the village, banked impossibly to the right and roared back in toward them in a classic gun run configuration.

"Hallelujah," said a voice in his headphones.

In order to fire, the Cobra gunship had to drop its nose and make the gun run in a tilted forward attitude, which is exactly what it did. Some of the men in the back of Webb's Huey could see the Cobra suddenly spit up every grenade, rocket and round of minigun ammunition it had left on board, burst on target, dead on top of whoever had been shooting at them. Once again, what was left of the jungle launched itself skyward in spasms of flame and smoke. And once again, the Cobra disappeared as quickly as it had come.

"Who *was* that masked man?" mumbled Webb, holding the nose down, picking up speed. "I didn't even have a chance to thank him." He pulled the chopper to the left across the river, out over the open water.

"Come on, you bastard," grunted Godwin, as though leaning forward in his seat could make the laboring machine go faster.

Webb kept it on the deck to gain whatever airspeed he could, right along the water, rotors lifting up fantastic spray, then he pulled up, a wicked cyclic climb between the trees, taking the occasional jolt as his rotor blades brushed the surrounding foliage. He roared through the jungle, as low as he dared, lower than most of them would dare.

Gripping the cyclic and collective, his feet dancing on the pedals, Webb whizzed through the world in a whole new way. In a shuddering revelation, he understood temporary insanity, because he was certifiable by any standard he could think of. He knew he was in for a court-martial, if they didn't just summarily execute him and get it over with.

In back, Watson and his gunner did what they could for O'Connell. "How is he?" Webb asked, his helmet finally in place, his headset plugged in.

"Not too good, sir," said Iglesias. O'Connell was gray and unconscious, coated with mocha mud the way they put chocolate frosting on a birthday cake, ominous red streams trickling down his face because of the rolling around, and bleeding from a few other places that nobody was sure of. He smelled like he was already dead.

But Webb got them home, calling in from a few klicks west, ignoring the section leader's frantic questions on the radio, dripping hydraulic fluid from most of the linkages, controls stiffening up, nose down, wind blasting into the cockpit, bringing it in as close to the base hospital as he could, almost into the laps of the waiting medics.

Dozens of hands reached into the cargo bay, eased O'Connell out into the air, somehow got him on a stretcher. They were gone in an instant.

Watson and his crew tumbled out the back, shaken, blood pressure peaking, driving the adrenaline through their systems like a hammer, but they were otherwise unharmed.

"Hell of a ride this boy gave us," said Watson to Heller, the rotund section leader who'd appeared alongside of them, puffing from the run.

"Mr. Webb," said Heller between puffs. "I've been (puff) ordered to (gasp) inform you that (choke) the troop commander will see you (gurgle, snort) tomorrow at oh-eight-hundred hours (puff) regarding your highly probable court martial."

CHAPTER 20
THE MAYOR OF AP DO

Monday, May 25, 1970

"Fuck this shit," muttered D'Amato. In spite of the noise of the Huey's rotor blades, Foster knew what he said because of the way his lips moved, and because he'd heard the phrase countless times, starting that very first day during the mortar attack at Tan Son Nhut.

Of everyone in the outfit, Foster liked D'Amato best, and he couldn't exactly figure out why. He liked all of them, actually, except Huggins, who he thought was an insect, but the feisty Italian kid from the Bronx went about his work with a strange kind of subversive glee. Foster, looking at everyone and everything around him as possible fodder for the award-winning feature film that he was destined to direct as soon as he got out of the Army, stored D'Amato affectionately in his dramatic memory. The kid's character would find his way into a Foster screenplay, someday.

What Foster didn't like about D'Amato but accepted in spite of himself was that D'Amato absolutely hated to get up in the morning. Foster knew plenty of people like that, but D'Amato had elevated not getting up into an art, or at least an avocation.

When the DASPO version of reveille sounded, D'Amato would first complain that he'd spent the night fending off the pernicious side effects of the orange malaria pills. Of course, he had also stayed out in the bars until the last second of the last minute of curfew, flirting with the tea girls, teaching them every obscene Italian phrase he knew, so morning was a heartless time of day for him. That particular morning, Former Sergeant First Class Harris, who apparently never slept, had hauled D'Amato bodily out of bed, propped him upright, and frog marched him to the shower. Unfortunately, the DASPO shooting schedule forced them all out of their cots at vile hours. The little projects Berner hatched for them were the most vile of all.

The colonel's newest and so far most pathetic attempt at self-promotion called for Foster, D'Amato, Ironman, and Svoboda to hunker down in the back of an Outlaws Huey at a time of day the chopper pilots called zero dark thirty, and, escorted by a fireteam of two Cobra gunships, fly out to film a village with the unlikely name of Dam Long about 30 clicks west of the city.

Much to Foster's annoyance, Berner wanted them to shoot live sound, so he'd been forced to include Huggins, the new soundman. Gangly and gap-toothed, Spec-5 James Lee ("call me Jimmie") Huggins had made Foster realize that there are people in this world who emanate such intense waves of insane energy, who broadcast such fuzzy currents of craziness, that you can feel their presence even if you can't see them, for he was surely one of those. Several times in the past week, Foster had felt the skin on his neck start to move by itself, and turned around to find Huggins, standing much too close, staring at him. He'd been in country less than two weeks, and was already giving everybody a bad case of horripilation. Worst of all, he chewed tobacco, and was never without a plug of Bull o' the Woods or Apple in his cheek. His teeth were stained brown, and sometimes a hideous fluid of obscene color seeped from the corners of his mouth. When Huggins was around, Foster would catch himself holding his breath without knowing it. He always knew when the PX ran out of chaw, because Huggins would dip into Mamasan's stash of betel nut. Huggins' teeth would turn from a grungy brown to putrid red. A dead giveaway.

It was bad enough that Huggins had made clear his loathing for Svoboda the minute he'd walked into the villa, and even worse that Foster had to bring him along on the shoot.

Huggins was sent over to replace Davidson, who Foster had ordered back to Hawaii because he'd single-handedly started a riot in the Cho Lan market place. Foster's dim, struggling hope that Huggins would be an improvement had already been destroyed by the events of the last ten days.

Foster was constantly amazed at how much some of his

countrymen hated the Vietnamese, how these solid American soldiers dripped with bigotry and prejudice. The departed Davidson was one of them, and the stunt he pulled in the marketplace could have lost the war for the Americans all by itself. He'd been in Saigon less than six weeks, and every other word out of his mouth was gook, or slope, or dink or dwarf. Foster didn't understand it, and certainly couldn't allow it, but all the lectures and explanations and discourses he'd given Davidson about hearts and minds and the brotherhood of man and how it's a small world after all ultimately did nothing to quell the bigotry burning in the man's gut.

In the Cho Lan marketplace, packed with busy Vietnamese, and certainly some Viet Cong who had put the war aside for a few hours to do some shopping, he'd started mouthing off to one of the street vendors who he was convinced had cheated him. The poor woman made herself even smaller than she was as she bore the brunt of his hateful tirade, not understanding a word as Davidson told her exactly which unspeakable sex acts Vietnamese women were good for, one of which had so mortally offended Thi Lanh at the Magic Fingers. But he had no idea of the surprising number of Vietnamese who spoke English, at least enough to understand the humiliation he was throwing at her, and even if they didn't get the words, his tone came through loud and clear. A crowd started to build around him, gradually transforming itself into a mob, people pressing in from all directions, yelling back at him, pushing, waving fists. He was too stupid to be scared. After all, he was bigger than they were, and even though there was one of him and several hundred of them, he considered himself evenly matched. After all, they were only gooks, and he was an American, by God.

Things got ugly very fast, and one of the other troops pushed his way through the crowd to go find some MPs. Hands clutched at Davidson, and he was dangerously close to pulling out his .45, which would have been the ultimate idiocy, when a mortar rocket dropped into a warehouse not fifty yards away. Pieces of splintered wood and jagged metal sliced through the air, cutting down the people on the fringes of the mob, and giving the rest of them more important things to think about.

Foster took a deep breath, a nervous habit he'd acquired since he arrived. If not for the mortar round, he would have been writing to Davidson's parents, telling them softly how their son had made the ultimate sacrifice in defense of his country and its support of democracy in Southeast Asia, and how proud he was of him.

In the early light, the brute machine beat the air northward, and Foster marveled once again at the beauty of the land below. If you didn't know there was a war going on, he thought, you wouldn't know there was a war going on.

Abruptly, the sound of the engine changed and the trees started getting bigger as the chopper dropped toward a clearing next to a group of huts in the distance. They all gave each other a grim secret look, all except Huggins who didn't know any better, because of the first thing they learned when they started traveling regularly in helicopters. They were passing through the kill zone, coming into range of possible small arms fire from the ground. As long as they were high, they were relatively safe, except for something bizarre happening to the machine itself, which wasn't unheard of, but once they got this close to the ground, a couple of rounds from an AK-47 or captured M-16 could easily bring a nasty surprise up through the floor. It wouldn't be the first time.

But not, thank God, today. The Huey landed in a swirl of dust next to Berner's chopper, which had beat them there by a few minutes. The Cobras stayed overhead, pilots straining their eyes into the jungle, looking for tiny twinkling muzzle flashes, or the puffs of smoke that signaled a mortar attack. Ambushes were everywhere.

What were they doing there? Berner's stock answer: they didn't need to know. The camera cases, reflectors and boxes full of 16mm film were secured to the walls of the cargo bay with the omnipresent bungee cords, D'Amato and Svoboda crouching among them, hanging on. Foster watched Huggins staring at Svoboda, wishing desperately he could have left one of them back in Saigon. Huggins was a hater, too, but he was too busy hating Svoboda to hate the Vietnamese. In fact, Huggins hated foreigners in general, and Svoboda in particular, because of his accent, and the fact that he was in the Army of the United States of America. Like Berner, Huggins was convinced that Svoboda was a communist.

Foster was a patient explainer, but it didn't help. They were short of personnel -- again -- and the rest of the troop was shooting background footage of wrecked vehicles for the traffic safety film.

What, thought Foster, one more time, are we doing here? He was sure that Cecil B. DeMille hadn't started out this way. They'd landed on the outskirts of a typical village, smaller than most, hooches grouped around a small central area in no particular order, a pen for pigs and a disappointed-looking water buffalo on the other side of a peculiar twisted tree. Some more hooches a few hundred yards off, just before the tree line. Three low hills beyond that. Even at the early hour, the place was alive. Children played in the dirt. Women tended the animals, men moved in and out of the hooches.

"Is too much guys," Svoboda muttered.

"What do you mean?" Foster asked.

"All the time we go to villages, we see boys, we see old men. Guys are gone. Fighting for ARVNs. Or VC. Here are all young. And look, you see those women in the field with the water buffalo? You know why do they walk behind the animal?"

"Uh, no."

"They do not. Women walk in front always, because of land mines. If they step on a mine, at least papasan still has his water buffalo."

Colonel Berner cut into the discourse on the relative value of women and water buffaloes when he waddled up to greet them, causing Svoboda to ease back toward the Huey, and Foster to brace for the attack. Berner was as round and moist as ever, perhaps a bit more of each, one of those people who don't take the heat well, giving off an aura of clammy dampness and...something else. Foster's nose twitched, but he couldn't place the peculiar odor. Through every one of Berner's pores oozed the almost visible smell of the garlic and cayenne pepper capsules he made himself swallow every morning because he thought they purified his blood. His high forehead glistened in the morning light, and his pale blue eyes bobbed and floated in their sockets.

"At ease," he said, though nobody had made even the smallest twitch toward attention. "This is Sam Thuoc, the mayor of the village. And his sons." Trailing Berner, swimming in his own effluvium of eager anticipation, was a short, toothy Vietnamese man about forty, round as Berner was, accompanied by two taller men in their twenties, all smiling, genial and friendly. The mayor had a full head of slicked-back gray hair and gave the impression that he was really glad to see everybody, but *really glad*, like he'd been starving for months and they'd just knocked on his door holding a huge pizza with everything on it. His white teeth dazzled at them as he seized each of their hands, pumping gratefully, his words of welcome streaming enthusiastically from his lips, head bobbing and bouncing.

This elaborate effusion of welcome was interrupted by a sudden sound from the sky. They all looked up at once as a dead-black Huey came roaring in over the tree line, not more than 25 feet off the ground. It had come from the downwind side of the village, so nobody heard it till it was right on top of them, screaming above their heads, burying them in swirling red dust. A steep turn out past the village put the Huey over onto its side, but it straightened out and stomped itself perhaps a bit too decisively onto the ground next to the other choppers. Colonel Xoan bounded out of the right seat, white scarf trailing behind, grinning like a kid who'd just jerked off for the first time. His customary lieutenants allowed themselves to be swept along behind him, waddling in his wake.

"I love that," he said to nobody in particular. "Where else can you have so much fun? Are we ready to shoot?"

Svoboda and D'Amato unloaded the rest of the gear, D'Amato moving twice as fast as anyone else, and Huggins toyed with his Nagra tape recorder. Xoan and the mayor, brotherly love filling the air between them, shook hands and bowed and hugged and kissed and chattered. Berner looked on, smiling uncomfortably, like a woman at her husband's high school reunion, presenting a pleasant face, but not understanding a thing. He wandered over to Foster.

"Sir," said Foster. "Can you tell me our assignment?"

"See that man, soldier?" Berner said, directing Foster's gaze toward Sam Thuoc. "Very important guy. Xoan tells me he's a front line defender in our effort to wipe out the epidemic of drugs that's ravaging our brave young soldiers."

"So you've been working with him?"

"Never saw him before. But Colonel Xoan loves his ass. The Colonel says they grew up in the same village. Been talking about him for months. A hundred per cent behind us, dedicated, yes, sir."

"And why are we here? Sir."

"Xoan says the mayor's going to let us use this village as a base for our efforts in the countryside. Apparently, this place is some kind of crossroads. Drug caravans come through here all the time, so he's putting the whole place at our disposal. See those burlap covered cases? Heroin. Sam Thouc and his men captured 'em on an ambush a few days ago. That's what this story's about, and when we're done, we're flying the whole stash back home so Colonel Xoan can dispose of it. I'm gonna have you shoot that, too."

Berner dragged Foster along behind him as they walked around the cloth-covered bales squatting on the ground. "This is gonna make a sensational press briefing, so I want some great film of me -- us -- shmoozing this guy out here, showing off all the dope we captured. And stills. Tons of black and whites. Make 'em good, because I'm sending this to every newspaper and wire service in the States. Sound is critical," he said, turning to Huggins. "I want to hear every breath. Got me?"

Ironman used one of the larger camera cases to bulldoze his way through a gaggle of kids, popped it open and pulled out the black, bulky Arriflex film camera. D'Amato snapped on a magazine of film as Huggins hooked up the long pointed Sennheiser microphone to his Nagra. He never took his eyes off Svoboda who was loading up the Hasselblad for the still shots. In moments, with practiced skill, they were in business, ready to make a film that would later prove to have not even the dimmest relationship to anything Berner mentioned.

D'Amato, Huggins and Svoboda followed the three men everywhere, Ironman hauling the gear along behind, sweating in the intolerable heat, while Foster grabbed and carried what he could, because everybody always helped. He didn't have much directing to do, because they were shooting documentary style, just grabbing footage of whatever was going on. His job would start when they put the whole mess on the editing table and tried to make some sense of it.

Sam Thuoc herded them through the tiny village, introducing every single one of the sixty-three children, women, and young men who he said were courageously standing guard, defending their homes against the vicious depredations of the Viet Cong, North Vietnamese Army, and other villains to be named later. Xoan, Berner and Thuoc posed for pictures with every last one of them, hugging babies, shaking hands. Svoboda took dozens of grip and grin shots with their arms around each other, best buddies, off to fight the drug wars. They posed in front of the bales, recording a self-congratulatory conversation between Xoan and Berner as Sam Thuoc smiled benignly from the sidelines. The DASPO troops dogged their heels, burning up thousands of feet of Eastman Kodak's finest 16mm color reversal film. Berner appointed himself director for the day, and if he didn't like a take, he had Foster shoot it five or six more times. It was rumored among military photographers that General MacArthur did the same thing upon his triumphant return to the Philippines. He made his entrance six times in the same day. Once because he promised he would, and five more times because he wanted the shot to be perfect.

Berner bustled around in front of one of the hooches, fantasizing that he was Howard Hawks or Alfred Hitchcock, setting up a shot, making a frame out of his fingers just like real directors do, while Foster watched in amazement through the Arriflex viewfinder. When the hair on the back of his hands started moving by itself, he looked up to see Huggins propelling himself toward the camera, the Nagra tape recorder slung over his shoulder.

Huggins had been acting like a lower life form ever since he arrived in country, making Foster dig deep for some of the leadership lessons he'd slept through during his officer's training at Ft. Gordon, and it was all because of Svoboda. Huggins loathed him with all the passion his shriveled soul could encompass, detested him with a power that absolutely uplifted and nourished him. His upbringing in a small hamlet tucked away in the mountains of some mid-Atlantic state had instilled in him a fear of outsiders, a xenophobia so radiant it could have powered a battleship, or at least a light cruiser. Huggins thought that Canadians were goddam foreigners. Vietnam was the cruelest assignment the Army could have given him.

Svoboda, to his credit, put Huggins in the same class as Colonel Berner and ignored him. When Huggins tried to pull rank, Svoboda automatically told him to fuck off, and the situation would land in Foster's lap. Like now.

Foster looked at Huggins standing in the red swirling dust, thin and angular, ragged scrofulous mustache dripping with beads of dark brown tobacco juice, light blonde hair, and blue eyes that burned with fearsome fire.

"What is it this time?"

"Sir, I ain't workin' with that commie bastard motherfucker no more. He's a foreign person from another country and he don't belong in the Army of the United States of America."

Foster took a long, slow deep breath. Then another. He would try one more time.

"Huggins, he's an American citizen, just like you are, and he took an oath to uphold, protect and defend, just like you did. I'm ordering you to work with him. If you don't you'll be violating a direct order, and the penalties for that offense in wartime are pretty stiff, if you know what I mean."

"But sir, he's trying to poison me."

"*Poison* you?"

"I got proof."

"Uh...Colonel Berner," Foster shouted back toward the group, "we have a small technical problem with the tape recorder. We need about five minutes." Then he turned to Huggins, transfixed in spite of himself by the lunatic electricity coming out of his eyes. "Come on. Let's take a walk."

During their previous discussions on the depressingly same subject, Huggins would tell Foster about his friends at the FBI, who had the real dope on the communist conspiracy to undermine our precious way of life, and then he'd walk off muttering to himself, going upstairs to listen to Porter Wagoner and Dolly Parton records till three in the morning. Foster didn't much want to hear the FBI story, or any other story for that matter, but he had no choice. Huggins was holding up the shoot, Berner was throwing evil glances in their direction, Xoan's troops wanted to start loading the bales into Berner's chopper, and everybody else was standing around waiting. He turned to face Huggins, preparing himself for the worst, and he got it.

"Svoboda is giving me diarrhea," Huggins told him.   This was a new one.

"And how does he do that?"   Foster wanted to add a "pray tell," but resisted the urge.   "You said you could prove it."

"Sir, he's from Europe, and them Europeans got different germs than we do.   It's called...um...intestinal flora.   I looked it up.   Last night at dinner, I thought I saw him take a drink from my glass.   Like a fool, I drank from it after he did, and today I got the shits, er, the runs.   Sir."

"This is Vietnam, Huggins.   Everybody's got the runs.   I've had 'em since I got here."

"Not me.   I never had 'em before, sir.   I know it's because of them foreign germs.   Yesterday I'm fine, then I get infected with some of his bacteria, and today I get the trots.   This morning I almost fell through my asshole.   It all adds up, sir. Don't you see?"

Foster didn't see.

"Remember in 'Doctor Strangelove,' where the Russians tried to take over the US by putting fluoride in the water?"

"That was a movie, Huggins."

"But it's the truth!   The Russians *are* doing it.   And Svoboda is attacking me in my intestines."

"Huggins, the diarrhea is from the malaria pills.   Everybody has it."

"I don't take the pills.   That malaria thing is just like the fluoride in the water.   Communist inspired."   Berner was glaring at them, wondering why they hadn't touched the tape recorder.   Foster tried one more time.

"Look.   Here's what you do.   If you're so sure Svoboda's infected, tonight after dinner, steal his water glass.   See, commie germs are different than ours, and his glass will be crawling with them.   Send it to your friends at the FBI. They've got special machines that can analyze it down to the molecular level.   They'll tell you the truth."

Huggins' face brightened.   "With your permission, sir, I'll do just that."

"Great."   Huggins slung the tape recorder over his shoulder, picked up his microphone and bounded back toward the group.   Foster closed his eyes and took another one of his deep breaths.

The production took over seven hours because Berner

made them shoot everything five or six times, but finally, he pulled himself up to his full five feet six inches, and uttered the phrase directors love to say: "That's a wrap." They never wrapped so fast in their brief military lives. They moved like they were under fire.

"Let me see the film footage as soon as you get it," Berner told them, peering into the cargo bay with his head folded into his shoulders as the blades spun up. "And the black and white stills...eight by ten glossies, maybe 200 of 'em for the press corps and the papers."

The igniters caught, the blades picked up speed, and the chopper started dancing on its skids. Berner had to shout louder.

"And about those black and whites of me with the mayor. Can you make about a dozen wallet size?"

CHAPTER 21
MAJOR SIGAFOOS

Monday, May 25, 1970

The desk in the office of troop commander Major Abraham Sigafoos was only slightly smaller than the great state of Pennsylvania, but a lot flatter. A vast expanse of refulgent mahogany, it wasn't simply a desk, it wasn't simply the Major's desk, it was The Desk, the distilled essence of everything a troop commander's desk should and must be. Major Sigafoos loved his desk, and spent an unsettling amount of time in his office with the door closed, hunched over with the softest cloth he could find, rubbing linseed oil into it the way you'd massage your favorite sex partner when you've got a hotel suite in Bangkok, a magnum of Dom, and a quart of warm baby oil.

As a result, he couldn't put any papers on it, since sooner or later the oil would stain them. He kept all those bothersome documents -- and the Army being what it is, there were thousands of them -- on a specially reinforced table under the far window, in supremely tidy stacks, all the same height, lined up with punishing precision.

In front of that desk, that overwhelming, intimidating desk, stood Warrant Officer Samuel Taylor Webb, properly awed, in the grip of gastrointestinal disaster brought on not by the orange malaria pills, but by naked fear. Actually, "stood" isn't exactly the right word, because he was postured into the stiffest, most rigid brace he'd hit since the TAC officers put him up against the wall in flight school. His abdominal muscles were tight as a hospital bedsheet, his shoulders square to the very millimeter. You could bounce a quarter off his ass. Inside, though, he thrummed with the kind of fear you experience only when faced with a death sentence, or worse, life in Leavenworth. For a government facility in the land of the free and the home of the brave, the place had a very third-world reputation.

Can you feel it? The depth of the shit you're in? That cold sticky dampness right around your hips? You're up to your ass, compadre, and that skinny maniac behind his square mile of mahogany hasn't even started dishing it out yet.

Shut up.

Next to Webb, all stiffed up as well, stood Parker, his platoon commander, breathing noisily in through his pinched nose, and out through his clenched teeth. Webb could see the veins in his neck, moving like little snakes.

When they were shown into the office, the major was standing behind his disproportionate desk, his back to them, looking out the window. Finally he turned around with the precision of a Radio City Rockette. Webb couldn't decide which Sigafoos to look at: the real Major or his twin brother reflected in the desk.

Sigafoos was small and wiry and lean, skinny almost, with a small intense nose and two small intense eyes, very brown, with receding gray hair that rolled back in tight little marcelled waves from his forehead.

Look at that. Even his hair is tight. Shit, you can almost hear him buzz from all the way over here.

Major Sigafoos was 38, but looked well over fifty, probably because he took himself so seriously. He moved with a barely controlled fury that made Webb fear he would spontaneously combust, right there on the carpet.

"Mister Webb." He said it the way you'd say "terminal cancer."

"Proper military conduct forbids officers from insulting, demeaning, or otherwise humiliating the troops under their command." *What the fuck is this*, Webb's voice inquired, without patience.

"The code forbids me, Mr. Webb, to call you an asshole. As a commissioned officer, I am sworn not to tell you what a dick-headed, insubordinate jackass you are.

"Luckily, the military still allows me to take young men who violate regulations, disobey direct orders and commit atrocities during wartime and hang them out to dry."

Webb's voice said, *Excuse me? Did somebody mention war crimes?* Webb started shaking harder, visions of Nuremberg and a cell at Spandau prison dancing in his head like sugar plums. They could give you the one next to Rudolf Hess, said his voice, and you'll come out when you're 104. He almost wished he could hit that brace even harder, so that nobody would see him shake. Did he violate the rules of engagement? Absolutely, and he did so with a totally inappropriate boyish brio, a youthful enthusiasm, a verve that even the most combat-hardened would admire. Disobey a direct order? That, too. Several of them, in fact. His friend was in trouble, he had a chance to save him, and he did it. But *war crimes*? Who put that on the list? Who did he kill that he wasn't supposed to?

"That," continued the Major, running a hand over the top of his desk, leaning over to look at his reflection deep within the surface, "is exactly what I'm going to do to you. Put your ass in a sling and hang you out to dry. If there was a way I could chain you to a rock and let the vultures pick out your liver, I would."

What a great guy, said Webb's voice. Lets his anger get in his way a little, maybe. And you remember when Mom made you read that Goldberg or Goldfinch guy and that myth about Prometheus? Bullfinch, that was it. Nice literary reference on the Major's part.

"Mr. Webb, did you or did you not knowingly fly your gunship across the border into Cambodia yesterday at approximately 1500 hours?"

"Yes, sir, I did." Webb would try to pitch his voice lower for the next answer.

"Did you attack a squad of NVA soldiers?"

"You bet your.... I mean, uh, yes, sir. I did."

"Did you, during this operation, order your wingman also to fire on those troops?"

The affirmative responses just kept on coming. *Why the hell is he asking you all this*, the voice whispered, *if he already knows the answers?*

"Did you further disobey direct orders to report your activities and return to base?"

"Sir, I was having radio trouble." Yeah, and I was a little busy killing the enemy, which I thought was kind of the whole idea in this part of the world. Oh, and I was rescuing an American aviator, too.

"Did you lose a helicopter in the process?"

Well....

"Pretty serious charges. Disobeying a direct order under combat conditions. Could earn you a court martial, no problem. Maybe even your own personal firing squad. You been in country, what, three-four months?"

"Yes, sir."

"Jesus, mister," the major said, almost to himself, "around here, it takes most men twice that long to fuck up big as you did. Do you have any idea how many treasonous bastards were desecrating the streets of our nation's capital yesterday? A hundred thousand, screaming filthy things at our Commander in Chief. It's just your kind of screwup that puts traitors like them over the edge."

Sigafoos turned toward the door. "Birdwell!" he shouted, and the door burst open immediately, as though the major's executive officer had been standing right outside, listening. He had, of course, been doing exactly that. He stared at Webb with unabashed curiosity, and not a little deformed delectation, the way you might look at an ant on a sunny sidewalk under a magnifying glass.

Damn, major, said Webb's voice, *where did you find THIS guy?* Birdwell matched the Major perfectly, the same tiny intensity, the same fluttery, anxious aura of imminent detonation. He and his boss could have been twin cousins. The desk now reflected both images, making the place look crowded. Webb sensed that a tribunal was underway.

"What do you think, Birdwell," the major asked. "Do we send this smartass to Leavenworth for thirty years on the rockpile, or....?"

That last"or" hung in the air like passed gas. What was the "or," Webb wanted to know.

The XO looked Webb up and down through little round wire glasses, holding his clipboard tightly to his narrow chest.

"With the major's permission. I believe that Mr. Webb's actions should properly be reviewed by...um, higher authority. At least at the squadron level."

Sigafoos was crushed. He gave Birdwell an evil look, his shoulders slumped, and all the wind went out of him. He'd been so looking forward to moving his figurative bowels all over this poor unfortunate miscreant that the idea of having the punishment taken out of his hands was almost too much for him. But he knew Birdwell was right. The XO had kept him out of trouble before.

Sigafoos peered once more into the surface of his desk, as though he expected to encounter in its depths eternal verities that only he could comprehend. When his reflection failed to give him the judicial guidance he was looking for, he looked up slowly, his thin, lipless mouth breaking into a thin, lipless grin. People who try to grin with no lips look like they've been sliced across, right below the nose. Sigafoos had excellent teeth, and they glittered, like icicles hanging from the roof of his mouth, white and cold.

He sat down, dwarfed by his hand-stitched burgundy leather executive chair, and ran his bony hands lovingly over the fine-grained sweep of dark wood.

"Colonel Houle at squadron is a former CO of mine. I'm sure I can convince him to pay special attention to this matter. Okay, Webb. You're assigned to squadron HQ pending further action. Dismissed."

"Sir," Webb ventured. "With the Major's permission, may I say something?"

"No."

"Sir, since my ass is grass anyway, and with all due respect, what about the other chopper, the black one with no markings?"

Sigafoos suddenly looked up. "What chopper?"

"A black Cobra. It blew away the village once, and then, when we were trying to get out, it came back and wiped out a .51 cal."

"You were hallucinating. I'll put that on the list of charges against you."

"Sir, everyone saw it"

"Then everyone was hallucinating. Get out of here."

Webb and Parker came back to attention, did a crisp about-face and headed for the door.

"By the way, Mister Webb," the major said. Webb stopped and turned, one hand on the knob. "You might like to know about your friend."

"Yes, sir. Please."

"He'll live. They pulled two bullets out of him. One in the leg and one in the ass. He may never walk again, but he's got a slim -- I say again, slim -- hope. The bullets were ours. The gooks didn't shoot him. You did."

By the time Webb was halfway back to the hooch, his voice was in full form. *Could have hauled your ass out of there in a wheelbarrow,* it said.

Funny thing about the voice. It had been with Webb for a long time, and he never thought there was anything strange about it. Of course, he knew about people who "heard voices," but the one in his head never told him to pull out his eyes, or kill women, or shoot up a fast food joint, or do anything weird, and he was fairly certain that everybody had a whisper, a conscience, a moral compass, somewhere inside that advised them, whether it expressed itself in actual words or not. So he didn't consider himself too terribly unhinged. Sometimes he heard it loud and clear, five by five, right up in front of his head, but other times it was barely a mumble. He heard it best when it told him the bad news. That night it came from just outside his left ear, and he heard it very well, indeed.

This is what it said.

Second time, right? You saved O'Connell, sure, but you shot his ass up in the process. He could die, thanks to you. Worse, he could live. Spend the rest of his life on wheels, or hooked up to the machines. But still, he's one of your friends who actually managed to survive your fumbling attempts at rescue. So far, anyway. Besides, if you didn't shoot O'Connell, maybe the black Cobra did. And they were trying to help. That is, if there even was a black Cobra.

He didn't need the voice to tell him the rest. At times like this, the locked away things are the first ones up from the cellar, like the taste of a bad lunch.

CHAPTER 22

DEPARTMENT OF THE ARMY
HQ U.S ARMY STRATEGIC COMMUNICATIONS COMMAND
SIGNAL GROUP, HAWAII
APO San Francisco 96557

DRPQS-R   May 27, 1970
COMMUNICATIONS NUMBER 06-10

SUBJECT: DOD FILM PROPOSAL

TO: FOSTER, LEON B. 266-90-4235
     2LT MOS 8511 MOS
     US SPECIAL PHOTO DET.
     Pac. (W1X9) APO SF 96558

Lieutenant Foster:
Once again, I must caution you against submitting frivolous film proposals to the DASPO office in Honolulu. I have just received your revised version for the Army Big Picture series, in which you actually expand on the "horror" of drug abuse in the military. Regardless of the information you think you have on this subject, continuing to submit such proposals could be considered an act of insubordination.

Let me make this plain: you can not and will not produce a film containing any references to drug abuse in Vietnam. It is the position of the US Army that this situation is both minor and currently well-controlled. Assistant Secretary of Defense Daniel C. Henkin recently testified before Congress that intensive investigation developed no evidence that units in the field were under the influence of marijuana or other narcotics. Is your information more accurate than his? I think not.

I also must inquire as to why you have demonstrated no progress on the Land Clearing/Defoliation film. The Army

Chemical Corps has gone on record proving that Agent Orange is completely harmless, and is aiding greatly in our war effort. This project is much more worthy of your attention. We suggest that you and your film crew spend as much time as possible in areas where this chemical is being used, so that we may continue to assure the American people of the value of this important tool.

I have also been informed that the three-part series on mortuary science is behind schedule. Why?

FOR THE COMMANDER

Col. H.T. Frye
Adjutant
DISTRIBUTION
D-Plus FAO, ATTN: IA Br.

* * * *

Wednesday, May 27, 1970

DASPO was responsible for producing two kinds of films: the scripts that the Department of the Army sent from Washington for them to shoot exactly as written, which could be anything from Hazards of Vehicle Operation to a documentary on Sammy Davis Jr.'s. tour of the country. Most times, an order would come down with instructions that said "do a film on tanks." It was up to people like Foster to come up with the central idea, write it, get it approved, and shoot it.

The second kind of film was the target of opportunity. If Foster or any of the DASPO officers came across an activity they thought was worth filming, they did it. They were authorized to take as much equipment as they needed, as many men, as much per diem, as they deemed necessary to get the job done. If it turned out they needed more, they asked for it, and got it.

The mortuary cosmetology film was the second type and it was D'Amato, not surprisingly, who had seen the cinematic potential, practically the moment he arrived in country. Everybody in Saigon walked around with the disturbing knowledge, somewhere in the back of their minds, that the morgue on the base at Tan Son Nhut was the largest facility of its kind on the planet, there being no shortage of corpses in Vietnam. D'Amato got interested. He wrote up a proposal for a film, submitted it, and received word that it had been enthusiastically approved by the commanding officers in Hawaii. D'Amato's concept called for them to spend an indeterminate amount of time at the mortuary doing not one film, but a three-part series documenting the advances in mortuary cosmetology achieved during the war. Funeral directors, like other professional groups, were quick to avail themselves of the unique career advancement opportunities provided by the mutilation and fatality of combat. They came from all over.

When the DASPO crew arrived at the mortuary, they found it to be the coldest place in Southeast Asia. Worst of all, everybody in the building was dead, with the exception of the inexplicably cheerful civilian technicians and the head mortician, a man in his sixties named Lazslo Kapusta.

Lazslo Kapusta, under contract to the United States government, was an American from Cleveland by way of the former Austro-Hungarian Empire, the fifth in a long line of undertakers, the death care profession being one of the most hereditary occupations in the world. In the States he would have insisted on the title of Funeral Director, but in Vietnam he didn't direct funerals. He just made sure the fallen ones were as presentable and complete as possible for their tragic trip home.

He was a tall, individual, angular and pale, with sunken cheeks, bloodless lips, a chilling smile, hair as black as deep space, and a widow's peak. This is too easy, thought Foster when he met him, because Kapusta would have gotten the undertaker's part in any movie you were casting, and was fated for his profession if not through heredity or experience, then by his looks alone.

D'Amato's concept called for them to film the mortuary operation from top to bottom, and they started outside: the body bags, which Kapusta insisted were called "morgue packs," that came in from the combat zones, and were unloaded like sacks of produce from the choppers, the "transfer cases" (*not* coffins!), rectangular aluminum boxes, thousands of them, stacked outside the facility ten high as far as the camera could see. Gleaming silver in the sun, they symbolized more about the war than Foster ever wanted to know.

As they got set up to shoot, Ironman and Weinberg started to move one of the transfer cases, and almost dropped it, because it was unexpectedly heavy. Something shifted inside. They froze.

"Holy shit!" Ironman screamed. "There's somebody in this one!"

They stood around, shaken, and looked at each other. Nobody was brave enough to open it, so Foster sent Weinberg inside to bring out one of the technicians.

"You guys are a hoot," the tall, gangly tech drawled when he bent over the case. "All's it is are these rubber wedges we stick in there to keep the remains from rolling around...." He threw the catches, pulled the lid up, and his eyes went wide. There was a body bag, sorry, a morgue pack lying in there, and it looked like whoever was in it weighed about three hundred pounds. Covering his nose, the tech carefully ran the zipper down, revealing hundreds of clear plastic bags, each about the size of a loaf of bread, filled with white powder.

"Shit," said the tech. "Not again. You guys don't move. I gotta go call the MPs."

Foster pulled the bag open wider and stared. Jesus. What a great way to ship the stuff. Last place anybody would look. He told Ironman to run off some film of the hoard. "We'll give it to Colonel Berner," he said. "Might be worth a few brownie points." Svoboda shot a roll of stills.

The MPs arrived in four Jeeps, sirens screaming, and finally let the DASPO crew get back to work. But inside the mortuary, the sights were even worse than they feared.

"You zee," said Lazslo Kapusta, leading them through the facility, "we get dese boyz in bad shape."

"Dead is about the baddest shape you can be," whispered Ironman."Not true," said D'Amato. "Remember those poor fuckers in the hospital? Their skin was falling off."

They watched, leaning on each other and holding their stomachs in tight as the techs threw the morgue packs on chrome tables, cut the clothes away, hosed down the bodies to remove the dirt and blood, then set about establishing their identities. Fingerprints. Dental impressions. One of the techs was eating his lunch, a tuna fish sandwich on pumpernickel, lettuce, no tomato, sitting at one of those dreadful chrome tables, inches from a dead body that looked like half of it was made of raw hamburger. He didn't seem to mind. But Kapusta was ready for the reaction of people who had never seen the process before.

"Dun't vorry," he said, opening a corpse's mouth and sticking his finger inside. "He ain't gonna bite you. YOW!" Screaming, he jerked his hand back, shaking it and cursing. Weinberg fell back against D'Amato.

"Chust kidding. Come zis vay."

He walked briskly in front of them, not looking back.

"Sometimez they are missing certain pieces of their parts. Zis is not like some poor bastard is shot in a bar on Saturday night. Not the clean simple car crash. On the battlefield, is not possible alwayz to bring everything back.

"Zo here," he said cheerfully, leading them to a huge silver-doored storage locker, "ve have de spare partz."

He threw open the door, and treated the DASPO team to a freezer full of human anatomy, broken down into all its components. There were men's arms and legs, feet and hands, of every color, size and description. "Of course ve match the complexion as close as ve can...."

Foster closed his eyes and tightened his stomach muscles with all his strength. Not as bad as the hospital, maybe, not as bad as live people with flesh turned to jelly by napalm and white phosphorus, but the sights grabbed Foster and the crew in a cold fist, and squeezed. The people in the hospital were Vietnamese. He pitied them, but they were not his. Besides, he'd been in country a short time, and between the jet lag and dysentery, nothing he saw seemed real. But this...? Americans. Kids. Pieces of them. Maybe even somebody he'd known in high school, or college.

And some of his crew were new in country. They hadn't seen the hospital, and they'd definitely never seen anything like de spare partz.

Events slid even farther downhill when Kapusta showed them what mortuary cosmetology was all about. Their stomachs spoke, telling them that chronic dysentery and the agony caused by the orange malaria pills were mere pinpricks compared to watching somebody rebuild a dead man's face from the eyeballs out. Brilliantly lit. In sharp focus. Close up. The film hummed through the camera. Hours of it.

It took ten solid days to film enough footage for the three part series D'Amato had dreamed up. After the cheerful tutelage of Lazslo Kapusta, Foster knew he needed to get very drunk, or die, or both.

* * * *

In spite of the horror of it, or maybe because, the slices of life he was encountering at the hospital and the morgue deepened Foster's appreciation of his circumstance to an encouraging degree. They weren't combat photographers, but they'd flown in and out of the upcountry firebases plenty of times. Saigon was good. Inside the villa walls was better.

For the grunts living in a hole out in the shit, and for those exiled to firebases, the nights were the worst. First of all, in the monsoon season, which seemed to last most of the year, it rained so hard they couldn't see the man in the foxhole next to them, and they spent way too much time covered by thick, oozy mud. Then, whatever ground or hillside or rice paddy they'd fought and died for during the day would be given back, and after that, there was an excellent chance that mortars would come raining out of the black sky, or the Claymores would start erupting in the dark and a horde of VC would come tumbling across the perimeter. They called it "zips in the wire." At sundown, there was the small comfort of a few warm beers while sitting around a hooch or a bunker, if the slicks had even brought any in that day, but mostly the dark was a damp, uncomfortable time, reeking and foul, where eyes were strained forcing sight into the darkness, watching for movement in the jungle, looking up every once in a while, as if they could see the rockets before they arrived. Watching. Waiting. Hoping for one more wakeup in the morning.

But Saigon was the ultimate balm for the savaged soul. There, the hours after sunset reverberated to frenzied, hebephrenic merrymaking, especially for troops in outfits like DASPO. The nights in Saigon were a time of the darkest magic, a time when bizarre beings with glowing eyes, pointy teeth, and superhuman senses of smell slithered out from the city's moister, darker places. They appeared in the streets, in the bars, in the boom-boom rooms with writing all over the walls. Magical women appeared, like the kind that wafted across the verandah of the Continental Hotel. At night, everybody from generals to PFCs consecrated themselves to forgetting where they were, what they were doing, and what might be going on with their families and lovers back in the World, often with stunning success. The night life of Saigon, even on the bases, was custom-made for those who sought sweet blindness, temporary insanity, total loss of ego. For some, it was a godsend. For many, an absolute necessity.

There were, of course, some Americans who resisted the temptations of the boom-boom rooms, the massage parlors and the tea bars. But aside from those two, thousands of GIs and civilian contract workers emerged after dark, like bats swarming out of a cave in New Mexico, and descended on the city, greeting the blackness with a fervor that bordered on the sacramental.

The DASPO troops, living where they did, had ready access to Saigon's attractions, but so did many others. Most of the old French-era mansions owned by military or government officials were rented out to other non-combat Free World Force military units from various countries. Then there were civilian employees of American and international companies that maintained the communications networks, charter airlines, weapons systems, and all the other killingly complex, obscenely expensive machinery that modern warfare requires. Equipped with a full complement of cheap domestic labor and long nights with nothing else to do but drink in a bar, drink in your quarters, or get stoned, the villas tended to become like fraternity houses. Weekend parties were necessities of life, and miscellaneous celebrations tended to erupt spontaneously four or five other nights of the week as well. Everybody came, and they drank or smoked till the darkness enveloped them. In the villas, every night was homecoming, New Year's Eve, the Super Bowl, all three.

Much of the entertaining was done for the pure pleasure of pure pleasure, but when Former Sergeant First Class Harris and the officers and NCOs who ran the DASPO villa put together a list of privileged invitees, they generally had more self-serving purposes in mind.

If they needed a new air conditioner, which they weren't

authorized to have in the first place, the 55th Maintenance Battalion NCO and his group would likely grace the balcony for a cocktail hour that sometimes extended well into the next morning. If somebody had a special yen for corned beef, or a real steak, the honor of the commissary staff's presence would be requested. If special support was needed for a particularly tough film assignment, members of the Free World Forces would receive a cordial invitation.

But some nights there were no parties, no swarms of people running up and down the stairs chasing the hookers. On those nights, especially after shooting at places like the hospital and mortuary, Foster and the rest would repair to the rooftop terrace, sit back in their chairs, open a few cold Heinekens, fire up a fatty, and surrender themselves to the sweetness of the night.

CHAPTER 23
DOUGLAS IN WINTER

Wednesday, May 27, 1970

Sometimes, when you think you can't fall asleep, you do anyway. You don't know it, but you lie through a kind of twilight that lets visions and memories seep out through the cracks in the cellar door of your psyche. Webb, crunched on his cot with a pillow over his head to drown out the noise of artillery fire, thinking of O'Connell down in the jungle had just that kind of non-sleep. The sickness in his stomach from the virtual waterboarding by Major Sigafoos had not gone away, and he thought he was getting sick. Malaria was common, so he'd taken a handful of pills that were supposed to prevent it. What they did was give him the chills, the sweats, and nightmares. He tossed on soaking sheets.

* * * *

Monday, February 1, 1954

It had been cold, so cold that Douglas didn't want to walk across the lake to school. Probably about sixteen degrees that Monday, the fourth morning of a brand new 1954. It had snowed all night. Taylor Webb loved the way it looked, like a Christmas card.

He started calling himself Taylor the year before, when he decided he couldn't bear to be a Sammy, no matter how much his father loved Samuel Taylor Coleridge. He'd been sick of the "Rime of the Ancient Mariner" since he was four, but he had to admit he liked the one about Xanadu. It sounded so good when his father read it to him.

"If we can't skate, we'll be late again," Douglas complained, wiping his nose with the back of his mitten, leaving a gleaming trail across his face. "You remember what Old Raisinface said. You want to sit through fourth grade one more time?"

"Come on, we'll make it." Taylor loved the lake. From his backyard, it stretched at least two miles to his right and left, but it was narrow where he lived, and the school was just on the other side. In the summer, they had to bike around it, but when it froze over, they could skate across. But no skating today. Too much snow on the ice from the night before.

Taylor pulled his wool cap down farther over his ears. "Come on, Douglas. We *will* be late if you stand here pissing about it."

Douglas was his best friend. They'd lived next door to each other ever since the first grade. Their fathers worked together at the brewery, both top brewmasters. Nobody called him Doug, or Douggie. His mother insisted he tell everyone his name was Douglas, and never to answer to anything else. She said it was more proper and dignified.

Together, they looked kind of like Laurel and Hardy. Taylor Webb was tall for his age, fair and skinny, but his friend was plagued by a common problem for a nine-year-old: residual baby fat. It just wouldn't go away. He was short, too, which made it even worse. His hair sat on top of his round head like black fur on a cue ball.

Most fat kids Taylor knew around school were objects of the very most cruel kind of derision...the nine-year old boy kind. But not Douglas. He was funny, he was outgoing, and he was a brilliant dancer, baby fat or not. He was in all the school plays, and they picked him to narrate the school Christmas pageant, even though he was Jewish. Everybody liked him, except when it came time to choose up sides for baseball.

"Come on," Taylor insisted, pulling at his friend's coat.

"I think we should go back inside and ask Mom to take us."

"I think you should get your fat butt off this porch and come with me."

Taylor Webb was born to lead. Douglas couldn't resist. He gathered his books close to his chest, wiped his nose one more time and reluctantly set off across the snowy backyard toward the shore of the frozen lake.

The storm of the night before had blown itself out, so it was

quiet and still, with the kind of razor dryness in the air that
freezes the little hairs inside your nose. The new snow lay on
the ground like it did the night good King Wenceslaus looked
down. It crunched under their feet, a fine powder. Taylor
loved it.

"Shit," Douglas complained. "Now we'll have to shovel all
this up tonight before we can go skating."

"It'll do you good. Take off a little of that pork." Taylor was
the only person who could say anything to Douglas about his
weight.

"Yeah? Well, look at you. You ain't got no ass at all. Just
a flat place back there. Don't it hurt you to sit? You...."

It was the last thing Douglas said before he started trying
to scream. With an abrupt lurch, and a high-pitched squeal,
the ice gave way beneath them. For some reason, Taylor fell
to his left and landed on a solid spot, but Douglas went
straight down into the black water, the surface opening like a
trapdoor on a gallows, then crumbling, the cracks radiating
out around him, pieces breaking free.

"Taylor...it...help."

For a second, Taylor couldn't do a thing. His throat closed
up tight, his heart beat furiously against the cage of his ribs,
crazy to get out. He made little squeaking sounds and stayed
where he was, on his hands and knees, his books strewn
around him, bright red and blue rectangles on the brilliant
white snow.

"Douglas! Can...you make it over here?" Choking, Taylor
lay down on his stomach and tried to inch himself toward the
hole, stretching his arm out till he thought it would separate
from his shoulder altogether. But Douglas was just *this much*
too far away, and every time Taylor got close, the ice below
him would shift, crumbling a little bit more, and he'd have to
skitter back.

Douglas' snow suit was soaked through with freezing
water, and he floated a little less well with each passing
second. The whole scene took place in an eerie kind of
silence, because Taylor was so panicked he could barely
breathe, let alone speak. And Douglas felt the first insidious
effects of hypothermia so quickly that his body didn't have the
resources to let him scream. He could make only little pants
and squeaks and grunts as Taylor reached for his straining

hand, reached harder, as hard as he could, screaming inside, but he never quite got there.

He looked up. Could he run for help? It was just about as far to the school as it was back to the house. His head turned wildly, searching for a tree branch or anything he could stretch out to his friend, who panted in the water, a little less of him showing than before. They were in the middle of the lake. There was nothing.

More frantic squirming on his belly, a few more futile reaches, their wooly fingertips barely inches apart, Douglas not screaming, not yelling, just a soft moan as his clothes became soaked enough to pull him suddenly down, a bubble, another, then black water framed by white ice, smooth and shiny and cold, very cold.

He didn't remember a thing after that, not the crazed stumbling run back to his house, not the glass he broke as he charged through the back door, not his mother's face as she knelt on the warm kitchen floor, trying to get the story out of him. He stood in front of her, clutching her apron desperately, out of breath, choking, but finally he made her understand.

He didn't remember the sirens or all the trucks, or his father rushing home early from the brewery, or the men who swarmed through his yard, running out to the lake. His mother wouldn't let him watch an hour later when they finally dragged Douglas out of the water accompanied by the shrieks of his maddened mother, and lay his body on the ice, a sodden black form, very still and cold in the bloodless light of January's midmorning.

CHAPTER 24
MEET THE SHADOWS

Friday, May 29, 1970

Webb arrived at the Shadows much the same way Longacre had, and in much the same state of dislocation and confusion. He, too, walked Troung Minh Ky Street from end to end, climbed the improbable stairs of the Magic Fingers Massage Parlor, was greeted by the same mysterious Vietnamese man who spoke perfect American English, and ultimately found himself confronted with Major Sanderson deep within. There was the same walk across the street, the amazement at the living quarters, and the same subversive serenade from the DASPO villa next door. Disappointingly, large-breasted blonde nurses were nowhere to be seen.

It fell to Longacre to fill Webb in on the hows and whys of the Shadows, even though he still wasn't too certain himself. After the episode with Juan Wayne, he, like many others, began to have Serious Doubts.

Webb barely had time to get his gear stowed in his room at the villa when Longacre hauled him out the door.

"Where are we going?"

"The racetrack. Don't ask me why, because I don't know. But on the way, I'll buy you a beer at the Continental and get you up to speed on what we do."

Longacre absolutely loved living in Saigon, especially after all the time he'd spent in the boonies. One of his favorite haunts was the bar in the Continental Hotel. He decided it would be a good place to tell Webb the story. A few drinks made the unbelievable a little less so.

Webb followed him through the alien streets, having been in Saigon only six hours, transported there in a swirl of activity on orders from Major Sigafoos. He barely had time to say goodbye to the Vampires. All he knew of Vietnam in three months had been the air base and Tay Ninh, but Saigon was a *city*. It was teeming with closely-packed storefronts, most of them run by Indians, and especially Sikhs, who seemed to have cornered the haberdashery business. Tall, big-boned, bearded and turbaned, they could make a custom suit for you in a day, if you had anywhere to wear it.

So many people on the sidewalks, and he couldn't help noticing how many were missing pieces of themselves. The amputee count was noticeably high. He'd never seen that before, but then, he'd never been so close to the culture, either.

"Everybody tells us the war is winding down," Longacre said to Webb as they walked down Troung Minh Ky Street in the lowering dusk. "But from where we sit, it looks like it's speeding up.

"American casualties are lower, if you can believe what they tell you, thanks to Vietnamization and the raids on Cambodia. You know about the raids on Cambodia?"

"You might say." Longacre steered him through the slightly cooled and slightly quieter streets, past the innumerable and inevitable vendors, some of them actually living in the indentations they'd scratched out of the villa walls on the block.

They walked down Tu Do Street, the 42nd Street of Saigon, the Times Square, where every narrow door led into a shop or a bar. The bars were the kinds of places where you could walk in and know instantly that everybody in the room, everybody, without exception, was on the take, on the make, doing the Saigon Hustle more or less well, covering the angles, making the deals, buying and selling. If they'd all been dealing just weapons or drugs, or merely selling children, the atmosphere would have been considerably more lighthearted.

"See that building on the traffic circle?" Longacre pointed a bony finger as they dodged their way across the street. "JUSPAO. Joint US Public Affairs Office. Every afternoon they hold a press briefing to explain what's happening with the war. They call it the Five O'Clock Follies. You ought to go.

"Now this place here, well, this is the crossroads of Southeast Asia." Longacre led Webb up to the verandah of the glittering Continental Hotel, just across the street from the old Opera house that the French had built, which was now the Vietnamese Senate. He took the steps in three long strides, but Webb needed five. "You want to know who really runs the war, you're looking at 'em."

Webb knew at once it was true. He was only 24, a little older than the average soldier in Vietnam, and not terribly attuned to the subtle energies and influences that places like the Continental constantly soak up over the years and then slowly release into the atmosphere like low-level radiation. But he certainly could feel...something. Mystery. Danger. People on unfathomable errands, plotting international plans.

On the sidewalk that ran past the verandah, mutilated Vietnamese war veterans begged for spare change, limping up to the tables on the verandah, holding out their hands, tapping people with their stumps to get attention. There didn't seem to be enough fingers to go around.

The Continental Hotel was home to every type of character that breeds during long term warfare in exotic climes, especially when vestiges of empire cling to the locale like tattered finery. Senior officers in civvies, trying to pretend that everyone took them for British businessmen, men in aloha shirts, dozens of Indians, who, it was said, actually controlled the commerce of the country. Women who were so beautiful that they came to life only at night, because you'd never, never see them during the day. French, Germans, Scandinavians, Vietnamese women in *au dais*, women who exhibited the very most fortunate mix of the French and the Asiatic, floating across the salon with heads high, as though they breathed only the bouquet of the heavens.

In the background, the occasional bang, gunshot, ciclo backfire, explosion, a constant noise, like the muffled hum of traffic on a distant highway.

The Continental was an antique place, a venerable place, in the French style, of course, as were most of Saigon's important buildings, with open colonnades, grand windows rounded at the top, terrazzo floors, disheartened ceiling fans hanging from long stems, everything white and totally authentic, even down to the Sydney Greenstreet type who surveyed the room from an obviously privileged table in a far corner overlooking the crowded sidewalk, his back to the wall.

Webb examined him from his seat, staring over Longacre's shoulder as he talked.   A beefy Caucasian with a faintly Germanic or at least Eastern European look, reddish face, overhanging stomach, the inevitable white suit.   Every so often one or another shadowy figure would approach him, bow down to his ear, give him a little Peter Lorre whisper, then melt away.   Some of them came from inside the hotel, others walked in off the street, still others leaned over the railing in the hot night, exchanged a few low words, and then disappeared into the darkness.

Webb was to see the man almost every evening, sitting in the heavy night air like the caterpillar on the toadstool, immaculate, manicured, dry and powdered, reading a Vietnamese newspaper, or *Paris Match* or *Dei Zeitung*, or *L'Observattore Romano*, or the *International Herald Tribune*, always rolling between his fingers a fine crystal snifter.   In Webb's imagination, the cognac cost $80 an ounce.

What was the import of all those comings and goings? What dark decisions were handed down from that chair, or from the little alcoves and corners that surrounded it?   The place had an atmosphere you could pick up with a spoon, palpable and real, the same kind of feeling you'd get in the dining car of the Orient Express, or on a narrow side street in the Casbah.   It was vintage Agatha Christie.

Well, ain't this just the shits, said Webb's voice.

"Ever fly Cobras?" Longacre asked in a very low voice, fumbling in his sport coat pocket for a Marlboro.

"Nope. Our platoon never got them."

"Well, you're gonna fly 'em now.   Here's the story.   Every one of us, including you, is here because we fucked up somehow."

"I didn't do anything wrong."

"Me neither.   But they could have just court-martialed you and thrown you in the stockade.   Why didn't they? Because you fucked up in a special way.   My guess is you could have either gotten a medal for what you did, or a firing squad.   If your little half-assed exploit hadn't turned out the way it did, you'd be up the ass.   But the guy lived.   You didn't leave your friend on the battlefield.   The military admires that, much as they hate to admit it.   You qualified.   All of us, you, me, Larue, Larson...fucking up like that, it's an art."

He fell silent, looked around the verandah. Webb was squirming to ask Longacre what he'd done to earn a place in this dubious unit, and how the hell he knew about the adventure of the O'Connell rescue, but something told him he should wait a while, maybe forever. A slight breeze came up, ruffling the napkins under the dark green bottles of Heineken that sat on the white marble top table sweating in the night. The smoke from innumerable black tobacco cigarettes floated gently toward the street. Curious lavender smells drifted past.

"You know what a shadow unit is?" Longacre asked, suddenly getting down to business. His voice was very low.

"You mean, like...secret missions?"

"I mean like secret missions that stay secret. No medals. No records. No heroic stories to write back home. We're a complete gunship platoon. Got Huey slicks, Cobra gunships, a few LOACHs, even a Chinook to sling load those suckers out of there when we get shot down. Which is a lot. Operate out of a compound on the base, very restricted. We are, you might say, highly confidential."

"Why are we so secret?"

"Cause no one knows about us except them who can't talk anymore and them who give the orders."

"What kind of orders?"

"Well, see, that's the secret."

"Who gives them?"

"That's a secret, too." Webb gave up. Ours not to reason why.

"Okay, but why would they put a fuckup like me in that kind of unit?"

"Why? You were lucky. If you couldn't fly gunships, you might be on the rockpile right now. We need a good gunny or two. Seems like we keep losing 'em. Besides, with an atrocities rap hanging over your head, they know you'll keep your mouth shut."

Here, said Webb's voice, *is a perfect example of how the worst thing that could happen becomes the best thing that could happen.* When he first got to Vietnam, he was floored that they let him fly gunships, let him be a "real" combat troop, taking part in the "real" war. It was exactly what he wanted, at least until he'd found out what it was like. But he'd stepped right into it, feeling sorry for the slick pilots, driving ash and trash around the sky all day in their fat sloppy Hueys, with no protection except for two birdfart M-60's. Webb had learned how to fly and shoot at the same time and he loved it, because his Huey had rocket pods and machine guns and a thumper on the front that threw chunky little grenades.

Then came Tay Ninh, and O'Connell, and he found himself larynx-deep in Very Bad Shit. His punishment? Transfer to a secret gunship platoon that flies Cobras. He felt like Br'er Rabbit when the fox threw him in the briar patch. He'd fucked up by the numbers, and was being viciously chastised, severely punished with a delicious cold Heineken on the verandah of the country's finest hotel, assigned to a gunship unit that didn't exist. War, his voice told him, is great. It's combat that's hell.

He leaned back in his chair and took a slow, deep, profoundly satisfied breath, suddenly feeling very good about himself. Over Longacre's shoulder, the Sidney Greenstreet character removed a stack of Vietnamese piasters about two inches thick from his coat pocket and pushed it across the table to a man wearing a filthy turban.

"There are two more things I need to tell you." *Here it comes.* Webb clenched his teeth.

"Our cover is that we're civil engineers. You'll catch on."

"Civil engineers. Okay. And number two?" Webb gulped with a whisper as the man in white pushed another stack of MPC currency across the table.

"We're under the direct command of the Vietnamese."

"We're *what?*" It came out louder than he intended. Heads turned, even the man in white froze midway through stuffing a wad of bills into his pocket.

"Shhh! Our theoretical commanding officer is a guy named Colonel Xoan. He gives us our targets, plans the missions, points us at what he wants destroyed, and we destroy it."

"But...how...I mean...."

"They say it's drug interdiction. Stopping the flow of opium from the golden triangle, and the flood of heroin that so many of our fine young American boys seem to like so well. You'll see. Can't answer all your questions tonight. Don't think I could if I wanted to. Easier if you just find out as you go along. Rest of us did."

"Okay," Webb persisted, "but tell me this. What's this shit with the cover and civilian clothes? Why don't we just wear uniforms?"

Longacre sucked the last out of his cigarette and deliberately mashed it out in the clear cut glass ashtray.

"We don't wear uniforms because we don't exist. At least not on any chain of command chart. People know there's some kind of unit doing some kind of drug police work, because it was announced. But nobody knows who we are, or what we do, exactly. Safer that way."

"Wait a second. You guys fly Hueys, right? And Cobras?"

"Yup."

"But if we're a shadow unit, what kind of markings do the choppers have?"

"Markings?" Longacre smiled. "You gotta be kidding. Secret is secret. We got no markings."

"So all your choppers are...?"

"Dead black. No numbers, no nuthin'."

"Well, I'll be fucked," Webb said, leaning back in his chair and taking another long, cold Dutch beer swallow.

"Remember," said Longacre. If anybody knew who we are or what we're doing, some drugrunning motherfucker who didn't want us around would waste us in our sleep. So if anybody asks, you work for Municipal Planning and Engineering Management Corporation, home office, Silver Spring, Maryland."

"And what, exactly, do we do for Municipal Planning and Engineering Management Corporation, home office, Silver Spring, Maryland?"

"We're under contract to the Vietnamese government to design solid waste disposal facilities."

"You mean like...?"

"We survey and develop the new waste management systems that this country will need in its bright new capitalistic future. When we win the war, our Vietnamese allies will be able to take a comfortable dump on modern toilet fixtures anywhere in the country, thanks to people like you and me. So congratulations, son," smiled Longacre, sticking out a skinny hand. By reflex, Webb took it. "You're now a highly-paid professional in the dynamic field of sewer design and construction."

CHAPTER 25
THE RUFF PUFFS

Monday, June 1, 1970

At the five o'clock follies, Colonel Berner, his round face moist as ever, his vast expanse of forehead gleaming in the anemic light of the JUSPAO briefing room, stepped up to the podium and announced yet another high point in the Vietnamization of the war.

"Yesterday," he said, motioning with his prized pointer toward a well-worn map of the country, "the Regional Force/Popular Force, who we all know as the Ruff Puffs, claimed one of their biggest victories of the war. In a brilliantly co-ordinated series of raids on Vietcong positions south of Danang, they killed 125 enemy soldiers, and took an equal number of prisoners."

He went on, attracting the divided attention of maybe half the correspondents in the room, to explain how this dazzling victory was one more stunningly conclusive bit of proof that the administration's policy of Vietnamization was succeeding beyond anyone's most naively optimistic expectations.

"I have personally called upon our Special Photographic Operations unit to produce a documentary film showcasing the rigorous, intensive training these troops have undergone, and how their valiant efforts are contributing to the eventual but inevitable victory of the allied forces. The project is already under way, and I'll have the film to show you in just a few days. That concludes the briefing....."

But the reporters had already started wandering toward the double doors at the back of the room, and happy hour at the Caravelle.

* * * *

"What I want to know is this," said Weinberg, his face glowing green in the reflected light of the villa's dining room walls. It was time for the evening production meeting and bitch session. "Whatever happened to the shoot we were supposed to do for Berner? The one where Xoan destroys all that dope we brought back from Dam Long?"

"I called him on that," said Foster. "He told me Xoan went ahead and burned it without telling him. He was really pissed. However, I'm proud to announce another one of Berner's asshole ideas. A film on the Ruff Puffs."

"Tank Gott," mumbled Svoboda, "At least ve don't haf to go to combat."

D'Amato ran his fingers through his Brylcreemed hair and put his elbows on the table. "Bet your ass we do. How are we gonna show what the Ruff Puffs are doing if we don't get out there with 'em in the shit? Sign me up!"

"Wait a second," Foster said, leaning back in his chair to relieve the uncomfortable pressure around his waistline. Mama-San had curried a wicked noodle for dinner, and he could already feel the beginnings of a meltdown. "There could be a way around this. D'Amato, maybe you feel like running off into combat situations because Berner wants to impress the brass, but we don't. We're all brave young American boys, but it's not our job. How many times do I have to tell you? We're not combat photographers. You want to mix it up in the jungle, I'll sign your transfer to the 221st Signal Company. You can go up to Long Binh and take all the crispy critter pictures you want."

"I just think we're missing a big chance," pouted D'Amato. "There's an awful lot of production value in combat."

"He's got a point," observed Weinberg. "If we were making a feature film, it'd cost millions to stage a war like this."

"We could fake it," Ironman mumbled into his beer.

The group turned to stare at him.

He peered at them, his long, narrow face glowing in the light. There were many peculiar things about Ironman, but the strangest was that he didn't sweat. In the steaming tropical paradise of Saigon in summer, he was always dry. His washed out eyes blinked at them.

"You know...stage it. Write out a scenario, get a shitload of Ruff Puffs, dress half of 'em up like Charlie, take 'em out to a hamlet someplace and let 'em go through the motions. We'd probably have to rehearse it a few times first, block out the battle sequences, you know, like 'Sands of Iwo Jima.' This way, nobody gets hurt, especially not us. It'll be fun. Besides, Berner's never been near combat in his life. He won't know the difference."

"Ya," Svoboda joined in. "But the brass, they will."

"Fuckem," said Ironman. Nobody could disagree with that.

Foster thought about it for a few seconds. The DASPO mission was definitely not combat photography, and Berner knew it. It was just like him to fuck them over, sending them to dangerous places where they weren't supposed to be, even as he tried to use them to his advantage.

"Well," he said. "Tomorrow we'll get the Ruff Puff commander on the horn, you know, the one who was working with the Anzac Battalion in Phouc Toi. Let's see if he can lend us a hundred men, and fifty pair of black pajamas."

Thanks to the able and subversive assistance of Former Sergeant First Class Harris, it took them less than a week to set up the shoot. Foster found himself, along with Svoboda, Weinberg, Ironman and D'Amato, in a small village about twenty miles outside Saigon, surrounded by almost a hundred enthusiastically grateful Ruff Puffs. Grateful because they didn't have to go on any raids that day like everybody else, they didn't have to get shot at, they didn't have to worry about getting one more wakeup. Not that they wouldn't have, but thanks to Foster, all they had to do was play war games all day long and go home. They were ready to worship him as a god.

But Foster didn't have time to be happy about his eager and willing extras or his deified status in their eyes. He'd stayed awake for three nights on his narrow cot, thinking about only one thing: if he was going to run around with a bunch of soldiers dressed up like VC, he'd have to make sure every command in the immediate area – the immediate *world* -- knew exactly what they were doing. Given the fuckups he'd seen so far, and the dozens more he'd heard about, he was certain that, no matter how effectively he communicated up the chain of command, there'd be at least one trigger-happy chopper jock somewhere who wouldn't get the word. Some asshole would see fifty men in black pajamas scurrying around beneath him and open fire, or call in an air strike or a couple of A-7s full of napalm. There was little chance any of them would come through the exercise alive, he thought. It might actually be safer to follow the Ruff Puffs into battle.

Foster looked down at the incoherent notes that Berner had sent him. Why doesn't this man believe in typewriters, or secretaries? The Public Information Office must be crawling with them. But no. Berner had to write it all out longhand, in a spontaneous spidery scrawl. A prescription instead of a script.

"Here's the idea," Foster told his crew, and the Vietnamese interpreter assigned to the project. "Charlie attacks this hamlet, and we see our troops sounding the alert, picking up their arms, and taking defensive positions. Everybody to my right will be Charlie, so if somebody could hand out the black pajamas....?"

When the "enemy" Ruff Puff troops saw their costumes for the drama, a noticeable stiffening ran through the crowd. Most of them hated the VC, and nobody had told them that wearing the costume was part of the deal. The Ruff Puff troops who were already VC didn't want to wear them because they knew, as Foster did, that if even one unit in the area didn't get the word about what they were doing out there, friendly fire would pour from the skies.

But D'Amato, acting as assistant director, finally got everyone organized, and Foster spent most of the day doing what he loved best -- telling actors and cameramen what to do, even if he had to do half of it with simultaneous translation. Sometimes, film shoots just kind of bump along from shot to shot, but sometimes a miraculous thing happens. Everyone on the set gets into the rhythm, the events of the day flow perfectly, one to another, and the process becomes a sort of bizarre religious experience. One scene leads naturally and inevitably to the next, the cameraman and crew are reading your mind, the actors get the timing right on the first or second take, and life is wonderful.

That was exactly the kind of day Foster was having till the Cobras showed up.

"Hey, there they are," said Webb. He was high in the back seat of his Cobra, flying as aircraft commander this time, enjoying himself hugely, with Longacre in the front, on his way back from yet another practice session outside of town. They'd spent the afternoon blasting huge anthills with their miniguns and rockets. The anthills were imposing brown cones that stuck up from the grass, five or six feet high, and they made terrific targets. Best of all, they were self-renewing. No matter how much the pilots shot them, the ants built them back up in a couple of days, so they could go back and blast them again.

High to his left, Harrell and Shortstop followed. It was a slow day, and they'd come along for fun.

Webb was learning how to line up with the target, lower the nose, establish proper airspeed, and fire his weapons, all at the same time. He didn't think he'd ever be as good at it as Longacre.

"That's them DASPO motherfuckers," said Longacre.

The Shadows, like other units, had gotten the word. Webb could see the camera setup, the reflectors on stands, and even Foster, in the middle of a gaggle of men in black pajamas, pointing and yelling.

"I hate them guys," Longacre mumbled.

"I know," said Webb.

"I have the aircraft," Longacre told him. "Harrell, let's orbit here. Left turns."

"What are we doing?" Webb wanted to know.

"Just watch."

Foster looked up at the clatter. All the other choppers coming over that day had just gone right past.

"Great. D'Amato, are you sure everybody knows we're here?"

D'Amato swore he'd been thorough. He'd either called or been to visit every command in II Corps, he'd made lists, checked them twice, talked to everybody personally. "But those choppers don't have any markings," he observed. "I dunno where the fuck they're from."

They all started waving up at the sinister machines, smiling, grinning, even those who had the misfortune to be dressed in the pajamas, who desperately wanted to run and hide in the jungle, but knew if they did, it would just make matters worse.

The Cobras widened their circle, broke off, and started

back toward them. The pointed noses of the aircraft dipped a bit, directing the miniguns and rocket pods toward the ground. Toward them.

Foster had been in country long enough to know that when a gunship drops its nose, flaming hell is sure to follow.

"Heeeeeeyyyyyy!" He yelled, jumping up and down and waving, barely holding on to his clipboard. His normal coating of sweat suddenly turned cold.

"Heeeeeeeeyyyyyy!" yelled every single one of the 96 Ruff Puffs, and the six DASPO troops on the crew. But the choppers kept on coming.

"We're gonna die," screamed D'Amato. "We're gonna fuckin' die."

Fuckin' die is the last thing Foster wanted to do. Please, he prayed, not like this, not at the hands of some asshole chopper jocks who didn't get the message. The barrels of the grenade launchers, the gaping holes of the rocket pods yawned at him. Then, when the Cobras got into perfect firing position, they pulled up, and racketed over the village about 20 feet in the air, leaving everyone on the ground covered with red swirling dust.

Longacre's voice giggled in Webb's headset.

"Always wanted to do that. You have the aircraft. Take us home."

CHAPTER 26
DEAR BENNY

Tuesday, June 2, 1970

Hi, Benny,

It's kind of late, and I've had a long day, so I'm going to make this short and stupid. The cassette is almost full, and I should be able to mail it to you in a day or two.

If my voice sounds funny or my words run together, it's only because I learned about the five levels of intoxication tonight, and I'm not going to tell you which one I achieved. Just got back from the Number One club, where I listened to the Blue Jets sing the latest songs from the Philippine hit parade, watched our boys and a bunch of American civilians drink up the whole place, then we stopped at a new recreational facility called the Pink Palms, and they weren't talking about the kind of trees that grow in Florida. It's like the Magic Fingers, except the girls use their whole hand.

You're not letting Mom listen to any of this, are you?

Vietnam and the war get more amazing by the minute. The longer I stay here, the more I find out, and the more I find out, the more I think I really should be writing about what's happening here as a movie script. You can't make this shit up.

I'm sick about those guys getting blown apart out in the boonies while there are so many people here in Saigon really living it up, making huge amounts of money on the black market, juggling the currency, dealing drugs, God knows what they're doing. Worst of all, D'Amato submitted an idea to the Department of Defense for us to shoot a major documentary about the mortuary facility on the base. The DOD loved the concept, we just finished shooting it, and that made me even sicker. On a more optimistic note, it's nice to know that not all of the coffins – excuse me, I mean "transfer cases" – not all of them contain dead people. Some are sent home filled with dope.

I'm also sick – and pissed off -- about all the American civilians running around here. These guys are having way too much fun. Don't remember if I told you about those oddballs who live in the villa next door? The ones who try to look like they just got out of college? I've got a feeling they're into some kind of stuff, but I don't know if it's drugs or hot condoms, or guns or what. I've seen them come and go a few times, and I'm more convinced than ever there's something really twisted going on over there. As if we should talk. The DASPO villa is the center of the perversion universe. But there's a wrong number there someplace, and I just can't put my finger on it. One thing I'm sure of, those guys aren't designing any sewage systems. We're planning a huge party in a few days and I'm thinking of inviting them over, just so I can look at them close up. They all look like assholes, or CIA, but we'll see.

You know me, I'm a pretty friendly, talkative type, right, and I'm not shy about meeting people in bars. Not the tea girls, because they'll cost you fifty bucks before you know it and all you get is maybe a little squeeze on the leg. I'm talking about foreign service people, contract workers, troops attached to all these weird divisions I never heard of. I run into tons of them, and every single one tells me something about the war I didn't know, some tell me things I didn't want to know, and if half of it's true – if a *tenth* of it's true – I'll probably wonder about it for the rest of my life.

Like tonight. I ran into Call Me Norman again, the guy I met the first night I was here. Remember? Shithead graduated law school, walked into an Army recruitment office, told them he was a lawyer, and they said, "Sign here, Captain." Must be nice.

He was either still drunk or drunk again, and launches into all this incredible shit about how maybe half the people in the Army are either doing drugs, selling drugs, recovering from drugs, thinking about drugs, stealing drugs, or some damn thing. And he's supposed to prosecute all of them, plus the people who are dealing the black market, boosting weapons, and playing really complicated games with the currency. It could take the rest of the year.

You know, in 1965, around then, the military didn't even

have a single jail in Vietnam. Nobody was committing crimes, and those that did got shipped to Okinawa for court-martial. That's sure changed. This call me Norman guy is one of the flood of lawyers that came over a while back attached to the Army, and he hasn't slept since. Too many cases, not enough people. Some guy fucks up and they want to prosecute him, but the witnesses to whatever he did got transferred and he can't find them, or they got rotated to the states and the Army won't bring them back to testify, or they're not in the service any more. Or some silly fuck shoots one of his buddies at a firebase in the middle of the jungle and Norman can't get there to investigate because he damn sure can't travel over land, and the Army won't fly him up because they need space in the choppers for troops and supplies. He isn't exactly a priority.

Then, if he does get to the fire base or wherever, the guys he needs to talk to are in the field, and some of them don't come back. Lots of people getting away with doing lots of shit. I'm glad I don't have his job.

The conversation got really interesting when Call Me Norman started talking about the drug situation, because I got a peek into that whole world about as soon as I got here. Now, you know about my roommate in college, Dave the druggie? Okay, so I smoked a few times with him, but I never saw anything like what goes on over here. Norman says MAC-V did a survey a few years ago to find out the availability of drugs in Cholon – that's kind of the Chinatown of Saigon – and in the area around Tan Son Nhut. They reported 29 outlets for pot, opium and heroin, and believe me, they never got close to counting them all. The report said that just about anybody who dealt with the public had it for sale. Bar girls, shop owners, pedicab drivers, hotel clerks, you name it. By the way, before we got here, the Vietnamese government never had any laws against marijuana. Now they do.

There's talk about the Army forming some kind of drug abuse task force, and their main priority is supposed to be destroying the stuff at its source. When he told me that, I laughed so hard half a Heineken came out my nose. We did this film where that asshole Colonel Berner interviewed some Vietnamese colonel who's supposed to be working on drug interdiction with his own secret platoon of helicopters, but all that stuff comes from the Golden Triangle. Think we'll invade Burma to stamp out a few warlords up in the mountains someplace? Besides, it would put half the Burmese government out of business. So I don't know what they're going to do. All I know is if I stand down on the corner waiting to cross the street for more than five seconds, some mamasan or cowboy – that's what we call the teenage boys who come up behind you on a ciclo, knock you down and steal your money – some cowboy will come up and try to sell you something, or slip a vial of opium in your pocket as a free sample. I'm sure that most of the Vietnamese are as decent as anybody, but the war brings out the worst ones.

Here's something else that makes me sit and shake my head. If you're a civilian employee and you commit a crime, they can't do anything to you. Seems there was this guy working for an American company who tried to steal 36,000 batteries, but they caught him and he was tried and convicted by MAC-V. He appealed, and they had to let him go, because the military doesn't have any jurisdiction over civilians unless it's a *declared war*, which this, as I'm sure you know, isn't. Norman referred me to the Uniform Code of Military Justice, found in Title 10, Subtitle A, Part II, Chapter 47 of the United States Code, and I think I'll look it up. All they can do is fire civilians who commit crimes, and bar them from working in government related jobs. So they can smuggle all the heroin and opium they want and nothing much will happen. Some of the fired ones go back to the states, but others stay here and find some other way to make a living that doesn't involve the US government or the military. Of course, if a guy is arrested by the Vietnamese, the Americans can't – or won't – do anything, and the guy's fucked. He can wind up in a hole in the ground, like Uncle Dung.

I can't keep my eyes open. Hope I can mail this soon.

Weirdness, Benny. All is weirdness.

CHAPTER 27
THE RACETRACK

Tuesday, June 2, 1970

The racetrack in Saigon, another relic of the city's French heritage, could hold 15 or 20 thousand people, but there were only a thousand or so in the place, and none of them had come to bet on the dark horse. The crowd was fairly quiet, for a bunch of soldiers, because now that the war had spilled completely over into neighboring countries, now that the ARVNs and Cambodian mercenaries were battling for places like Kompong Speu just southwest of Phnom Penh, now that Americans were getting shot at over there, they didn't have a whole lot to say, and sat, for the most part, in sickly silence.

The stadium was a shallow empty bowl, rough wooden slatted benches all around, dotted here and there with the khaki of the American troops who had been summoned to see some kind of show. Nothing was left of the actual track except a tattered brown oval. Nobody was racing horses in Saigon at the time, social conditions as unsettled as they were. If anybody ever found a horse, they ate it.

What had once been the infield was covered with a carefully arranged maze of concertina wire, gleaming spiky whorls of the stuff in rows, jumbled from one side to the other about 40 yards deep, with thin wire holding it together just like a base perimeter. Tin cans were strung all along the wire, probably filled with pebbles or small pieces of scrap metal. Nobody had any idea what was going on.

Sanderson was there, and Larue, who'd left the villa a few minutes before them.

"What do we have to see this shit for," Larue said. "We could be at the steam and cream instead, the old hot oil treatment, it's a perfect night."

"Throw a towel over it," said another troop, a skinny guy, about five-six, with curly black hair.

"That's Shortstop," Longacre said. "And Zemina, who we call Z-Man. This is Harrell...Larson...Martin, but he pronounces it "Mar-TEEN...." The names went on, a blur of handshakes and faces. Webb didn't worry about it. He'd learn them all later.

"What the fuck are we here for?" Martin asked nobody in particular. "What are they gonna show us we don't already know?"

"It's okay, Carlos," put in Z-Man. "You already know everything. Especially if it has to do with the female anatomy."

"You do mean the human female?" asked Harrell.

"Any female. Señor Martin could get it up for mold and lichen, if they had sexes."

"They do," said Martin. Webb looked around at the new faces. Which of them was flying that anonymous Cobra the day he rescued O'Connell? Which one had saved his ass? Or were there other shadow units in Vietnam, other mysterious black gunships?

A squeal of feedback from the ancient loudspeaker.

"Gentlemen," said the echoing voice, "as you know, the NVA and VC are constantly changing their tactics in their war of aggression on the peaceful, democratically-minded people of South Vietnam. They are still attacking towns and villages in traditional ways, but terrorism, infiltrations, and booby-trappings are becoming more and more common. So tonight you're here to see a demonstration of sapper infiltration techniques."

"Oh, peachy," muttered Larson.

A platoon of MPs filed onto the field from either side, taking up positions along the outer edges of the razor wire.

"At the north end of the stadium you see Quai Ng, a Viet Cong Chieu Hoy and former sapper."

The US had a program in Vietnam that assured safe conduct and amnesty to any VC or NVA soldier who surrendered. They were called Chieu Hoy. The idea wasn't terribly successful, though every so often they would come up with someone like the little man who appeared on the racetrack infield that night. Nobody had even noticed him before, but as soon as he was introduced, the night air erupted with a roar of hoots and boos and catcalls, foot stamping, whistling, screaming. Here was the enemy, the worst of the enemy, in their midst, and if any of them had been able to get to the field, they would have terminated him instantly, with extreme prejudice and plenty of justification. He'd certainly terminated enough of them.

There wasn't a man in the place who didn't hate the Viet Cong, and they especially hated the weaselly Chieu Hoy like the one who stood before them, hated them with a peculiar mixture of fear, disgust, and admiration that none of them would dare admit. Men like Quai Ng were so quiet, so invisible, that you could wake up one night and find him standing next to your bunk, long knife in hand, smiling the Reaper smile. They were deadly men, ghastly silent, and every troop in the place would have gladly cut Quai Ng's balls off one at a time with a dull spoon. Worst of all, he was a traitor.

The announcer waited until calm was restored.

"I said *former* VC sapper. He is now working with our forces, and is here tonight to show us what he does best. Just to give you an appreciation of the enemy, in case you don't already have one."

Longacre held his fist in front of his mouth like a microphone. "And yes, Ladies and Gentlemen, Quai Ng, formerly of the VC, responsible for numerous American deaths, will now perform for our pleasure. Step right up and see the Chieu Hoy defector who now suddenly loves America and wants to fuck your daughter..."

"Can it, Longacre," said Sanderson. Harrell picked up the commentary.

"Watch in amazement as he demonstrates how he used to murder us in our beds, but due to a sudden change of heart and a desire to live regardless of which side he's on, he will now present an amazing display of sneaky, cunning, slimy dexterity and grace, right before your astonished eyes."

The purpose of the evening gradually became apparent. The MPs were positioned around the field elbow to elbow, so that nobody could get from one end to the other without going through the glittering, treacherous razor wire. Quai Ng, however, was apparently going to attempt exactly that. Webb couldn't wait.

The little man stood at the end of the stadium farthest from the Shadows, wearing nothing but a pair of shorts and sandals, his narrow hairless chest gleaming with sweat. He carried a bayonet, long and dull gray under the feeble stadium lights.

"Boy's in somewhat good shape," observed Larson, sucking the last hit out of a Pall Mall. And he was. Ng didn't have the painful skinny no-arms-no-chest build of most of the Vietnamese they'd seen, dead and alive. He wasn't heavy, he wasn't muscular, but his conditioning was readily apparent. He looked strong the way steel cables look strong.

"The cans you see hanging on the wire are full of pebbles," resumed the announcer, "and there are small bells scattered through the maze. Can we have it quiet, please." Then the lights went out.

"What is this," Z-Man whispered. "Some kind of magic show?"

Webb blinked. All he could see was the glow of Larson's cigarette against the sky as he flipped it away, and stuttering yellow flames of Zippo lighters flaring in the darkness all around the stadium. There was almost no light anywhere else. The announcer's voice rattled in the darkness, amid the distant buzz of ciclos and motorbikes.

"Quai Ng has been specially trained in infiltration techniques, and he is now teaching our forces how to defend against them. It's been our experience," continued the voice, not without irony, "that NVA and VC forces are particularly skilled at getting into places where we don't want them."

"Something of an understatement, there," muttered Z-Man.

"And that is why Quai Ng thinks he will come to America and dick our American daughters," Longacre continued.

"Quai Ng," said the announcer, "has told us of his colleagues who pride themselves on how many sleeping American throats they've cut." A low murmur from the crowd. The announcer didn't talk for long, because just as Webb's eyes were getting used to the darkness, just as he was able to pick out the dark forms of the MPs standing along the sides of the field, the lights came back on and Quai Ng was standing, shorts and sandals and bayonet, at the exact other end of the field, now closest to Webb. At his feet were five of the bells that he'd stolen from the wire, and two tin cans of pebbles. Nobody had seen or heard a thing.

"What a performance!" exclaimed Harrell, still doing his announcer thing. "So, from WRVN, this is Raymond Harrell saying, cut off my dick and call me Shirley."

Webb looked at Larson. Larson looked at Shortstop. And when Major Sanderson spoke, everybody looked at him.

"Dangerous man. Very dangerous man. Xoan's gonna love him."

CHAPTER 28
THI LANH'S BABY

Thursday, June 4, 1970

Weinberg came back to the villa with good news. He'd taken precious time away from his latest artistic interpretation of a mackerel to find a place for Thi Lanh to live. She'd been camping at the villa for about two weeks, slowly recovering, ever since Foster had brought her home from the hospital. A Catholic religious organization ran a home for women who found themselves in her particular circumstance, and as soon as she was well enough, they'd welcome her into the fold.

Foster was delighted. He didn't begrudge her his help, but he was in charge of two film crews, and even when somebody else watched her, the moans and mumbles kept him up all night. All he ever expected to do was give her a hand, but she turned out to be like a pair of shoes left too long at the shoemaker. If nobody claims her in thirty days, do you throw her away? Foster couldn't wait to tell her about her new home.

"No! No go without baby!"

Baby?

"I have baby. Little boy, very small. Must get him."

Baby?

Apparently so. A six month old named Ki. Thi Lanh had given him to an old woman, kind of a nursemaid, nanny, babysitter. Before the old crone would give him back, she would want money.

"How much money?"

"In dollars, maybe five hundred."

"Five hundred dollars? Why?"

"I need money, my boyfriend need money to start business so I leave him, she give me money. Now I must to give her more back."

"You hocked your baby?"

"?"

"Never mind." Deep breath. He thought, wait till I tell Benny about this.

He put the situation on the table at dinner that night. They were supposed to be planning a sequel to the film on the Vietnamese National Police, the White Mice, since everyone back in Washington had been highly complimentary about the first one. Foster and the rest thought it was most shameless piece of unabashed bullshit they'd ever produced. If he'd known the word "meretricious," he would have used it. The Department of the Army had given them a lot of static about the unfortunate cemetery desecration incident, because the police captain had complained, but otherwise, they had a green light for a followup.

When Foster had finished, they all just sat there, looking down at the table. Predictably, nobody wanted to kick in fifty or a hundred dollars a man to help her get the baby back.

"All due respect, Lieutenant," said Huggins, spitting an unspeakable brown wad into an empty Coke can. "But y'all brought her in here your own self." Foster didn't need to be reminded.

"Well, I'm open for suggestions."

"You want baby back?" asked Svoboda. "We take him."

Huggins glared at him and sneered. "We can't do that, you dumb...."

"Enough." Foster didn't want things to get ugly, didn't want the MPs around, and God knows he didn't want to deal with the QC, the South Vietnamese Military Police. Most of all, if anybody got arrested, or a gun went off, or some other unthinkable thing happened, Berner would find out, and shoot him.

"Looky here," said Huggins. "If this old bitch is buying and selling babies, she ain't gonna want no trouble from the QC either." Foster hated himself for admitting it, but Huggins was right.

"Besides," Huggins said, "I think we can make this real easy. I got a idea."

"Dis is vonderful," Svoboda whispered to Foster. "He don't know how to spell QC and now he writes a script."

* * * *

Ironman squinted at the piece of paper under the dim light that flickered across the alley. Like all alleys, the place was a catacomb made up of sheds, huts, and lean-tos, built along the walls, stacked one above the other as if they'd fallen randomly from above. Americans who wanted to desert or go AWOL went there to disappear themselves. Eyes peered out at them. People drifted across their path, appearing from nowhere, and disappearing the same way. The shadowy figures running across the rooftops reminded him of that chimney sweep dance number in *Mary Poppins*, which he'd seen about six years earlier. Ironman could barely decipher what he'd written when Thi Lanh told him where the baby was. They would have brought her along, but didn't want to move her. She'd described the child to them as best she could.

"This way," he said, and headed for a dubious wooden staircase that ran up the side of a weathered building, one of the more permanent structures. The banister and balcony railings were loose, and they walked softly, as if they thought they'd weigh less up on their toes.

Ironman went first, then Huggins. Foster wanted to leave him at the villa, but the plan was his idea, and it was brilliant. Besides, if things got sticky, they could well have need for his kind of unbridled reptilian perversity.

On the second floor, Ironman counted doors. He pushed open the fourth one.

"Who you!" the old woman demanded. "Who the huck you?"

"Nice talk," said Ironman. The woman was the twin of the one who worked at the Magic Fingers, anywhere from seventy to a hundred and six, bent, gnarled and twisted.

He and Huggins found themselves in a single big room with bare wooden floors, and the first thing they smelled was the horde of babies, every single one desperately in need of a new diaper. They were scattered on the floor, some of them crawling, some on their backs, some wrapped up in cloth and blankets. Only about nine of them were crying. Above the wailing and screaming, the old woman repeated her inquiry.

"Who the huck you? What you want?"

They tried to explain they'd come for Ki, the son of Thi Lanh.

"Okay fine. You give me five hundred sixty dollar. Green."

"No money," said Huggins.

"No money, no baby." She yelled it more than once, practically jumping up and down, her white hair flying out to the sides as she trembled.

"C'mere," said Huggins, dragging her by the arm over to the dingy window that looked down on the street. "Look."

The woman was cut off in mid-shriek. In front of the building the street was overrun by police. Dozens of White Mice, more dozens of QC, even more MPs, Jeeps, vans, paddy wagons, the works. Huggins' most truly inspired idea was to have Foster shoot scenes for the Vietnamese National Police sequel that night. They scheduled about fifty or sixty police to be in the film, and on the way to the shoot asked them to wait in the street while they made a quick stop "to scout a new location."

The poor woman's jaw opened, then it closed. She made small wheezing sounds in her chest.

"See that girl?" Huggins said, pointing to Young Dung, who sat glumly, with her arms folded and head down, in the back of a Jeep they'd positioned directly under the window. They'd brought her along for effect. D'Amato's idea.

"She sells babies. Got caught. Now they take her to jail. Cong Song island. Tiger cage. Ten years. You want to go?"

She didn't. After some more shouting back and forth, she picked a small wailing bundle off the floor and almost threw it at him.

"Huck you!"

"Let's go," Foster said. He had elbowed his way into the room through a crowd of dour-faced onlookers who had crowded into the doorway, and they were getting edgy. He had cleared a path for Huggins.

"*An maia u lon!*" the woman yelled at them. "*An maia u lon!*"

They rushed down the stairs, not being delicate this time, and ducked under the balcony. The woman's voice echoed off the surrounding buildings.

"You hucking numba ten GI! You forget something!"

Ironman looked up and yelled "Incoming!" just as the old bent woman, in a show of uncommon strength driven purely by rage and fury, held a baby's crib above her head and threw it over the railing. It crashed into the courtyard and splintered in the dirt at their feet. They kept running.

"*An maia u lon!*"

Svoboda was waiting in the Jeep up the block. They stood there for a second, catching their breath, chattering with excitement, Foster clutching the squirming bundle. He turned to Yak Dung, cowering in the back seat.

"What was that old woman yelling at me?"

"I...I...don't know how you say. Eat blood of..." She pointed to her crotch.

Meanwhile, Weinberg tried to explain to the bewildered and concerned QC captain that they were borrowing the baby from its mother because they needed him for a scene in the child care film they were going to start shooting the next day.

"This is him?" Svoboda asked. Foster held him out. Round face, huge eyes, pursed lips, cute and drooling and ominously fragrant. "How you know she gives you the right one?" They all stopped talking at once. Foster, stricken, pulled the blankets apart.

"Well, at least he's a boy." On the way back, he decided that if Thi Lanh told him it wasn't her baby, she'd have to go back and get him herself. But it was, and she cried over him for an hour. They gave her five painkillers to make her stop.

CHAPTER 29
THE SHADOW COMPOUND

Saturday, June 13, 1970

So far, so good. Webb liked the Shadows fine. Not only because it was better than life on the rockpile at the most famous Federal institution in Kansas, but also because he didn't have all that much to do. The war was very different for those who lived in Saigon, and the first two weeks had been a delight. He'd hung around the villa and their totally private hooch on the base, they'd had some jolly sport with the petrified DASPO guys on the mountaintop a few days before, he'd flown along on a few totally non-dangerous missions -- though his voice never stopped telling him the next monumental Rat Fuck could be just around the corner -- and was blissfully free of that intestinal terror he'd experienced flying gun runs out of Tay Ninh. No cement in the stomach, none of that nervous twitching of those intimate, involuntary muscles down below, except for the occasional bouts of dysentery that the bowels of every American were heir to. Of course, there was none of that old adrenaline rush, either, no sense of real purpose or direction or accomplishment, but he didn't want to admit that to himself, and his voice had been strangely silent on the subject.

What could be bad? He was learning to fly Cobras, he lived in a villa, didn't have too many strangers shooting at him. Of course, Saigon was a steambath, but there was plenty of cold beer, the Magic Fingers right across the street, and he didn't have to wear a uniform. There was the small matter of those asshole film guys on the other side of the wall, but he could live with that.

Shit, said his little voice. *If you'd known things would turn out like this, you'd've committed high crimes and misdemeanors a lot sooner. This place is like one of those 1940's black and white matinee movies, you know, intrigue and adventure in exotic locales. Deception and double dealing, trickery and treachery, knavery and slavery.*

He was especially fascinated by the way people urinated in the streets. It was apparently a fairly common practice, but the men of Saigon -- and many of the women -- had elevated it into a kind of folk art. The day before, he'd seen a young man standing between two cars, one foot up on the bumper, reading a magazine, his unit hanging out of his shorts, draining the vein without a care in the world. It was the casual nonchalance of it all that charmed him the most.

                                    * * * *

The Shadows compound was tucked away in the very farthest corner of the sprawling airfield at Tan Son Nhut. In the seven years since the Americans moved in and took over, the base had become, quite literally, the busiest airport in the world, playing host to an endless river of screaming machines that appeared out of the sky around the clock, delivering all the necessities of war, hot off the American military-industrial assembly lines.

As a result, the Army Corps of Engineers, the Seabees and whoever else does military construction work had expanded and enlarged and augmented the place until it was, by any measure you'd care to use, a medium-sized city. Even the par 3 nine-hole golf course reserved for Vietnamese Air Force officers was enlarged to 18 holes. And at the very outskirts of that city, in the boondocks, on the other side of the tracks, next to the largest and busiest mortuary on the planet, squatted the Shadows compound.

One low gray building and a maintenance hangar. Three sets of high fence, small windows. On the apron, a line of Hueys and Cobras, even the Chinook that Longacre had promised. No markings anywhere, no sign outside proclaiming the clandestine name of the unit. When Webb first saw it, his little voice had piped right up. *If anybody thought about this*, it said, *the place stands out like an unmarked police car.* But then, there were plenty of buildings on the base trying too hard to be anonymous. Nobody knew what went on inside any of them. Nobody asked.

They had thrown him into it right away. No time for the formalities of check rides, area orientation, special training. The war wasn't going exactly the way President Nixon was leading everyone to believe, the Lam Son 719 operation and the events in the A Shau Valley were fresh and wet in memory, and things were feeling a bit desperate. His new colleagues did spare the time to teach him to fly the Cobra, about a week, running practice missions in the front seat while Longacre or Sanderson flew as aircraft commander, high up behind him. He hated that tiny armchair cyclic Cobra co-pilots had to fly with, the little shift-knob-looking thing that came up out of the armrest, instead of a real stick, nice and thick and solid and manly, like the one between your legs in a Huey. You flew those things with your whole arm. The tiny stick made you fly the screaming machine with your fingertips, as if keeping a helicopter in the air wasn't difficult enough.

Most of the Shadows went off on Colonel Xoan's mysterious little missions while Webb practiced gun runs in his Cobra. Fortunately, during those first weeks, they all came back. He'd met the seven pilots who lived in the villa the night of the sapper demonstration, and after his little tete-a-tete with Longacre at the Continental, they promptly initiated him into the joys of Saigon night life, most particularly at a place called the Vietnamese National Air Force Officers' Club.

The Vietnamese actually did have an air force, once, when Nguyen Cao Ky was in charge, until he went off to become Premier for a while. Then he was booted out by President Thieu, who gave him the position of Air Marshall without a whole lot of aircraft to marshall. The South Vietnamese Air Force had nice uniforms, however, and most of the pilots, like Colonel Xoan, wore flashy white scarves around their necks. And they had the advantage of one effective intelligence weapon: the Saigon tea girls at the VNAF club. They knew more about what the Americans were thinking and doing than the Americans did.

But the tea girls didn't get much out of the sewage engineers from Maryland. Webb, Longacre, Larue and the rest bullshitted them unmercifully and at enormous length about flow rates, fecal consistency and other, more esoteric waste-related topics which they made up completely out of

their own alcohol-addled heads, until the girls got bored and
moved off to find somebody more interested in screwing than
in sewage, like Svoboda, or, as a very last resort, Colonel
Berner.

When the Shadows got moderately shitfaced at the VNAF
Club or on the verandah of the Hotel Continental, they talked
about the war, and what assholes the demonstrators were,
and the happenings at Kent State. They may not have all
believed in the war -- though Webb certainly did -- but they
were soldiers, they were in the military, and they were doing
their job. The only thing they didn't talk about was why each
of them was in the Shadows instead of languishing behind
high walls in the middle of Kansas making little ones out of
big ones. Webb was dying to know.

He took his orders from Major Sanderson. Col. Xoan, their
Vietnamese commander, or advisor, or whatever you wanted
to call him, was still a mystery. He was more of a shadow
than they were.

CHAPTER 30
THE SHADOWS VILLA

Sunday, June 14, 1970

Larue absolutely could not believe his senses. Sitting, quiet and composed, in the salon of the villa was Quai Ng, the sapper from the racetrack, dressed in a clean white open collared shirt, a pair of beige slacks and sandals, a small canvas bag resting on the floor beside him.

It seemed like yesterday that they'd seen his chilling little demonstration at the stadium, and they jammed up in the doorway to get a closer look.

"The fuck is this?" asked Longacre, of nobody in particular. Webb elbowed his way into the group, looked at the man more closely. Seeing a Vietnamese in the villa was like walking into church for midnight Mass on Christmas Eve and finding a rabbi up on the altar.

"The fuck are you?" Longacre wanted to know.

Carefully, Ng folded the Playmate of the Month back into the copy of *Playboy* he'd been skimming through, and stood up. He was a bit taller than most Vietnamese, with a broader face. His eyes were wide apart and fairly large, giving him an air of curiosity, or wonder.   Straight black hair, combed directly back from his high forehead.   He looked almost professorial.

"I am Quai Ng." Webb goggled at him. This was too much. For a month, his own existence had been like one of those good-thing-bad-thing jokes.   He'd been charged with war crimes (bad), shipped to a nonexistent helicopter unit (maybe good), found himself living in improbable luxury (very good...he even liked the music that was pouring over the walls at that moment from the DASPO villa next door), was under the command of a mysteriously remote Vietnamese colonel whom he'd still not met (bad), learned to fly not only gunships but Cobra gunships (good), posed as a sewer engineer from Maryland (not that bad), and now there was a "former" enemy sapper sitting in his living room (possibly very bad). He suddenly recalled another book his mother insisted that he read: *Alice in Wonderland*. *Curiouser and curioser,* his voice remarked.

Quai Ng spoke English with a very proper British accent, the merest trace of Vietnamese in his inflection. Had the Shadows been more linguistically sophisticated, they'd have detected just a touch of his French schooling as well. "Perhaps you have seen demonstration at the racetrack?"

"What demonstration?" Longacre asked. "We're sanitation systems engineers. You know what that is?"

"You're in the wrong place, boy," said Larue. Ng's equanimity was undisturbed.

"I was ordered to come here. I am to see Major Sanderson."

"Why don't we just shoot him now?" asked Longacre.

"In a minute," said Webb.

"I'm Sanderson." He lumbered down the stairs, pushed his bulk through the doorway where Webb and the rest were gathered, gaping at Ng as though he were a huge cockroach, dripping with mucus. "And I don't know a goddam thing about this."

Quai Ng offered him a handful of papers.

"What the hell's this?" Sanderson accepted the documents with his fingertips, turning them this way and that as though they were written in Albanian on rotten banana peels.

"This is all in Vietnamese," he said. "So I don't know what the fuck it says, and I don't know who you are. You damn well better know something about solid waste treatment. Besides, we don't need no sappers in this platoon. So what are you doing here? And how do you know about us?"

"I am sorry to say it is a mystery to me, as well. Where are my quarters?"

Everybody in the room had the same thought at the same time. Their lives were full of thrills already. A former -- or supposedly former -- VC sapper bunking at the villa was one they didn't need.

"I don't want this motherfucker staying here," muttered Longacre. Then he glanced at Ng, who looked him in the eye, a reaction none of them expected from a Vietnamese.

"Perhaps you do not understand. These are my orders. I have promised loyalty to the Republic of South Vietnam and risk my life as well as the lives of my family in the north for doing so. Please, where are my quarters?"

"Z-man, see if you can get Col. Xoan on the horn," said Sanderson. "Sit down over here, Houdini. I got a few questions for you."

Ng smiled. "Houdini. Yes." It was clear he recognized the reference.

It didn't take the Shadows long to put together a kangaroo court, the sort of tribunal you'd experience if you got stopped for speeding at 3AM in some Bull of the Woods back country hamlet where everybody had married their cousins and there weren't enough teeth to go around. But they were only trying to protect themselves against an enemy troop whose surreptitiously lethal skills had been demonstrated in the most convincing terms. All they knew was they had this little neatly pressed bronze-faced man, a stack of papers they couldn't read, and a painfully acquired though discouraging lack of sympathy for the Vietnamese people in general no matter which side of the DMZ they hailed from. Some of the antipathy came from personal experience, some was handed down by those who'd gone before, a lot of it was just plain xenophobia. It had been a very long war, and many of them were a bit fed up with Far Eastern culture in general, and things Vietnamese in particular. Unfortunately, the only Vietnamese the Americans had contact with were either enemy troops who were trying to kill them or criminal civilians who were trying to scam them or sell them drugs. They never met the decent ones.

They grilled and roasted Quai Ng for hours, and got even more severe when Z-man came in with the word that he'd found Col. Xoan on the verandah of the Continental Hotel. It was true. Xoan had pulled some very long strings and gotten Quai Ng assigned to the Shadows. He'd mentioned something about using the sapper to scout villages outside of Saigon, look for suspicious traffic, caravans, or other types of activity, strange square packages covered with cloth lying around on the ground, that sort of thing. He was supposed to be some kind of one-man advance intelligence unit.

Quai Ng was 34 years old, though nobody in the room

could really tell, and in phenomenal condition. Even if they hadn't seen him half naked in the stadium it was obvious that he could probably do one-armed pushups on his fingertips all day long if he had to.

Webb just had to find out how he did it.

"Pigs," replied Houdini.

"Pigs? What do you mean, pigs?"

"When I leave my position at the university...."

University? Webb had never made it to any university. Was it possible that this...*gook*...had more education, possibly more privilege, than he did?

"When I leave the University in Hanoi," Houdini continued, "I go back to my family's pig farm to the north. There, I teach my body to lift the animals and carry them. First I start with very young pig, carry him around for hours. He grow every day, get big and fat. I carry him every day, so I get strong. I know I will need to be strong."

Apparently, raising pigs was a profitable endeavor, at least on the scale that Ng's family had practiced it. He'd been to school in Cambridge ("I very much love the Shakespeare," he had said) and Paris, receiving his degree in electrical engineering from the Institute Polytechnique. He told them all this in a quiet voice with an excellent accent and passable grammar, no caricature South Vietnamese here, no gook talk, and as they listened they stared at him like he was some kind of completely new life form, which, to them, he was. Mouths opened, jaws dropped, at least figuratively. Neither Webb nor Larue nor Z-Man nor any of the Shadows had ever met a Vietnamese like him. He caused them to shift uncomfortably in their prejudices and on their chairs, sitting first on one cheek, then on the other.

Even though they didn't exactly realize it consciously, Quai Ng was causing all their preconceptions to squirm around in their heads, old ideas sliding liquidly on each other like intestines in the process of digestion, rearranged by the insidious magical stirrings of Houdini's long spoon. Unwillingly, they were finding how much of what they knew was wrong, or at least not a hundred per cent right, and they didn't want to admit it.

He spoke in a quiet voice, looking down at the table most of the time, but unafraid to look directly at any of them, even

Longacre, who sat there radiating hatred in waves you could almost see, like the shimmering heat that rises from a black tar road in summer.

Quai Ng told them all of it, how he'd been positive the Viet Cong would bring the joys of Communistic society and the people's state to the south of his divided land. But he got a lot less positive after the Americans began plodding in. The round-eyes, carrying their hundreds of thousands of tons of war toys, their airplanes and helicopters, their B-52s and aircraft carriers, their toilet paper, Polaroid One Step, and Johnny Walker Black, were an obviously irresistible force. His reasoning was characteristic of his people. The only way to win was to apply a different kind of force, indirectly, which the full-speed-ahead Americans would probably not understand. "An ancient principle," he said, almost smiling, "to turn the power of your enemy back upon himself."

He read the English newspapers, and the French ones. The course of the conflict became clearer to him than to most. His decision was made almost without him knowing it. He had to help in the fight as best he could.

There in the narrow room, around the long table with its stained and scored top, bathed in unkind light, Ng gradually told them the whole story, a war story from the other side, one they'd never heard before. It took hours. Soon, they stopped asking hostile questions. Then they stopped asking questions altogether, and just listened. He was talking in terms they could understand -- all except Longacre -- because each of them had made the same decision for similar reasons, and they couldn't explain why they'd done it any better than he could. Like him, they just knew they had to help.

"When I joined the fight, I knew two things. I wanted to help, and I wanted to stay living."

"Now, there's a sound policy," put in Larson. Webb elbowed him in the ribs.

"To stay living in a war, you must have the best special training. Sappers stay alive, unless they have a suicide mission. They are very effective, and they are very hard to kill. I think I am doing something worthy and glorious, but the ugliness, the torture, the..."

"Brutality?" asked Webb. He saw O'Connell, huddled and bloody in his tiger cage.

"Brutality is a good word. War is brutality, no? But my people -- it is unfortunate -- are accustomed to it. We have been fighting for...a very long time." His voice sounded like it. He gazed blankly around the table. "They steal children to carry drugs so they can have money to buy weapons. They put heads on sticks in the village. You kill a man, you kill him. To cut off his penis and put it in his mouth? This offends me."

"'Specially if it's your penis," observed Longacre. He was far from convinced.

"Then there is the drugs," said Quai Ng with a hint of regret, "and the corruption. Your people want this country to be democratic, but we do not understand the word the same as you. Voting? You think the peasants believe they may vote and choose who next will steal their land and their money and their sons? Here, everything is done by relationships. Family. Brothers and sisters, cousins, in business together. There are black market people, drug lords, like Wo Minh, who we are fighting. But those who fight him are family to him. Nobody knows. Even those Vietnamese who work for you have brothers and cousins who fight you."

"Even you?" asked Longacre.

"I have been away from my family so long," said Quai Ng, "I do not know who to fight. Besides, I see NVA and VC do more cruel things every day. "And every day I say, if we do these things now, what will we do when we win? How you fight for power is how you use it when you get it. Is it really possible to fight for good by doing evil things?"

"So you came over because you think the South Vietnamese are such good people?" asked Webb. The sarcasm was hard to miss. He wasn't as stubborn as Longacre, but Quai Ng would have to walk the walk for a long time before Webb got convinced.

"I do not come because South Vietnamese are so good. But I think perhaps they are a bit less bad. In this country, these are the choices."

CHAPTER 31
MEET LT. FOSTER

Monday, June 15, 1970

Webb's good-news-bad-news saga continued. He got word that O'Connell was out of danger -- finally, after a whole month -- and there was a reasonable chance he'd walk again. "But he'll never win another mambo marathon," the sergeant told him. It was an event worthy of celebration, but his joy, intense as it was, had its limits. As he started flying missions planned and directed from afar by the invisible Colonel Xoan, his voice made soft breathy noises in his ear, pointing out the ethical contradictions of the war, and the emotional dimensions, all of it triggered by Quai Ng's impromptu seminar. The voice had become more insistent of late, and he would not have been surprised if it had started speaking to him in Hebrew.

Before the Cheu Hoy appeared, Webb had begun to feel pretty good about things, sitting on the veranda of the Continental, or in the bar at the Caravelle with his beer and peanuts, looking out for Colonel Xoan but never spotting him, reflecting on how lucky he was. Then, over one of those cold green Heinekens, he was told how Longacre had to gun down some Caucasian in cold blood. After that there were a few missions to obliterate sorry little villages that didn't look like they needed obliterating, and that made the voice whisper not louder, but more intensely, talking through its teeth, still, thankfully, in English. He was flying gunships, true, but there was no heat of battle, no mission objective to accomplish, there was none of the typical justification ("Well, the bastards were shooting at ME!"), or rationalization for what gunship pilots did to earn a living. There were brown faces looking up at them from the village as the ominous shape of his Cobra rose up over the treeline. There was

Longacre's sorry little line of people on a paddy dike, smiling and waving, hoping they'd live to see another day. They didn't.

For the life of him he couldn't figure out how the Shadows had anything to do with the relatively noble goal of stemming the flood of heroin into the country. It was hard to find drug addicts among helicopter pilots, because flying stoned demanded a type of profound insanity that not even they were capable of, but he was as aware as anyone about what was happening around him, especially since he was living in Saigon. He'd had the same experience as others on the streets of the city, incessantly approached by people selling a complete selection of stimulants and depressants. But something tugged at the sleeve of his soul. He'd never seen a drug caravan, or found any hoard of narcotics piled in a hooch, or seen anybody who remotely looked like a drug smuggler. He might not have known what one looked like, but still...

So with decidedly mixed emotions he sat next to Longacre at the bar, eyelids at half-mast, a beer in one hand and a shot of Johnny Walker Black in the other. With increasingly blurred vision, Webb saw O'Connell in the cage. Longacre, in similar condition, was looking at Juan Wayne sprawled in the mud, that ridiculous little hat floating on the brown water. God knows what Larue saw when the numbness set in, or Harrell. But he was positive they saw something. He ordered another shot.

In spite of Webb's depressing visions, the Shadows, like all troops in Saigon, thought just about any event was worthy of a celebration on Tu Do Street. Coming home alive from a mission, getting through the night without a mortar falling on you, the sun going down, or coming up, for that matter, there were a million reasons to rejoice.

Webb's favorite place -- and everybody else's -- was the Number One club, because they had the best band in town, a rock and roll combo of six Vietnamese brothers and sisters who called themselves the Blue Jets. Unfortunately, the siblings could play only one set of American songs: the soundtrack from "Hair." Their father had bought them the album, and they'd learned all the lyrics phonetically, with dubious results. They played and sang the whole show every single night to a club jammed with foreigners who were so drunk they didn't care what the words sounded like, and didn't even care that "Hair" was a goddam hippie musical, full of longhaired peaceniks and disgusting frontal nudity.   In fact, the people who enjoyed the act most of all were the NVA operatives and Viet Cong officers who dressed in civilian clothes and packed the place to amuse themselves at the decadence of the Americans.

The American military command was thankful that the Vietnamese civil government didn't have fire marshals, because the Number One was ridiculously crowded all the time.   It didn't take long for them to realize how simple it would be for a VC sapper to walk into the place with a satchel charge and blow himself up, taking half the high ranking officers in the city with him.   It never occurred to them that the VC would never do such a thing because the place was much too full of their own officers.   But when Saigon's most famous restaurant was blown off its barge in the river for the third time, some influential senior Americans posted MPs to guard the place.   The troops fought over the duty, because the ones stationed at the front door were allowed to frisk the hookers.

Webb and Longacre, accompanied by Larue, left the bar and tried to make their way across the dance floor, packed with Americans and their Vietnamese "girlfriends" for the night.   They were approaching what Larue called the fifth stage of drunkenness.

"The first stage of inebriation," Larue had explained to Webb earlier, over their first shot, "is you get intelligent.   Start talking sports, statistics, and you're right about everything.   There ain't nothing you don't know.   Second stage, you get beautiful.   You look around the bar, realize you're surrounded by a bunch of ugly fuckers, and you're the best looking sumbitch in the room.   Third stage is wealthy.   Start buying drinks for people you don't even know.   Forth, you get talented.   You discover you sing better than Elvis, and louder, too.   Fifth stage, you get invisible.   Start dancing on the tables, thinking nobody can see you."

Webb had already decided how ugly everybody was, except for the exotic Vietnamese women who periodically rubbed their breasts against his back as they brushed by, convinced

Longacre that Bobby Orr was the best hockey player who ever lived, ("bastard scored 37 goals and 102 assists with the Bruins this season…"), bought at least one round, and sung "Lucy in the Sky With Diamonds" three times. He had no urge to dance on the tables, but every desire to disappear. The Blue Jets were singing "Hair" for the hundred and twenty-first time.

"Dis is a drowning of the haze of a curious…." The kids sang with more spirit than harmony, and yet more harmony than talent, but were still considered the best band in Saigon at the time. Webb had seen "Hair" with his mother on Broadway, and the tune, if not the lyrics, brought back memories. Longacre wasn't listening. He was muttering into his beer about the assholes from the villa next door, who were grouped around a distinguished looking Vietnamese man about fifty years old in a corner next to the stage.

Corporal D'Amato, watched closely by Foster and Weinberg, was hard at work. The Blue Jets was the only group that Former Sergeant First Class Harris hadn't been able to put under contract. Partly because their father, Mr. Mu, was smart enough to know that Ed Sullivan had been off the air for years, and partly because, pronunciation aside, the kids were so popular they could have their pick of bookings at any club in Southeast Asia.

"You ever seen 'Hair'?" D'Amato shouted at Mr. Mu. He admitted he'd never been near Broadway.

"These kids could be huge," D'Amato insisted, and Mr. Mu agreed.

"Big like Beatles," he observed.

"Bigger than Beatles, but they're doing this all wrong." The two men had had this conversation many times before, due to a bet that D'Amato had made with Former Sergeant First Class Harris.

When D'Amato arrived in Saigon his acquisitive senses immediately started to percolate. Like many others, he became increasingly alive to the abundant revenue streams and profit centers a wartime environment offered to those who had the talent of combining enterprise with deviousness. Former Sergeant First Class Harris was his idol.

D'Amato wound up in DASPO because he'd stolen a camera when he was sixteen. He didn't particularly want a camera, but it was there. Then he stole some black and white film and went around Brooklyn taking pictures of everything, any face he could find, closeups of brick walls, shots of garbage in the street, kids playing stickball, the library, whatever. His mother found an envelope of prints in his drawer and sent one in to a photo contest from the local paper. A shot of an old woman sitting on the front porch with her young grandson. His mother didn't know that her son had snatched that same woman's purse two years earlier. He remembered that she had an interesting face, found her address in her wallet, stalked her, and went over to take her picture.

First prize. Everybody became unexpectedly ecstatic, praising the photo's sensitivity, perfection of artistic vision, the subtleties of light and shade. "Hey," said D'Amato to the newspaper editor when he accepted the award, "all I did was point the fucking camera and push the goddam button. What's the big deal?"

They gave him a $500 savings bond anyway, which he promptly browbeat his mother into cashing so he could buy a new camera and some basic darkroom equipment. When the money was gone, he broke into a photography store a few blocks away and replenished his supply of chemicals. He had no idea why everybody made such a fuss over his pictures, because what he was doing was so easy for him, but he knew a ticket out of Brooklyn when he saw it. He stole a bunch of photography books (it never occurred to him to check them out of the library) and by the time his draft notice caught him sleeping on his mother's sofa, he was good enough to strut into the Selective Service office and get himself assigned to the Army Photographic School at Ft. Monmouth, New Jersey. To D'Amato, the blood and broken bodies, the missing limbs of combat, the napalm victims in Cong Wah Hospital were fringe benefits that he never expected but thoroughly appreciated.

D'Amato thought that "Hair" was the greatest musical of all time, especially the second act when everybody took off their clothes. He'd bet Former Sergeant First Class Harris that he could convince the entire band to get naked, and had been working on Mr. Mu for a month. This night was the deadline.

"You don't understand," D'Amato shouted over the band's heartfelt rendition of "Late The Sound Shine Ing." "In the play

they take their clothes off. That's what makes it so special."
Mr. Mu had heard this from D'Amato every night, but still
wasn't convinced. Former Sergeant First Class Harris was
close by, already counting the money D'Amato would owe
him.

"Look, every band has a gimmick. The Beatles have long
hair, they have Ringo, an Indian guru. Jimi Hendrix sets his
guitars on fire. All your kids do is sing. If they take their
clothes off, they're famous overnight. We need to set them
apart from other Vietnamese rock and roll bands."

"There are no other Vietnamese rock 'n roll bands," Mr. Mu
replied. But as the drinks kept arriving and as the night wore
on, the father finally agreed. "But only the boys," he insisted.

Not good enough. D'Amato counted out a bunch of
twenties into the Former Sergeant First Class's steak-sized
hand, and had himself another glass of creme de menthe.

* * * *

It was just before curfew when Webb and Longacre rounded
the corner of Troung Minh Ky, on the way back from the
Number One Club, the VNAF Officers' Club and several other
despicable bars along Tu Do Street, leaning against each
other for mutually alcoholic support, serenading the
neighborhood with a fullthroated rendition of the ditty of the
day:

> *A marvelous thing is the penis,*
> *Filled with blood both arterial and venous.*
> *Its turgid condition*
> *Assures intromission*
> *And the transfer of fluids between us.*

The lights on the high walls of the villas flooded the street.
Anyplace Americans lived in Saigon was always as well-lit as
they could make it. About halfway down the street, at the far
corner, a gaggle of Vietnamese boys hunched over something
on the sidewalk. A high-pitched whirr of conversation swirled
through the air.

"The fuck's those gooks up to?" Longacre mumbled.

Webb had become accustomed to seeing young children on
the streets at obscene hours, so he barely looked up from the
cracked pavement, where he was placing one foot meticulously
in front of the other.

"Who gives a shit? Are we home yet, daddy?"

The streets of Saigon were full of "cowboys," Vietnamese boys in their early teens who were quick to grasp the opportunity the conditions offered them to make a quick buck. They all had ciclos or Hondas, and one of their favorite pastimes was to ride up behind an American walking on the street, knock him down, and rob him. Webb was watching them apply this technique to a form slumped on the sidewalk.

"Jesus, I think they're rolling somebody. Come on." Longacre seemed to sober up instantly and started to run, leaving Webb with no visible means of support, so he collapsed sideways into some low prickly bushes along the wall. It took him about thirty seconds to haul himself to his feet and make his way over to Longacre. The gang of boys had scattered.

"Hey, pal, are you okay?" Longacre kneeled over the form of an American in civilian clothes, curled up in kind of a fetal position on the sidewalk. He gently rolled the man over.

"That tickles," he mumbled. Then he opened his mouth, threw his head back and eructated a huge, fetid, palpably miasmic cloud of what could have been beer, pickled eggs and fish sauce. Surprised and overwhelmed, Longacre fell backward and landed painfully on a broken piece of pavement. Webb reached down to pick him up, lost his already tenuous hold on his balance, and wound up sitting next to him, both men goggling at the supine form. They were the only three people on the street. In the distance, the ciclos made their perpetual high-pitched buzzing racket.

"Fuck," said Longacre, looking more closely. "He's one of those assholes from DASPO next door." He pushed himself to his feet and started walking away. "Come on."

"What, are you just gon' leave this silly sumbitch lying on the sidewalk?"

"Bet your ass," Longacre spat. "They're all dickheads."

"Wait a second. I think I know this guy."

"Great. Then you can take care of him." Longacre turned his back to Webb and weaved off down the street, supporting himself with one hand against the once-white villa wall, plodding toward the black iron gates. Webb squinted at the form lying in front of him. He started seeing two of them, maybe two and a half. He tried to focus, and to remember that when they'd sat through the mortar attack at Tan Son Nhut, he'd been a Warrant Officer on the way to Tay Ninh. Now he was supposed to be a skilled sanitation engineer. Fortunately, Foster was too pickled to recognize him.

"I'm Princess Grace of Monaco," he mumbled. "And you?"

"I'm Eleanor Roosevelt," Webb said. "Shit." He fumbled around inside the man's shirt and pulled out his dog tags. Foster Leonard M. 207395018. Jewish. B Pos.

"What's the 'M' stand for?" Webb asked. For some reason, he needed to know.

"Moses. Heard of him? Something of a folk hero to my people."

"Rings a bell. Listen, we gotta get you home. Can you get up?"

"Can I get it up? Not after what Li did to me over at the steam and cream tonight. I got a rosy red reproducer. Come back tomorrow, okay?" He belched again, deeply, wholeheartedly, the upheaval issuing from somewhere in the very basement of his being. Fish sauce, for sure. Perhaps a Hershey bar and a few tequila shooters. Webb couldn't be sure.

"Longacre was right. You *are* an asshole. But if I leave you here those kids'll take you apart and sell the pieces. Come on."

It was a struggle, but Webb managed to haul the eructating Foster to his feet and maneuver him down the block the way he'd once moved a refrigerator when he had to do it himself. It was the alcoholically poisoned version of the blind leading the blind.

An EM unlocked the gate of the villa and pulled the chains off the bars with a harsh rattle. The two men staggered through into unkind light and the incredible noise of Hilda the generator. Webb struggled his burden up the steps to the front door just as Jack and Little Shit came yelping and drooling into the yard.

"Ooooh, Lieutenan' Foster! Hello, sir! You late night." Yak Dung greeted them with the happiest of grins, his teeth looking like Chiclets coated with rotten seaweed. They gleamed from the light above the door.

"Uh, Lieutenant Foster isn't feeling well. Where can I put him to bed?"

"Oh, no worry, sir," grinned Yak Dung. "Lieutenan' Foster sick like this alla time. We take care. You no worry."

"You gonna be all right?" Webb asked.

"Roger that," said Foster, slurring a bit. "This is my faithful retainer, Yak Dung. Serves my every need. Been with the family for generations. Well paid and loyal. I guess I should thank you for helping me out."

"I guess you should."

"Okay. Thank you for helping me out. Fuckers got my wallet. Must've had two thousand piasters."

"Lucky they didn't cut your balls off. Night." Webb retreated through the door, closing it behind him. From outside, the sudden howl of Jack and Little Shit split the night as they once again tried to close in for the kill. The gate clanged.

"Hey," Foster said to Yak Dung as the tiny man and his outsized wife heaved him up the stairs, "Who was that masked man?"

"I no understand," said Yak Dung.

"I mean, the fucker didn't even tell me his name."

"Fucker have name Samuel Taylor Webb," the tiny man wheezed, struggling under his burden. "Live villa next door."

Foster was too drunk to ask him how he knew.

CHAPTER 32
FIRST SERGEANT GOODHARDT

Thursday, June 18, 1970

About two weeks before the MPs dragged Huggins out of the villa screaming into the night, First Sergeant Goodhardt arrived in Saigon, in a preoccupied frame of mind.

The First Sergeant had been in the Army for over 23 years and for the last five of them he'd had *de facto* responsibility for a gaggle of frustrated Fellinis and harebrained Hitchcocks, had seen them come and go, all of them convinced that someday they'd be up on a stage in Hollywood walking the red carpet and thanking the Academy. So he was depressingly accustomed to having his intestines devoured by chronic misgiving practically around the clock. By the middle of June, however, he was worried enough to hop a MAC-V flight out from Hawaii. Squeezed into his seat for the long ride, he'd reviewed all the reasons why he should get to Saigon at once. He hadn't been there for a while, and his office at DASPO's Pacific headquarters was getting smaller every day. He'd heard rumors that the unit's unorthodox and unmilitary lifestyle was starting to take its toll, and was especially concerned after he'd seen the footage they'd shot at the mortuary. He obsessed about Foster, who he pictured as some kind of lost soul, because they'd sent him over without even a nebulous idea of what he was supposed to do. Foster had originally been assigned to the Army Pictorial Center in New York, which he loved, because the Center was in the old Astoria studios, where Frank Capra had worked, along with other directors he worshiped, where a casting director had once told Paul Newman he'd never make it as an actor. But the Army closed the studio down, and Foster had traveled all the way to Washington to personally wangle himself an assignment to DASPO in Hawaii. Lastly, Goodhardt had been keeping up to date on the escalating problem of drugs in the military, and was convinced that if anybody in Vietnam was getting stoned, it was certainly the DASPO crew (they were), and since they'd just submitted a proposal for a sequel to the mortuary cosmetology film entitled "Dance of the Body Bags," he was afraid they were all becoming addicted (they weren't).

Those, he'd convinced himself, were his official reasons for the trip. Unofficially, however, like nearly every career military man on active duty, he was about to follow a moderately devious though completely legal course of action that was not only common during wartime, but virtually expected. While in country, he would re-enlist for his last tour of duty. The Army would give him a $10,000 bonus, as it had when he'd done the same thing in Korea, made even more substantial because it was taking place in a combat zone and the IRS waived taxes under combat conditions. And during his trip, he'd make every effort to clock six hours of flight time, which would make him eligible for a month of flight bonus pay. And since all of this was going to take place in wartime conditions, he would also receive a bonus of one month's combat pay. He was a patriot, a warrior who had devoted his entire life to serving his country. He deserved it.

But Goodhardt had plenty of real worries. Usually, each DASPO team was commanded by a Captain or an experienced First Lieutenant. The detachments in Bangkok and Seoul had only one team, but Saigon had enough action to warrant two. They were short on the position of "officer/filmmaker" because nobody expected Garcia to become gator bait, and certainly hadn't expected the flood of shooting assignments that had come through in the last month, partly because of Colonel Berner. So Foster, a lowly Second LT, found himself, strangely in a strange land, responsible for not one but two teams of petty thieves, frustrated artists, lifelong misfits, alleged communists, part-time ichthyologists, truly talented filmmakers, and virulent xenophobes. To beset him further, the unit was being swamped with ever more pitiable requests from Colonel Berner, whose job, and desire for personal advancement, were becoming progressively more desperate as the war threatened to wind down. He was frantic with the worry that it would all be over too soon and the Army would make him take a real job.

So Goodhardt took it upon himself to fly over, get Berner in line, pick up a signing bonus, and take Foster under his wing. At least that's what he'd told his superiors.

"Really, Top," Foster had told him on the phone -- Goodhardt liked to be called Top, so everybody did it because it was better to keep him happy -- "there's nothing to worry about. I've got it all pretty well under control." Watching Goodhardt get off the plane, Foster actually did feel like he was in control of just about everything except his intestines, because his immunity to chronic flatulence and insistent diarrhea had long since deserted him, and the bright orange malaria pills they were all required to take were intensifying the effect. Except for Huggins, who refused to take them because he thought the pills were a government conspiracy to keep the soldiers drugged, impotent, and compliant.

"Lieutenant," said Goodhardt after the salute and handshake, "lemme tell ya why I'm here. First, I think me and Harris can help improve your air conditioner situation. And second, I may be able to get Colonel Berner off your back." He didn't say a word about checking around for drugs, or the re-enlistment bonus. "Could I ask you to drive by the paymaster's office?"

Ah, so now it's official, Foster thought as he put the DASPO Jeep into gear and steered it onto Cong Ly toward the entrance to the Military Assistance Command office.

Foster dropped him off. When Goodhardt made his way back to the villa later that day, he clutched in a hairy fist his re-enlistment bonus, a roll of cash big enough to clog a Clydesdale. For some reason Foster was never able to discover, old sergeants always took their bonuses in cash. Tradition?

The next thing Goodhardt did, after walking down every hallway in the villa expecting to detect the smell of smoldering loco weed (he didn't, because the troops had been warned, and they usually smoked on the roof, anyway) was to verify Foster's preparations for DASPO's much-needed next bacchanale. If there hadn't been a debauch in the offing, Goodhardt would have manufactured one. However, Foster's depression and horror over the time they spent in the mortuary had already prompted him to begin planning a feast day. It was scheduled for two nights hence.

"You been here a couple months," Goodhardt said in a voice like a grinding wheel, looking up at Foster through a jungle of eyebrows. "You should know just about everybody by now. Who did you invite?"

"Well, there are the darkroom guys from the 7th Air Force photo lab, they bail my ass out all the time, there's the sergeant from supply who got us the golf balls and Day-Glo paint we needed for that venereal disease film, remember 'Genital Warts and You?' And some guys from next door who saved me from a Vietnamese ass kicking."

"Guys from next door? What unit?"

"Well...they're not actually with any *unit*..."

"*Civilians?*" He said it the way you'd say "toddler-molesting slime drenched spawn of Satan."

"Well...yeah. Some guys who say they're going to build sewers when the war's over, or...."

Goodhardt gave him a frigid, piercing look from eyes that had suddenly become tunnels into the Pit. Foster didn't know what the look was for, but he found out in a hurry.

There are people who divide the world into two groups, and people who don't. Goodhardt was one of the former. He'd been in the Army so long that his field of focus had narrowed only to his fellow soldiers. Civilians (and commissioned officers, for that matter) were, to him, a separate species, or entirely different life-forms. The fact that civilians even lived on his planet was surely just an oversight on the part of the Supreme Commander. Even if there were absolutely nothing remotely military about the merry DASPO crew except on the rare occasions when they wore their uniforms, Army was still Army. Then, conceded Goodhardt, there were maybe the other branches of the service, and then, down at the bottom of the ocean with the whale shit, was everybody else.

So, on top of all the running around he'd have to do getting the air conditioners fixed in time for the party, he needed to scare up some *real* soldiers in response to, and as an antidote for, the presence of godless non-military personnel on the sacred ground of the DASPO villa.

But first, the air conditioners. Goodhardt had almost broken Ironman's back with the huge cartons he'd brought over from Hawaii. Sixteen cases of Polaroid film.

When he cleared customs, the Military Police made him

open all the cartons, because the drug and black market situation had become so lunatic. Not long before, there was that 7th Air Force colonel who had been arrested for smuggling heroin to the states inside hollowed-out plaster elephants. But Goodhardt's shipment didn't attract that much attention. It was film, it was going to a photographic unit, and besides, Goodhardt had a hand receipt directing him to deliver it to DASPO. The MPs didn't know that DASPO never used Polaroid film, except to shoot location stills, or capture unusual sexual performances. Svoboda went through tons of it, taking pictures of his naked Vietnamese girlfriends. But for some reason the demand for that particular commodity was high everywhere else in Vietnam, exceeded only by the ever-escalating value of Pepto Bismol. Supposedly, you could buy Polaroid film in the PX, but they never seemed to have any, and it was worth about four times the sticker price on the street. Goodhardt loaded Huggins and all the film into a truck, gave Huggins an automatic weapon called a grease gun with a 30-round clip, and invited him along to stand guard, because Huggins' demeanor impressed him as soon as he walked into the villa. He was gung-ho, eager, very much On Our Side and best of all, he looked dangerously insane. When they came back six hours later, he presented Foster with six brand-new, one-ton Westinghouse wall units. Jesus, Foster thought. Why did they pick James Garner to play the scrounger in *The Great Escape*, when there's guys like Goodhardt around?

That night, as they sat on the roof recovering from installing all the units, Huggins tucked a plug into his cheek, wiped some thick brown spittle out of his mustache, and told them the story of his day. Svoboda had disappeared into the Magic Fingers, or the Nimble Touch, so Huggins was a bit less crazed than usual, but nobody noticed. He felt so good that he stepped into the role of host, passing out bottles of Heineken to everyone.

"First, he takes me to the commissary. There's a mess sergeant over there he did some deals with a few months ago. He gives him three cases of film, and we get twenty pounds of cream cheese, fifty bags of frozen bagels, and some of that shitty pink smoked fish the kikes eat...."

"Lox," Foster felt obliged to help him out.

"That's what they are. Locks. Then we go to the PX liquor annex, and he gives up three more cases for two cases of ten-year-old scotch."

"Bullshit," put in D'Amato. "There's no such thing as ten-year-old scotch in this country."

"Yeah, there is, but you'll never see any. The sergeant who runs the PX gets it from some Vietnamese guy who deals all the booze in the country and keeps it in back. Anyway, from there, he drives us to the motor pool, and trades five cases for an air conditioned Ford sedan and a signed blank authorization form...."

"Wait a second," Weinberg said. "Let me get this straight. By now, you got lox, bagels, cream cheese, scotch, and a car, right?"

"An *air-conditioned* car. And four cases of film left. Which he takes to the NCOIC at the 427th Maintenance Battalion. The guy's name is Shlomo Deutsch."

"That explains the lox and bagels," said Weinberg. Huggins didn't get it.

"This is where it gets really good. This guy Deutsch has air conditioners up the ass, and Goodhardt's ready to give up everything we got for them, because why not. But if he can get away for less, he'll do it. Goodhardt tells him we got them locks and bagels, plus a case of scotch, for ten air conditioners. The guy laughs at him and offers three. Goodhardt throws in the rest of the scotch and asks for five. Deutsch gives up one more. Goodhardt ups the ante, throws in three cases of film, and tells him about the sedan, which can be his for only three more units, but Deutsch laughs at that, too, because he knows he can't drive it without an authorization form. Goodhardt slaps the signed form on the desk, the guy just about falls over, and loads us up. Plus, we got one case of film left over for ourselves, which he's gonna trade with the hookers for the party."

Huggins, feeling important, offered the group another round. Foster took out a pad of paper and began to scribble a list of everything they'd need for their grand post-mortuary celebration.

CHAPTER 34
DAVE IS MY NAME

Friday, June 20

"The problem with going to sleep," Former Sgt. First Class Harris explained to Foster, "is that the second you do, you wake up in Vietnam again." Foster actually saw the logic of that, which is why he chose to escort Sgt. Goodhardt to the Number One Club after the latest production meeting instead of crawling into the questionable comfort of his cot. The top kick immediately disappeared into the sea of bar girls, and Foster found himself once again seated next to Call me Norman, the JAG attorney he'd met shortly after his arrival.

The place was packed. Unfortunately, the Blue Jets were off that night, but the walls rang with the sound of another band, composed of five middle-aged Vietnamese men who called themselves "The Boston Quartet." They were hacking their way through a new song by John Denver.

"Make me Joan, Can Tree Rose...."

"What the hell are they singing?"

"I'm guessing it's 'Take me home, country road,' but who the fuck knows," Call Me Norman said. "This is my new best friend." The man packed into the bar next to him could very well have been his twin cousin. Same big wet eyes, same glasses, same doughy physique. Foster estimated that he was in the "intelligent" phase of intoxication.

"Dave is my name," he said, struggling to extend his hand through the crush of people. "Ketchum, Idaho."

"He's with the JAG, too," Call Me Norman explained.

"What'd they do, bring in reinforcements?" asked Foster.

"Need 'em," said Dave Is My Name.

"What is it this time? More black-market Pepto Bismol?"

"It's still Walter Crawley," said Call Me Norman. "The more

we investigate the more we find out that he practically runs the fucking war."

"Doin' a shitty job," said Foster.

"Actually, he's doing a wonderful job...for Walter Crawley," said Dave Is My Name. "Got the most efficient logistical, procurement, and distribution system in the country. All his goods get where they're supposed to go when they're supposed to be there."

"Better than us," Foster observed.

"You make movies, you got a sense of story and dramatic structure, right?" asked Call Me Norman.

"I'm an 8511, so I suppose I do."

"Want to hear about regional warfare for fun and profit?"

"Do I have a choice?"

It didn't take a college degree to notice the corruption and wheeling and dealing that the war had produced. DASPO dealt in it by necessity, like Sgt. Goodhardt's recent shopping trip, or they'd never have finished any of their films, but that was small stuff. The real level of the industry was marked not by what you saw, but by what you didn't. You didn't see the PX shelves stocked with the abundance of the American consumer economy that came into the country every day at Cam Ranh Bay, Da Nang, and Bien Hoa. You didn't see all the traditional creature comforts of war that GIs yearned for, like Pepto Bismol to quell the intestinal rebellion caused by the malaria pills. You didn't see the huge displays of photo film at the BX, which was the one thing the troops wanted as much as that precious pink fluid. Foster wasn't the only one who appreciated the abundant photo opportunities of warfare. But it wasn't there.

And where were the radios, cassette recorders, cameras and stereos? Not on the shelves of the PX, but on little makeshift tables on the streets of Saigon, Nha Trang and a hundred other places.

You didn't see the liquor, either. By some logistical miracle, the Johnnie Walker Black and the Wild Turkey never made it to the shelves, but the Old Fartblossom did. How did all this stuff, asked Dave is My Name, get into the country through the military system and then out the back door?

"Walter Crawley," muttered Call Me Norman.

"Ever notice," asked his new best friend, "how the roofs of the huts around here are made of Coke cans?"

It was true. Most people who managed to piece together shelter or even build a house roofed them over with sheets of imprinted aluminum used for cutting and rolling into soda cans. There were red and white roofs made of Coke material, green and yellow 7-Up roofs, and even Budweiser roofs. The colors created a riot of artificial gaiety among the maze of huts and hovels.

USAID gave Walter Crawley a contract in 1967 to provide building materials that would help raise the standard of living of the people blessed enough to get any. He was, after all, the logical choice. Favored by the Colonels, bright, witty, probably the only person in the country who, because of the accidents of his upbringing, could perfectly bridge the two cultures.

They gave him $6 million, and never saw it again. He fulfilled the literal terms of the contract by finding 6,243 pounds of surplus aluminum can material with defective imprinting. The supplier was dying to get rid of it, and Walter drove the bargain with a sledgehammer.

"USAID was furious," said Dave is My Name, "but they couldn't touch him." Foster couldn't keep himself from asking why. It was his fifth beer.

"He has friends in high places," muttered Call Me Norman. "The pie is very large around here, and there are slices for everybody."

Then there was the whole boat thing. Over time, Crawley had made contacts with Navy chiefs who ran PBR boats on the Mekong. He was from the Midwest, and knew how to talk to them. Even troops who hated the Vietnamese couldn't help liking Walter Crawley. Gradually, materials that were supposed to flow upstream began flowing downstream, offloaded at obscure inlets along the river. Food, weapons, ammunition, other supplies. The sergeants got their cut to spend on R&R in Bangkok, Walter's Swiss bank account swelled comfortably, as did his "charitable trust" in the Cayman Islands, and the colonels were perfectly happy to let Walter run the underside of the Vietnamese economy, as long as they didn't have to do it themselves, and as long as their foundations and dummy corporations received the proper consulting fees.

Crawley had a knack for working his way to the top. He

didn't deal with individual BX managers, he found the *capo di tutti capi*, the man who ran the managers. They worked hard together to assure that very few bottles of really good scotch ever saw the shelf of a Base Exchange.

Foster was reluctantly impelled to question one more time. "Why don't you bust him?"

"He isn't breaking any laws," said Dave Is My Name. "And if he is, nobody cares about a bunch of liquor and cameras. It's only money. Besides, the military has other things to worry about."

"Hey!" Call Me Norman leaned over and peered into his face, gifting him with a breathy zephyr of cheap booze. The Number One Club floated on a sea of it. "You're in DASPO, right? Whyntcha make a movie?"

"Yeah," said Foster just before he passed out. "Why don't I?"

CHAPTER 34
THE DISCOVERY AT THE VILLA

Saturday, June 21

Outside the gate of the DASPO villa, enjoying the relative quiet of the evening, three erstwhile sewage engineers with Quai Ng in tow shuffled their way through the clusters of people on the sidewalk. Longacre was so distrustful of Quai Ng he didn't want to leave him alone in the villa. Besides, he reasoned, the man may be Vietnam's best pig lifter but he knew nothing of the American way of raising hell. Tonight, he told Ng, the Shadows were going to teach him how to hang loose.

"Why are we going to this thing?" Longacre mumbled. "I hate these fuckin' guys. And I'll tell you what. If they play 'We Gotta Get Out of This Place' even one time, I'm gonna personally cut off every swingin' dick in the building."

"It won't be so bad," Webb said. "So they're not combat troops. Neither are we, remember? But...have you seen some of the women that come through there?"

"Yeah," Larue said. "Some of 'em got better mustaches than us." Larue, ever uncharitable and mean-spirited, was referring to some of the female volunteers from the Red Cross, affectionately known as Doughnut Dollies.

"American women have mustache?" Quai Ng asked.

"The ones over here do," said Larue.

"Can it," shot back Webb. "Tomorrow's mission could turn into our next Rat Fuck, so how about we carpe the old diem, huh?"

"Cop the what?" Larue asked.

"Never mind. Tonight you could get a mercy fuck from some generously endowed Caucasian woman, so don't complain." He reached up and yanked the bell cord.

Pavlov would have been proud. At the sound of the bell, an

obscene harmonic chorus erupted from Jack and Little Shit, the former taking the bass and the latter howling the high end, causing Ironman to grab his tire iron and hurry toward the gate. Webb and his buddies would need an escort through the courtyard, protection against the rapturous leg-fucking that the dogs would inevitably attempt. Since Ironman had started smearing the hounds with crankcase oil they'd fallen in love with him, and he was the only one they'd obey. But he still needed the tire iron, just to get their attention.

The Shadows raced up the stairs and stumbled through the front door, Ironman slugging it out behind them. Longacre almost fell backwards when Yak Dung recognized Webb, and emitted one of his gorgonzola grins.

"This is the guy I was telling you about," Webb said as he shook Foster's hand. "Lenny, right? This is Longacre, our... chief engineer, and that short yet handsome fella is Larue, our, uh, hydrologist." Foster leaned forward and looked at Larue a little closer.

"Don't I know you from somewhere?"

"No. You don't." Foster backed off.

Larue and Longacre looked around the entryway of the villa, trying to decide if theirs was nicer. He didn't know where to look first, assaulted as he was by the riotous collage of black and white photos that wallpapered every square inch of available surface. The walls in the dining room were full of them, both sides of the stairwell, everywhere. It was a visual history of DASPO in Vietnam, what are called production stills, film crews in every possible situation, making Hollywood magic with cameras, tripods, lights, reflectors, in the city, in the countryside. Some were their normal 8x10 size, others had figures cut out and pasted over each other, troops who rotated in and out of the villa over the years had written degrading obscene captions in black marker pen. Webb thought he even recognized the old Vampire hooch at Tay Ninh, but couldn't say anything.

The Australians were next to arrive. Goodhardt had met them on a previous trip in Phuoc Toi province, and looked them up again, because he knew they'd provide a perfect military balance to the civilian heathens who Foster had invited.

The Aussies were Special Air Service, and though Foster would never have said it publicly, he believed they ate their dead. He was both horrified and impressed when Jack and Little Shit bounded up to them in the courtyard. But instead of the vicious attack that Foster expected (and had grown to relish as much as the rest of the troops), the two brainsick animals flipped over onto their backs and spread their legs to have their stomachs rubbed. They knew their own.

Foster had found out about SAS troops the hard way. A few weeks before, his team had been assigned another in an endless series of films on Vietnamization, this one called "Images of War," and spent a day with an SAS platoon leading some ARVN troops on a search and destroy mission. He'd been sitting in the red dust at the landing zone with D'Amato, Svoboda and a red-faced spindly new guy named McSwan, when seven of the largest Australians on the planet showed up humping backpacks the size of Volkswagens.

"Check this out," D'Amato said. "These guys must have a fuckin' arsenal in there." His eyes shone with his love of military hardware. "Bet they got Claymores and LAW rockets and RPGs and enough ammo to last a month. They ain't gonna let us get caught with our pants down. Maybe they'll let me shoot one."

A nice safe feeling, all those explosives.

The Hueys dropped the whole group off in the middle of godforsaken nowhere, and the crew followed the Aussies along a jungle trail, dragging themselves and their equipment in the heat and muck for almost two hours. Finally, the SAS lieutenant called a much-needed halt, and the aspiring filmmakers collapsed on the ground. Every member of the SAS squad laid his monstrous pack carefully down, opened it up, and pulled out quart bottles of hot beer.

"Where's the ammo?" Foster whispered to D'Amato.

"Where's the guns?" D'Amato whispered back.

The Aussies just smiled, offering the 110-degree brew to one and all with foamy generosity, not disappointed that Foster and the squad turned them down. "No worries, mate. Just more for us, is all. Bruce, take a look round and see if you can find any of those grasshoppers. The crunchy ones." His eyes glittered madly at Foster from under his wide brimmed hat. "Salty little fuckers. Great with beer."

It was all he ever needed to know about Australian grunts, but now, Goodhardt, out of spite and revenge, was bringing them into the DASPO sanctum sanctorum to participate in their hallowed rituals and neutralize the odious presence of civilians.

The feature of the villa that most impressed the party guests was the array of women standing on the stairs. They were four of the most adorable, most petite female escorts Saigon had to offer, size five girls in size four bodies, laminated into outfits that would give even Frederick of Hollywood a fierce erection. A symphony of spandex, hot pink asses, high, pointed electric blue breasts, long straight black hair, and full-lipped smiles that dripped with delicious and not very expensive promise. They'd spent half an hour on the ground floor with Thi Lanh, who was installed in an armchair, plaster-covered leg elevated, cooing and squealing over the baby. One of the Aussies pulled Foster aside.

"How much for the one in the cast?"

Even more impressive and wonderful to Webb was the sight of three unmistakably Caucasian women, precious and rare beings, who, unlike most of them, weighed in at well under a hundred thirty each. Longacre stared open-mouthed, and when the colossal stereo on the second floor started belting out the Young Rascals' version of the American military anthem, he didn't even mind.

"The bar's on the roof," said Ironman. But they already knew that, because the Australians had gotten there ahead of them, and the upper floor was already resonating to dull thuds. Plaster dust drifted down.

Longacre put his mouth next to Webb's ear. "I might come to like these guys after all."

"Ladies first," said D'Amato, and followed the women up the stairs.

"Don't strain the neck like last time," said Svoboda. D'Amato liked to let girls get two or three steps ahead of him on the stairs. He was one of those men who put women on a pedestal so he could look up their skirts.

Gradually, the place filled up. The lox and bagels sergeant from the motor pool, some troops from the maintenance battalion, others from the quartermaster corps, most of them with their Vietnamese "girlfriends" for the night, very valuable to DASPO in their quest to get the oddball items they needed for their film projects. Before too long, there were about fifty people on the roof, and some couples already wandering around the hallways on each floor, looking for a little privacy.

Drinks were poured, courtesy of Weinberg and D'Amato, introductions were made, joints were ignited.   Magically, magnetically, the four Vietnamese ladies that Harris had hired gravitated toward the sewer engineers, and the American girls edged closer to the impressive bulk of the Australians. Goodhardt kept his distance because after 23 years in the Army he could spot a soldier, even those who try to convince him they're "sewer engineers." He could tell that Webb, the plain-looking guy with the receding hairline, was a little on edge, but couldn't figure out why.

Webb had a reason. Before this, the Shadows had kept mostly to themselves, drinking together in clubs or at the Continental and Caravelle, not mixing with anybody outside the group. They had a cover to maintain, and it is the nature of people who hide behind false identities to suspect that others live in similar states of deception. Were these guys really a photography unit? All this camera equipment, the film editing machines, the projectors...could be a cover. Besides, the Shadows were fond of saying among themselves they didn't know shit about waste management, so there was at least a minimal risk that they'd blow their cover as the evening's promise of reduced mental capacity was gradually fulfilled. But the promise of lubricious sex was too good to pass up. As one of the Vietnamese girls tucked herself under his arm and put a delicate hand on his ass, he hoped nobody would screw up.

Larue found himself with two giggling companions, since it was generally DASPO procedure to invite more women than men, and was, in fact one of the few procedures the outfit actually followed. The one adorning his left side, Kim, boasted the roundest posterior on the immediate premises, and Larue was doing his best to support its heft and proportion with one of his hands. On his right, Li gave his bicep a breast massage, and the evening hadn't even started yet.

"What is a...hydrologist?" Li asked.

"I study wet things," grinned Larue. "Got any?"

More drinks, a few more hits, the night growing darker around them. When he sensed the atmosphere was right, First Sergeant Goodhardt and his two bosom companions, Kiat with the dark hair and Johnny with the Black Label, put their plan into motion. He looked around the terrace with his eyelids at half mast, inspected the bulky Australians who were filling their laps with American Red Cross girls, and purposefully threw down the gantlet.

"Gentlemen!" he ventured. "And ladies." He wrapped his tongue carefully around each word.   "I have served my country proudly in the United States Army for 23 years, four months, eight days, and seventeen minutes, and there's one thing I know for sure. Nobody standing on this roof tonight can out drink a man from DASPO."

Well, the Aussies looked at him like he'd just called their mothers pig-fucking whores.   They instantly stood up, dropped their women on the floor, and curled their hands into fists the size of dinosaur haunches.

Webb glanced at Longacre. Larue looked at Webb. What kind of bullshit was this? These guys shot pictures for a living, for Christ's sake. Or said they did. They weren't real soldiers, and that meant they certainly couldn't be real drinkers. Of course, waste management engineers were, as a group, probably not known for their alcoholic prowess either, and normally would never rise to this kind of blatant bait, but cover stories tend to wither and die when helicopter gunship pilots are challenged on this level.   They were trained as soldiers, not undercover agents, and they'd kept their secret as best they could. Besides, the missions assigned to them by Colonel Xoan had become so maniacal that they lived with the conviction every one would be their last, and were not about to take such an affront lightly.

Larue stood up first, dropping Li and Kim on top of the American girls who were struggling to get up off the floor. Webb stood up, and Longacre. They were thirsty, and eager for the fray. The Aussie sergeant just looked at them and licked the foam off his mustache.

"Didn't know that blokes who spend their lives mucking about in sewers would be much for a drinking contest."

Webb gave Longacre a precautionary kick. "Listen up, pal," he said. "See this guy here? His grandfather's got a city park named after him in Butte, Montana. So watch it." Foster just looked at him.

"Top," Foster whispered, turning his back to the group. "Are you nuts? These guys go on search and destroy missions with fifty pounds of beer on their backs. They've been drinking since they came out of the test tube."

Goodhardt blinked innocently at him. "Lieutenant, these men are our guests. We can't back down now. The honor of DASPO is at stake, here."

"Tell ya what, mates," the Aussie Sergeant said. "This is how we do it down under. We sit around a table, much like the one I saw downstairs, and each man tells a war story. Everybody takes a shot before each story, and one after. Man with the best story wins, if he's still conscious. What do you say?" The girls looked at each other with a common understanding that transcended all cultural boundaries and united them in gender. Soon, they'd have a sodden group of unconscious males on their hands. No sex tonight, unless they wanted to stay up on the roof and cut somebody out of the herd, or enjoy each other. Li and Kim and Kiat were relieved, because they'd gotten half their fee up front. Janette, Linda, and Renee felt otherwise. They'd been hoping for a different kind of party, because the only men they ever saw were either soldiers missing pieces of their bodies, or doctors missing pieces of their minds. They could never decide which was worse.

Totally confused, Quai Ng asked Longacre, "Is this what Caucasians do for fun at home?"

"Men," muttered Linda in disgust, and lit another one of the joints she'd bought downtown. Twenty for five dollars, machine made, rolled just like cigarettes, sealed with cellophane in a real cigarette pack.

"Here," she said to Renee, "care for a marijuana Marlboro? Soaked in opium." Renee couldn't resist.

When she lit it, and Foster smelled the famous smell, he flashed on the sailor who had sat next to him on the flight over from Hawaii. The guy talked to him for ten solid hours, and told him he was going back for his third tour.

"Third tour?" Foster was incredulous. "Why in the world would you go back there three times?" The sailor answered him in one word.

"Dope."

"Dope?"

"Shit, yeah.   You can stay fucked up for a whole year. Everybody does it."   Foster didn't believe him.   Not until he saw the two pot plants growing in barrels outside the USAID Narcotics Advisory Office in downtown Saigon.

"Three men on a team," continued the Aussie sergeant, starting downstairs. "Looks like three teams. DASPO, us and the sewer rats. You pass out, your side loses. You puke, your side loses. But you can name your own poison." Foster, D'Amato and the rest didn't trip over each other more than five or six times getting the table set up and handing each man the bottle of his choice. Some of the people from the roof came down to watch. Webb took Seagram's. Longacre was a scotch man, but the best they could do was Cutty Sark. Larue went for the Bacardi. Foster, sensing he'd be one of the first to fall off his chair, asked for a white wine spritzer.

"You get the tequila," said the Aussie sergeant, and Foster was in no position to argue.

"Hey!" Foster shouted.   "This bottle's got a worm in it. Wait! TWO worms."

Actually, it was mescal, and the cheapest possible brand, at that.   There's nothing more purulent, thought Foster, not even in Southeast Asia during a war, than bargain mescal.

"It's okay," said the sergeant. "They ain't worms. They're caterpillars. You eat 'em, you see God."

"Why do they put those goddam things in there, anyway?" Foster asked, holding the plain unlabeled amber bottle up to the light and swishing it around.

"This particular kind of caterpillar," the sergeant explained, warming to the subject, "is found only in the blue agave cactus plant of your American southwest, and in Mexico. Real mescal is made from the blue agave, so those little buggers are your guarantee of authenticity."

"I'll have one," said Renee.

"What's the prize?" Webb asked.

"Prize?" The Aussie stared at him with washed-out blue eyes.   "Honor. Prestige. Glory. I'll explain it to you sometime."

Longacre lurched forward, aiming straight for the Aussie's throat, but Larue grabbed him at the last second.

"Sorry, sergeant. You know how it is in the sewers." He sat Longacre down.

"Glory? I'll give him a glory enema," Longacre muttered. "How many missions has *he* flown?"

"None," Webb reminded him. "And neither have you."

The hookers had gotten up from their tangled mass of arms and legs, pulled their skirts down as far as possible, which wasn't very, and settled into position behind their man of the evening. Either they were lending moral support, or getting ready to pick pockets once oblivion had arrived. The American girls poured themselves a few more drinks and pulled up chairs. They weren't about to do touchy feely on Foster or anybody else, because they didn't think it would get them anywhere. Janette actually headed for the door, thinking she'd get back to her quarters before curfew, but when she opened it, the howls of Jack and Little Shit convinced her to stay inside.

CHAPTER 35
WAR STORIES

Saturday, June 21

"Heads," announced the Aussie sergeant. "We go first." Each of his men ripped the top off a can of Bud and gulped it down in one long swig. "Just to show you what nice guys we are," said the sergeant, pouring Johnny Walker Black into three shot glasses, "we'll spot you the first round." The Aussies inhaled the shots, refilled them, sat back, and two belches and one fart later, were ready to begin.

"'Kay. One day we take a lorry down to the beach for some R & R," the sergeant said, his eyes swimming beneath the long black eyebrow that ran from one side of his forehead to the other. "And we get into this soccer match with a bunch of ARVN."

"Kill any?" Former Sergeant First Class Harris wanted to know.

"Don't interrupt, mate. I remember them all wearing these funny little yellow bathing suits. Looked like they all had bananas for dicks. They was small and fast, and messed us up pretty well on the pitch, but they bought us a couple cases of Ba M'Ba after the game, so they turned out okay."

"Kill any?" Goodhardt, this time.

"Next day, we went out on this long range recon mission, trying to get a look at VC mountain, you know just north of Vung Tau.

"We're crawling about up there for maybe a day and a half, and we finally come across a fresh trail, so we follow it. About an hour later we just about fall into a VC encampment, maybe twenty-thirty of 'em. We're lookin' at 'em through the binocs, and Hagen here says, 'These guys look familiar. I seen 'em before.' I says, 'Yeah, you waxed a bunch of guys last week looked just like 'em.' He says, 'No, I mean it. Look.'

I grab a look, and it's the whole team of banana dicks we
played soccer with two days before. All of 'em VC. Guess
they came down to the beach for R&R just like the rest of us,
mixed right in. Can't tell 'em apart without a uniform,
anyway."

"What happened?" Svoboda asked.

"Since they all looked like they had bananas on their dicks,
we harvested the whole crop. Want to see 'em?"

The group demurred.

Quai Ng sat apart, consuming the first scotch anyone in
his family had touched since the Ming Dynasty. He slurped it
just Like Colonel La had slurped his Coke but with more
intoxicating effect. He licked up the first one in no time, and
ambled unsteadily toward the bar for a refill.

"Okay," said Foster. "I'll tell you about the scaredest I've
ever been."

"I can't wait," mumbled Longacre.

"We were shooting a film on the Ruff Puffs," Foster began,
and launched into the tale of how he had fifty Vietnamese
dressed in black pajamas running around on the hilltop, and
how worried he was that some asshole chopper jocks might
not get the word and would come by, raining down death from
the skies.

"And that's almost what happened," he continued.
"Suddenly these two black Cobras, not a marking on them,
are circling our position, we think they didn't get the word,
and we're waving and yelling at the fuckers. They drop their
noses, and I just knew we're gonna get the shit shot out of us,
D'Amato's yelling about how we're gonna die. Finally, at the
very last minute, they pull up and head off in the other
direction."

Longacre laughed so hard that beer came out of his nose.

"It wasn't that funny," said one of the Aussies.

"What's wrong with him?" Goodhardt asked.

"Nothing," Webb said. "Nothing." He handed Longacre a
handkerchief.

The Aussie sergeant looked at the liquid dribbling down the
front of Longacre's face. "Waste of good beer, you ask me."

"I got one," said Goodhardt, and each man at the table
filled his shot glass. It was a little more difficult for Foster,
since one of the Vietnamese evening companions had

insinuated her hand down the front of his shirt and was working her way southward, but he didn't spill much, and the caterpillars stayed in the bottle.

"You guys may not know this," Goodhardt said. And turning toward the Shadows, told them, "And you certainly don't."

"Let's get the choppers in the air," whispered Larue, "and put some Willie Peter into this goddam place." The unadulterated disdain that emanated from the Aussies and Goodhardt and Harris was getting on his nerves. Sure, dumping on civilians was common enough in the Army, even the ones who were living there trying to help out. But if you were in country and not actually in the war, that just wasn't good enough for some people.

"We been doing a lot of films illustrating the brilliant success of our Commander-in-Chief's Vietnamization policy. So they sent a unit down into the Delta to shoot some scenes and I figure I'll go along to show these kids that I ain't so old I can't hold an Arri BL on my shoulder."

"What kind of gun is that?" one of the Aussies asked.

"It's a camera," Top replied.

"How do you kill gooks with a fucking camera?" another Aussie chimed in. "Smack 'em on the head with it?"

"We weren't there to shoot them," said Foster. "We were there to shoot them. So..."

"Forget about it," said one of the Aussies. "Sounds like a shit story to me. Take a drink. Start again." So Goodhardt took a drink, Foster poured himself another mescal, Larue belted whatever he was drinking, and McSwan weighed in with the following:

"DASPO teams have security clearance, but I think I can tell this without having to kill you later. Last time I was here, we got secret orders to go to this mountain in Thailand. Took us two days by mule, five guys, all our equipment, three native guides, and about a dozen of the stinkingest most fucked up mules you ever saw. Fleas, ticks, mosquitoes, snakes, every kind of vermin on earth, and that doesn't include the two-legged ones with guns waiting for us in the jungle. We were scared shitless the whole time. We never got secret orders before, and that meant a secret mission, and that meant we were all going to die.

"We get to the top of the mountain and walk straight into this village of Montagnards. These guys are living in huts up on poles, maybe seen two white men in their lives, teeth all black from chewing betel nuts, loincloths, it's like stepping back in time a thousand years."

"Montagnards," said one of the Aussies. "Nasty smelly bastards. Great fighters though."

"So here in the middle of this practically prehistoric village, appears this American Sergeant Major. The guy looks like he just walked off a recruiting poster, he's all pressed and creased and starched, I can't imagine how he did it, and he's got fruit salad all over his chest.

"'Gentlemen', he says, 'your assignment is to shoot a film on the health and personal hygiene programs we are about to institute in this village."

"'Okay,' I say. 'We can do that. What kind of health programs you got in mind?'"

"'We're introducing a new stannous fluoride tooth decay prevention program.'"

"But...Montagnards don't have teeth," said Goodhardt. "At least not so's you'd notice."

"Bingo. But that didn't matter to the Sergeant Major. We set up the camera, and he gets a bunch of these little guys formed up in the middle of the village. He's got two enlisted men with him passing out toothbrushes and tubes of Crest or some shit, and he's teaching them how to apply the paste to the brush, one, two, now brush upper left for a count of four, lower right for four."

The American girls, now with their eyelids at half mast from the liquor and pot, just sat and listened, but the hookers were fascinated. They consumed their Coca-Cola bar-girl style from tall glasses by lifting out the chunks of ice with long soda fountain spoons, and sucking the Coke off it. That way, they could nurse one for an hour.

Then it was Webb's turn, but none of them could actually tell a story. Webb wondered how the rescue of O'Connell would play to this crowd, Longacre would have told the one about Juan Wayne, but they had to pass. By acclamation of everyone at the table, it cost them two shots. Since they had to do two shots, everybody else did them, too. Stories followed one another, each more outrageous and ridiculous than the last, and all of them as true as they needed to be. Weinberg scurried around the table snapping black and whites for the wall display till the Aussie sergeant threatened to feed him his camera. Inevitably, the scotch and mescal and pot and whatever else took their toll, the hookers got impatient, the spectators drifted away, heading back to their quarters because of the curfew, and the party started dissipating.

Eight drinks and most of an opium-soaked joint had made Larue irresistible to Renee, especially since the Aussie she'd been working on had fallen off the balcony, and was lying in the courtyard bushes with Little Shit sniffing at his crotch and planning to consummate the relationship. She decided if she waited for him to make his move, she'd be drunk and stupid and alone for the rest of the night, and she'd rather be drunk and stupid and with somebody. Anybody. So she struggled to her feet, put an arm around him -- she was six inches taller than he was -- towed him down the hall into the projection room and arranged him on the lumpy sofa. His senses hadn't abandoned him completely, so he was conscious enough to enjoy her hands inside his shirt and feel some vague stirrings in his reproductive regions. She unbuttoned and unzipped him with more than moderate competence. He even retained enough eyesight to admire the way the light glistened off her red hair when she leaned in for a closer, more personal inspection of the area directly below his belt buckle. Warm breath on his thighs, something hot and moist where he needed it the most...he closed his eyes, letting the sensations build, fighting their way through his diminished capacities. His eyelids flickered open, gaze wandering improbably across the nuthouse collage of photos stuck to the ceiling. Then, just as the dedicated efforts of Renee's wicked mouth started to pay off, he opened his eyes all the way, and saw something that put a cruel stop to the whole ecstatic process.

Larue jumped up so fast he almost dislocated Renee's jaw and cost himself a few inches off the top. She fell back onto the floor, startled and drooling and screaming.

"What?" she yelled. "What's wrong?"

Larue, eyes wide, held on to his pants and climbed up on the sofa, staring at the ceiling.

"Holy shit."

"What? Was it the teeth?"

"Here. Hold on to the sofa," Larue said, climbing up on the arm, then onto the back, stretching toward the ceiling.

"Was it the wart on my tongue? Most guys like it."

Renee had been in Vietnam for over a year, and she'd seen lots of strange men do lots of incredible things, but nobody had ever jumped up in the middle of oral sex before. Still, she was what the boys would call a good sport, game enough to add her weight to the seat of the sofa while Larue balanced on the back and pulled an 8x10 glossy off the ceiling just before the alcohol kicked in again and threw him to the floor. He sat there, genuinely shaken, and stared at the image in front of him.

"Holy shit."

"What?" Renee was mystified, and not a little alarmed. "What did I do?"

He fought his way to his feet and lurched through the door, banging his shoulder painfully against the wall, staggered down the hall, and crawled up the stairs to the roof.

Renee watched him ricochet out of the room. She took a deep breath, shook her head, pulled up her slacks, and wiped her mouth on her sleeve.

While Larue was surrendering himself, however unconsciously, to Renee's moist mouthings, Foster was grappling with Li in his room and Longacre was turning Janette upside down, bestowing sensations on her that she'd imagined only in her most private and fevered delirium. Webb, disappointingly, remained on the roof of the villa trapped by Linda, who told him immediately how committed she was to remaining faithful to her boyfriend back home. She'd been in country three whole weeks.

Just your luck, said Webb's voice, which had been curiously quiet till Linda started her peculiar harangue. *You always get the ones who want to talk*. Which is exactly what Linda had been doing for the past half hour, and with every word she said, Webb's eyes got wider, and his grip on his chair tighter.

She was a tall, thin, green-eyed brunette from Tennessee, with high, tight, assertive breasts, full lips, and the longest legs he'd seen in years. He'd visited with his share of delicately-built Vietnamese women, all of them gorgeous, but he'd been feeling the need for the company of a female who was more his own size. He was, in fact, willing to put up with almost any amount of talk to get Linda onto the sofa, until she got around to the topic of her father.

"He was a good man," she said. "Worked hard all his life. Used to take me hunting, and when we were alone in the woods, he'd tell me how people were like animals being hunted, except they were the hunters. Some got shot, and some lived on."

"Huh?"

"Like my relatives, for instance. Momma had six brothers and sisters, daddy had five. Some of them died of disease, some from accidents. Some got eaten by animals, and some got married."

"Wait a second. Your relatives got eaten by animals?"

"Well, yeah. Some of 'em. Daddy useta say it's the fate of all living things. Some of us become food, and some get made into rugs. Some are coats, some are shoes. Some of the coats wear out, but others last for years. How do you explain that? The clothes that wear out become rags. My father taught me all that."

"He must have been quite a guy," Webb observed, sliding his chair back a bit. "I'd better go see where Larue is....."

She grabbed him by the arm, hard. "I guess you must have missed the point."

"I guess I did. What was it?"

"We're all being persecuted. Hunted. Me in particular."

"Webb!" Larue stumbled up the stairs, holding up his pants with one hand and the photo with the other. "Look at this!" He dragged Webb away from Linda, just in time, over to a corner of the terrace.

"So?" Webb said as he turned the picture into the light. "Isn't this that asshole Berner from JUSPAO?"

"Right. And the guy in the middle is Colonel Xoan."

"It is? How do you know?"

"I saw his picture in some stuff Sanderson showed me, while back."

"Okay. Who's the third guy?"

"No idea."

"So where are they? And what are they doing there?"

"That's what I want to know," said Larue. "Where's Longacre? And your buddy Foster?"

Webb stumbled down the stairs behind Larue, leaving Linda sitting there with her drink, her half-eaten relatives, and her forlorn sense of persecution, falling along the hallway, throwing open one door after another, interrupting who knows how many imaginative couplings, until they found Longacre. He was sharing a sexual posture with the ecstatic Janette that made Larue stop just inside the doorway and stare in awed admiration, wishing he had a camera. It took a while to pry them apart, partly because Janette didn't want to let go. They showed Longacre the picture.

"What's this?" They told him.

"Holy shit." Semi-naked, drunk, crazed, achingly erect, he untangled from Janette, led them along the hall to Foster's room, and charged through the door.

"Where did you take this picture?" Larue demanded.

"Mrpfh," answered Foster, a consequence of trying to talk with his mouth full. He rolled off Li, pulled a sheet around both of them and sat up, squinting at the light that flooded in from the hall. Longacre pushed the glossy in front of his face. Foster was too fuddled to look at the puckered scars on Longacre's shoulder and stomach and wonder how a sewer engineer could get himself shot so many times.

"Can't this wait?"

"No," said Longacre, and Foster could see that he meant it.

"Some village up around Tay Ninh. That's Colonel Berner, the asshole from JUSPAO. And some guy named Xoan who's in charge of this drug interdiction unit. Supposed to have his own platoon...."

"Who's the guy in the middle?" said Webb.

"That's the mayor of the village. Sam Twat, or something. Sam Thuoc, that's it. Seemed to be huge buddies with Xoan. Put the whole place at his disposal as a drug interdiction point. Anything else you want to know?"

"They are loving cousins." Everybody stopped talking and turned toward the door. The voice belonged to Quai Ng.

"You mean kissing cousins?" asked Webb.

"Yes. Sorry." He moved uncertainly into the room and pointed at the picture in Webb's hand. "These men. They are related. But he is not Sam Thuoc. His name is Wo Minh."

Foster's eyes went wide, remembering the filmed interview when Xoan was telling the camera how Wo Minh was a combination of Satan, Hitler, and Attila the Hun. The sanitation engineers, too, looked at Quai Ng in stunned disbelief.

"How...how do you know?" said Longacre.

"I know him from Ho Chi Minh Trail. He and Xoan grow up in same village."

"You sure?" said Longacre.

"At one time, it was my job to know these things."

They shut up and looked frantically back and forth at each other like scared little sparrows, not realizing how much, in that brief moment, they resembled Moe, Larry, and Curly. Longacre pulled Larue and Webb down the hall and initiated a spirited discussion about whether or not to tell Foster who they really were. Their military training prevailed, and they decided to wait. Larue flung the door open again, and again Foster fought his way out from under his date.

"What's all this about?" said Foster. "And why do you care? This guy have something to do with sewers?"

"Yes," said Larue.

"Yes, what?" asked Foster.

"What happen?" asked Li.

"Yes, this has something to do with sewers. If this guy is who Quai Ng says he is, he's connected to..."

"Uh...some industrialist who's out to corner all the sewer contracts in the country." Webb was tap dancing as hard as he could.

"Right," Larue agreed. "He's a...um, competitor. The deal's worth a billion dollars to our...company."

"Maybe this Berner guy is in it with him," Longacre suggested.

"And this Xoan guy, too. A billion dollar sewer scandal. This could be big. Real big."

"Can we have this picture?" asked Webb.

"Sure," said Foster. "I got more."

"How many?"

"Many as you want. We have the negatives." Li put her tiny cool hand between his legs. "Now, if you gentlemen will excuse us?"

CHAPTER 36
HUGGINS GETS THE CALL

Monday, June 22

"Anybody got any ideas?" The hot light over the table in the Shadows villa made the crags on Sanderson's face look like canyons. They probably had actually gotten a little deeper after Webb showed him the picture, and after he started really thinking about what it could mean.

They'd passed the piece of shiny black and white photo paper back and forth across the table until it had gone limp. The shot was still clear and sharp, though, beautifully lit, high contrast, crisp. You could have run it in a magazine. Svoboda had truly captured the magnetic presence of Colonel Xoan as it radiated off the paper.

The opposite of love is not hate, and the opposite of good is not evil. The opposite of love is indifference, and the antithesis of good is evil that masquerades as goodness, or hides behind it. It is the Devil quoting Scripture, the dagger concealed in a crucifix. It is the face of Xoan, grinning at them.

The enormity of it squatted on their shoulders and drove their gazes into the table. Nobody could even look up. Z-Man usually had the first word, and often the last, but no words came to him that night. Harrell sat still, listening to his stomach clutch itself as the implications sank in. Larue, Longacre, all of them thought the same thing. Bad enough that their supposed commanding officer, a pillar of the Army of the Republic of Vietnam, had his hands in the pants of the region's most popular drug lord. Actually, that part didn't bother them so much, because they'd already seen far more imaginative examples of corruption on both sides. In Vietnam, the opportunities grew, like the pot plants, everywhere. The MAC-V colonel who'd been taken down for smuggling heroin back to the states inside plaster elephants, and Ellsworth Bunker, the US ambassador, had a chief pilot who'd been arrested with $8 million dollars' worth of heroin in his airplane. There was a multitude of ARVN officers who spent most of their time running steam baths, massage parlors, hookers, black market Pepto-Bismol, doing unimaginably base things that the Shadows couldn't even dream of.

But this? *This*? It's one thing to be a soldier, a highly motivated pilot and warrior, but to have someone take your skills, your training, your equipment, your loyalty and obedience and patriotism...your *country*, and pervert all of them in such a satanically depraved way? That, as Longacre would have said, is a horse of a different wheelbase.

The longer they sat there, the more they stewed in the rich rancid soup of betrayal. It boiled up inside them like fetid gases in a swamp. Conversation was difficult, but they desperately wanted to talk about what to do with -- and to -- Colonel Xoan. There was no mention of reporting him to the authorities, no due process, habeas corpus, evidence, burden of proof, innocent until proven guilty, none of the cornerstone concepts they themselves lived by and had sworn to uphold, protect and defend. And absolutely not a word – not a *syllable* – about kicking the situation up the chain of command. There was only that shiny black and white square, grinning, mocking them, from the rough wood table. It was an image that spoke to them the way that famous shot of the Hindenberg speaks, even today. Or, the Marines raising the flag on Mount Suribachi. More to the point, it screamed vile things about the fundamental nature of war itself, and this war in particular, which had already generated other equally memorable, and equally distressing, images.

Sanderson managed to keep the lid on, partly because he was of a cooler head by nature, and partly because he knew the old saying about the recommended temperature for the serving of revenge. First, he made them talk about supporting evidence.

"Think about where this comes from. Bunch of weird film guys who live next door. We don't know where this village is, or why they were there, or any of that shit. Before we get our undies in a bunch and one of you does something stupid, we ought to check this place out."

"Fine," said Harrell. "Where is it?" Nobody knew.

It became instantly apparent that somebody from DASPO would have to take them there, as much as they disliked the idea of asking Foster and his crew of anarchists for help. Besides, Quai Ng could probably find the place on his own, had, no doubt, lived there at one time and spoke the local dialect. But one other thing became apparent. If what they were looking at was what they were looking at, they needed to bring back some strong evidence, preferably of a photographic nature. That's where DASPO came in.

"But that means blowing our cover," said Longacre. He didn't like it, especially the idea of revealing the truth to a bunch of assholes. He tried to keep from feeling like some kind of ungrateful bastard, because thanks to Foster and the party, he had practiced advanced kundalini with Janette the entire previous day. Of course, if it hadn't been for the party, they wouldn't be sitting there in the half light, staring at Colonel Xoan's perfect white grin. We waxed a lot of people, Longacre thought, and I'm gonna get 'em all back from you.

"I wouldn't worry about blowing cover," put in Webb. "This is gonna surprise the shit out of you all, but those *assholes* next door have top secret clearance."

"I agree with Webb,' Sanderson said. "Besides, what do you think'll happen when Xoan decides to pull the plug on our little sewers for freedom operation? We'll be lucky to find a sewer to hide in ourselves. Or he'll order us into a situation we won't get out of. And I'm sure thatassholecolonelberner will make our demise look like a heroic suicide mission at the Five o'Clock Follies."

That dumbed everybody down. "I got some thinking to do," Sanderson said. "Let me check into this and then I'll make a decision."

The last and most important item came before the board: finding Colonel Xoan. Only Sanderson and Larue had ever actually seen him, and then only briefly, meeting him in the bar at the Continental. Mostly, they never had any idea where he was. Another reason to ask the DASPO crew for help. They'd spent more time with him than anyone.

"I'd sure like to ask him a few questions," Z-Man said.

"Hard ones," said Harrell.

"True-false or multiple choice?" That's when they realized

how little they knew about Xoan, and how blindly they'd accepted him. Where did he live? Where was he based? What was his unit? They never saw him in the bars, and they saw everybody in the bars. Of course, they wouldn't have "known" each other, but where was he? All Sanderson's orders came over the phone, Xoan's weird accent immediately recognizable.

"Excuse me." The mild voice came at them from a far corner of the room, and it made them all sit up. Quai Ng was squatting on the floor against the back wall, invisible by habit more than desire, blending into the very paint. They'd forgotten he was there.

"Colonel Xoan. I know where he is."

"Yeah," said Longacre. "I just bet you do."

"Then let's go get him," said Webb, standing up.

"Soon," said Quai Ng. "There will be a time."

* * * *

Sanderson did some checking around and discovered that Webb was right. The DASPO troops had top clearance, incredibly enough, and all of them traveled on diplomatic passports, the kind with the purple cover, the same kind that the Secretary of State and cabinet officers carry. So he made the decision.

Later that evening, right around that magic hour when the city begins to subside and the new aromas come out, Sanderson walked over to the DASPO villa with Webb at his side. Sanderson was dressed in his Ivy League best, khaki pants, Madras shirt, looking much the way Webb had seen him that first day in the Magic Fingers. He looked across the street at the stairway up to the massage parlor where his whole adventure had begun. It was years ago.

To their surprise, the gate was open, and to their further surprise, the courtyard was full of people. Two Jeeps, maybe six oversized MPs, Ironman to one side of the door, holding Jack and Little Shit in check by straddling them and jamming a crowbar across their throats, Foster on the front steps next to some tall skinny soldier. There wasn't a lot more room.

Oh, shit, Webb's little voice said. I bet they're getting popped for drugs. From what he'd seen at the party, it was the most obvious possibility. Foster, on the other hand, when he saw the Jeeps drive in, was petrified that they'd found out about the small yet impressive arsenal Former Sgt. First Class Harris kept under the beds upstairs.

They were both wrong. It was Huggins they asked for.

"Are you James Lee Huggins?"

"That's affirmative, sir. Boy, am I glad to see you guys."

The largest MP peered at him from under the big white letters on the front of his helmet.

"Yeah? Why's that?"

"Well, you're here to take away that commie Svoboda, aintcha? Treacherous bastard. Put his ass in the stockade where it belongs? Deport him, maybe?" Huggins couldn't help giving them a gap-toothed, tobacco-juiced grin. Brothers in arms.

"Well, not exactly." The grin was unrequited.

"But didn't the FBI send you the test results?"

"Corporal Huggins, did you, on or about the sixth of last month, package up a bag of human vomit and send it to the FBI office in Washington?"

Webb could see Huggins' chest expand.

"Yes, sir, I certainly did. That should be all the proof you need."

"And did you, a week later, send them a similar bag of excrement?"

"Excrement?"

"Feces, soldier. Did you mail the FBI a bag of shit?"

"Yeah, in case they didn't have enough puke. Lemme tell ya', it wasn't easy to get. Didja get the letter? I sent a letter."

"You're under arrest. Come with us."

Foster had to hold onto the doorway to keep his legs under him. He had no idea that Huggins would, so to speak, stoop that low. He'd told Huggins to send in Svoboda's water glass, just to quiet him down that day at the village. He never expected it to get this far. But he *had* noticed Huggins running into the bathroom right after Svoboda came out. Two or three times. Strange, because when it came to dysentery, Svoboda splattered the bowl worse than any of them, and nobody *ever* followed him into the bathroom.

It took them about three seconds to slap the cuffs on, another three to load him in the Jeep, and two more to clamber in around him. Sanderson and Webb stepped back as the two vehicles wheeled around, kicked up another load of dust, and bullied their way into the traffic on the street.

Webb climbed the steps and found Foster on the floor, tucked into the womb pose, teary-eyed, wracked with spasms of hysteria, howling and breathless, the kind of laughter "Variety" would call "boffo yoks."

"What was all that about?" Webb asked, putting an arm under him and pulling him up. Foster could barely stand.

"It's a long sad story with a very happy ending," said Foster, wiping his eyes. "What are you guys doing here?" *Tell him*, said Webb's voice. *Tell him how everything he thinks you are is a lie.*

"Lenny, or should I say Lieutenant, I want you to meet Major Alvin Sanderson."

"*Major* Sanderson?" Foster finally stopped laughing and tried to struggle to his feet, still giggling.

"At ease. Is there someplace we can talk?"

CHAPTER 37
D'AMATO CASHES OUT

Friday, June 26

The Shadows had grudgingly adjusted to the presence of Quai Ng, more or less. Longacre's attitude, however, had a considerable distance to go. Most of the troops were still suspicious because if he'd come over from the enemy, if he'd betrayed the North Vietnamese, he was obviously capable of doing the same to them. In spite of himself, Webb mistrusted him less than the others, but only slightly. He had a reluctant respect for the wiry Quai Ng. The man exuded an air of confidence, self-possession that, at 26, Webb could only aspire to, no matter how much he thought that combat had made a man out of him.

Besides, Quai Ng knew everything about the strange world they found themselves in, and could even make them understand -- some of them -- why the people on that part of the planet had been fighting each other since prehistoric times, and how various superior foreign cultures (such as the French and the Americans, for example), certain that they alone were capable of straightening the whole thing out, had come. And gone.

But one day, after diminishing their mistrust just by being himself for longer than they could stand it, he severely shook their faith.

After Sanderson's heart-to-heart with Foster, he had sent Quai Ng on a reconnaissance mission to the village where DASPO had shot the pictures of Colonel Xoan and "Mayor Sam Thouc." He returned and told them a story you'd believe only if you'd recently fallen off the proverbial turnip truck.

"Nothing is there. It is not even a village."

They were in the Shadows compound on the base, where it

was always a bit dark, so Quai Ng couldn't see the expression of dumb incredulity on Sanderson's face.

"What do you mean? We saw the pictures, and the DASPO guys told you where it was. Foster even ran the film for us. Xoan was there with Wo Minh and thatassholecolonelberner. What do you mean it's not a village?" The other Shadows were not as vocal, but they shared the sentiment.

Quai Ng looked around the room. "I should explain more," he said, demonstrating his estimation of his audience. "The hooches are there, the animal pens, the paths, but it is not a village. Nobody lives there. Nobody has ever lived in that place. No recent fires, no food, no animals."

"A ghost town?" asked Larue, but Quai Ng was unfamiliar with the slang, so Larue spent five minutes briefing him on the old west.

"Ah! No, not a ghost town. It is not that people were there, and left. It is more like...what do you call the place where you film motion pictures?"

"A studio?" ventured Harrell.

"Sound stage?" said Webb.

"A set?" asked Longacre, against his will.

"Yes! A set! Made especially to look real in pictures. There are buildings, but they are not to be lived in. They are false."

Webb was just about to say "That's impossible," but remembered he was in Vietnam. Instead, he picked up the photo Foster had given him at the party.

"This village?"

"The same," Quai Ng assured him. "You see this bent tree? Three small hilltops in the distance?" The Shadows handed the photo around one more time, just to be sure. There, in the finest print the photo lab on base could produce, was the face of Xoan grinning out at them, his left arm around one of the most notorious opium lords in Laos, and his right around one of the most dimly witless commissioned officers in Vietnam. They were grinning, too, such good friends, having a wonderful time.

"Come," said Quai Ng. I will show you."

"Well, I'll be a buffalo fuck," whispered Sanderson.

* * * *

The next day, Svoboda, Ironman and D'Amato muscled the

camera cases into the back of Longacre's Huey, sliding them across the cargo compartment. Every so often, at unpredictable intervals, Svoboda let out a short sharp snort of amusement, as his mind went back time and again to the image of the handcuffed Huggins being spirited away by the MPs. He was sure he'd remember that scene on his deathbed.

Shortstop strapped the gear to the walls with the ever-present bungee cords that decorated the inside of the chopper. For helicopter pilots, and just about every other troop in Vietnam, bungee cords were probably the most effective and infallible pieces of equipment they owned.

"See?" D'Amato said to Foster. "I knew they weren't sewer engineers."

He'd seen Webb carry Foster in from the street that night, and immediately took him for some kind of spook. When Foster told D'Amato who Webb was, he just laughed.

"That guy builds sewers for a living? Forget about it." *Fuggeddaboudid.* Foster himself had been suspicious for a while anyway, and many beery evenings were taken up with extensive, imaginative and often obscene discussions on the topic of Who Are Those Guys? Now they knew.

Foster watched his crew with half his attention, following Webb around as he pre-flighted the other Huey. Behind the next revetment, Larue and Harrell were inspecting their Cobras.

"Pretend I'm an idiot child," Foster said, "because I still don't get it. We're going back to this village where we took the shot of Colonel Xoan, but it's not a village?"

"That is correct," said Quai Ng.

"But why do you want us there?"

"To confirm it's the same place," said Major Sanderson. "Besides, if Xoan's working with that drug lord, we're gonna need a whole bunch of pictures to prove it."

"And if Berner's involved," said Foster, "That would make me feel like Jimmy Stewart at the end of 'It's a Wonderful Life.'"

"Me, too," said Longacre.

Webb closed the last panel and signaled to Larue in the Cobra. "Let's go."

A short flight to the north, noisy and smooth, with the deep green of the jungle rolling beneath them, Longacre in formation trailing low and to the left, with Shortstop and Z-Man aboard, two Cobras hanging in the air to their sides, keeping watch. The beauty of the countryside could turn ugly in a heartbeat, and, on many occasions, it had.

"There," said Quai Ng, over Webb's shoulder.

"That's it," said Foster.

They fluttered to earth in the inevitable choking cloud of red dust about a hundred yards from a small circle of hooches. Farther on, maybe another hundred yards, were more hooches, set near the treeline where the jungle started.

"You sure this is the place?" Webb asked Foster.

"This is the place." They jumped out of the cargo bay and started pushing camera cases toward the door. It was much too quiet. Sanderson stood by the chopper, his eyes straining toward the treeline, where trouble would come from, if it came. Webb would swear that Quai Ng was sniffing the air.

Same place, for sure. Three little hills, gnarled tree just on the edge of the settlement, and from the air, the twisted bend in the river about half a mile to the north. No mistake.

"Jesus," said D'Amato, "This place looked awful real last time we were here."

It didn't any more. Foster, Ironman and Svoboda carried the gear to the middle of a circle of hooches. Webb stood with them, while Z-Man stayed back at the choppers with Longacre, keeping them ready for takeoff, just in case. There was always a just in case.

Movie sets are a little creepy. When you walk onto one, like the back lot of a studio or a sound stage, you step into a completely new, and extremely convincing, reality, suddenly finding yourself on a perfect New York street, say, or an Italian village square in the 14th century. Foster had felt that peculiar dislocation the first time he worked on the huge soundstages at the Army Pictorial Center in New York. Weird. You stand outside a castle, but even though the massive, authentic-looking stone walls fool the eye, they do not fool the subtler senses. The texture, shape and color may be perfect, but the wall exudes no gravity, no sense of age, or history, or itself. So it was with the village. The hooches were perfect, but it was all different without the people. There was no humanity or personality. No bedding, food, clothing, no sense of human habitation. If Disneyland had a "typical authentic

Vietnamese village," perfect and sterile and manufactured, this is how it would look. When the people were there, as they had been on Foster's last visit, the illusion was totally convincing. Everyone had been deceived.

Quai Ng, his eyes wide, crept silently among the structures, sometimes in sight, sometimes not.

"This was the 'mayor's' hooch," recalled Foster. "We shot the stills of him with Xoan and Berner right over there, in front of the tree. They had a huge pile of bales. Drugs they said they seized in an ambush."

"And this place was full of people?" asked Sanderson.

"Sure. Maybe fifty-sixty of them, with pigs, chickens, kids, goats, old mamasans. Just like any other village."

"All from central casting," observed D'Amato. "This place is givin' me the fantods."

"Yeah," said Foster. "Are we safe here?" They'd shot at several uncomfortable locations in the past few weeks, sometimes being carried off into the boonies on one of Colonel Berner's demented pet projects, to spend the night at some tiny firebase that floated like an American island in a vicious sea of Vietcong, or joining an ARVN patrol at a landing zone in the middle of the jungle. He saw the guards and the wire and the Claymores and the artillery emplacements, realizing there were people just like him living that way day and night, and he was never just a little scared. He had only one kind of fear, and it was intense. He'd heard the stories. He wasn't a combat troop, but he was smart enough to know that things like death could happen anytime, anywhere.

"Nothing to worry about," said Webb, though he should have known better. "We got two Cobras in orbit, and nobody spotted anything in the jungle when we landed. Let's have a look around."

But there wasn't much to see. Everything was as Quai Ng had told them. The hooches seemed old and well-used, but now they knew what they were looking for, and they could tell the structures had been built to look that way. The only sign of real habitation was in the crude empty animal pen, where the pigs had been wallowing. A few small paths led off toward the treeline and the other hooches, and then disappeared into the jungle. It was silent, except for the sound of the Cobras, keeping watch from on high.

"Ve take some pictures," Svoboda declared.

"Let's set up the Arri," Foster said to D'Amato. "I want some film of this. And put that 300 telephoto on it, so we can get a look at what's over by those hooches. Svoboda, you do the stills."

D'Amato popped the spring clips on the silver-gray camera cases and handed the chunky black Arriflex film camera carefully to Foster. Svoboda set up the tripod, and Ironman brought out a few 400-foot magazines of film.

"Damn," Foster said as he snapped the camera into place on the tripod. "It sure looked real the last time we were here. I can't believe somebody would build a village, bring in pigs and chickens, get a bunch of extras to act like peasants...."

"Or peasants to act like extras," Ironman observed.

"Maybe they were making a movie," D'Amato put in.

"Yeah, and maybe we were making it for them," said Foster.

"Place'd make a great location," said D'Amato. "When I do my first Vietnam feature...see, there's two guys who meet in the war, but they get separated...."

"They each think the other one's dead...." chimed in Ironman.

"Because they was running from the bastard Communists," said Svoboda, and they were off, doing what they did all the time, spinning plots and screenplays out of everything they saw. The war was a cinematic place to be, and they were trying to save up all the intense images, all the millions of stories, because each of them had a movie in him, or a book, or a documentary.

Foster held the slate in front of the lens. The film humming through the camera sang in D'Amato's ear. His Arriflex was the little brother of the cameras used to shoot major movies, and he loved it. He was always stunned at the quality of the film equipment the government showered on them. Hasselblad still cameras, Steenbeck editing tables, Nagra recorders. First class professional stuff, every single piece, just like Hollywood, and he got to play with all of it, thanks to the abundant generosity of the American taxpayer.

Foster watched as D'Amato squinted into the viewfinder, panning the camera around the village, focusing in on the hooches in the distance, then on a water buffalo near the treeline. Foster was so taken with the composition, the perfect light, that he didn't realize how odd it was to see a water buffalo loose in the field. The animals were prized possessions. Those who owned any – even one -- were rich, and leaving it alone would be like leaving a brand new Cadillac unlocked, with the keys in it, in the worst neighborhood in town at three in the morning. But Foster was rapt...the benign black animal, head held low, grazing peacefully, rays of late afternoon sun providing backlight, thank you, God, the greatest lighting director of them all, the whole scene in a radiant halo. The golden light shimmered thick on the trees behind the beast, and the grass waved gently in the foreground, leading the eye deeper into the frame. Fuck the war movies, D'Amato thought, this was art. Briefly, he entertained thoughts of going to work for National Geographic after the war, then thought better of it. He wanted to be a combat photographer, because he knew he'd never be out of work.

"What's over there?" Foster asked, pointing toward the four hooches in the distance. D'Amato panned slowly over, seeing them in bright detail with the telephoto lens, and discovered that Quai Ng had been right all along. The hooches closest to them were real, but the ones along the treeline were fakes, just the fronts of the buildings with nothing behind them. A movie set if there ever was one, built to fool the camera, and the eye. All he could do was marvel at the sharp, magnified, glistening image on the ground glass of the viewfinder. Somebody was a genius. But just as he was about to lift his head and tell Foster how impressed he was, something else appeared in the perfectly-framed composition.

In brilliant magnification, clear as the air around them, also rimmed with a golden halo of sunlight, a small, painfully thin man wearing a flop hat, T-shirt, and shorts materialized in the tall grass as though he'd just popped up out of the ground, which he probably had. Instinctively, D'Amato pointed the Arri at him and zoomed in for a close-up, seeing the man's face in the cross hairs of the viewfinder like he was standing five feet away.

He was old-looking, but probably not old, with an upper lip that curled over his top teeth, giving him the visage of a very pissed off rat. His skin was the color of a saddle, his eyes tiny slits next to the flat bridge of his nose. As D'Amato squinted into the viewfinder, rolling the collar on the lens to get better focus, the frame was filled by a large black circle. It took D'Amato a second or two, but he finally realized that an AK-47 rifle has two ends, and he was looking down the wrong one.

It was the last thing he ever saw.

Crack! Crack! The film camera exploded on top of the tripod, and so did the entire right side of D'Amato's head, blood, brains, metal, film, everything bursting open in puffs of misty crimson. Foster happened to look back at D'Amato at exactly that second, in time to see pieces of camera and skull flying skyward, inches from his face. The idea of reaching for his gun and shooting back never once occurred to him, partially because he'd never seen a man's head explode before and partially because he'd never been a combat troop and his instinct didn't kick in. But Webb and Sanderson thought of it at once.

"Get down, you asshole!" Webb shouted, and every asshole got down, Foster standing there for a stunned second, then having the presence of mind to throw himself to the ground at the base of the tripod, landing inches from D'Amato's ruined, staring, jittering face. He couldn't bring himself to close his eyes and shut out the horrid, reddened image. Clumps of D'Amato's hair lay on the ground next to him, bits of blood and bone sticking to his shirt. He was dead, but he hadn't stopped moving.

Svoboda grappled for his .45 and muttered "Goddam pigfucking bastards," spraying rounds in the general direction of the sniper, who had instantly disappeared after squeezing off his two lethal shots. Ironman scuttled through the dust toward what was left of D'Amato and the camera, hugging the earth as Webb and Sanderson sent their rounds whistling over his head.

From above, the Cobras dipped their noses and rolled in. Either they saw what happened, or Longacre called them in from the Huey. Foster buried his face in the dirt as the Cobras let go with everything they had, and the earth just yards away erupted with bursts from rocket explosions, grenade launchers and mini-guns, every shot right on the mark. Harrell and Larue buzzed above, laying down suppressing fire while Webb and Sanderson shouted for everybody to get back to the choppers.

Ironman put every one of his 130 pounds into slinging D'Amato over his shoulder and staggered toward the Huey. Foster, forgetting all the cases of expensive equipment they'd brought, ran alongside with Svoboda, trying to help, but Ironman wouldn't let go. D'Amato, cruelly ruined, dripped blood and sticky fluid and pieces of raw meat and greasy kid stuff down the front of Ironman's shirt. He was slick with it, but he kept running. Webb cranked up the rotors of the Huey just as they hurled themselves into the cargo bay. He pulled the shuddering machine into the air, turbines screaming, but nobody heard them over the sounds that Foster was making as he looked into D'Amato's mind in the most sickeningly literal sense. The floor of the cargo bay ran red, everybody holding on as best they could while the machine tilted forward, picking up airspeed and struggling for altitude.

In the back, Sanderson slammed on a headset and keyed his mike.

"Shadow Six to Shadow Two," Sanderson said in the radio. "Did you get him?"

"Don't know," said Larue from above. "If he made it back into the jungle, or into a tunnel, he's gone."

"Roger that. Go ahead and flatten this fucking place."

The Huey climbed above the kill zone and wheeled around to the right as the Cobras rolled in on a series of racetrack runs, showering the imitation village with high explosive. Flames burst from the hooches, the treeline bathed itself in orange fire, and in moments there was nothing left.

Foster sat on the floor of the cargo bay, clutching the padding on the wall, breath coming in short, tight gasps, looking down at the one empty eye D'Amato had left. "Oh," he said. "Oh."

Svoboda and Ironman squatted on the other side, stricken faces looking at Foster for some kind of help, solace, encouragement, leadership. But he'd never seen anything like this before in his life, and all he could say was "Oh."

He'd seen wounded troops when they shot their films in hospitals, he'd seen the napalm victims at Cong Hoa, remembered the arm of Garcia sticking out of the crocodile's mouth. He'd taken in the piles and pieces of dead at the mortuary, each of the scenes becoming more real than the last, each of them wearing away his innocence and optimism, each one showing him just a little more of the real war. He'd always known there was a war going on, and regarded its consequences coldly from the sidelines, a thing to be recorded on film. He saw it only for its dramatic potential, its compositional possibility, through layers of lenses, on a brilliant, expensive viewfinder made of the costliest ground glass. Ironically, the camera's viewfinder had crosshairs in the middle, just like a gunsight. But until this moment, until he looked down at the red mess of D'Amato in his lap, the action, the excitement, the dying had always been something to be photographed and assembled. He worried so much about getting the shot. Any filmmaker worth his salt would walk over his grandmother to get the shot, because he might never have another chance. Then, the film editing process required him to review all the glistening images, and impose structure on them, put them together, each scene like a word in a sentence, in a sequence that made narrative sense. But nothing could make sense out of this.

There were so many people in Vietnam who couldn't wait to get out in the shit. Webb, for example, and Longacre. But Foster had always felt just fine where he was, in Saigon, getting drunk and stoned with the rest of them, having some cute massage parlor dolly give him intensive genital therapy two or three times a week, living in decadent French luxury on a windfall per diem.

But now he was sitting in blood and brains. Not a movie this time. No special effects, no carefully planned pyrotechnics, no clever makeup man creating wounds and scars with latex and spirit gum. No more jokes about who died falling over a tripod, and who died laughing. Life had suddenly started imitating art, and he was so stunned, so speechless that he couldn't answer when Webb called back, "Hey! Is he gonna make it?"

No, Foster had to admit to himself. He's not gonna make it.

"*Borzhemoi!*" whispered Svoboda. Russian was one of the many Slavic languages he customarily cursed in.

"Fuck this shit," said Ironman.

"Hey," said Sanderson. "Where's Quai Ng?" He said it just as Longacre's Huey burst into flame and went down.

CHAPTER 38
THE JUNGLE

Saturday, June 27

Now, if this isn't just the biggest mind fuck, thought Longacre, sitting in the dark about a hundred yards from what was left of his Huey, which was pitifully little.

Not bad enough that Shortstop is dead, faded away in my arms while I watched, listening to the wet sucking sounds from his chest as the lights went out in his eyes. Not bad enough that the crash pushed the console right through his body, so the radios are gone, too. They don't work right when they're full of lung tissue and stomach bile. Z-Man gone, everybody dead except me and the one person who ought to be dead, that goddam gook sapper bastard Houdini, sitting quietly across from me in the dark. Not a scratch on him.

Bad day. Very bad day. After they'd flattened the artificial village and wheeled around for one more run, they felt the heavy *chunk!* of rounds coming up from somewhere in the darkening jungle below, and it got them in the tail rotor, plus a couple of other tender places.

The chopper lurched into a spin on the rotor axis, fire and smoke and hydraulic fluid streaming out into the sky, black like the blood of a harpooned whale. The linked M-60 rounds in the cargo hold started going off, the fireproof silver blanketing that lined the walls demonstrated just how fireproof it wasn't. Longacre thought Z-Man was on fire when he jumped, just plain unassed the chopper at about five hundred feet, diving into the sky. It was better to believe that he'd taken a round and fallen out, but Longacre had been in Vietnam a long time, and knew he shouldn't make assumptions like that. He hardly knew Z-Man was gone, because he and Shortstop were busy at the time, wrestling with the controls in the middle of blazes and sparks and acrid burning smoke.

"Are we fucked?" Shortstop asked.

"Yes," Longacre replied.

No autorotation, no controlled crash where he can slow the aircraft down, drift to the ground keeping the nose up, then, just before he hits, yank that collective upward, right into his armpit, cushion the impact by making the blades take a big bite of air. There was none of that. They simply fell out of the sky, plummeting, plunging, thirty-two feet per second squared, strapped inside a flaming mass of metal. Luckily, there wasn't much ammunition left on board, or much fuel.

The other Huey and the two Cobras wheeled overhead, but the canopy was so thick that it swallowed the chopper whole, and there was no place for the others to land. Besides, Webb had to get that wounded troop back to base, and one of the Cobras had to escort them. The other Cobra couldn't land, and even if it could, wouldn't have been able to take wounded men on board.

Longacre had passed out from the pain, and the smoke grenades had been crushed along with the chopper, so he couldn't pop one to mark their position. Even worse, it was getting dark, and the other aircraft didn't have enough fuel to orbit their position for very long. They knew exactly where he was. They'd be back in the morning. He was sure of it. Now, all he had to do was live through a night in the jungle, in enemy territory. Longacre thought about the times he'd been hunting with his father in the most remote forest, but there had been no tigers in the forest, and he'd never spent a moonless, cloudy, dripping night under smothering Southeast Asian triple-canopy jungle.

When Longacre went down, Webb's craziness, suppressed since the rescue of O'Connell, kicked in with long-delayed vengeance. He already had serious fetishes about leaving troops on the field and rescuing (or not rescuing) his friends in trouble. But the dark was rising up at them from the earth, they were low on fuel, Longacre had been thoroughly absorbed by the jungle, and there was no place to land. He hadn't popped any smoke, they couldn't raise him on the radio. Normally, they would have called in the coordinates so a search party could be ready to go in the morning, but they had nobody to call but themselves. It was the price they paid for admission to the glamorous world of covert operations. So they continued on to Saigon, ready to return at first light, hoping to find more than merely pieces of recent human beings.

* * * *

Quai Ng blinked at Longacre. They'd been sitting across from each other for at least half an hour, it was hard to tell, trying to get over being thrown from the chopper.   Dazed, disoriented, Longacre had no idea how he'd gotten out, how it is decided who survives and who does not.

"How did I get here?" he mumbled.

"I pull you out," Quai Ng said, meeting his eyes.

"What the fuck you looking at?" Longacre demanded.

"We can not stay here," said Quai Ng, quietly. "They know where we crash. They are not so far away. Soon they will come for us. For the rockets and M-60s."

"Let 'em come," whispered Longacre. He cradled his M-16 in his arms. At least one weapon had survived the crash. But what was that funny piercing pressure on the left side of his chest? Ribs? Heart?

"You are foolish. It is not possible to stay here. Already it is too late. We must go."

"Yeah? Where?"

"I know where we are. We go west."

"West. Into Cambodia? That's a brilliant idea."

Quai Ng stood over Longacre and looked down. His broad face was smeared with dirt and blood. He had little cuts all over him, tiny dark streams, blood and sweat, ran down his slight but well-defined chest, soaked into the waistband of his thin cotton pants.

"I am sorry for Shortstop and Z-Man," he said, almost under his breath. Longacre said nothing.

"We must go. Now. If they find us, we are dead men. It will not be pleasant. I....I know what they do."

"I'll bet."

Captured is the worst thing to be, but Longacre's current situation ran a very close second, and he knew it. The middle of the jungle, shot down (for the very first time, actually), at night, no gear, no food, one clip in his M-16, six rounds in the .38 at his hip, huge aching pains in his chest, the worst headache of his life, and nobody to help him except one potentially treacherous Asiatic. On top of it all, his mouth tasted like the bottom of his grandmother's feet, and the pressure on his bowels was making him curl his toes. Something was definitely broken inside.

"They are coming now," Quai Ng said. "We must hide."

"I don't hear a fucking thing," Longacre whispered in spite of himself.

"No, you would not. Can you walk?"

Gasping, Longacre tried to heave himself to his feet, but sharp spears of pain in his chest drove him back to the wet ground. "Leave me here. I'll take care of those assholes."

"I will carry you."

"Right. You'll never pick me up."

Quai Ng smiled, though Longacre couldn't see it. "I will pretend you are a big pig."

There was no choice. The little man helped him stagger to his feet, lifting him slowly, with surprising ease, even though Longacre's vision turned red from the pain. Searing white lances shot through his chest. He had broken two ribs when he was about twelve, after one of his father's little reprimands, and he recognized the feeling. Three, maybe four. Hurts like a motherfucker.

Limping, dragging Longacre with him, Quai Ng made his way into the jungle, trying to put as much distance as he could between them and the crash site. He walked as though he could see in the dark.

"You must be quiet," he hissed.

"I'm bein' as fucking quiet as I can," moaned Longacre through clenched teeth. He could barely walk, bent over, leaning on his rifle, Quai Ng's right hand holding him tightly, painfully, under his left arm.

Quai Ng was desperate to smother the noise of their escape. Behind him, he could detect the rustlings of troops moving through territory that was totally familiar to them, closing in on the wreckage. Closing in on them.

He released Longacre and the tall thin man sank to the ground, lying on his back, barely stifling a groan.

"Be very quiet," Quai Ng cautioned. By that time even Longacre could hear the sounds of the NVA troops, not a hundred yards away. Scurrying silently, the sapper covered him with handfuls of leaves and small branches. If it hadn't been so dark, Longacre would have seen him picking the vegetation carefully, so as not to leave a trace. All he could do was lie there on his back in the dark, more frightened than he'd been since his father brought home the new razor strap, grinding his teeth from the tight pain of his shattered ribs, his eyes hurting with the effort of trying to see, feeling the leaves and branches drifting down, burying him alive.

"What....the fuck are you doing?" Quai Ng finished the job with five or six handfuls of rotting vegetation over Longacre's face.

"You call me Houdini. I can make you disappear."

"Jesus," groaned Longacre, "this shit stinks."

"Keep *quiet*. It covers you very good. No matter what happens, do not move. I will come back." And he dissolved into the night.

God damn, thought Longacre. God double damn. The night was absolutely still, except for the occasional hoot of a monkey or some other, more sizable jungle creature. Lying there under the earth, he couldn't help remembering all the stories he'd heard about the pit vipers and kraits and pythons that seethed through the jungle. You got bit, you were dead in three seconds, and there was nothing anybody could do. There were worse ways to go. He could hear footsteps, whispered conversation, rapid and high-pitched.

Longacre lay there, abandoned by Quai Ng, alone in the night, buried under the leaves and musty rotten smell of the jungle floor. His breath was soft and shallow because he didn't want to make the slightest noise, and besides, it hurt too much.

The troops began to spread out from the crash site, so quietly that Longacre could barely hear them, but he did, because every single sense, all of his body's will to live, was focused on those tiny noises.

Closer, now. How many? Two, maybe three, and they were *right there*, murmuring through the undergrowth. A foot came down not six inches from his left ear. The other NVA stepped over the mound of jungle filth, putting one foot directly between Longacre's outstretched legs, right in his crotch. He stopped, whispered something, then moved on.

Longacre permitted himself a small shuddering breath. The feet stopped again, not far away, not far, *there!* just past him.   He could only imagine what they were doing, looking around in the dark, trying to find at least one live American to play with.   They'd seen three bodies.   They knew there had to be one more.

A whisper came from the distance, and Longacre held his breath again as the feet shuffled past him one more time, a little farther away.   The sounds became softer, then melted into the jungle.

Quai Ng was back in seconds digging through the mound of rotten stuff, helping him to his feet.

"They are gone," he hissed.

"Then we're safe?"

"You are very funny, Longacre.   They will be back first light.   Night is long in the jungle.   We must find a safe place from snakes and tigers."

"Tigers?"   Longacre had heard that the jungles were full of them, and even seen pictures of some that had been killed by door gunners, but he'd never seen one outside the zoo in Oklahoma City.

"The NVA have killed many small animals for food.   Tigers have nothing to eat, so they are very hungry all the time.   We would be safe in the trees, but you cannot climb.   Come."

If it had been dark in the jungle, it was even darker down in the tunnel.   Quai Ng had dragged him through the dense undergrowth for at least two klicks, his ribs slicing pain into him every step of the way, until they stopped by a clump of bushes.   In seconds, he had pulled them aside, revealing a narrow, dark forbidding hole in the ground.

If Longacre had been any less long and bony, he never would have fit.   The tunnels were made for the small-staturedt Vietnamese, and even some of them had trouble moving around down there.   But Quai Ng managed to slide him down into the earth feet first, burying him for the second time that night, then crawling in after him, carefully pulling the bushes back over the hole.

"If this ain't the goddamndest thing," Longacre said under his breath, but his voice was loud in the dead blackness.   All he could hear was the sound of Quai Ng's breathing.   "What do we do now?   And where the holy fuck are we?"

"Old VC tunnel.   No longer in use.   This was big bunker that got bombed, fell down.   This is way in."

"Yeah? And now what?"

"I know clearing maybe two-three klicks from here. Is the only place close to where we have crashed. When they come back, they must land there to search for us."

"You know this area pretty good."

"As you say. This is my....turf?"

It was quiet for a long time in the moist, loamy smell, like the fresh turned Oklahoma fields after a rain, though minutes seem like days when you're lying underground in absolute blackness with the pain of three or four broken ribs to deal with. In such complete dark, when there is nothing to see, your eyes provide their own visual stimulation, giving you little electric bursts, blue and red and green, sometimes white, whisking across the retinal screen. There was no sound except for Quai Ng's breathing, and the sick wheeze as Longacre tried to force air into his damaged chest. It wasn't getting any easier. He was going to die.

"Longacre?"

"What."

"Why do you hate so much?"

He would have been perfectly happy just to lie there all night in the dark, comforted by his pain, not talking, especially not carrying on deep emotional conversations with this mysterious little man to whom he now owed his life.

"Hate you, you mean?"

"Not just me."

What was this? Small, innocent questions, four or five words, one syllable words at that, words from ordinary conversation, ones that took him places he didn't want to go.

But Quai Ng had asked, hadn't he, laying himself open for the full force of Longacre's long-suppressed fury. In a way, it was a good thing his ribs were broken, or he would have started stamping around, waving his arms and screaming. He was warm, starting to feel feverish, a little dizzy, hungry, disoriented from all the darkness and all the pain, very much out of his depth. He couldn't feel much of himself, he was convinced the darkness was becoming deeper still, there, in the utter blackness, under the earth. He was dying, for sure.

"Far as I can tell," he whispered, "you guys are nothing but a bunch of yellow mini-niggers. Got no fuckin' class, you eat that *nouc mam* shit at every meal and call it food, Jesus, who ever heard of making sauce out of rotten fish? You live in shit, you piss in the streets, the guys who run your government are all crooks, and you been killing each other for fucking ever." Longacre wasn't much of a reader, but he did know that the peoples of Southeast Asia, and Indochina in particular, had been at war among themselves in one form or another for the last couple of millennia. "Now you got us doing your killing for you. That's supposed to make this godforsaken country safe for democracy? If you guys got the right to vote tomorrow, you wouldn't know what the fuck to do with it. You think Mr. Nguyen down in the rice paddy's gonna understand government of the people and by the people? Give me a fucking break." Hot metal bolts of pain shot through Longacre's chest as he got worked up. "Aaahhh....fucking goddam Asians, if it wasn't for you, I wouldn't be in this hole in the ground."

"That is very true," Quai Ng observed, but Longacre missed the irony, heavy as it had been.

"Hadn't been for you, my father...he...." Another spasm of pain. Abruptly, he stopped talking. Again, the two men sat in the dark, Longacre's breath rattling in his chest.

"You think we are all the same."

Longacre was going to tell him that they *were* all the same, all the yellow-skinned races who teemed over that particular part of the planet. Let 'em go on killing each other, for another thousand years if they wanted to, because back in Oklahoma nobody gave a rat's rectum what the gooks did, and he firmly believed what his daddy had made such a great effort to teach him, out there in a real woodshed, on a real American farm. There's certain bunches of people in this world who need killing, and we know who they are. Gooks for sure. And the blacks. He respected the Jews, for some reason. But that's what this whole Vietnam thing is all about.

And yet, he had to admit one overwhelming fact. He was alive, though probably not for much longer. The heart still pumped, the lungs still sucked air (in limited amounts), and when that NVA had put a foot down in his crotch, he discovered that his bladder still worked.

Quai Ng weathered the storm of Longacre's xenophobic invective, because he was prepared for it.

"Is that all?" he asked.

Longacre didn't answer for a long moment. He was livid with pain, spending his last night on earth, and was maddened that it was so completely black in the cave, because if he started losing consciousness he wouldn't be able to tell. Fall asleep, he said to himself, and you're dead.

"Well...there is one other thing..."

CHAPTER 39
DEAR BENNY

Saturday, June 27

Dear Mom and Dad and Benny,

This tape may take a while, because I don't think I'll be able to tell you the whole story all at one time. Your son is no longer a virgin. I know what you're thinking Dad, I should have lost it in high school or college and you're right, I did. This is another rite of passage. A different kind. Yesterday afternoon I saw a man die. One of the men in my unit, one of my team members, a photographer named D'Amato, was killed while we were out on a shoot.

I'm still shaking and you know how I try to make a joke out of everything, but if I try it now.....

I never saw anything like that before. All that keeps coming to mind is going with Mom to Malter the butcher's shop when we lived in Kansas City and watching him lift a chunk of bloody meat over the counter to show Mom how fresh it is, but this side of beef had a name.

I guess what Captain Blank told me when I came to Hawaii is no longer true. I had asked him if anyone in DASPO had ever been killed. You remember the joke about the guy getting killed falling over the tripod, and the second guy dying from laughing at him. Well, I came inches from being the second guy. I know I shouldn't tell you this, and Mom has probably fainted by now, but the truth is I'm having a little trouble remembering exactly what happened. Kind of blocked it out, I guess.

We flew up to a village north of here to shoot some film about a drug interdiction mission. There's this Viet Cong guy. Well, not anymore, he's what they call a Cheu Hoi, which is a polite term for a defector, and he's supposed to be working for our side now. Anyway, he's one of these people who crawls around the jungle and infiltrates places and does reconnaissance missions, and he went up there snooping around, but he came back to this chopper unit he's assigned to and told the guys over there....but all along I thought these chopper guys were building sewers. See....sorry, I'm running on.   Well, why not, I haven't stopped running since I came close to paying a courtesy call to our long-departed ancestors from Austria or Poland or wherever we came from.

Anyway, the Vietnamese guy, Quai Ng, tells this chopper unit that the village is not really a village but a movie set. We're friends with the chopper guys who told us they were here to plan and build new sewers after we'd won the war. But that story was a bunch of water buffalo droppings, because they're actually ...well, never mind. Anyway, they smell some kind of rat when they see the photos we had taken at the village and coupled with what Quai Ng told them, they decide to go up there and see for themselves and take us along to shoot some film so they can prove whatever it is that's going on.

I just listened to what I said so far, and I don't think it's making much sense, but I'm going to keep trying.

Normally, we wouldn't be involved but it's all because of thatassholecolonelberner – sorry, Mom -- Colonel Berner, who you've heard me mention several times before. See, he was in the pictures along with the Vietnamese Colonel who's in charge of the drug interdiction program and another guy who we find out is some kind of drug lord with his own private army, and he owns half of Burma or something. No, this isn't a Flash Gordon hallucination, this is for real and none of us can understand why all these guys are together and why a village which was there one day with people and hooches and pigs and water buffalo and we saw it with our own eyes, is suddenly only empty buildings.

So we go back to the village in a few choppers with some Cobras escorting us, and found exactly what Quai Ng told us we would find...nothing. The place was deserted. So we figured we would just shoot some footage and get the hell out.   D'Amato must have seen something he wasn't supposed to see and while he was focusing his lens, a sniper took a shot at him. Part of what was his head ended up running down the front of my jungle fatigues. I just stood there looking at it until more shots rang out, and I started to run.

Dad, remember when I ran the mile in high school? I was never any good, but yesterday I broke four minutes including a jump or two at some high hurdles.

We loaded what was left of D'Amato on the chopper, and brought him back to base. He...he died in my lap.

When I got back to the villa, the first thing I did was take a shot of scotch and another and another. I hate scotch. Then I started searching for words to write home to D'Amato's folks, because I'm his commanding officer, and I was there, and it's my job. All I could think of was Van Heflin doing the same thing in 'Battle Cry." He had a script, and a pretty good screenwriter, but it took me the better part of a bottle to come up with the words, and then I discovered there aren't any. How do you tell a mother about the death of her son? I didn't know D'Amato's parents. I didn't even know if he had parents. I didn't even know D'Amato except for the short time I spent with him since I came to Nam.

I was stupid. I thought not knowing much about him would help me get through what just happened. But it didn't. It was like that time I was stationed at the Army Pictorial Center. Remember? Every officer had to pull Notification of Kin Duty once a month. There are a lot of New York kids in Vietnam, especially inner city ones, and a lot of them were dying.

One Saturday night, some Major from the Chaplain's school called me and told me to go meet some sergeant at an address up in Harlem, and spoil some family's day by telling them their kid wasn't coming home from the war. The only consolation was that he hadn't been killed in Vietnam but in a freak car accident outside the gates of Ft. Riley, Kansas.

I told the Major that he should call the Judge Advocate General's office instead, and start court martial proceedings right away, because not even the US Army was going to send my Semitic Caucasian *tuchus* to Harlem near midnight on Saturday to bring home that kind of news.

Well, he apologized and told me he thought I was black

and he would get someone else but would it be okay if I handled the SA Duty. Survivor's Assistance is where you help the family get the deceased's personal effects, medals, and serviceman's life insurance. I said fine.

So I end up doing everything there is to do for the soldier's family including making arrangements to bury him in a military cemetery since they couldn't afford any other kind of funeral. I had to help bury this young GI who had only been on active duty for a whole ten weeks of basic training. He was reporting to his new assignment at the Artillery School in Ft. Riley.

When I went to process the papers for his SGLI policy so his folks would receive the $10,000, the Army said they had no record of him being in the service.

I must have knocked on a dozen Army agency doors with the same spiel. "I just did an SA job on a young black soldier who is now buried in one of country's finest military cemeteries and the Army is saying he never existed."

Finally, I get a call one day from some clerk at Ft. Benjamin Harrison asking me where could they send the money. It turned out that when the kid was in the auto accident, the taxi he was in burned to a crisp. Not only did he become toast but so did his 201 file. About the only thing which survived was his dog tags. Finally, a second set of his records ended up at Ft. Benjamin Harrison and the matter was straightened out.

Why the heck did I tell you this story? Oh, yeah. It didn't bother me when this kid died. I never knew him. I never saw him. I even felt good about trying to help his parents out. But, D'Amato I knew. I ate with him, worked with him, went drinking with him and did just about everything else young guys do when they're trying to blow off steam in a war zone. Then I watched him die.

And, I'm damned if I understand why it happened. He didn't have to die, sure didn't deserve to. I guess that's true of everybody who's getting killed around here. He was looking through the camera when he got shot. What was the last thing he saw? Scares me to think about it. And it shames me, too.

When I was in college I had to take this science course where they taught us how Florida is made of limestone, and there are these rivers that run through underground caverns. Sometimes, they eat away the stone and the ground caves in, making sinkholes. They can happen anywhere, like in the middle of a town. I remember once a sinkhole opened up around Orlando somewhere and swallowed a used car lot and a bunch of stores.

That's what it's like here. Up till now, we were all having a pretty good time back in Saigon, on solid ground, with the bars and the...the...other forms of entertainment. Never mind. But we've been walking around with a huge river of war running under our feet, and yesterday...the ground opened up.

Don't worry, I'll try and remember what Mom said no less than five million times, "Don't mix in with other people's business." But Mom, you don't understand. Before D'Amato's death, it wasn't my business. That's when I should have remembered what you said. But the war has made it my business, whether I like it or not. I'm the one who has to write the letter.

The day I arrived in Saigon, there was a mortar attack, and I found myself in a bunker with a bunch of guys who had obviously been here a while. I was amazed at how old their faces looked, even though most of them were kids, younger than me. Well, when I was brushing my teeth a little while ago, I looked up quickly in the mirror and something in my face is different.

Now, I look like them.

CHAPTER 40
THE STORY OF ABRAHAM RADO

Saturday, June 27

Longacre could have started his musings with "once upon a time" and it would have been appropriate, but he didn't. This, more or less, is the story he told Quai Ng.

About two years ago (he said), there was a man named Captain Abraham Rado. He joined the Army in 1959, and knew exactly how his life was going to turn out. The first thing he did was volunteer for every weapon and tactical combat school the Army offered, almost like he knew one day he'd need the training. He was one of the first junior officers selected to join the brand-new Green Berets, and to him, it was like being transferred to heaven. Then, when the government started sending "advisors" to Vietnam, Rado knew at once that he'd been called to his destiny.

"How do you know of this man?" Quai Ng asked.

"You shut up, and I'll get to that." When Longacre started talking, the penetrating pain diminished, even if only slightly. He wanted to continue, even though he knew Quai Ng wouldn't understand half of the story he was about to tell.

The really strange thing about Abraham Rado was that he'd been born an orthodox Jew, but when he was about six, his entire family was wiped out by a drunk driver while they were walking home from synagogue after Yom Kippur services. The car missed him by inches, and he watched his parents and older brother die on the side of the road before help could arrive.

Of course, he was taken in by relatives, the orthodox community being extremely close-knit, but the anger and trauma of the tragedy made him what you would call a difficult child, and even though he spent eleven years wearing a prayer shawl under his clothes, growing earlocks and a beard, and studying the Torah all day long, he constantly seethed with the dedication to free himself from the restrictions that any orthodoxy inevitably imposes. Through his teen years, only an extremely rigid social structure kept him under control. He went through the motions till he was seventeen because he was smart enough to realize he had no choice, and then he disappeared into the Army. He looked older than he was.

By the time he was transferred to Ft. Bragg, he knew more than practically anyone about guerrilla warfare, and was so good at it they made him an instructor. He was 22, teaching men twice his age about a kind of combat he'd never experienced. And when, in August of 1963, as an American advisor, he took his first breath of Vietnam's crystal air, Abraham Rado, first Lieutenant Green Beret, 5th Special Forces, knew he was in the right place at exactly the right time.

He was eager to put his skills to the test. For some reason, Green Beret training had been a cakewalk for him. He had a talent for it, he was physically strong beyond his size, and he was well equipped for the things he'd be ordered to do. Mission after mission, in command of squads of American and Vietnamese Rangers, Rado would return with minimum casualties and maximum intelligence. The better he got, the longer and more dangerous his missions became. He made Captain two months after his arrival in Nam and ten months before the normal time in grade allowed.

"How do you know this many things about him?"

"We...spent some time together." Longacre peered into the dark. He couldn't make out Quai Ng's face.

"Yes? Where?"

"This is my story, so you let me tell it my way."

"Please."

Leaping Lena was the MAC-V code name for a select number of Vietnamese and CIDG warriors. The Civilian Irregular Defense Groups, pronounced SID-gee, were originally created by the US mission in Saigon to be a paramilitary force made up of the country's various ethnic groups. This included tribes like the Rhade, Jarai, and Mnong, whose major purpose was to keep the other tribes like the Montagnards from going over to the Viet Cong. The Montagnards were important because they occupied some of the largest strategic areas of the country. The groups were reorganized in 1964 under the name of Operation Delta, the embryo of what would later become the LRRPS, Long Range Reconnaissance Patrols. The mission of Leaping Lena was to create an ongoing special reconnaissance unit capable of conducting the most hazardous and critical missions inside the country. Later, the units would cross the lines and move operations into Laos and North Vietnam. Rado was one of the first men selected.

The assignment was easy, to lead a heavy LRRP mission into an area north of the A Shau valley. Usually, a LRRP team was composed of five or six specialists, but when there was the possibility of extensive enemy contact, they increased the team to ten. Most of Rado's men preferred the short team, because it was harder to hide ten men in the jungle. But a heavy team had the added advantage and comfort of an M-60 machine gun.

On the evening of November 23, 1963, Rado led his team in a prayer. They were so far out in the bush they hadn't heard that their Commander in Chief had died in Dallas, or they would have prayed for him, too. His men kissed their crosses or St. Christophers and he kissed his mezuzah, the only part of his religion he retained, and then all of them melted into the jungle.

It was a recon mission, cutting to a point about 20 kilometers northwest of the A Shau Valley to monitor the movement of troops and materiel down the Ho Chi Minh Trail. There were reports of heavy traffic, and Rado was glad to have nine men behind him instead of four.

The A Shau was located in Thauthien Province of I Corps near the Laotian border. Rado knew it well as a principal entry point to South Vietnam from the Ho Chi Minh trail. The NVA and Viet Cong used this canopied jungle path to carry everything down from the North by any means they could. Bicycles were a favorite method.

As American involvement slowly deepened, and as the North Vietnamese increased traffic along the trail, the valley became a critical area of operations. Later, it would be the target of repeated major attacks by allied forces, especially the 101st Airborne Division. The area was vigorously defended.

But on November 23, 1963, all of that was far in the future.

They arrived at their observation point, a small hill overlooking a slice of the Ho Chi Minh trail, and dug in. Not more than a few hours later, a caravan of elephants rumbled past, led by a gaggle of Montagnard tribesmen. Rado knew that the Montagnards hated the communists worse than anybody, and were friendly to the few American advisors they'd met crawling around in the jungle. Best of all, they always knew where the VC were, and didn't hesitate to share the information. The VC, after all, customarily drove them from their homes, forcing them to relocate entire villages.

The patrol called in the caravan's location, and were told it was probably a village on the move. Rado checked through his binoculars and couldn't see that the elephants or tribesmen were carrying any weapons. The beasts were loaded with ragged women and children clutching pots and pans and whatever other belongings mountain people took with them when they moved their village to stay ahead of the VC who terrorized them.

"This happened many times," said Quai Ng. "We discovered many deserted villages."

"You gonna let me finish this, or not?" wheezed Longacre.

"Yes, please. Continue talking. Do not sleep."

Longacre didn't know if he was asleep or not, because it was absolutely perfectly dark in the tunnel. His body throbbed, much of him had gone numb, either from injury or lack of motion, and he was terrified that some broken blood vessel, somewhere inside him, was pumping blood, bit by bit, into his chest.

Over the radio, the operations officer in charge ordered Rado to intercept the caravan and see if he could get any information about VC patrols or weapons movement in the area. Rado didn't like the idea, but the OIC assured him they were the same Montagnards who'd been stopped by another LRRP team north of their position a few days earlier. He was wrong, and Rado paid for the mistake.

For the only time since he'd been in the jungle, his judgment deserted him, and he took the word of an intelligence officer he'd never met. When he led his team down the hill to stop the caravan, the jungle exploded around them. Instantly, six of his men were dead. The other three went down next to him, and somehow, in the middle of small

arms fire coming from every direction, he pulled one of them
to safety off the trail, went back, carried the second one into
the cover of the jungle, then went back again, and picked up
the third. Then he disappeared.

The Army gave Rado the Congressional Medal of Honor
posthumously, which is the way most people receive it, on the
testimony of SFC Windon, the only surviving member of the
team. It took him five days of crawling through leech infested
terrain behind enemy lines to make camp and tell his story.

Windon told the officers at base camp that he, Rado, and
the other two survivors had agreed to split up and rendezvous
at a point they knew a few klicks on the other side of the
Vietnamese border. Their wounds weren't serious, and they
knew they could make it, but Windon was the only one who
did. The other two were discovered by a patrol some weeks
later, nailed to trees with their tongues cut out and their eyes
hanging from threads of rotting flesh. Rado was never found.
Officially he was presumed killed in action.

But he was, for better or worse, very much alive, and in the
custody of a small unit of the North Vietnamese Army. The
caravan they'd intercepted was conveying huge amounts of
raw opium from Burma through Laos to the laboratories into
Cambodia. The "refugees" on the elephants were camouflage,
unfortunates who had been kidnapped from their villages.
They'd been given the choice of dying or spending a few days
riding through the jungle on elephants and being released at
an unknown location. Most of them chose the latter, even
though they knew they'd probably be killed anyway. Rado,
his two leg wounds making it impossible for him to navigate
the jungle quietly despite all his hard-won skills, passed out
from loss of blood, and was captured by the caravan guards
hidden in the jungle. When he came to, he found himself face
down in the red dirt at the feet of the leader of the caravan, a
warlord named Wo Minh.

He absolutely could not understand why they didn't shoot
him on the spot, but the slightly cross-eyed Cambodian who
dressed Rado's leg wounds turned out to be quite expert at
the job. Bullet wounds were common in the drug caravan
trade, and he'd had plenty of practice. He gave Rado some
kind of bark or root or herb to chew on which miraculously
dulled the pain, made him dizzy, and he passed out again.

Next time he came to, he was being handed down from the back of an elephant and delivered over to an NVA patrol.

He didn't understand a word of the language, but he could tell some kind of deal was in progress. The caravan leader was huddled with the NVA officer, whose six men clustered behind them in their khaki shorts and pith helmets, AK-47s at the ready. There was much pointing, gesturing, and some raised voices, but apparently agreement had been reached. The NVA officer wanted the drugs, but Wo Minh talked him into taking the American instead, and he had to agree because the drug runners had superior firepower.

In the bamboo tiger cage, his leg slowly healed. He was ready for death every day, but it never came. Rather, he became the NVA captain's most treasured possession, and his favorite form of entertainment.

They let him out of the cage for only a short time each day, and kept him closely guarded. The captain spoke some English, and when he wasn't threatening to kill him, shouted convoluted streams of propaganda in his ear. Rado, his leg slowly healing from the daily application of some foul-smelling herbal concoction the cross-eyed drug smuggler had left with them, realized that if he could prove to be of value to the NVA, they might keep him alive. He wouldn't be a traitor, he'd be meeting his obligation as a POW to survive.

One day, when he was out of the tiger cage, escorted by three guards for a short walk, he stopped suddenly on the jungle trail and motioned for them to be quiet. They brought their rifles up, suspicious of any move he might make. Slowly, painfully (since his leg had not yet healed completely), he squatted down to the fetid floor of the jungle, his hand shot into the undergrowth and came out with a four-foot snake. The edible kind. The guards' eyebrows went up. They couldn't tell one snake from another, assumed all of them were poisonous, which most were, and kept their distance. But this American knew the difference, and could catch them with his bare hands. He'd suffered through the nastiest jungle survival training in the world, and could bite the head off a live lizard, if he had to, or drink duck's blood. Back at the base camp, they put a pistol to his head, cautiously handed him a knife, and watched him expertly fillet the snake and turn it into a surprisingly tasty ragout.

From that day on, he was the official forager of the best fed unit in all of North Vietnam. He tracked down and caught all kinds of small animals, and prepared them in ways that used the indigenous herbs and other vegetation in the most imaginative and appetizing combinations. They kept him for five years, never once going near a city or major base, moving his cage every few days and guarding him around the clock, at first because he was a POW and then because of his position as chief forager for the unit. Sometimes they lowered him into a maze of tunnels and he spent weeks under the earth without ever seeing the sky. At night, they'd take him out to hunt for larger animals with a bow and arrow. He moved with the company as if he were one of them. He learned their language through osmosis and brute force, and memorized everything he saw. He never had any idea where he was, but knew that he'd be able to use all he learned when he escaped. Unlike most other prisoners, he spent no time worrying about his family, because he didn't have any, or about what his captivity might be doing to his wife and kids, because he didn't have them, either. What he did have was a strange re-awakening of his faith, and he spent hours in the darkness reciting pages and pages of prayers and scripture in Hebrew, all perfectly memorized from his very earliest childhood, from Genesis right on through to Deuteronomy. When the NVA soldiers tried to learn English words or phrases, he would teach them Yiddish instead, because his only source of amusement was listening to the captain say things like *gay cocken offen yam* (go shit in the ocean) or *kish mier in tuchus* (kiss my ass) in Yiddish with an Asiatic accent, thinking he was learning the language of his enemy.

Meanwhile, he absorbed every jungle marking the NVA and VC had devised to warn their own about Tu Dai, the Vietnamese marking for booby traps. He so amazed the captain that they forced him to teach jungle survival to the recruits they kidnapped from the villages. He didn't consider it helping the enemy, or giving aid and comfort, because it was keeping him alive, and teaching him things he'd be able to use later. He thought of it as counterintelligence, and never doubted that he would escape. When he did, he would be able to turn every bit of it against them.

"To escape is very rare," Quai Ng said, his voice close in the dark. He was right. Up to that point in the war, fewer than 30 prisoners of war had ever escaped from the NVA or the VC.

"Rado did," said Longacre, looking at the green glowing face of his watch. He could barely move his arm. Thankfully, the watch had survived the crash. It was 3:15 in the morning. The air in the tunnel was hot and fetid.

"How did he do this?"

"He just ran away."

Rado developed plan after plan to make his escape, and it made him furious that he never had the chance to try one out. He was well aware that his timing would have to be perfect, and he was patient enough to bide his time until the right set of conditions was presented to him. He was kept by the same little platoon the entire time. Don't these guys ever go home, he wondered. Don't they ever return to base? Don't they have families, or go on leave? They didn't. They just stayed in the jungle, planting booby traps here, killing some villagers there, "recruiting" young boys from hamlets and sending them off to other units, increasing their numbers. Unlike the Americans, they had no one-year tour of duty. They would stay in the jungle till the war was over, one way or another. In spite of himself, Rado began to respect them.

Over the last year, before his escape, they had increased to almost thirty troops, had somehow gotten rudimentary uniforms, guns, and ammunition resupply from patrols who transported them along the trail, and had allowed Rado to train all the new "recruits" in jungle lore, because he was better at it than they were. Maybe they thought they'd won him over, because he made every effort to behave as if they had. Maybe they came to believe that the communist ideology the captain preached to him every day in fractured English finally had the desired effect. He'd learned their language so well he could make jokes and puns in it, and could quote the sayings of Ho Chi Minh in a convincing Haiphong accent. Unknown to him, rumors had spread down toward the south about an American traitor who lived among the NVA, helping them on their maneuvers in the jungle. According to the stories, this turncoat had killed at least fifty Americans himself. Or a hundred. Nobody knew who he was.

When the escape plan came to him, it was, like most good ideas, elegant in its simplicity. For days, he turned it over in his mind, applying to it the same sophisticated questioning techniques the rabbis used in arguing obscure points of Talmudic commentary. He waited, reviewing the plan again and again. He had come to understand the jungle after being hauled through it for years, and believed he knew where they were. If he was right, escape would be easy. If he was wrong, escape would be death.

The patrol had just "drafted" several teenage boys from an unfortunate village.   He was instructing them in jungle navigation and concealment, running drills to reinforce the lesson. He divided the group of unwilling recruits into two, and told the veterans to watch them, fashioning a game of hide-and-go-seek. They'd made him a whistle out of bamboo, and when he blew it, the recruits stumbled into the jungle, trying to become invisible as quickly as possible. He blew it again, and the veterans scattered, going after them. Rado looked around. They had left him completely alone, and he quietly melted into the jungle in the opposite direction.

He ran for four days, in what he hoped was the direction of A Shau, because he was convinced that he wasn't all that far from where he'd been captured. He was in excellent shape. His wounds had healed completely long ago, he grabbed whatever furtive exercise he could, and when he fed his captors, he managed to save the most nutritious parts of the jungle rats for himself. He'd lost thirty pounds over the years, but he was running for his life.

He kept telling himself an American fire support base was just over the next hill, beyond the next clearing, but it wasn't. He continued south, knowing the captain was after him, easily keeping his sense of direction in the jungle. On the fourth day, dysentery took hold of him. He'd been careful of the roots and berries and grasshoppers and bugs he picked off the jungle floor to eat, but something got him. He didn't care. He'd lived among the North Vietnamese for five years, and he was going home.

On the morning of the fifth day, Rado heard the percussive sound of a chopper in the air. He peered through the jungle into a clearing and saw the most welcome and most surprising sight of his life...an American Chinook landing on the far side of a small stream, disgorging a platoon of grunts from its belly. He didn't actually know what year it was, nor did he know how far his country had committed itself to the war. Certainly, he'd heard choppers and aircraft in the sky when he was a prisoner, but he'd never seen so many American troops in one place at one time. He was going home.

With a yell, he started running toward the chopper but took no more than ten steps when he threw himself to the ground to avoid being cut in half by the grunts, who all opened fire at once with their M-16s. His uniform had fallen apart years before, and he was dressed in whatever his captors gave him. Khaki shorts and a shirt. He didn't look that much like an NVA troop, but he was all the way across the clearing, the grass was high, grunts couldn't see him clearly, and besides, they were jumpy.

His drop to the ground had not been entirely voluntary. He'd been shot again, this time by his own men. Blood poured from his shoulder. It hurt like hell, but he could stand the pain. He turned around, dragging himself along the ground, trying to make it back to the tree line. Behind him, he could hear the rustle of feet through the elephant grass and knew that within moments he'd be killed by some gung ho grunt or captured again by the NVA who would be crawling through the jungle. Apparently, some regular forces had heard the chopper land and were closing in to get a piece of the action.

With no place to go, Rado started screaming at the top of his lungs "Rado...Captain...POW...just escaped."

It was no use. The enemy in the jungle started shooting at the grunts, pinning Rado down in a blistering crossfire. But suddenly the treeline exploded in a fabulous burst of flame thanks to two Huey gunships that rolled in and rippled a series of rockets into the far side of the clearing.

It was over as fast as it started. Rado was losing blood, getting dizzy, his vision turning to black and white. Above him swam the round moist face of an Army colonel, pale high forehead, no neck, baggy eyes. A black corporal hauled him to his feet. Hot fire lanced through his ruined shoulder. In his weakened state, it occurred to him that the colonel looked a hell of a lot like Broderick Crawford.

"Get this drug smuggling motherfucker taped and tied!" the colonel yelled in a shrill, high-pitched voice.

"I'm American," Rado gritted, barely conscious. "Rado, Abraham, Captain Special Forces. I've been a POW for five years! I just escaped."

The major hit him viciously across the face with his sidearm. "You lying fuck. Your ass is mine."

The black corporal turned to the high pitched voice and said, "Colonel Berner, this guy is American."

"And a low life drug smuggling deserter. Didn't you see how those gooks were trying to rescue him?"

"Sir...I think Turner is right." This from a tall thin warrant officer with long bony arms and fingers.

"Shut up, Longacre."

"Sir, I think they were shooting at him, too."

"Tie and gag him. That's an order. You just fly my goddam chopper and I'll let Intelligence determine what kind of drug smuggling son of a bitch he is. Load him up. Got me?"

Turner, Longacre, and two other troops bundled Rado back to the Chinook, but just as they got to the door, machine gun fire burst from the treeline again, this time from the other side of the clearing. Bullets ripped into the side of the aircraft. Rado got another one. Longacre got two of his own.

"So you have known Colonel Berner before already?" Quai Ng asked.

"Yeah. He was running around doing public information, stories for the Stars and Stripes, stuff like that. "Guess he thought this Rado guy was the story that'd make his reputation."

"What happened?"

"I got the rest of this second hand, because I took two and went down. But we got back to base, and Berner came to find out he beat the crap out of a wounded Medal of Honor winner who was missing in action for five years, then tied him up and gagged him. Fucked his career. He wanted to make sure things didn't get too public, so he somehow pulled strings to get me and Jackson out of the way. Don't know what happened to Turner, probably transferred him to the north pole, but when I got out of the hospital, they assigned me to the shittiest platoons, flying ash and trash around the most fucked up parts of your wonderful country. Thatassholecolonelberner did it, I know he did. Spent two years fucked out in the boonies, thanks to him. He was probably hoping they'd kill my ass."

"How could he do such a thing to you?"

"He knows all the wrong people."

"But why do you know so much about this man Rado?"

"We both got medevaced to Hawaii. I spent six weeks in the bed next to him. He talked both my ears off."

It was cool underground, but little beads of smelly sweat clung to Longacre's skin. He was feeling warmer. The sharp pains in his chest had arranged themselves into a regular convulsing throb, like the dull beat of drums at a public execution.

He never did tell Quai Ng about his father, because he fell asleep, or fainted, or somehow lost a significant part of his consciousness. When he didn't answer, Quai Ng reached over to gently run his hand over the hot forehead, bent his ear to Longacre's face to check his breathing, then sat back and closed his eyes.

Quai Ng dreamed of nothing, but Longacre's night was a time of feverish figments, a time of hazy images doing a stuttering *danse macabre*, flickering pictures on the wide screen of his mind, times and events he'd long since forgotten or suppressed. But they never disappeared completely, always lurking someplace down in the pit, behind the walls he built, behind the doors he had long since pushed closed with his shoulder and locked with the big rusty key. In his sleep, the walls came down, and all the doors opened wide.

Flash. A first memory of his father, a shockingly skinny man, gaunt and haunted. They didn't tell him anything until he was "old enough to understand." but it was all about World War II, about fighting the Japanese in a place called Bataan, and what those people had done to his father in that place. They waited a long time, but when they told him, he wasn't old enough to understand. Even in 1970, at 26, he wasn't old enough to understand things like that. He could never be. Nobody could.

"Longacre, we must go. It is dawn." Quai Ng's voice played across the screen like the rest of the dirty little pictures. He said it again, then a third time. Gradually, the sound filtered in. Longacre pried open his eyes. It wasn't easy, and as soon as he did, all the pain came flooding back.

Quai Ng pushed the foliage away from the tunnel entrance and hauled Longacre's gaunt, broken body up into the pre-dawn darkness. There was no gentle way to do it, but by that time, Longacre was so feverish and so deeply into shock, and so numb from the constant beat of the drum that he couldn't have cared.

Somehow, Quai Ng pulled, pushed, carried, dragged, tugged and towed him northward through three kilometers of jungle, farther into Cambodia, to the clearing he knew. He almost killed himself doing it, because Longacre, even at his lankiest, weighed almost twice as much as he did. He was like an ant on the sidewalk, struggling along with a burden on his back ten times his size.

Longacre's face was very hot, his flight suit soaked with foul-smelling sick sweat and urine, and he babbled incoherently about Oklahoma, the tigers in the zoo, his almost-daily trips to the woodshed, Abraham Rado, and the Japanese on Bataan, another bunch of fucking little yellow men, who were responsible for all his pain.

But they got there, and Quai Ng was right. He made Longacre comfortable under a tree and didn't have to wait more than half an hour before the jungle revealed itself to him in the first light of day. Then minutes later, they heard that unmistakable sound in the distance, coming right for them, just above the treetops, Webb and Harrell and Larue and all the rest, a slick down low and two unmarked Cobras a few hundred feet higher, hanging in the air.

The Cobras orbited while the slick flew a right hand pattern around the clearing and settled in, light on the skids, just in case of surprises. Larue and Harrell jumped out, but before they could wade ten feet into the tall grass, Quai Ng struggled toward them from the treeline, carrying the inert form of Longacre in both his arms, tight against his chest.

CHAPTER 41
THE BOXING OF COLONEL XOAN

Monday, June 29, 1970

After Longacre had been safely medevaced to Hawaii for the second time in his military career, Quai Ng finally told them The Time Had Come, and Colonel Xoan was due to be weighed in the judgment. Ng started the process by leading selected members of the Shadows on an expedition toward their quarry through some shadows of his own...the unfathomable back streets of Saigon. If he was the bloodhound, they were the posse of backwoods deputies, struggling to keep up as he guided them on a Dantesque excursion down to the ninth circle of an unknown land. Into the bowels of the city they went, through places where no American would ever dream of venturing, threading their way through an overwhelming convolution of alleyways and dark spaces between buildings they never would have set foot in by themselves, past huts and shacks stacked one on top of the other, feral eyes peering out of them from ominous darkness within, open fires, pigs and poultry, steam, smoke, mud, dampness, vapor, sweating, squeezed between walls, attacked by thousands of odors, some that smelled like colors, and some that smelled like nothing they could possibly imagine.

Every once in a while Quai Ng would tell them to wait, and duck into a shack or scurry through a hole in a wall, leaving them alone in the wilderness of rickety structures. Almost instinctively, they stood back to back, Webb, Larue and Harrell, and put their hands on their .45s. Quai Ng had made a lot of points when he staggered out of the jungle with Longacre, but as they looked around themselves in the alley, they realized that they could disappear in that place, vanish completely, and nobody would ever know.

Finally, Quai Ng conducted them through another narrow

alley to a dark flight of stairs that led down under an old villa. Webb looked up, and saw that the place must have once been palatial. There were sculpted scrolls and leaves around the windows, elaborate decorations along the roofline, the home of a minister, maybe, or a province chief.

"He is down there," Quai Ng said. The disintegrating stone stairs, overgrown with vines and weeds, blotched with mildew, streaked with rust that dripped down from the old metal handrail, led down into unfathomable blackness.

"Where the fuck are we?" asked Harrell.

"This building is a...you would say recreational club?" Quai Ng told them.

"You gotta be kidding," said Larue.

"I ain't going down there," agreed Harrell.

"You first," said Webb.

"I cannot. But it is safe. The place is owned by a man named Walter Crawley. People know better than to make trouble here. The colonel will not be expecting you. He is...occupied."

Of all the Shadows, Webb was more comfortable with Quai Ng than most. Perhaps it was his Midwestern neighborliness, his human nature, or those old Sunday sermons about forgiveness and brotherhood back in Milwaukee that had stuck with him on some subliminal level. But still, he wasn't so sure about going down those stairs, into that darkness, just because the wiry Vietnamese said it was okay.

Webb threw one more barbed look at Quai Ng, searching his black eyes, and decided to let his human nature prevail.

"Follow me."

Down the stairs, the stone crumbling under their feet, easily through the plain door at the bottom because of the ancient broken lock, and a dead stop inside when they heard, from down the hall, the unmistakable sounds of a man suffering incredible physical punishment. Groans, screams, the sickening, unmistakable sound of heavy vicious blows against soft unprotected flesh.

They took out their guns. Webb followed the sound around a corner to a thin strip of light that leaked from under a door at the end of the hall. Behind that door, something unthinkable was going on.

"That son of a bitch," Larue hissed. "Who's he got in there?"

More sounds of impact from behind the door.

"Let's find out," said Webb.

Harrell took a long look at the door.   He was understandably hesitant to shoot his way in, because he had no idea who might on the other side, or upstairs.   Once, on R&R in Bangkok, he found out you can't go crashing through a door with your shoulder the way they do on television.   That discovery, and the regrettable events that followed it, were part of the reason he'd been relegated to the Shadows.   But the door he was looking at seemed relatively new, cheap, probably with a hollow core.   So he crashed through it with his shoulder.   Webb and the others tumbled after him, pointing their weapons into the room and yelling, "Nobody move," or its equivalent.

Nobody moved.   The mysterious Colonel Xoan did wiggle a little bit in spite of the command, because he was hanging by his feet from an ancient wood ceiling beam, naked and sweating, with his hands tied behind his back.   The two Vietnamese hookers didn't move, because three Americans with guns had come careening into the room, and they weren't even going to twitch.

"Now, this is very pretty," said Harrell.   The two women were the kind of killingly beautiful creatures who waft across the verandah at the Continental, or magically appear on the streets at night.   Gorgeous Eurasian Vietnamese call girls with the shiniest black hair, bright red lips, each of them looking no more than fourteen years old.   The impression of their age was due partly to their diminutive size, and partly to the French schoolgirl uniforms they wore.   White blouses with blue diagonal striped neckties and a navy blue vest, heartbreakingly short navy skirts with just a hint of white cotton panty peeking out underneath, white knee socks and patent leather shoes, the kind Americans call Mary Janes. On their hands, the ladies wore bright red 12-ounce boxing gloves.

Webb walked over to the pendent Xoan, inspected the angry red blotches and bruises on his midsection, leaned down and looked him in the upside down face.

"You twisted little devil." He straightened up and faced his men. "See? Everybody in this country is having a good time but us."

Xoan, even though he was hanging upside down playing human punching bag, even though his ribs ached (deliciously) and even though he sported the grandfather of all erections that pointed emphatically at the floor, somehow retained his commanding aura, and barked orders to the two women. They both moved toward him at once, but the government-issued firearms changed their minds.

"Out," said Larue, and the two women started for the door.

"No," said Webb. "His boys could be right upstairs."

Xoan started screaming at the women, at the Shadows, at life in general. He knew exactly the depth of the shit he was in, hanging there, his head two feet off the floor, his ribs and kidneys aching, wishing he'd hired bigger women who could hit harder. He looked up at his penis, a traitorous organ that stared at him with one teary unblinking eye, though the stare was not as fixed as before. Harrell looked frantically around, seeing the place for the first time, and discovered that it was a regular little dungeon paradise, liberally supplied with straps, cuffs, gags, and other instruments of erotic immobilization, no doubt purchased by Colonel Xoan on his many trips to Paris. (The colonel did, in fact, know of a delightful bondage boutique on the Boulevard de Charonne just across from the Père Lachaise cemetery.)

Larue grabbed a black leather ball gag from a hook on the wall, knelt down to the colonel's bobbing head and stuffed it in his mouth. He used a few more of Xoan's imaginative leather accessories to immobilize the women, and took his time doing it. "Somebody'll find you in a day or two," he assured them.

Webb went to the other wall and found the little winch that the hookers had used to hoist Xoan to his undignified yet undeniably stimulating position.

"Let's get him out of here," said Webb. He did not let Xoan down gently.

CHAPTER 42
THE RETURN OF THI LANH

Wednesday, July 1

Foster was glad to have his room to himself again, and glad that Thi Lanh had been bundled off, baby and all, to the Blessed Sisters of Perpetual Consolation or whoever they were. The DASPO troops all congratulated themselves and each other on their bravery, their good deeds, and their contribution to Vietnamese-American relations. The shoots were going well, Berner was safely contained for the time being, D'Amato's belongings and his remains had been shipped home, Foster, holding back tears, had written the obligatory tragic letter to his family, Huggins was locked up in some VA mental health facility in Virginia, and Foster felt good enough to dig into a new film proposal for the Army Big Picture series. They even had a rare day off, all their projects either in preproduction, waiting for film to come back from the lab, or in transit. Things were quiet. A perfect day to sit at his desk and work on his new script.

"Lieutenant, somebody here," Young Dung mumbled, and sulked out of the room.

It was Thi Lanh. Only a few days had gone by, but she was walking on her crutches with the ease of constant practice. Svoboda crowded into the room right behind Ironman. Weinberg, interrupted in mid-fish, came stumbling down the stairs. Hugs all around, and high-pitched squeals from Thi Lanh.

"How are you doing?" Ironman asked.

"Very nice."

"How do you like living with the Sisters?" Weinberg asked.

"Oh, I not there no more."

No? And why not?

"Sisters very mean. Bad to me."

"What are they doing to you?" Ironman asked. He had run into a couple of nasty nuns during his school days.

"They no let me out to do trick, make money for my brother. They get SO mad. I go away from there. Live with girlfriend. Some GIs like girl with crutches, pay extra. I make money."

Foster's stomach started to retreat to the south, feeling much like it did when she first showed him the mangled leg.

"You mean the sisters wouldn't let you turn tricks out of the convent?" Foster asked.

"No! You believe it?"

"Where's your baby?" He almost didn't want to ask.

"I give him back to mamasan. You remember. No work. Need money. Mamasan give me money for baby."

"Wait a minute. You hocked your baby *again*, and now you turn tricks and give the money to your brother?" Ironman, in spite of himself, wanted to know.

"You bet. He buy pills and hash oil, some joints, sell them on the corner. I give him hundred dollars, he make four hundred. So quick. Good money, huh?"

Ironman and the rest had unconsciously taken a step back from her when she started telling the story. The silence in the room roared in their ears, not even the persistent sound of the ciclos from the street penetrating their shock, disappointment, and emptiness. A thank you would have been nice. While some of them felt they deserved it for staying up all night, listening to her mumble, and changing the green sticky dressings on her leg, others, like Foster, knew they hadn't helped her for the gratitude. But the realization that all their efforts, all their innocent good intentions were worthless, hollowed them out for a brief, black instant.

"Come with me," said Svoboda. He started urging her to the front door.

"You mad at me?"

"Mad? No. Not mad."

Ironman ran ahead to contain the dogs. Svoboda escorted her across the gravel courtyard to the front gate, let her out, and started to clang the black wrought iron shut behind her when he was interrupted by three men pushing their way through the opening. Ironman recognized Colonel Berner at once, because everybody in Saigon knew him by sight, so when Jack and Little Shit came barreling around the building, eager for a good leg fuck, he stepped back and let it happen.

"God DAMN!" yelled Berner. "Get this beast off me!" The dogs left the other two men alone, partly because they were dressed in civilian clothes and partly because they were scarier-looking than the hounds themselves. They wore dark grey suits, white shirts, skinny black ties. Nobody in Saigon dressed like that, ever.

Ironman let the dogs have their way as long as he could, then two whacks with the customary tire iron made Jack release Berner's leg, and the three men climbed the front steps, where Foster was waiting at the door, not without a certain degree of puzzlement.

"Lieutenant Foster," said Berner with a sick, ominous smile. "I'd like you to meet Agent Russell and Agent Calhoun. They're with...an agency of the government."

The two men were as alike as Call Me Norman and Dave is My Name. Same height, same build, same clothes and hair, same intense expression around the eyes. Clearly, thought Foster, these were men entrusted with Important Matters. Foster shook their hands, and wondered how they could be so cold when it was around 400 degrees outside. As he walked them into the relative cool of the dining room, the rest of the crew scampered out of sight, but stayed close enough to listen in. Foster did not miss the sour expression on Berner's face as the colonel took in the relatively luxurious surroundings of the villa.

The agents got right to the point.

"Where is Colonel Xoan?"

"Is he lost?" Foster felt like someone had filled his stomach with hot rocks. These men are with a "government agency?" Okay, which one? Which acronymic organization spawns spooky motherfuckers like this? What were they doing here? Why had Berner brought them? And what in hell made them think he would know anything about Xoan? Berner sat across from him with a "boy, you in a heap of trouble" look on his face, enjoying it.

"Just answer the question, Lieutenant."

"I have no idea. The last time I saw him was with Colonel

Berner here." The two agents turned to glance at Berner for an instant, then turned their dark gaze back to Foster.

"Do you know the name Walter Crawley?"

"Who doesn't?"

"Do you know who he is?

"From what I heard, he runs the war. Drugs. Black market. That's what they say in the bars."

"Have you ever heard of a man named Wo Minh?"

"Sure. Colonel Xoan says he's the biggest, most evil drug lord in Southeast Asia."

"Have you ever seen him? Been with him?" Foster paused, just for an instant. Had these guys seen the photo from Dam Long?

"Me? How would I get to see him?"

"Excuse me," Berner chimed in. "What's this all about?"

"Thank you, Lieutenant," said Russell, or Calhoun, as both men got to their feet. "Colonel Berner seemed to think you would be able to help us. Clearly, he was mistaken. Colonel, let's discuss this back at your office. We'll find our own way out."

CHAPTER 43
SAD NEWS FOR BENNY

Thursday, July 2

Hi, Benny,

Let's see...I told you about our party, even though I couldn't remember much of it, and I told you who the guys next door turned out to be. And I told you that the MPs came and took Huggins away. I'm still celebrating about that.

We're still fighting Colonel Berner on every front, and his buddy Colonel Xoan with the drug interdiction movies. Haven't heard much about them the past few weeks, though. Wonder what's going on. We were supposed to do a piece on all the drugs they found in that fake village once they brought them back to the base, but Berner never called. Speaking about Berner, he dragged some spooky guys in dark suits into the villa the other day. I'll save that story for later, but it was the same day that hooker Thi Lanh came back. Also a story for another time.

Remember that captain Call Me Norman I run into once in a while at the Number One Club? Well, he had himself duplicated, and now there are two of him. His twin calls himself Dave is My Name, and I can't go anywhere in Saigon without seeing them. The other night, I'm walking past the Continental Hotel downtown, and Dave is sitting on the veranda. He was shitfaced as usual, and wanted to buy me a beer. I didn't especially feel like it, but he was buying, and it's a violation of the Uniform Code of Military Conduct to refuse free beer. They can execute you for it.

One beer turns into six or so, and all I hear is more Walter Crawley. I'd love to party with that guy. Dave makes it sound like he's responsible for nine-tenths of the black market profiteering that's happening around here, all the steam and cream parlors, the war itself, the attack on Pearl Harbor, and the extinction of the dinosaurs, too.

They don't care that he's in bed with some corporation called Maredem that's skimming zillions of dollars out of the clubs and slot machines on the bases, and they don't care that this company is owned by a bunch of American colonels and top sergeants. No, everybody's trying to find out how much Walter has to do with the drug trade. They might as well ask how much screwing has to do with making babies. Vietnam, it seems, is a family business, and the way Dave tells tell it, Crawley is a favorite cousin. One of his relatives is a colonel in the Vietnamese Air Force, such as it is, and there's another mysterious cousin who may or may not be a legendary drug lord in Laos or Burma.

If any of that is true, I'd like to meet him, because he probably had something to do with D'Amato getting killed. Maybe he didn't pull the trigger, but it wouldn't surprise me if that fake village was his idea.

Anyway, Dave gave me an earful about Crawley and how he practically runs the country, and I just got tired of it. I got up to go, and it took me three tries.

Then I remembered about Call Me Norman, and asked Dave where he was. They were always together.

"He took the big ETS," Dave says. That usually means discharge, but not this time. They found him in the barracks, dead of an overdose. Needle was still in his arm.

I said, "I never thought he was the type to do drugs."

"He wasn't," said Dave.

CHAPTER 44
COLONEL XOAN TAKES A DIVE

Friday, July 3

"We shoulda brought the DASPO guys and a couple of cameras." Larue's voice crackled in the headsets as he climbed the Huey up through 2500 feet. "This guy's a real sight."

He was referring, of course, to Colonel Xoan, who at the hands of the Shadows, was in the process of having his fortunes seriously reversed.

In the basement playroom, Webb and Harrell had wrestled the dangling Xoan into a shiny green morgue pack. Foster had informed them of the correct terminology when he gave them the bag, since he'd learned it from Lazslo Kapusta at the mortuary. ("Here ve have not ze body bagz. Ve have only ze morgue packs. Ve have not ze corpses, ve have only ze remainz.") It was the most logical and readily available form of packaging they could think of, and DASPO was sitting on about a dozen of them, which Svoboda had commandeered after they finished the mortuary film.

"Shoot loot," he said. "Besides, you don't never know."

They zipped Xoan up and hustled him to the base in the back of a Jeep, then subjected him to uncomfortable repose in a closet at the anonymous hooch next to the mortuary, in a state of accelerating anxiety. Now the Colonel was lying blindfolded on the cold vibrating cargo bay floor of a Shadows Huey. He knew it was cold because he could feel the oily metal all along his quivering body. He was relatively certain he was naked, but the scrap of filthy black cloth tied much too tightly over his eyes made it hard to tell. There was a strong wind blowing through his crotch, though, which he rightly took as a clear indication that his exposure was in direct proportion to his vulnerability. He was in a helicopter, he couldn't move his arms, he couldn't move his legs. Tied up, he concluded, half in panic, half in anger. He did not find the tied up part terribly unpleasant.

He couldn't speak, either, which was the third thing he found out.

The racketing cargo bay was full of people, as many as could fit in the laboring machine, because they all wanted to celebrate the July 4th weekend with the colonel. Larue was flying because he lost the toss. They all wanted a piece of Xoan, and would have gleefully taken slices of his mortal meat with knives, dull spoons, broken glass, even fingernails if they'd allowed themselves to. Martin, being of Spanish extraction, hoped to be awarded an ear and a tail. But they had one serious problem, and it was almost Zen in its nature: how do you coerce a man who loves pain? ("Whip me!" said the masochist. "No!" the sadist replied).

The flight was Webb's idea, and its implementation gave him a skybox seat, squatting next to their huddling captive at the finale of his private little drama. If he'd been a bit more literate, he might have said something like, "Oh, how the mighty are fallen," because there was the once-mighty colonel, naked, sweating in spite of the cool air, tangled up in a confusion of 100-mile-an-hour tape and baling wire.

So this is one of the most powerful men in Vietnam, said Webb's voice. *All look the same naked, don't we? But your ass is much nicer than his.*

Larue kept the Huey in a slow circle. They were northwest of Saigon, around Go Dau Ha (which the troops called "Go To Hell" for lots of reasons).

"Ready?" Webb gave Col. Xoan a little tickle in the armpit. "Put the headset on him." Harrell reached over to slap a pair of cans on Col. Xoan's head, wiring him into the chopper's intercom system. The pale naked figure jerked at the touch, his strangled sounds becoming more emphatic, if not more persuasive. The microphone jutted out in front of his sealed lips, poisonous, like a snake. Webb untied the gag, and Col. Xoan, in his gratitude, instantly unleashed a heartfelt outpouring of vituperation in French, Vietnamese and even a few words of Hmong.

"God *damn*," said Larue. "Fucker don't have to scream in my ear, does he?"

But he did, at length and in detail. After the incoherent screaming, he produced a rhythmic river of Vietnamese invective, beautifully cadenced and as well articulated as his vermilion fury would allow. After having his little sex session so rudely interrupted, and spending a day and a half bound, blindfolded, gagged and semi-conscious, his balls aching from release denied, he was making his outrage known in the strongest, most incomprehensible terms. Harrell gave him a little nudge with a stick, one time, right on the head of his tool, but the colonel's rage was a stronger stimulus. He started cursing in Cambodian, Thai, and a language spoken only by a tribe of 12 people in the Shan state of Burma.

Then Harrell demonstrated why they'd brought him along in the first place.

"Holy shit, colonel!" he screamed at the top of his lungs right into their government issued headsets. "There's a scorpion on your dick. Jesus, how did he get in here? Hold still! I'll get him!"

A lightning quick motion, a snap at the wrist, and Harrell unleashed a whack on the head of Xoan's unfortunate organ that sat him straight up.

"Ooooohhhhh. Do that again."

"*Coño tu madre!*" whispered Martin. "You were right. He likes it."

"Can you hear me, Col. Xoan?" asked Webb, giving the Colonel time to remember how to breathe.

"What is this? Who are you? Why you are doing this? Where are we?" He would have added several more questions, but for the sensation of Harrell's stick around his genitalia.

"Let me go. Release me now. This is an order."

"He just won't give up," marveled Larson.

"You cannot harm me, whoever you are. The police and army will crawl up your ass. For this, you will die so very badly."

Larson couldn't take it. "Hey, the first step is a real biggie, son. And we ain't the ones all tied up."

Col. Xoan's chilling confidence did not desert him.

"You fuck yourself." Strong words, said Webb's voice, from a man lying bound and blindfolded and naked. "We do this all the time," Xoan continued. "Blindfold some joe, take him in chopper five feet off the ground, throw him out, very scary. I am not scared. You fuck your own self."

Harrell and Larson each grabbed Col. Xoan in a sweaty naked armpit, rolled him on his stomach to the lip of the open cargo bay door, and pulled the grubby strip of cloth away from his eyes. He feasted on the luminous sight of his beloved native land, rice paddies twinkling golden warm in the early sun, spread out like a buffet a full statute mile straight below.

Larson yanked the blindfold abruptly back into position and they wrestled their captive, shrimplike in his nakedness, into the depths of the chopper. It was windy and noisy and he trembled, struggling against the tape and the wire that cut into his arms. He was relieved to discover that most of his body still retained sensation.

"See? You could become part of your country in a very literal way."

"You will not kill me." Question? Statement?

"All due respect, sir, but allow me to point out that every troop in this chopper, plus the many we had to leave behind, wants you dead." Webb sat back on his heels for a moment. "You're responsible for the deaths of Shortstop, Z-Man, and a couple others. Plus all those people you had us wax for nothing, plus the guy in the funny hat, and Longacre never did get over that one. Plus the guys who almost took me out in Cambodia while I was trying to save one of my buddies. And maybe we should count that poor son of a bitch film guy from DASPO, too. We all want you dead, but none of us can think of a way to kill you that's slow and disgusting enough."

"That is because you are Americans."

That one caused Webb and Harrell and the rest to exchange uncomfortable glances. Yes, they wanted him dead but no, they really didn't want to do the killing. The conversation around the table after they saw the photo proved that to them.

"He got a bunch of us killed," yelled Larue that night. You never met Nutcase and Carpenter...." Even after talking the matter over in punishing detail, they couldn't decide exactly what to do, except find him and snatch him. They wanted to hear his story, and they didn't much mind leaning on him a little, but nobody could bring himself to use the word "torture." Longacre would have, but he was in some hospital in Hawaii.

"Really?" said Webb.

"Your blood is not cold enough. Yes, some of your men demonstrated a bit of talent at My Lai, but...."

"Hey," said Larson. "You wouldn't exactly be the first guy we ever killed."

Col. Xoan allowed himself a small chuckle. "Soldiers, yes. Killers, yes. But you do not execute people."

The glances got more uncomfortable. On one hand, they told each other, God knows Xoan wouldn't be the first person they'd waxed during the war. They were gunship pilots, after all, and they almost always hit what they aimed at. On the other hand, though, as closely as they were involved in the shit, they rarely stayed on the scene long enough to see the awful consequences of the hot metal and white phosphorus and high explosive they threw around. But then, they'd never shot film at Cong Hoa hospital, either, seen the red liquefied flesh lying on white metal beds. For them, it was a few rockets into the treeline, the enemy machine gun fire would stop, they'd fly on. Gunnies rarely landed to inspect the heaps of bleeding melted meat they left behind. War was one thing, the furious combat, the kill or be killed, but one-on-one cold-blooded murder? Termination with prejudice or without? That's where most of them drew the line. They remembered that South Vietnamese police chief and the way he blew that prisoner's brains out on a main street in broad daylight. They didn't see themselves that way. Most of them wound up in the Shadows for doing the right thing the wrong way, and the experience had tempered their attitudes enough to let them see a little more deeply into their own characters, especially as they contrasted to the society they found themselves in. If they wanted to kill the enemy eye-to-eye, they'd have volunteered for the Pathfinders or Rangers, or some kind of job that let them in for a little hand-to-hand, bring them up warm and personal, feel the lubricious wetness, hear that soft choking sound, when they slip in the knife.

Strangely enough, the actual legal barriers to the act were the furthest thing from their outraged sensibilities. Fuck the law, they said as they thrashed out the issues during their highly charged and highly unaccustomed ethical debate.

Every single one of them was in the Shadows because they'd gone against orders one way or another. But this, though they never stated it directly, may not even have known it directly, was just too intimate for them.

"No matter. You will not kill me." More confidence, now, in Col. Xoan's thin, reedy voice. Did he know the American mind that well?

"Oh, yes we will," said Webb. "It's a long way down, ain't it?"

Suddenly, the colonel didn't seem so sure. "Why are you doing this?" Even in the tinny headsets, even above the roar of the turbine over their heads, they all could feel the quaver in his voice, that bitter taste. "Tell me."

"Jeez, I almost feel sorry for him," Larson muttered. Harrell threw him an electric look. "Hey, I lied, I lied, okay?"

They were passing through 5000 feet. It was getting cold, and the colonel was starting to show a little blue tinge around the edges.

"Fifty-five hundred," said Larue from the right seat.

"I think that's high enough," said Webb. "Don't you, colonel? At least you'll have plenty of time to think on the way down."

"No. Please."

"Then tell us about your deals with the Cambodians."

"No."

THWAP! A smack on the penis from Harrell. An "ooohhh" from Xoan.

"What were you doing in that village? What's this buddy act with Wo Minh?"

Silence.

THWAP!

"Ooooohhhh...yesss."

"Where do you get the opium from? Who did you sell it to?

Nothing.

THWAP!

"Ahhhh...thank you."

"Cut it out, Harrell," said Webb. "Or make him pay you for it. Xoan! Do the Americans help?"

A brief snort of laughter, then static in the headsets, nothing more. Col. Xoan had seen, in places, the compassion of the Americans, which he took for weakness. He'd seen their hesitation to kill his countrymen for him, which he took for cowardice. He'd seen their kindness toward the children, which he took for naiveté. After all, the children carved poisonous punji sticks in their classrooms. He hated Americans, but he was more than moderately convinced they would not simply murder him in cold blood. Most of them would never understand the joy, the immense satisfaction, of execution the way he did. Xoan still didn't see why everybody got so upset when the Saigon police chief blew that VC's brains out on the street.

Harrell and Larson grabbed him under the arms.

"Sorry Colonel," Larson screamed in his face. "This headset is property of the U.S. Army and if we can't account for it, we get in trouble. You on the other hand...."

They ripped the headset off his ears, and pitched him headfirst out the door, just the way you'd throw a mean drunk out of a bar. They couldn't grab him by the collar and belt, but they managed a creditable bum's rush in spite of it.

Xoan hung in the air for the merest second on the still morning air, bathed by the downrush from the rotors, awash in the dawn's early light, smooth and golden, hands behind his back, ankles together, hunched into a little ball.

He hung there, weightless. Had his situation been any different -- if, for example, he'd been wearing a parachute -- he might have thrilled to the exhilaration of free flight the way ardent skydivers do. Some of them even exit their chosen aircraft naked, just to capture the sensation Col. Xoan was experiencing at that very moment, but he was in no position to appreciate it.

And then he dropped. Straight down, except for the mild forward motion imparted by the chopper.

In those films, when skydivers sail through the golden air, it looks like they're soaring, or hovering, or really flying. They're not. What they *are* doing is *dropping*, falling directly toward the exact center of that huge gravitational mass below them, plummeting toward the hard surface of the immovable planet, straight down, 32 feet per second squared, until they reach terminal velocity. Xoan did exactly that.

It didn't take long to fall the first 200 feet, but it felt like a lifetime to Col. Xoan. It *was* a lifetime, because certain fervent images burst forth from his spasming mentality, his brain, recognizing the circumstances of impending death, feverishly trying to outlive itself, flinging bright pictures on the screen inside his eyelids, fast, so fast, quicker than an instant yet perfectly recognizable for all that. In this kind of situation, your life is supposed to flash before your eyes. Xoan discovered that it was true.

The Huey was making only about 10 knots forward speed, so Webb and Harrell and the rest still had a good view of the naked colonel as he dropped.

It hadn't been easy. Harrell had stayed up all night, scrounging all over the base for bungee cords. He stole as many as he could find from the choppers, most of them only a few feet long, so they'd had to tie hundreds of them together to give the colonel just the experience they wished for him. Some were black, some red and black, some green and black, so when the colonel began his downward journey all those colors flashed past them as the cords tied to his ankles unraveled along the green metal floor of the Huey.

"The other ends *are* tied to the skids, aren't they? asked Webb, of nobody in particular.

"Little late for that," observed Larson.

They could find only about 200 feet of bungee cord, but Larue put the chopper in a dive as Xoan descended, and went down right along with him. So he fell about 4,000 feet before the bungee cords kicked in. He couldn't even scream, because sheer panic and imminent death had put his windpipe completely out of business.

But after an eternity he suddenly felt the grip on his ankles, the bands began to stretch, another hundred feet, and another, his fall gradually slowing, tearing pain at his ankles, then *oyooyoyoyoyoyonnnng!* The cords stretched as far as they could go, then the heavy elastic repealed the law of gravity, at least for the moment, so Col. Xoan snapped back and started falling *up*, rocketing back toward the chopper at an alarming rate.

"Shit," said Webb when he saw Xoan starting back up. "Think he'll go through the rotors?"

"Hope so," said Larson.

He didn't. He hung in front of the door for just an instant, turned toward them, one side of the blindfold slipped down over his cheek so he looked at them through one glittering, maddened eye, then down he went again, various fluids, which the body tends to release in near death situations, trailing behind him.

As soon as he realized he wasn't going to die, he had a most characteristic thought: *Interesting form of interrogation. If I live, I would very much like to try this on someone.*

The Shadows couldn't take it any more. That last glance did them in, Xoan hanging naked and one-eyed in the air, just outside the cargo door. Huge explosions of laughter came up from tight bellies, hoots, yuks, even a guffaw or two, partly a release from tension and the incredible hostility they felt toward the man bouncing in the air, and partly because they thought Vietnam had showed them just about everything, but this naked man floating outside the cargo bay door would give them plenty to talk about at the reunions.

Col. Xoan made it about three-fourths of the way back up to the chopper before gravitational inevitability set in again and he started falling in the direction everything is supposed to. And again, the law of elasticity cradled him in its arms, launching him improbably upward. Down, then up.

"Hope his ankles hold up," muttered Harrell.

"Hope they don't," said Webb. "If they're not broken now, a few more round trips should take care of it."

They watched him bob up and down five or six more times, until their faces hurt so much from laughing they had to pull him in. Larson had wet himself, and that made them all laugh even harder. Hand over hand, Larson and Harrell dragged him back into the aircraft, doing absolutely nothing to keep his head from bumping painfully on the skids and on the floor.

He was wet, soaked with urine, phlegm, mucus, black bile, yellow bile, and other, less-mentionable fluids and solids. He was cold, shaking, his ankles were bleeding, and he was hyperventilating so hard he could have sucked a golf ball through a garden hose. From the floor of the chopper he looked up at the Shadows with wide, crazy eyes.

"I knew you would not kill me," he said, and passed out.

CHAPTER 45
THE LONG STRANGE TRIP
OF COLONEL XOAN

Saturday, July 4

"He's gonna have a hell of a headache when he wakes up," Larson said.

"That'll be the least of his problems," mumbled Webb, who still hadn't gotten over his profound rage at Col. Xoan's betrayal, but then, neither had any of the others. They were even more outraged by, and not a little envious of, his ability to stand up to what they did to him in the chopper.

Their first fumbling attempt at coercion, as entertaining and inventive as it was, had pretty much backfired, and the question was really what to do with him next. They wouldn't be able to keep him disappeared forever.

The Shadows had sat all night -- again -- around the table in the villa, trying to decide that very thing. It cost them a night's sleep and an unconscionable amount of alcohol, but they were too angry to go to bed, and there was so much adrenaline in their systems that the alcohol didn't work. They were nowhere close to a resolution.

Meanwhile, the hapless colonel, having fallen as only the mighty can fall, lay naked and blindfolded, again bound hand and foot with 100-mile-an-hour tape in the body bag at the bottom of the closet in the compound.

It was a curious thing. They were eight men, eight soldiers, helicopter gunship pilots, professional warriors who had killed hundreds of the enemy during their tours in Vietnam. Each of them had wound up in the Shadows because they were too far outside the box for the normal ordinary Army, and they sat around the table mute, looking at each other.

"You mean to tell me," burst out Larue, "that we can't decide what to do with one sleazeball, treasonous, white-slaving, gun-running, drug-dealing, scum-sucking, black-marketing motherfucker?"

"I thought the bungee thing would get him for sure," mumbled Webb.

Sanderson patted him on the back. Everyone thought the bungee stunt was incredibly creative, and had actually congratulated themselves when Webb thought of it, but it didn't work, and they were stuck for an encore.

They refused to worry about the fact that Xoan was connected to the regime at the highest levels. To associate freely and fearlessly with people like Wo Minh he would have to be. The Shadows didn't know it, but at that very moment, distempered members of the President's elite private guard were searching for him. They'd already been to the playroom in the basement of the mansion, because it was one of Xoan's favorite hangouts, and were deciding where to look next.

The Shadows cared even less about the potential international incident they'd have on their hands if anyone found out a secret American helicopter unit had kidnapped and tortured a high ranking member of the Vietnamese ruling elite.

And they'd already made up their minds before they snatched him that he should be brought to justice, or severely punished, flogged in public, castrated, something, but the question was how. Leaving him to the Vietnamese or the American military system was completely unthinkable. They would just bury it as they had tried to bury My Lai. The only way that atrocity came to light was because some DASPO photographer had gotten the shot and sold the pictures to the press. No, Xoan had to be tried in the court of public opinion. It was the only way.

The Colonel's deeds cried out for vengeance the way Caesar's wounds did, and the Shadows, not being disposed to wait for him to be punished in the afterlife, were more than ready to take things into their own hands. They had, without hesitation, already done so.

Webb hadn't been witness to the kind of horror shows some of the others had seen during their stay, but he'd heard the stories in blistering detail: the wet bag treatment, the skinnings, the beheadings, the severed ears and other assorted organs, sexual and non. But none of them really had the stomach to deliberately do any of those things to Xoan except for Longacre, and he was still critical. They sensed, somewhere on a nonverbal level, that torturing him would put them down in the gutter where he was, and they didn't want that. Killing in combat was one thing, but now they had to wrestle with all those twisted ideas of justice and fair play American boys grow up with. Xoan, despite his condition and his circumstance, probably knew what was taking place. He had them figured pretty well.

They eliminated the obvious. No field telephone generator attached to his balls, no slowly drowning him by putting a wet burlap bag over his head, no rats, or pit vipers or custom beds of punji sticks. Nothing like that.

"Maybe there's a way to make him do the job for us," opined Harrell.

"Commit suicide?" asked Larue. "There's a thought."

"If Longacre was here, he'd pull the bastard's intestines out hand over hand before his eyes," Webb put in. "Too bad we don't have any truth serum."

"Maybe we do." Harrell's eyes were bright.

"Truth serum right here," muttered Larson. He was on his ninth can of beer, or his fifteenth, but his mortal anger kept him from getting actually drunk.

Harrell pressed on, his startling gray eyes glittering under the light above the table. "I think we'd all agree that the colonel has a serious personality disorder."

"Roger that," muttered Larson.

"As his doctor, I believe he can be cured only by one unique therapy. I prescribe a good ten hours of chemically induced paranoid schizophrenia."

"LSD?" breathed Larson, incredulous, sucking up the last of his thirtieth Pall Mall. "We don't do that shit."

"Well?"

The idea started sinking in. "I'd like to see him hugging a drool bucket the rest of his life," muttered Larue.

"We don't even have to fold, spindle or mutilate him," realized Webb. "No cuts, bruises, marks or scars."

"Damn," said Anders. "Too bad."

"I'm not so sure about this," said Larue.

"Oh, absolutely," Anders replied. "We already tried the

holistic approach. Let's drug his ass. It's the American way."

The conversation escalated from there, spinning out intricate scenarios where every conceivable advantage was taken of a captive who would be in the process of losing whatever delicate grip on reality he may have had to start with.

"Yeah," said Larue. "But where do we get the stuff."

"I think I know," Webb muttered. He pushed himself back from the table, struggled to his feet, and headed out in the direction of the DASPO villa.

The Shadows concluded that the drug should be administered under carefully supervised conditions, so they set about creating the proper atmosphere of clinical inquiry. It was about four in the morning, but none of them were tired. Larue had already completed another secret procurement mission, but not before muttering about what kind of incision he'd like to make on Xoan, how those warm living intestines would flow out of the colonel's belly onto the ground, all wet and pulsing and squirmy....

"Jesus, cut it out," Webb finally told him. "You sound like Longacre. Now give me a hand with this thing."

By breakfast, everything had been arranged. The "controlled conditions" were in place. Col. Xoan, still taped hand and foot, still blindfolded, rested uncomfortably inside the small, well-used refrigerator that Larue had managed to "borrow," and which now sat in the middle of the Shadows building on the base. All the food had been dumped outside the hangar, and the shelves removed. The Colonel was cramped, he was cold, and the blower unit kept him that way while providing him with a marginally sufficient supply of air. The Shadows had decided not to be unnecessarily cruel.

Webb had come through. He'd returned earlier in the evening with some tiny squares of blotter paper ("Raspberry Delight," he'd informed them), which Anders had stuffed in Xoan's mouth. Then he taped his mouth shut. One of those tabs would keep a normal GI nicely crazed for about 8 hours. Larue had given him four, sublingually. Likewise, they'd taped a throat mike to his neck, and secured the biggest set of Bose headphones they could find to his ears. The wires ran from his oblong white container to the stereo along the far wall. Larson had hooked in a microphone so they could talk to Xoan through the headsets, which, at some point, they would certainly want to do.

"We should probably leave him to himself for a few hours," suggested Larue, who seemed to know the most about things. "He needs introspection, meditation. Get in touch with his true feelings. Let's treat him to a little music. I think I know just the thing."

The stereo in the compound was every bit as big as the one Webb had seen in Berryman's room back in Tay Ninh, a glittering monolith of anodized aluminum and chrome, red lights, green lights, still and flashing, graphic equalizers with sliding switches and gleaming knobs, the very finest gear the Sansui company could devise, putting out over 500 watts per channel, capable of causing landslides, avalanches, earthquakes, and actual shifts in the weather patterns of the planet.

Much fumbling with the stereo, the clatter of bulky eight-track tape cartridges. All the flashing little lights came to life, needles jumped across dials, everything buzzed with energy and the unleashed power of virtually unlimited electronic amplification at its state-of-the-art finest. The hair on their arms stood on end and several lights dimmed in other buildings on the base.

All that power was directed toward only one goal. To play "I'm Enery the Eighth, I Am" by Herman's Hermits directly into Col. Xoan's head at top volume for three and a half hours.

"Wake me up when you think he's ready," said Sanderson. "I'm gonna make a few phone calls."

* * * *

By midday Col. Xoan had already heard both verses (the second being the same as the first) of "Enery the Eighth" a brutal number of times, and had been switched to "Sgt. Pepper's Lonely Hearts Club Band." Larson, who'd always wanted to be a disc jockey, was giving Xoan his own private little radio show, introducing each cut with some bright Top 40 patter through the microphone into the headsets.

"Hey, gotta walk, gotta talk, gotta move, gotta groove, gotta zing, gotta ding. This is Andy Larson, and I'm as short as I am tall, with stacks of wax for you and yours. Now, get ready to slip and slide, reel and rock, all you rock and roll maniacs, 'cause here's Ozzy Osbourne and Bllllllllack Sabbath!"

The kicking from inside the refrigerator had been vigorous at first, but gradually died down, letting some of the Shadows get a little sleep. Xoan had been quiet most of the time, probably overcome by mystic crystal revelations there in his dark, cramped box, mentally liberated, sensorily deprived, except for the interplanetary sounds coursing through his head. But when Ozzy started to sing, he began kicking again.

"I think he's cooked," said Larson to Webb as he shuffled blearily into the room. Webb looked around and saw some familiar faces. Foster was there, with Ironman and Svoboda. Foster had even managed to tear Weinberg away from his aquatic art long enough to be of some help. Svoboda put the finishing touches on a brace of lights, plugging them in to that hideously heavy converter they dragged with them everywhere. Weinberg set up the tripod and topped it with their trusty Arriflex movie camera.

"What are you guys doing here?"

"Major Sanderson called us," said Foster. "Said there was a target of opportunity...something we'd really want to get on film."

"Well, he certainly is a target, and you've got an opportunity. Besides, if we have pictures, nobody'll accuse us of abusing him too bad."

"Whatcha got in the fridge?"

"Not what. Who. Hope you got film in that thing."

In moments, everyone was there. They all wanted to be in at the finish. Sanderson bent down to open the refrigerator door.

"One second, please, Major," said Foster. "Lights!" Weinberg flipped a few switches and the place blazed white. "Roll sound." Ironman turned on his tape deck, waited a second and called out "Speed!" "Camera!" In a few seconds, Svoboda yelled, "Ve are rolling."

Foster looked toward Sanderson, cocked his arm back, and pointed. "Aaaaaand.....*action!*" The major yanked the door open.

"Phew," he coughed as he backed away. The Colonel had ripened. He was fecal, urinary, naked, sweating in spite of the cool air, eyes and mouth covered up in a mess of heavy tape, his shriveled penis barely -- very barely -- peeping out from a sparse nest of hair between his skinny thighs.

"Holy shit," thought Foster. Even in his refrigerated state, he recognized the colonel. He hoped that D'Amato was watching, wherever he was.

"He wiggles pretty good," said Harrell, giving Col. Xoan a little tickle near the right armpit.

"He's gonna wiggle even better," mumbled Larue. Since Longacre was in the hospital, Larue felt morally obligated to take his place. "Can I do it now? You promised, remember?"

"I remember," said Webb, reluctantly. "Enjoy yourself."

Smiling, Larue reached around and grabbed a tiny corner of the 100-mile-an-hour tape that covered Col. Xoan's mouth, then began to pull it off as slowly as he could, straight up, for maximum effect. The tape was made of metal, used to hold military machinery together, patch bullet holes in choppers, and once it was applied, only sandpaper could remove it. What it did to the Colonel's mustache is exactly what everyone expected.

"Yaaa," screamed Col. Xoan, in fear and cold rage. Webb slammed the door shut, cutting him off in mid-yelp. Larue held the tape aloft. On the inside, a pencil-thin mustache, every fuzzy hair of it, clung to the powerful adhesive like a caterpillar caught on flypaper.

"Can you do that once more," said Foster, "so I can cut in for a close-up?" Larue opened the door, slapped a new piece of tape across Xoan's bleeding upper lip, waited for Foster to yell "Take two," and yanked it off again.

"Got it," said Ironman. Larue slammed the door. "Jesus, I wish Longacre could see this."

Xoan didn't stop vociferating just because he was back in the dark. After the incoherent screaming, the microphone taped to his throat delivered a new flow of Vietnamese invective, more euphonious than ever, every sliding syllable exquisitely cadenced and as well pronounced as his fury would allow, perfectly reproduced by the expensive speakers. Ironman got every incomprehensible word of it on tape. Xoan was getting carried away, borne on the riptide currents of modern chemistry, lapsing at times into English, making his outrage known in strong, though incoherent, terms. He didn't stop until Harrell pounded on the side of the refrigerator with a long steel pipe.

"Lucy in the sky with diamonds," moaned Col. Xoan.

"Shit. He's completely around the bend." Sanderson's lips were tight. "Now we'll never get anything out of him."

"Can you hear me, Col. Xoan?" whispered Webb into his hand mike.

"Yes. Yes, I can," said Col. Xoan, a perfectly reasonable response from a man who'd spent the night overdosed on LSD, and having American rock and roll pumped into his head at 500 watts per channel.

"Webb? Is you?" Col. Xoan spoke blearily, distantly, which, given his condition, didn't surprise a soul. "I have a question."

"We'll ask the questions," said Webb. "But go ahead."

"Will you still feed me when I'm sixty-four?" He would have added more questions to the list but for Harrell's steel pipe beating against his chilly little box.

"I shall kill you personally for this," his voice was weak, but even through the speakers they all could feel the quaver, the hot fear, that bitter taste. "Please, what do you want? I can give you. Money? Godiva chocolate? I get you girls with kaleidoscope eyes. What is a kaleidoscope?"

When Sanderson spoke, his voice was grave, full of pity. "I'm afraid he's not making much sense, but at least he's alive."

"It would have been a tragic waste of life," agreed Larue.

"Why were you in that village with Wo Minh?"

Breakthrough. Something clicked with Xoan, an unexpected moment of lucidity among the drug-induced schizophrenia, perhaps, or maybe he was just giving up. In any case, he started talking, giving them a course in Contraband 101, reciting chapter and verse of the setup he was running with Wo Minh, Crawley, the CIA, and more than a few high-ranking Vietnamese and American military officers.

"Holy shit," exclaimed Harrell. "Are you getting all this?"

Foster, listening to the sound recording in his headset, smiled and nodded.

A normal acid trip, if a day of recreational blubbering paranoia can be called normal, has a point about six hours in

when the influence of the drug is at its maximum, before it
starts to slowly wear off. The user is said to be "peaking" at
this time. For better or worse, Webb started playing 20
Questions with Colonel Xoan just as the acid secured the
firmest grip on his synapses. He told them things he didn't
want to tell them. Things they didn't want to know. The
method may not have been as effective as sodium pentothal,
but the answers were a lot more entertaining, and more
interestingly phrased.

Yes, said Col. Xoan, I'm up to my ass in the drug trade,
and yes, I did send you to wipe out villages that didn't need it.
Who lived there? Oh, most of my competition. Thanks to
you, he said, I control over half the market. They're going to
name a bank after me in Zurich. Me and my cousin the
finance minister.

His transgressions, and Wo Minh's even more fearful ones,
came pouring out of him in a lysergic litany of chemical
craziness that gave all the Shadows, and the DASPO troops,
too, a feeling in their stomachs worse than any
gastrointestinal distress Ho Chi Minh could ever devise.
According to him, every man in the room was a war criminal.
Their attention was undivided.

A pause. A long pause. "I tell you what you want to know.
I cut you in on the deal. Big money. You do not kill me?"

"We won't kill you," said Webb. "We'll give you a blow bath
and steam job instead."

"Ohh, that would be nice," the colonel replied dreamily.
"What would you think if I sang out of tune?" Inside the box,
in the dark, his upper lip where his mustache used to be was
killing him, because it was fresh sensation. His arms and legs
had gone numb long hours ago, and in the absolute blackness
the acid caused fabulous colored patterns to race around
behind his eyeballs, showing him scenes from the war, scenes
from his childhood, random shapes and patterns. Larson had
been cruel, not stopping at the Black Sabbath album. He'd
sent Xoan several hours of Pat Boone, too, and even a Frankie
Yankovic polka tape he dredged up from somewhere, which did
the Colonel in absolutely. Then a few more hours of Herman's
Hermits. He felt...strange, outside himself. Take one hit of
acid, and you experience a peculiar sense of ego loss. Take
four hits, and God knows what you experience.

"I do not want to die," Col. Xoan said, like it was some sort of revelation.

"Okay. On my honor as an American soldier, as a Warrant Officer in the Army of the United States of America, I will not kill you."

"Somebody will."

"No doubt. But it won't be anybody in this room."

"Henry the Horse dances the waltz."

Webb threw a puzzled look toward Harrell, who everybody had tacitly decided was the resident authority on the effects of lysergic acid diethylamide-25 on the human brain. He just shrugged his shoulders.

"Who knows what evil lurks in the minds of men?" he asked.

Foster, who knew the story of the drug trade right from Xoan's own lips, or thought he did, whispered to Webb, "Ask him about the opium and heroin from the Cambodians."

Webb was getting tired of the whole thing. He opened the refrigerator door, holding his breath against the inhuman stench, and put his mouth right up close to the mike, his lips against the cold metal mesh surface. "Uhh...we know about the opium and heroin from the Cambodians."

"You know shit. Opium and heroin from Chinese in Burma."

Eyebrows went up all around. Webb paused for a second.

"Well, in that case we know about the...uhhh...guns."
Another wild stab.

"Ah, to the Laotians?" asked Col. Xoan.

"Yes," ventured Webb. "To the Laotians."

"You know shit. Guns to Cambodia. Not even guns. Rockets. Anti-tank. Beautiful. Big orange explosions. Very fine to see."

"Well, what the hell does go to the Cambodians?" burst out Harrell.

"Cambodians get money. Dollars from Saigon."

"What the fuck for?" Webb asked.

"So they can steal guns and sell them in Haiti."

What? Webb and Foster exchanged startled glances, eyes wide.

"What about that Juan Wayne guy?"

"He is a sucker of dicks," Col. Xoan replied. "Was trying to buy from poppy farmers of Wo Minh in Shan state. Cut our supply. Longacre eliminated him for me. Thank you, Longacre." Between the effects of the acid and the incessant clang of Harrell's steel pipe on the side of the refrigerator, Xoan told them everything, and most of it they didn't want to hear. It was the same as he'd told Berner in that interview so long ago, but this time they were getting the story from the inside.

Sandwiched between surreal verbal excursions and remarkable flights of obscene Vietnamese poetry which vastly entertained Quai Ng, it all poured out of his unleashed brain, total loss of ego opening him up like a rotten fruit. For an hour, he gave them a rambling yet comprehensive introduction to the Southeast Asian drug trade.

"Best part is," Xoan said, "you help me. I love that. Without the Shadows, I control nothing. This is why you will not kill me. You are more guilty than me. I." Then, out of nowhere, "After the war I am retiring to Switzerland," Xoan beamed. "I learn to yodel and play accordion. Would you like to hear?" Harrell reached for the pipe.

"Some other time," said Sanderson impatiently. "Finish the story."

"Other warlords and armies," said Xoan, "not happy with Wo Minh because he controls all distribution through me and cousin Walter."

"Cousin Walter?" asked Foster, sitting straight up. "Call me Norman should be here now."

"American air force, too. But so much competition! They want a part of the activity. Piece of the action? Crawley and Wo Minh tell them get fucked, because Minh has the finest private army in the area. I say tell them yes, then go to their village, kill their wives and fuck their children."

It all started making sense to Foster, thanks to the marketing courses he took in college. Wo Minh's competitive advantage gets sharper every day, because he can transport his goods by air, and two governments will make sure everything goes where it's supposed to. Even on the ground, he has the protection of Colonel Xoan and his very own American gunship platoon. For the others, the Chinese, the Wa, and the dozens of drug lords who control pieces of Shan State, it's a much riskier business. Their goods move on the ground, with only the protection they can provide for themselves, sometimes in caravans made up of hundreds of mules, and on the backs of children who they buy or steal from their families.

"Did you send us to attack caravans of children?" Webb asked.

"Of course. But not the mules. Children, we replace them pretty quick." The Shadows looked at each other, stricken.

"Ve haf three minutes," said Svoboda from behind the camera. Foster asked Webb if he could stop to reload the film. In the box, Xoan huddled naked and sweating, his eyes protected from Foster's movie lights by his blindfold.

It took a few minutes for Xoan to get back up to speed after Svoboda slapped in a new roll of film, but in mere moments the flow of bad news once again built into a flood.

"They call it tea money," Xoan put in helpfully.

"How do you spell that?" asked Foster, who was taking production notes.

"How does it get here?" Anders asked.

"It is a beautiful thing. From northwest Laos to Vientiane," Xoan rhapsodized, now telling the story dreamlike, a fairy tale full of charms and marvels. "It flows like a river. In Laos, refine to heroin, then we bring it to Saigon in VNAF and civilian transport planes. Sometimes they know, sometimes they don't know. Syndicates pay off government and military." Then he dropped another bomb. Everything was fine until the CIA decided they wanted the opium-growing hill tribes to help them fight the Communists. In return, American pilots started assisting with the complicated export process, and when they sold the crop on the other end, used the money to buy guns and uniforms.

"Who is Wo Minh?"

"You are very stupid. He is my cousin."

Wo Minh was particularly successful at the warlord and narco-insurgency game because at the bottom of it all, everybody supported him. The Thais looked the other way because he was always sending his private army against the Burmese, and that kept them busy. The Burmese liked him because he was making so many of their ruling generals rich. And even the DEA had a use for him. Wo Minh was a single, stark figure, the very model of a Southeast Asian jungle drug

lord, a black and white symbol, a focal point of their
continuing need for more funding, more personnel, and more
expensive equipment. They invoked his evil name at every
Congressional budget hearing.

"And Crawley?" asked Webb.

"Him, too."

"Him too what?"

"He is cousin of my cousin Wo Minh. In my culture family
is very important. How many second cousins *you* got?"

More whaps with the pipe, a few more selections from
Black Sabbath. Xoan poured out sad psalms of deception,
betrayal, clandestine involvement -- some of it official, some of
it not -- by the Vietnamese, the Thais, Cambodians, Laotians,
and fine upstanding American officials with wives and
children back home.

"Do our boys know about this?" asked Webb.

"Asshole," laughed Xoan, the first time he'd laughed in a
very long while, "your boys give us the airplanes. Pilots, too,
sometime. Your people give you to me, God bless them.
What you think, Air America is part of American Express
travel service?"

Xoan was over seven hours into his chemical journey, and
he couldn't seem to stop talking.

"Are you getting all this?" Foster whispered to Ironman,
who was running the tape recorder They could do no more
than sit in stunned silence as Xoan told them that the
American government had offered to buy up the entire opium
production of the Golden Triangle, because it was the
cheapest way to keep it out of Vietnam, and off American
streets. He mentioned all the agents he'd met, told them
about how deeply the Taiwanese were involved in it, because
it was their Nationalist Chinese army who was handling it all,
and how much the American government loved the Taiwanese
because they were anti-Communist. Round and round, drugs
and money, everybody gets a little. Xoan got a lot.

The drugs, however, were a mixed blessing. On one hand,
getting American troops addicted was a good way to
undermine morale and hasten the victory of the NVA. It also
deflected attention from the flow of drugs going back to the
States. The bigger the problems seemed in Nam, the less
attention all those registered voters would pay in the

American heartland. Xoan even explained how they were able to control the press through thatassholecolonelberner. However, the sooner the war was over, the sooner all the geysers of money would dry up. "Everybody is afraid," said Xoan. "Afraid the war will end too soon." Svoboda changed film again. This was too good to miss.

And the drugs weren't even the best part. With a dandy little war going on in Vietnam, the riches flowed to those who knew how to manipulate currency or work the black market. When the Americans arrived, the Vietnamese economy simply could not handle the flow of goods into the country. Black markets sprung up overnight. For years, the merchandise had flooded in. Most desirable, of course, was anything military. There was always a ready market among the perennially pugnacious factions that swarmed across Cambodia, Laos, Thailand and Burma. Each country had groups the American intelligence officers called the chow mein Mafia, buying up all the guns and ammunition and rocket launchers they could get their hands on, screaming on the world stage about how they deserved their own identity, and freedom from foreign domination so they could determine their own destinies and make deals with the drug lords without some round-eyes from the Western Hemisphere looking over their shoulders.

The warlords who moved their goods in the caravans had, over the years, assumed control of a chain of villages stretching from Vientiane down through Thailand, into Cambodia. It was easy. You simply walked in to the village you wanted and killed everyone, except the people who begged to become your slaves. They used the villages as storage depots and transshipment points. It's possible to accomplish much when you have your own army in a small native outpost in the middle of nowhere and a subdued population who loves you because you bring in food and build schools for their children, or simply because you let them live. When the Americans started building up in 1967 and 1968, people like Wo Minh seized the opportunity to open new markets, and extended their influence to the villages that ran in a more or less straight line from the Cambodian border toward Saigon. The Shadows were starting to get the picture. Foster noticed the expressions from Webb, Sanderson and the others.

"You mean," whispered Webb, "like Ap Do?" That was the village he'd told them to wax the day before they ran into Juan Wayne.

"Ap Do, where did it go?" chanted Xoan. "And where is Dong Pao now?"

"Jesus," said Anders. "He's been making us wipe out his competition. All those innocent people...." The silence was so complete that Ironman tapped his headset, thinking something had gone wrong with the mike.

"The heroin," pressed Sanderson. "When it gets here, where does it go?"

"To the Americans," Xoan laughed. "How many American troops addicted now? Ten percent? Maybe fifteen. You heard of watermelon man?"

"No," said Webb.

"Yes," said Foster.

"He comes on base to deliver. They buy, then you send them home, and they are addicts in America. We supply there also, we have international marketing connections. The NVA do not have to win the war. They just have to let you lose it. You defeat yourselves. Me, I don't give a crap who wins. Plenty of opium for everybody. Plenty of tea money, too." Then he threw up, going for distance as well as volume, and Sanderson, in disgust, slammed the refrigerator door shut.

Amid the heaving sounds coming over the speakers from Xoan's throat mike, the Shadows sat in the glare of the movie lights, silent, stunned and dumb.

Why hadn't any of them caught on sooner? Were they so "dedicated" that they'd jump at any chance to fly, to do their job, no matter what it was? Theirs not to reason why? Is this what comes of being a good soldier, of trusting your commanders, of obeying orders? How could this man have so perverted their dedication, their beliefs? Misdirected them, unleashed their power in the sick ways he did? Why didn't anybody above them ask questions? Who was really responsible for this terrified hallucinating asshole in the box?

Part of it, they realized, was the way the whole war was conducted. Nobody knew who the enemy was. They don't wear little signs that say "VC" or "Not VC." They had to depend on their ARVN "allies" to point them toward the enemy. If Xoan said that a village harbored the enemy and needed to vanish in a blaze of high explosive, well, it was his country, after all, and he should know. All he had to do was gesture.

Ironic. Webb had never flown a snatch mission, but Larue had, and Z-Man. They told him about all the Vietnamese, guilty ones, innocent ones, blindfolded, tied and frightened on the floor of a Huey, surrounded by Americans, by one or two of their totally unsympathetic countrymen. No due process, no trial by jury. Most of the accused wound up walking home from a thousand feet up. It bothered the Americans, most of them, but it wasn't their country.

"I've had about enough of this," Larue mumbled, reaching for his knife. Sanderson's hand shot over his shoulder and gripped his wrist, his eyes casting one long, meaningful look at the staring eye of Svoboda's movie camera.

Foster said, "Ask him about the smuggled comic books and Captain Midnight Secret Decoder Rings. Maybe he's got a scam going for those, too."

"What about all those innocent people in the villages we blew off the map?" said Sanderson, not wanting to know the answer.

"You Americans are very hucked up," the voice kept coming from the box. "You may never understand. Villagers support us, VC kill them. Villagers support VC, *we* kill them. They know. You read Machiavelli? We do. People are tool of those in power. What do you know of war? You amateurs. I spit on you, and on the filthy feet of your mother."

"You're pretty ballsy for a whacked out guy in a box," Webb said.

Up to that point, Xoan had been remarkably coherent for someone with all those tabs of acid under his tongue and eight hours in an antique Frigidaire. But it would take at least four or five more hours for him to come down, if he ever did.

"He's got the jabbers," opined Anders. "It's characteristic behavior. Uh, so I'm told."

Xoan really started rolling, the subject now being political science, putting out acidic elucidation about the consent of the governed and how could some stupid illiterate rice farmer outside of Tay Ninh decide for himself who his leaders should be, and that only fools wait around to get elected. There was more, much more, his philosophical insights into the politics of contraband, some startling opinions on the power structure of smuggling, choice words about his highly-placed brother-in-law, including chapter and verse on certain concealed bank accounts in foreign capitols, intimate details of his truly appalling inter-species sexual practices, the straight skinny about how this or that minister had disappeared and who had disappeared him, a veritable mother lode of underground information. He talked and he talked and he talked, the acid doing a better job than sodium pentothal could ever have managed, speaking from the cold dark confines of a little world all his own. The film hummed through the camera, and the recording tape rolled.

"Okay," Webb said, looking at Sanderson. "Now what do we do with him?"

"Excuse me," said Foster, watching Svoboda take the film out of the camera. "May I make a suggestion?"

CHAPTER 46
COLONEL BERNER MAKES NEWS

Sunday, July 5

Colonel Berner couldn't bring himself to do it, but he should have thanked Foster for that episode with the two agents. Back at JUSPAO, he had set up a projector and screened the footage of Xoan's interview, managing to convince Russell and Calhoun that nobody had any idea who Wo Minh was or what he looked like. After all, he'd spent years in Vietnam turning disaster stories into tales of glory, and he actually enjoyed the process. Besides, he was sure it was all just a misunderstanding.

It had been several days since the interview, but it was still a distasteful discovery when he looked up from his desk to find Foster standing just outside the door, shifting uncomfortably from one foot to the other.

"What do YOU want?" Berner was still smarting from the Colonel La incident.

"Sir. Sorry to bother you, but I wanted to know when you'd be ready for us to film that pile of drugs out on the base. You know, the stuff you and Colonel Xoan brought back from Dam Long?"

Berner just stared at him. Was it possible something was going on he didn't know about? Foster had done it to him before, but he still wouldn't accept the idea that Foster knew anything at all, let alone something he'd be interested in. But he considered himself a journalist, and couldn't help asking.

"What pile of drugs?"

"All the stuff that Colonel Xoan's outfit confiscated. I assumed the colonel would have informed you first."

Berner knew that DASPO officers had security clearance, and seethed about it. They had State Department passports, too, with purple covers that let them go pretty much wherever they wanted, whenever. He hated that, too.

"Oh! THAT pile of drugs. Of course. I was thinking of something else. Uh...we'll probably have a briefing on it...oh, let's say maybe tomorrow. I'll call you and tell you when to bring the crew. Dismissed."

Foster ducked out the door, his part of the plan finished. Berner reached for the phone. If there was a pile of drugs he didn't know about, he wanted somebody at Xoan's office to tell him what the hell was going on. Sorry, the colonel had been gone for several days. Apparently, he was conducting secret psychological warfare operation in the north. Or the south. They couldn't say.

Berner tried again, this time to the Shadows building. He'd never met any of Xoan's secret warriors, but somebody over there had to know something, and he wanted one of them in his office, right damn now.

About an hour later, "Captain" Samuel Taylor Webb presented himself, walking purposefully into Berner's office, hitting the kind of brace you learn from the TAC officers in flight school, and snapping off a razor-edged salute that almost dislocated his elbow.

"Who the hell are you?"

"Webb, sir. Captain Samuel Taylor Webb." Sanderson had pinned the bars on him just before he left the hooch, feeling that rank would give Webb at bit more credibility...and protection from people like Berner.

"And....?"

"Sir. I'm a helicopter pilot in Colonel Xoan's unit. We're called the Shadows." Berner was impressed. At least this kid looked like a real soldier.

"I know who the Shadows are, son. At ease. Sit down."

"All due respect, sir...." Webb stumbled over his words, just a little. "I don't think I should be here. This information is...delicate...we're not sure whether it should be released now or not."

"What is it, son?"

Webb's little voice piped up. *Foster was right. He really is an asshole. Go ahead. Set the hook, and if he calls you "son" one more time, deck him.*

"Our drug interdiction efforts over the past few months have been incredibly successful as you are aware from the huge cache of heroin we got at Dam Long. The DEA and everybody else is pushing for some big news, a success story...."

"Don't you think I'd know that better than anybody?"

"Of course, sir. But the fact is, we're sitting on a huge pile of opium, too."

"What?"

"And heroin. Lots more heroin."

"*What?*"

"Oh, yes, and several bales of marijuana. A Conex container full."

"I thought that stuff was destroyed," Berner said.

"Colonel Xoan was going to do just that but President Thieu thought it would be better to wait and let *you* plan the release of the story on discovery and disposal. Didn't Colonel Xoan inform you?"

"Of course," Berner replied, not having a clue.

"They say Colonel Xoan is on a psychological warfare operation in the north, but we can't locate him, and we don't know what to do with the...stuff. We sure don't want anybody to think it's ours, and the longer it sits around the more chance it'll fall into the wrong hands. We were thinking it might be a good idea if you announced the seizure now...."

Berner's mind took flight. Instantly released from the everyday, it soared aloft to the immediate rewards of being responsible for the biggest drug seizure in the history of mankind. His fantasy galloped through the future in a heartbeat, past his guaranteed instant promotion to Brigadier General, in front of the cameras as he praised and embraced his dear friend, Colonel Xoan. Further still, seeing himself in front of the cameras as press secretary to the Joint Chiefs of Staff. Or...the President?

"Look here, son. Colonel Xoan is a close personal friend of mine. He keeps me fully informed of all his activities."

Really? Webb's voice said. *Does he invite you to his little sessions with the schoolgirl hookers with the boxing gloves? Do you hang upside-down, too? You prick.*

Webb tried to tighten up on the line a bit. "I really shouldn't be telling you this, sir. We're dealing with highly confidential information, here. I think I should notify the DEA, or the MPs. I'm not authorized...."

"You let me worry about that. Where is it?"

"I'm not really sure I should...."

"Captain, I've been involved in this effort from the beginning. Colonel Xoan is one of my closest associates. I'm certain he'd give me full access to any information you have." Berner was getting furious. The biggest story of the year, he thought, and this putz wouldn't spill the beans. Come *on!*

"Very well, sir. But I'd appreciate it if you'd keep my name out of it."

"Of course, Captain." As if I'd let you have any credit at all.

"Now, what have you got, and where is it?"

"We've been seizing contraband for months. Our most recent effort was particularly effective." Webb allowed Berner to wring the information out of him. It was an astonishing stockpile of raw opium and refined heroin, once bound for the labs of Laos and the veins of American fighting men. It was now concealed in an undisclosed location on the base, tons of it. Webb made Berner spend another five minutes pressing him for the location.

"That's all well and good, son, but in my business a picture is worth a thousand words. I don't want to stand up in front of a room full of reporters and tell them all this without some kind of proof."

Reluctantly, Webb unfolded a photograph from his top pocket. DASPO had done a brilliant job on it, thanks to Weinberg's talented pencils, the shots they'd taken of the drug stash in the "transfer container" at the mortuary, and the technologically advanced darkroom at the 7th Air Force Photo Squadron, whose technicians had, on more than one occasion, enjoyed the delights of the DASPO villa. A little compositing, a little double printing, some artful dodging, and there it was, a thousand words at least, summed up in one photograph, black and white and glossy. A Conex container full of drugs if there ever was one. The Colonel's eyebrows went up. He could feel his heart banging on the walls of his chest, trying to get out. Alarmed, he even thought he was getting an erection.

"Of course, you understand that we're a secret operation," Webb told him. "And..."

"And what?" Webb's mouth opened and closed. He stammered, he stuttered. Whatever it was, it looked like he really didn't want to say it.

Berner gave him another push, just hard enough to let Webb reel him up to the boat, gaff him, and haul him over the side.

"There's...some indication Colonel Xoan might be involved in the drug trade."

Webb had argued with Foster for hours about putting that particular bait on the hook. Finally, Foster convinced him that Berner would never believe it.

"I don't believe it. Now, I like you, son, and I'm going to forget you said that. As far as I'm concerned, he's above suspicion. You accuse him, you accuse me. Got me?"

"I'm sorry I said it, sir."

"Where is all this stuff?"

"On the base, sir. It's a full Conex container."

"I can see that." He saw something else, too. Stars before his eyes, and on his shoulders, the direct result of triumphantly revealing the success of their efforts to the American people and the world. The closer he stood to the event, the more his visage would shine with reflected glory. Finally, with utmost reluctance, Webb told him exactly where on the base the container was, and Berner dismissed him. There were lots of calls to make.

First, he called every reporter he could reach, and commanded them to be at the JUSPAO briefing room at 1400 hours the next day. Then he called DASPO.

"Foster! I need a film crew tomorrow for a special news conference. Bring a print of the interview film we did with Colonel Xoan, because I want to run it at the briefing. And bring somebody who knows how to work a projector." Usually Major Perry, his XO, would run the equipment, but Berner had transferred him to a remote firebase surrounded by VC for bringing back the news about how well Colonel La had treated Foster.

* * * *

Berner was so excited that he vibrated. Standing on the tiny stage in the briefing room, his toes wiggled inside his boots, his fingers clasped and unclasped behind his back, he craned his neck as the reporters filed in for the special news conference. To his disappointment, none of the anchormen from the major networks were in town. It was nowhere near time for the five o'clock follies, so while the reporters shuffled to their chairs, there was a low buzz throughout the room: speculation on what could be so important, for a change. The crowd was twice as large as normal. He'd managed to get most of the press corps off the verandah of the Continental and into his briefing. Something of an accomplishment.

"May I have your attention, please?" Reluctantly, the reporters quieted down. Berner introduced the program for the afternoon by repeating in superfluous detail everything he'd said the first time he presented Xoan to the group.

"'This is an update on the drug eradication efforts I told you about a few months ago." Most of them had promptly forgotten. "And as part of the briefing, I have a surprise for you today." The buzzing in the room stopped. Through long experience, the reporters had discovered that Vietnam was full of surprises, all of them unpleasant. "We're going to take a field trip." Despair floated on the sea of faces like an oil spill.

"But before we get on the buses, I have a special film presentation for you. Even though my great and good friend Colonel Xoan is on a mission in the countryside, we are working closely together on his drug interdiction efforts, and he is featured in this special documentary piece that I myself produced and directed." A wet sound of disgust blurbled out of Foster's nose. He couldn't help it.

"This is important background information for what you'll see later today. I'm confident Colonel Xoan's keen insight and deep understanding of the drug menace in this part of the world will be of great help as you write your stories. Can we run...."

"Colonel," whispered a young lieutenant from the doorway. "You're needed outside, right away."

Berner puffed up, ever so slightly. He was needed. Right away.

"Let's roll the film, and I'll be back in a minute."

Berner hurried off to discover that there was some indeterminate problem with the payment for the buses he had ordered. Sanderson had slipped each of the Vietnamese drivers four packs of Polaroid film (courtesy of Foster) and told them to give Berner a hard time. "Make something up," Sanderson said, and they did. It took the Colonel over twenty minutes of screaming obnoxiousness to get it all straightened out, and then something else came up that kept him out of the room, then another problem, during which time the film uncoiled insidiously through the chattering projector. About fifteen seconds after it started, the normally blasé correspondents stopped talking among themselves and started paying attention. After thirty seconds, eyes widened, jaws dropped, they picked up their chairs from the back of the room and carried them closer to the screen. The last film Berner had shown them was a bunch of soldiers urinating in plastic cups. This was better.

The screen was vivid with the image of a naked Vietnamese man with a bleeding upper lip, filthy and wild-eyed, tied up inside a refrigerator. Several of the correspondents had been there when Berner introduced Xoan, but not many of them recognized him now. After the bungee jumping, the acid trip, the Herman's Hermits and Frankie Yankovic, he looked awful, even worse than most people do when they're being submitted to physically demanding interrogation. He was wet, bleary-eyed, and functionally delirious.

Foster and his DASPO crew had called in a dozen favors at the 7th Air Force Photo Squadron, and rushed the processing of the film they'd taken the previous afternoon at the Shadows hooch, then spliced it together with the footage of Berner asking questions from the interview he had conducted a few months back. On the screen, Berner was very full of himself, sitting in his golden Hollywood pool of light doing his best Mike Wallace. Xoan, his addled mind full of rampaging chemicals, crouched in the icebox and answered his questions with the painful truth. Several painful truths, in fact. Foster had handled the lighting perfectly, and the footage they'd shot of Xoan the previous day was an acceptable match for the film from the interview months before. The reporters couldn't tell that Berner and Xoan weren't in the same place, unless they realized they never saw the two men on screen at the same time. Nobody realized.

Svoboda and Foster had sat up all night cutting the images together so that Berner's questions from the first interview made sense with Xoan's answers from the icebox. Berner came across like some kind of cold-hearted sadistic bastard, sitting there all pressed and perfectly composed, his voice calm, casual and friendly, showing no reaction to the pitiful condition of the naked wretch in the icebox, no sympathy. Inhuman. Obscene.

"Colonel Xoan," Berner said, "the armies of the United States and Vietnam have done brilliant work here in Southeast Asia choking off the flow of drugs across the border. Can you tell us where these drugs are coming from?" His cordiality was coldly mocking.

Xoan's face was dreamy as the correspondents heard his answer from the previous night.

"Mainly from my cousins in northwest Laos to Vientiane. Refine to heroin, then we bring it to Saigon in VNAF and Air America planes. Syndicates pay off government and military." He told them, as he'd told the Shadows, how the CIA got American pilots to help fly the extract from the poppies so the hill tribes who grew it would help them fight the VC.

"Tell me, Colonel, from your vast experience combating drugs in Southeast Asia, who is the biggest dealer in the area?"

Xoan, babbling, told them about his dear cousins and business partners Wo Minh and Crawley, about the payoffs for the Burmese and Cambodians, about how he, Colonel Xoan, diverted ARVN arms and ammunition to Wo Minh's private army, how the officers and government officials who were supposed to be helping were actually helping themselves. He told them what tea money was.

Then he expanded on the theme of Wo Minh, and how the DEA really didn't want to catch him or stop him -- at least not right away -- because they used his depraved image as a focal point for their own presentations to Congress when they were asking for more and more money. They were thankful they could put a name and an evil face on what was essentially an abstract problem, presenting a concrete symbol, a quintessential Bad Guy, to the members of Congress, who had difficulty grasping these issues without such simplifications. Wo Minh was a singular, identifiable embodiment of the drug problem that even a member of Congress could understand. If he hadn't existed, the DEA would have invented him.

"Where do they get their troops?" Berner asked

"You Americans are very hucked up," Xoan said, and treated

the assembled multitudes to his cold-hearted Machiavellian speech. The fundamental flaws of democracy. People as pawns. "I spit on you, and on the filthy feet of your mother."

"I gotta write that one down," the Associated Press reporter said. On the screen, Berner pressed on.

"But I understand our Thai and Cambodian neighbors are doing quite a bit to help us."

Thanks to Foster's clever editing, Xoan told them about how much the Thais and Laotians didn't want to go after Wo Minh (like they told the Americans they were doing) because he was making so many people so very rich. They were all deathly afraid the war would end too soon.

"Asshole," laughed Xoan, "your boys give us the airplanes. Pilots, too, sometime. What you think, Air America is part of American Express travel service?"

Every terrible truth Xoan had told the Shadows was up there on the screen, with Berner moderating the discussion at his pompous best. His geniality and friendliness juxtaposed with Xoan's miserable condition was absolutely chilling.

The room was buzzing. Reporters wrote frantically, held up their cassette recorders to catch every word, whispered back and forth. Foster, who was quickly learning how to build dramatic tension and impact with his editing techniques, had saved the part about the drug caravans and their expendable children for last.

Just as the film ended and the lights came up, Berner, oblivious to what the reporters had seen, bustled back into the room.

"Colonel Berner!" yelled one of the younger reporters, jumping to his feet, ready to ask a lot of hard questions. An Australian stringer yanked him back down. "Not a word, understand?" The rest of them got the idea.

"Attention, everyone. The buses are ready. So if you could just follow me.....?" They all got up and shuffled out of the room, but nobody looked Berner in the eye, and sensing a delicious disaster, nobody said a word to him about what they'd just seen.

* * * *

The buses wheezed to a stop behind the mortuary, next to the Shadows building and the other anonymous structures, before a stack of Conex containers. These were huge shipping boxes made of heavy corrugated metal, each about the size of a small house, that once carried tons of food and supplies. Out on the firebases, GIs would bury them in the ground and live in them, creating cozy, if somewhat stuffy, apartments. At least they were relatively safe.

But the container the correspondents were looking at was set apart from the rest, just where Webb had said it would be, and Berner gazed upon it with a kind of fatherly pride.

He was the first one off the bus, and stationed himself in front of the huge container doors. Foster had sent his crew on ahead, and they were all set up. They had one camera covering the whole scene for the master shot, and Ironman scurried about with a hand-held camera ready to move in for the close-ups. Webb loitered in the background with the rest of the Shadows. There were lights, there were cameras, and everybody was ready for the action.

Berner looked around to make sure the attention of the reporters was undivided, pushed up the heavy catch with both hands, and swung the door open.

The container was so heavy, and the metal so thick, that they didn't hear the voice until the door creaked open that first little bit.

"You hear something?" said the man from CBS.

"Sounds like....singing?" observed another reporter. And it was. From the cavernous blackness within came a tiny voice, high and thin, a pure quavering voice singing in perfect pitch.

"I'm Enery the Eighth, I am, Enery the Eighth I am I am..."

Berner glanced uncomfortably around at the reporters, eyes wide, smile sick.

"There seems to be a problem. Wait one." He slipped through the door and disappeared inside. After a long moment he was back, struggling to close the huge door and throw the latch.

"Uh, I'm afraid we're going to have to postpone the..."

BANG! The container rang with the sound of hammering from within. BANG! And then a few more. The reporters looked at each other and started to press forward.

"Someone's in there!" It was Webb, yelling from the back of the crowd, hoping that Berner wouldn't recognize his voice.

"No...it's okay...I mean..." Berner looked around frantically.

"Open the door," shouted one of the reporters, then another, then Foster. Berner had no choice.

He had to put all his weight into it, and when the heavy steel panel finally creaked open, there emerged into the sunlight a completely naked Colonel Xoan, his hair standing out on all sides of his head like it had been electrified, which, in a way, it had, weeping, leaking from his eyes, nose, and selected other apertures, singing and falling into Berner's arms, kissing him furiously, wetly, on both cheeks, his forehead and ears.

"I am so glad to see you," he sobbed and slobbered. "My good friend, I love you so much."

"Colonel," yelled one reporter. "Exactly what IS your relationship with Colonel Xoan?"

Before Berner could take offense at the insinuation, the reporter held up the photo of Xoan, Berner and Wo Minh at the village. The Shadows had made up about three dozen prints and slipped them to the reporters, working from the back of the group.

"Is this Wo Minh in the picture?"

"And what is your relationship with Wo Minh?"

"Colonel, yelled another. "How much did you know about Xoan's activities?"

"And when did you know it?"

"Is this you in the picture with the biggest drug lord in Asia?"

"What is your involvement....?"

"How many.....?"

"Who are....?"

"Where is....?"

"Did you....?"

Berner, his forehead getting moister by the minute, was buried under a landslide of questions, inferences, innuendo, and sloppy kisses, struggling all the while to free himself from Xoan's passionate, sticky, grateful embrace. Cameras clicked in his face. Phallic microphones darted toward his mouth. The long lens of the DASPO Arriflex stared at him unmercifully. Ironman moved in for the closeups.

In junior high, Foster had seen a nature film, a time-lapse sequence of a dead field mouse being devoured by ants. This was the same.

Berner yelled at the reporters, trying frantically to untangle the still-hallucinating Colonel Xoan from his neck. The colonel had begun singing something unidentifiable from Black Sabbath's first album.

"I wonder," said Foster to Webb as the reporters closed in on Berner, "if the second verse is the same as the first?"

CHAPTER 47
AFTERMATH

Typical of the U.S. Military's method of resolving untenable situations, Colonel Herman Berner was credited with breaking up one of the most notorious drug smuggling rings in Southeast Asia, and promoted to Brigadier General. Three days after he received his star, he was killed in a terrorist bomb blast at the Number One Club.

Colonel Xoan and his cousin from the finance ministry were detained by the QC, brought to the presidential palace and issued priority orders and diplomatic passports to escort numerous cases of the president's personal effects to a bank in Switzerland.

Wo Minh bought himself a totally new identity and bequeathed his Army of mercenaries to his sons. He was able to establish himself as a restaurateur in the suburbs of Washington catering to strange and often perverse requests from some of America's most politically connected.

Still sporting an American passport, Walter Crawley bought a beachfront villa and a chateau on the border between Italy and Switzerland so he could be close to his money. He spent much of his time studying maps, trying to anticipate the next world hot spot where a man of his talents could find the greatest opportunities for profit.

Yak Dung was elected the first communist mayor of Ho Chi Minh City.

Former Sergeant First Class Harris retired from the army and within two years after the fall of Saigon, returned to ply his trade. He operates an adoption agency, and a travel service specializing in tours for war veterans.

Corporal Robert A. Holloway (Ironman) owns and manages a chain of men's gyms in California.

Harry Weinberg lives and paints on Sanibel Island in Florida. His painting "Halibut" was auctioned by Christie's for $850,000.

Kyle Longacre is a men's room attendant in a Las Vegas casino.

Corporal D'Amato's mother won $16 million in the New York Lottery in 1988 and established a scholarship foundation in his name.

Samuel Taylor Webb was sent back to Ft. Wolters, Texas as a helicopter flight instructor. He was discharged when a student pilot flew them into a tree, and owns an air charter service in the Upper Peninsula of Michigan.

Quai Ng was the last person left on the roof of the Pittman Apartments during the evacuation of Saigon. He was captured by the North Vietnamese Army the day after, and publicly executed.

Private James Lee Huggins established a people's militia known to the FBI as the White Aryan Brotherhood of True Americans for Governmental Freedom. He trains over 300 recruits at a base camp in the hills of Montana, though the exact location is unknown.

Murphy O'Connell recovered completely from his injuries, and decided to give acting one more try. He had bit parts on television programs such as "My Mother, The Car," and then became a stunt pilot for the motion picture industry.

Georj Svoboda owns six McDonald's franchises in Warsaw.

Leon Foster surprised himself by deciding to stay in the Army after the war, became the Commanding Officer of DASPO, and retired as a Colonel. He lives in Miami Beach.